TEMPTING ROWAN

TEMPTING ROWAN

Tempting Rowan

Copyright © 2014, 2016, 2017 Micalea Smeltzer

All rights reserved.

This book or any portion thereof may not be reproduced or used in any manner whatsoever without the express written permission of the publisher.

This is a work of fiction. Names, characters, businesses, places, events and incidents are either the products of the author's imagination or used in a fictitious manner. Any resemblance to actual persons, living or dead, or actual events is purely coincidental.

Cover Design: Emily Wittig

Photography by Regina Wamba

Edited by Wendi Temporado of Ready, Set, Edit

Formatted by Micalea Smeltzer

To anyone that's ever felt worthless or unworthy of love.

> FOR EVERY GOOD REASON THERE IS TO LIE, THERE IS A BETTER REASON TO TELL THE TRUTH.
>
> —BO BENNETT

PROLOGUE

I stare at the reflection in the mirror, not recognizing the girl I see. The fancy dress, the shoes, the hair—none of it's me. But take that away and I still don't recognize myself.

Who am I?

I don't know.

If I don't know, then no one does.

I glare at the girl in the mirror, hating her. The hate consumes me and I watch helplessly as my fist flies out, connecting with the glass. It shatters around me, crumbling to the ground just like my life.

Pain radiates from my hand up my arm. I look down and all I see is blood and all I feel is pain. For a moment, I'm reminded that I'm alive and I welcome the pain. But it's not enough. It won't be long until the numbness consumes me, swallowing me whole.

It's all I know.
It's all I am.
A shell.
A ghost.
I don't exist.
I used to be okay with that, but I don't know if I am anymore, and that's what scares me the most.

CHAPTER ONE

"Hey," my best friend Tatum poked my side. "Hey," she hissed a little bit louder. When I still ignored her, she exclaimed, "*Hey!*"

"Shhhh!" hushed a guy with his nose buried in a textbook.

"What?" I glared at her, mad that she was disturbing the peace in the library. I mean, honestly, I thought she could at least respect the obvious need to stay quiet in the library. Apparently not.

"Over there" —she nodded her head at something over my shoulder— "is Trenton Wentworth, and his eyes are *all* over you," she whispered, smiling excitedly. I wasn't surprised she knew who Trent was; in this town the Wentworths were practically famous—with the kind of wealth they had it was surprising that they still lived in this small town.

"What?" this time I gasped the word. "No." Her words had

poured a bucket of ice-cold water on me. It was like I couldn't escape the guy. No matter where I hid, he always popped up.

I refused to turn and look, but I felt his eyes boring into my back. Those blue eyes had once twisted my stomach into knots and with one bat of his lashes I would've come running. Even girls like me weren't immune to the charms of a guy like Trent.

"I have to go." I stood hastily, grabbing my books and pushing my glasses further up my nose. I didn't care if I had two more hours' worth of studying to do and would never be able to finish it at home. My desperation to get away from Trent was more powerful than my need to study ... and that was saying something.

I stumbled around the chair, and Tatum watched me with a dumbfounded expression. The chair I bumped into crashed to the floor. "Sorry," I mumbled, not bothering to stop and pick it up.

I had never told anyone about that night.

The night I gave into my desires.

The night I let Trent take a piece of me.

The night I ran from him.

The night my life was irrevocably changed.

I bumbled toward the exit and, in my haste, one of my books slid from my arms, landing on the floor. I was tempted to leave it, glaring at the treacherous book, but a tan hand was already snaking out and picking it up. The person placed it back on the stack in my arms and I swallowed thickly, refusing to look up. I felt his stare, and I *knew* it was Trent standing before me. Slowly, I looked up and my hazel eyes connected with his. Looking at him was like taking a punch to the gut—leaving me breathless with a pain I couldn't understand.

"Rowan," he beamed, and the way he said my name made

me squirm ... and not in bad way. But, oh, how I wished I didn't enjoy hearing my name leave his kissable lips.

I tucked a piece of light-brown hair behind my ear. "Trenton." I stared at his shoes. They were black motorcycle boots with heavy silver buckles. I wondered if they were real motorcycle boots or designer ones just for show.

"My face is up here," he said in that deep husky voice with a slight chuckle.

I forced my head up and met his eyes. His dark hair was longer on top and shorter on the sides. His chin was dotted in a light dusting of stubble like he'd forgotten to shave this morning. Beneath his leather jacket he wore a navy t-shirt and his jeans looked well worn, even though I knew he could afford new ones.

"What are you doing here?" I stuttered, looking around for a means of escape. I needed to get away from him before I did something stupid, like give into the temptation of Trenton.

Brilliant question, Rowan. I scolded myself when I realized what I'd asked him. Sometimes, words seemed to fly from my mouth without me thinking through what I was about to say. I really needed to work on that.

He chuckled, wetting his lips with the tip of his tongue. "It's a library. There's usually only one reason to be here."

"Usually?" I questioned with a raised brow. What other reason would one have for coming to the library?

His smile widened. "Well," he said as he leaned toward me, his lips grazing the shell of my ear, "if you're really quiet you can always have sex." He pulled back, laughing at my wide-eyed expression. "I always did have a naughty librarian fantasy." He looked me up and down and a blush stained my cheeks in what I was sure was an unflattering shade of red. My hair was pulled back, my tortoise-shell glasses perched on the end of my nose since my contacts had been bothering me today, and I was wearing a pencil skirt and button down top. It might not have been *naughty,* but I was dressed like a librarian since I worked here after classes and studied before going home.

"I really need to go," I explained, realizing that I was still standing in front of him like an idiot. I tried to push past him, but he ceased my efforts with a hand on my arm. His sweatshirt was rolled up, displaying the tattoos that covered his one arm. Tattoos I had been very intimately acquainted with once upon a time. I wondered if he even remembered.

"How could I forget?" he asked.

Oh, no. Did I say that out loud?

"You didn't have to," he answered my unspoken question. "I could see it in your eyes that you were thinking about that night."

I swallowed, my heart beating a mile a minute.

"You were the one that left," his voice held a tone of irritation. "You never gave me a chance to prove myself to you." His thumb rubbed circles on my arm, still refusing to let me go, and it was like he thought I was an animal he could calm with a soft touch.

"You didn't have to." I yanked my arm from his grasp and glared at him. "I know what guys like you want from a girl like me. You got it, okay? There's no need to keep up the farce of a good guy."

He stared at me with a look of shock. His mouth opened and closed, gaping like a fish. He was at a loss for words, and Trenton wasn't the kind of guy to be left speechless.

I took this opportunity for what it was and all but ran out the doors of the library. I had to get away from him. If I stood there a second longer I wouldn't be able to resist him. From the moment I first laid eyes on Trent, when I moved to Winchester my freshman year of high school, I'd been under his spell.

"Rowan!" he called after me, but I kept walking like I hadn't heard him. "You're the one acting like a player! So, what? I was good enough to fuck once but I'm not good enough to give a chance?" Those words hit me like a slap in the face. Not because they were true, but because they were so very wrong. Trent didn't know the *real* me. No one did. If he found out about me, about what I had done, he wouldn't want anything to do with me. I knew that, so I was only trying to spare him. It had been five years since we lost our virginity to each other on a school camping trip our sophomore year. I'd have thought by now he would've forgotten about me, but Trent wasn't like most guys. He actually *cared*. He was *real*. And he was *perfect*. I didn't deserve him; frankly, no one did. But for some reason, he thought I was someone worth caring about. But if he knew the kind of person I really was, he'd run as far away from me as his feet would take him.

I reached the sidewalk and turned to see him standing on the steps staring at me.

"Answer me," his voice was raised, but not angry. He sounded hurt and that broke my heart, because I was the one causing him pain. If he'd leave me alone, he wouldn't have to feel that way. But Trent wasn't the type of guy to give up. Whenever we ran into each other it was like he still cared about me, and I couldn't understand it. I ran away from him after we had sex and ignored him through the rest of high school. On the rare occasions when I was forced to interact with him, I was less than friendly. He needed to stay away. I couldn't afford to let him get close.

"Girls like me don't end up with guys like you," I told him and he flinched like I had slapped him.

"Guys like me, huh?" His jaw flexed. "Funny." He descended the remaining few steps and stood in front of me. He stared at me for a moment, anger and sadness stormed in his eyes. "Because somehow, in this situation—" he pointed to him and then me "—it seems like *I'm* the one that got used. Not you."

I glanced down at the gum-covered sidewalk. It was much easier to look at it than Trent's hurt face. I *never* meant to hurt Trent, but that's what I was doing. I wanted to keep him safe from the cruel world that I called home. He didn't deserve to have his view of life tainted.

"I wanted one night. That was it. And I didn't mean that the way you took it," I explained with a defeated sigh.

He grabbed my chin and forced my gaze to his.

"Then explain what you meant!" His intense blue eyes held me captive. I swallowed thickly, overwhelmed by his demand.

I swallowed. "Look at you!" My voice rose as my anger increased and tears threatened to leak from eyes. "You're, ugh —perfect and I'm—" I pointed to my librarian-esque clothes, mousy hair, and glasses. "Nobody."

His jaw clenched as he glared at me. "You're nobody? For someone that's so smart, you're incredibly stupid," he spat, shoving his fists into his jean pockets. "Whatever." He shrugged, turning and walking away. He shook his head back and forth, muttering under his breath. I knew he was pissed and a part of me wanted to run after him and tell him everything so he'd understand why we couldn't be together.

Instead, I let him leave, just like I always did. I watched until he turned the corner and let out a deep breath I'd been holding in. He was gone ... for now. But I'd known Trent long enough to know that he wasn't finished with me. He'd pop up again, and based on this conversation, I'd say sooner rather than later.

A moment later, the library doors opened and Tatum came running down the steps with my backpack clenched in her hands. I'd completely forgotten about it.

She stopped, looking quickly left and right for me. When she spotted me, she jogged my way and handed me my backpack.

"Where's Trenton?" She looked behind me, like maybe he was hiding there.

"He left." I stared at the last spot I saw him. A motorcycle roared to life somewhere, the only sound in the otherwise quiet town.

"Did he leave ... peacefully? Or did you make him leave?" she asked, tilting her head to study me.

I rolled my eyes. "You make me sound like a bitch."

"When you get around Trent, you sure act like one. Why do you hate him so much?"

"I don't hate him," I whispered, watching the little clouds my breath made in the cool air. I *wished* I hated him. It would make things so much easier.

"Really?" She tilted her head, pushing her blonde hair out of her eyes. "Because you sure act like it. I would *kill* to have Trenton look at me like he does you. Heck, I'd like for any guy to look at me like that."

I shrugged, avoiding her eyes. "He doesn't look at me in any particular way."

She snorted. "Are you fucking blind? He looks at you like he wants to lick every crevice of your body."

My eyes widened. "That's ..." I had no words.

She took a step back. "I love you, Rowan. I really do. But sometimes I feel like I don't really know you at all. You're so strange sometimes."

Her words didn't hurt my feelings. No one knew the real me, not even myself. If I were an outsider observing myself, I'd think I was strange too.

"My mom's going to be here in a few minutes to pick me up since my car's still being fixed, so you don't need to give me a ride." She backed away further. "I'll see you tomorrow."

I waved weakly, watching as she disappeared inside the doors of the library.

I adjusted my books so I could sling the backpack onto my shoulders and headed to my car.

Normally, after I finished working at the library I stayed past closing time to study. They knew me and didn't mind me using it, but Trent had messed with my plans. This also meant I hadn't had a chance to change out of my work clothes. I always changed back into my school clothes once my shift was over so I'd be more comfortable. I knew my mom wouldn't have done anything for my siblings. Everything always fell on me. I was like Cinderella, only Prince Charming was never going to put a glass slipper on my foot and take me away to his castle.

I unlocked the door to the old silver Honda Civic. It was a piece of crap, but it ran, so that was good enough for me.

I tossed my bag and books into the back and slid into the driver's seat. I sat there for a moment, counting my breaths and heartbeats. It calmed me for some reason.

I put my hands on the steering wheel but I didn't pull away.

I didn't want to go home ... I never did. But that didn't stop me from doing it anyway. Maybe I could have left, gone away, had a different life. But I wouldn't leave. I was chained to that house and a life I didn't want.

I was trapped and I was slowly being suffocated by all of it.

Sooner or later, everything would catch up with me and I'd willingly let it consume me.

"HI, MOM," I said when I walked into the house. I closed and locked the door behind me.

I turned, glaring at her passed-out form. Every single day of my life it was the same routine. I was always talking to the equivalent of a corpse. She was here in body and that was it. Even when she was awake she was drunk.

"Row! Row!" I dropped my bags down as my little siblings came running at me.

"Hey." I opened my arms wide, hugging them tightly. They were the only two things in this world that kept me going. "How was school?" I asked them, smoothing my fingers through Ivy's light-brown hair and then ruffling Tristan's.

"It was okay," Ivy's pale pink lips turned down in a frown.

"I got a gold star." Tristan pointed proudly to the sticker adorning his chest.

"Awesome!" I gave him a high five. "What did you do to get that?" I tickled his stomach lightly, making him giggle.

"I got an A on my spelling test!"

"Well, Tristan," I started, hugging him again, inhaling the

scent of his shampoo, "you're the smartest kindergartener I know. Have you guys eaten?" I asked, even though I already knew the answer.

They shook their heads and I sighed in disgust. If my mom didn't have me, I feared what would happen to Ivy and Tristan.

"Come on then." I stood, taking each of their hands. "I'll make us dinner. You guys can help me."

"I like helping." Tristan beamed up at me. His smile always managed to break my heart.

"I know you do." I lifted him onto the counter and then did the same with Ivy. She was only three years older than Tristan and getting a bit too big for me to be lifting her, but I didn't mind. Most days, I felt more like their mother than their sister. I fed them. I bathed them. I packed their lunches. I looked after them. I *loved* them. It was more than my mom had ever done for them or me.

There wasn't much food in the house so our options for dinner were limited.

"How's macaroni sound?" I pulled out a box of SpongeBob-shaped noodles and shook the box.

"Yay!" they cheered. I was lucky that they were easy to please kids.

I put water on to boil and crossed my arms over my chest as I leaned against the counter. "Who's going to pour the macaroni into the pot?" I asked.

Tristan enthusiastically raised his hand.

"It's Tristan's turn," Ivy agreed with a sad shake of her head. "I did it last time."

"That's nice of you, Ivy." I smiled at the little girl. "You can stir the cheese in. Would you like that?"

She brightened, smiling widely. Several of her baby teeth

had fallen out, making her adorably awkward looking. "I'm a good stirrer."

"Yes, you are." I leaned over, kissing the top of her head.

"Row! Row! The water!" Tristan pointed enthusiastically at the water beginning to boil.

I opened the box of macaroni and removed the packet of powdered cheese. I handed him the box and lifted him onto my hip so he could pour the noodles into the water.

He watched in fascination as the bubbles hid the noodles from sight.

"How long till it's ready? I'm hungry," he pouted as I sat him back on the counter.

"Not long," I assured him. "We'll eat and then I'll give you a bath and you can take a shower, Ivy."

"I don't want to," Tristan groaned. "Baths suck."

"You don't want to be dirty, do you?" I tweaked his nose.

"I'd rather be dirty than wet," he grumbled, crossing his small arms over his chest. His too small shirt rode up, exposing his stomach. I was going to have to start picking up some new clothes for him whenever I had some extra money.

"Stop whining, Tristan. You know it doesn't work with me," I warned him with a steely gaze.

His arms lowered and he let out a pent-up breath. "Fine. Will you read me a story tonight?"

"Don't I read you a story every night?" I countered with a raised brow.

"Yeah, but sometimes you fall asleep." He giggled.

"Sorry about that." I hung my head shamefully. I tried my best to be a parent for my siblings, but it was hard. I had school and work. When I got home it was late and I was exhausted. I wished I could afford for a babysitter to watch them, but I didn't have the money … not if I wanted to buy food. I already had to pay for Tristan to stay in after school care since he was only there for half a day. My stepfather was just as bad, if not worse than my mom. He didn't drink, but he constantly smoked in the house, had a lousy job, and was just plain creepy.

"It's okay, Row." Tristan opened his arms for a hug.

I held him close. It amazed me that two kids that had *nothing* could be as sweet as Tristan and Ivy.

I let him go and stirred the macaroni. When it was done, I strained it and put it in a bowl. I dumped the ingredients in the bowl and handed Ivy a spoon. "Stir, sweetie."

She mixed it as thoroughly as she could, but in the end, I had to help her.

"Ivy, why don't you get the plates?" I nodded my head at the cabinet that housed them.

"Sure." She smiled, eager to please me.

She grabbed three plates, hopped off the counter, and scurried over to the card table that served as our only eating surface.

I helped Tristan down and carried the pot over to the table where I loaded our plates with macaroni.

"Wash your hands before you eat," I warned them.

With heads bowed, they did as I said. I cleaned the pot and washed my hands before joining them at the table.

"It's good, Row." Tristan smiled at me with trusting eyes. It broke my heart every time I saw that look in his eyes. He and Ivy trusted me completely. To love them. To protect them. But how could I ever do those things when I wasn't a whole person? I was shattered. Broken. Unimportant.

"Thanks, Tristan." I ruffled his hair, hoping the innocent little boy couldn't see the darkness inside me.

"You're the best sister." He leaned into my touch, like a dog begging to be pet.

"Hardly," I laughed.

They helped me wash the dishes and then it was time to give Tristan his bath. After a lot of grumbling I finally got him into the warm water. I *really* wished I'd had time to change my clothes. Giving Tristan a bath in a pencil skirt wasn't practical. Damn Trenton Wentworth.

I let Tristan splash around for a few minutes before I washed and shampooed his hair.

"Pull the drain plug." I pointed to the stopper. He pulled it and the water began to whoosh out.

He stood and I helped him out. I wrapped a towel around his small frame, drying his body and then his hair so it stuck up around his head like a bird's feathers.

I led him down the hall to the room he shared with Ivy.

Ivy was reclined on her bed, playing with her dolls. "Shower, Ivy."

"I wanna play," she whined.

"Ivy. Shower. Now," I snapped. "I'm tired and I don't have the energy to argue with you."

"Fine." She slipped out of the bed, grabbing pajamas to take with her to the bathroom.

"Hurry back and I'll read you both a story," I said in a softer tone. I hated snapping at the kids, knowing they got enough of that from our mom—on the rare occasions she was awake—and step-dad.

"Okay," I heard her say as the bathroom door closed.

I grabbed the lotion and rubbed it into Tristan's body. "Which pajamas do you want to wear?"

"The dinosaurs!"

I shook my head. I should've known.

I pulled out the pajamas with different colored dinosaurs on them. "Lift your arms," I instructed.

Once he was in his pajamas, he climbed into his bed.

"Which story do you want tonight? It's your turn to pick." I rubbed my eyes.

"Um ...," he thought, placing a small finger against his lips. ""The Lion King"!"

I grabbed the Disney book and climbed into his bed, leaving room for Ivy on my other side.

She came into the room a few minutes later.

"Ivy," I groaned at the wet stringy pieces of hair framing her face. "You didn't brush your hair!"

"But it hurts!" she argued.

I sighed, slipping out of the bed even though it felt so good to rest my tired body. I grabbed the detangler spray and a comb from the bathroom.

Sitting down on the floor of the bedroom, I motioned with my hand for Ivy to sit in front of me.

After a moment of hesitation, she reluctantly took the spot.

"You have to brush your hair or it will only get more knotted," I told her, spraying her damp hair with the detangling solution. "I hate brushing my hair too." I worked the comb through the ends.

"You do?" She sounded surprised. "But your hair is so pretty and long, Row."

"I like it long." I shrugged, trying not to pull her hair. "But brushing it is a pain."

"Ow!" She grabbed her head when I brushed through a knotted strand.

"Sorry," I told her, kissing the spot in apology. "Better now?"

"A little."

"There." I patted her back when I was done. "See, that wasn't so bad, was it?"

"No," she admitted reluctantly.

I returned the comb and detangler to their spots in the bathroom before climbing back into the bed to read their story.

When I finished reading the story, Tristan looked up at me with wide eyes and Ivy snuggled closer to my side.

"Row," Tristan started, "I wish you were my mommy."

His words turned my stomach inside out. Both he and Ivy deserved better than our deadbeat mom, but they also deserved more than me.

"Why?" I asked, my voice barely above a whisper.

"Because," he said as he shrugged his small shoulders, "you do everything for me."

Even at five years old, Tristan was aware that our mother did nothing. It broke my heart that he and Ivy had to grow up with this. But I had too, and I didn't have anyone to look after me. That's why I did what I could for them.

"I love you, Tristan." I kissed his forehead. "Love you, Ivy." I kissed hers as well. "Goodnight."

"Night, Row." Ivy scurried over to her bed on the other side of the room.

I hugged Tristan and slipped out of the bed. I hugged Ivy too and closed their bedroom door behind me.

I leaned my head against the closed door. I was so exhausted, but I needed to shower and I had homework to finish since I hadn't done it at the library. Trent had ruined my whole evening. *Why couldn't he leave me alone?*

Choosing not to waste my energy dwelling on it, I pushed myself forward and into my room. It wasn't much of a room to be honest. It was more like a closet. My full-size bed took up most of the space and the closet door was always open because it was impossible to close it. The walls were painted a bright aqua blue and the bedspread was purple. It was nothing special, but it was *mine* and that's what mattered to me. I grabbed a pair of loose sweatpants and a sleep shirt.

I showered as quickly as I could, but took more time than I meant to because the hot water felt so good on my tense muscles. I never seemed to relax.

Before I headed into my room for the night, I checked on my mom. She was still passed out on the couch. I hated her so much, but she was my mom, and nothing could change that. I watched her for a few minutes, noticing the steady rise and fall of her chest. I wondered how someone that drank so much was able to breathe like a normal person. It seemed like her breaths should falter or something. I wanted to yell and scream at her to get off her lazy ass and be a mom. But I knew that was pointless. I'd yelled and screamed at her more times than I could count and it never did any good. It usually resulted in me getting slapped in the face.

With a scowl, I pushed myself away from the wall.

I closed my bedroom door, locking it behind me.

I slipped beneath the covers, glaring at the textbook lying on the bed.

I wanted to put off my homework until tomorrow, but it would only bug me and result in even more lost sleep.

I pulled the textbook onto my lap and began to read the assigned pages.

Thirty minutes later, when I finished reading, I had to write a short essay to summarize what I'd read. Honestly, you'd think professors would have better things to do than grade stupid papers like this.

We were supposed to type this, but I didn't have a computer, so I had to hand write it. I always did my typed assignments at the library before I went home. Hopefully I'd have time to type this up tomorrow, but tomorrow also meant even more homework. It was a vicious cycle.

Once the short paper was written, I tucked it into the pages of the book and dropped the book beside my bed on the thin strip of floor that served as the walking space in my room.

I reached over and turned the light off, bathing the room in darkness.

I lie in bed, unable to go to sleep even though I was exhausted.

I heard the front door slam closed and jumped.

My step-dad, Jim, was home.

I hated Jim with every fiber of my being, maybe even more than I hated my mom.

I listened to his heavy footsteps echo through the small house. When they started down the hall, I closed my eyes for a moment to ground myself.

Turning on my side, I forced them open, staring at the darkened shadow stopped outside my door.

I held my breath, counting in my head.

One, two, three, four, five, six, seven, eight, nine, ten.

Jim smacked me around some but nothing too bad. What I couldn't handle was when his eyes roamed up and down my body like I was piece of meat he wanted to devour. Even worse than that was when he touched me. Sometimes, when I was wearing a skirt, if I passed by him while he was sitting his hand would skim under the fabric and up my thigh. Other times his fingers would graze my butt or my breasts. He liked to play with my hair too. I'd thought about cutting it more than once, but my hair was the only thing I liked about myself and I refused to let him take that piece of me.

I held my breath, waiting for him to leave. When he finally did I was red in the face and black spots floated across my eyes.

I wondered how much longer he'd be satisfied with simple touches and standing outside my door.

I rolled onto my side away from the door and squished my eyes shut.

Behind my lids, Trent's image filled my mind. I couldn't escape him no matter how hard I tried. He was *always* there.

Pressing the heels of my hands into my eyes, I let out a groan. Why couldn't he leave me alone? Didn't he see that I was no good for him? I would never be able to love him when I couldn't even love myself.

CHAPTER TWO

I HAD THE SAME DREAM THAT NIGHT THAT I'D HAD AT least once a month since I was sixteen.

The twigs snap beneath my bare feet and my heart races in my chest as I try not to make a sound. It's pointless, though. My heavy breathing is bound to give my location away to the teachers. If they catch me sneaking over to the boys' tents, they'll send me home, and home is the last place I want to be right now. For one night, I want to be a normal teenager. I don't want to have to take care of Ivy.

I push all thoughts of my crappy home life away—for the night at least—and stop outside the tent I know is Trent's.

I swallow thickly, counting to ten.

One, two, three, four, five, six, seven, eight, nine, ten.

And then again.

I know that behind the fibers of the tent Trent is waiting for me.

Wetting my lips with a flick of my tongue, I reach out, grabbing the zipper between my thumb and index finger.

I slowly pull it up, easing the zipper open. I'm positive my heart is about to beat out of my chest. I count its beats, but not even the counting can calm me tonight.

When there's a hole large enough for me to fit through, I slip inside.

A hand reaches out and grabs my arm. I shriek as I begin to fall but the hand holding my arm releases me and comes across my mouth to stifle the sound.

"Shhh, Row," Trent whispers and the sound of his voice makes me shiver.

"Sorry," I mouth when he moves his hand.

He eases his weight off me and closes the tent. "I didn't think you would come," he admits, biting his lips adorably. His teeth are slightly crooked and there is a space between the front ones, but I think it only makes him more handsome. I'd never been attracted to a guy before I laid eyes on Trenton. He turned my insides to mush, but more than that, he was my best friend. When I moved here earlier this year, I'd been so scared. I'd never been the new girl before and I was shy. Making friends had never been easy for me. But Trent had taken me under his wing. I'd questioned his motives at first. After all, why would a guy as gorgeous as Trent want to be my friend? I quickly learned, though, he didn't have any friends. He was a loner ... an outcast like me ... and we clicked. Since I transferred to this high school in November, we'd grown closer every day. Our friendship blossoming into more. He wasn't my boyfriend—that was too simple of a word. He was my everything. My air. My gravity. He kept me centered. It was spring now, and with the blossoming of the first flowers, we'd decided to take our relationship to the next level.

His home wasn't an option for what we had planned and neither was mine. In fact, I'd only been to his house once, and he'd never been to mine. I didn't want anyone to know what I had to deal with at home. Some things were better left in the dark.

"Row." He flicks his finger against the end of my nose. "What are you thinking about?"

"You," I whisper.

"Me?" He grins crookedly. "Good things, I hope." His blue eyes sparkle when he talks. I like that he's always so animated. He's not like other guys that try to hide their feelings. He's real.

"Always." I reach up, cupping his face in my hands. A light dusting of stubble covers his cheeks.

"Are you scared?" he asks.

"Yes," I admit. I have no secrets with Trent.

"We don't have to," he assures me, pulling away.

"I know that." I grab onto his blue sweatshirt, holding on tight. "I want to. I promise."

He stares at me, unsure of if I'm lying or not.

"If you want me to stop what I'm doing at any time" —he closes his eyes as if his words pain him— "tell me and I'll stop, Row. I mean it. I don't want to pressure you."

"I want this," I tell him, wondering how many times I'll need to say it before he believes me.

He swallows thickly as a slow smile spreads across his face. Normally, the darkness would make it hard to see him, but his face is so close to mine that I see him perfectly.

"Here." He reaches for a pillow and lifts my head up to place it beneath me. "Is that better?"

"I was fine before." I giggle quietly from nervousness.

"I want this to be perfect for you, Row."

"It will be perfect," I grasp his arms as I speak, *"because I'm with you. I wouldn't want to do this with anyone else."*

Before I can talk myself out of it, I reach up and undo the zipper on his jacket. His eyes close as his breath falters.

Once the jacket is unzipped, I push it off his wide shoulders. He's left in a thin black t-shirt and my fingers greedily trace the lines of the tattoo on his arm. I've seen him without his shirt so I know that it starts at his shoulder and stops at his elbow. If you see it from a distance, it looks like an ocean scape, but up close you see that it's really different shades of blue in a watercolor design so it looks like it's dripping off his arm. I think it's beautiful, just like him.

"Row," his eyes open and his voice is shaky.

"Yeah?" I blink up at him.

"You're beautiful." He traces a finger over my rosy cheek.

I smile, knowing I'd been thinking the same thing about him.

I push my hands beneath the edge of his t-shirt and place my hands flat against his warm stomach. He's muscular, but not overly so.

I ease my hands back out and grasp the fabric in my hands, pulling it over his head. His baseball cap falls off his head and we both laugh.

"I feel like you're excited to get me naked." He chuckles.

"Maybe." I squirm at his gaze. I hate being stared at.

"I want to kiss you," he warns, his mouth lowering.

"Then do it," I challenge.

A quiet moan escapes me when his soft lips touch mine. I'm positive that no other guy out there is as good of a kisser as Trent is. It's just not possible. His tongue presses against my closed mouth and I open to let him plunge inside. My fingers pull at his hair, drawing him closer so his whole body is pressed against mine.

Warmth zings through my body at his touch and my hips rise to meet his. I gasp in surprise at the feel of his large length pressed against me. I honestly don't know why I'm so surprised. This is why I came here. So we could lose our virginity together.

"Trent," I gasp his name. "I need ..."

"What do you need, Row? Tell me. I'll give you whatever you want." He nips at my neck.

"You."

"You have me, Row. You'll always have me," he promises, and I know he means it.

I ease out of my t-shirt so I'm left in my bra and jeans.

"God, Rowan." His eyes heat as he stares at my breasts. "Who knew you were hiding those under all those baggy superhero t-shirts?"

"I like those shirts," I defend.

"I do too." He winks, kissing me again. His tongue snakes inside my mouth, flicking against my own.

My heart is still racing in my chest, even faster than earlier if that's possible. His large hand grasps my right breast and I gasp. I need more. I need him to make me feel alive. I need him to give me my freedom.

His hand moves over my stomach, stopping when he feels my belly button ring.

"You're pierced?" His eyes are wide as he looks down at me.

"Why are you surprised? You have tattoos and gauges," I comment.

"I don't know." He smiles crookedly. "I thought you were a good girl, Row."

"I'm far from a good girl," I admit.

"I like it." He slides down my body, flicking it with his tongue. My back bows off the ground in response. His breath is hot against my bare stomach and goosebumps begin to coat my skin.

His fingers find the button on my jeans and he flicks it open. With his eyes on mine, he eases the zipper down and pulls them off of me.

"God, you're fucking amazing." He eyes my long legs. "I want to be inside you so bad."

"Then hurry up," I whine.

"I don't want to hurt you." He bites his lip.

"I'm a virgin," I state. "It's going to hurt." God, boys could be so dumb.

"Still, I don't want to cause you pain."

"It can't be avoided." I wrap my legs around his waist and pull him flush against me. "I want this with you, Trent."

He swallows thickly at my words. "Maybe this was a bad idea—"

"It's not. This is the best idea we've ever had. You're my best friend, Trenton. I want us to experience this first together." I reach up, cupping his cheek in my hand and rubbing my thumb over his plump bottom lip. He playfully nips at my finger and I smile in response.

That seems to get through to him. "Together," he repeats.

He kicks his jeans off and removes the rest of my clothes. I'm a bit embarrassed, being completely naked in front of him, but it doesn't bother me as much as I thought it would.

He stares at me for one-hundred and sixteen seconds—I counted—before he finally removes his boxers and puts the condom on.

"Are you sure, Row?" he asks one last time, his jaw clenched and his arms stiff as he holds himself back.

"Positive."

He eases slowly inside me. My eyes pinch close and I grit my teeth at the feeling of tightness and pulling below. It hurts ... a lot ... but I know I can't make a sound for fear of the teachers discovering us. Plus, Trent would stop if he knew he was hurting me so badly.

"Almost there, Row." He kisses me as he thrusts inside the rest of the way. I guess he knew he'd need to muffle my small cry.

He holds himself above me, not moving, giving me the chance to adjust to the foreign feeling.

"Are you okay?" he asks.

I'm holding my breath, so I can't answer at first, but I nod slowly.

"Tell me when I can move."

"Not yet," I plead, my fingernails digging into his arms.

"Not yet," he agrees, kissing me slowly to ease my anxiety.

My body begins to relax and pleasure replaces pain. My hips wiggle and he groans.

"Row," he warns, his forehead pressed against mine.

"I'm ready. You can move."

He swallows thickly. "Tell me if it hurts and I'll stop."

I nod, biting my lip as he eases out a bit and then back in. It feels so good being connected to him like this. I never want it to end.

Sweat dampens our skin, making us stick together. I watch the muscles in his stomach clench as he thrusts in and out of me.

His breathing accelerates and I know he's close. I am too, although, my mom always told me to never expect any pleasure my first time. She lies, though. It's the only thing she's good at ... Well, she's good at getting drunk too.

"Row," he gasps, his thumb pressing against the throbbing nub. He rubs it in circles and my muscles tighten.

"Trent. Trent. Trent," I say his name over and over again. When I come apart, his mouth silences my cries. A moment later, he twitches inside me and I know it's over.

I'm not a virgin anymore.

He presses kisses to my neck before falling to the side. He wraps his damp body around mine and I close my eyes, smiling. It feels so good to be held like this. He brushes my long hair away from my neck. "I love you," he breathes, pressing tender kisses to the skin behind my ear.

Those three words drench my body in ice-cold water. It's a shock to my system and there's only one thing I know to do.

Run.

I sit up, grabbing at anything that might be my clothes.

"Row?" he questions and I refuse to look at him. I can't see his eyes right now. I won't be able to leave if I look at him. "Row? What did I do?" He presses a hand against my bare skin. "You don't have to say it back, but I thought you should know."

I don't say anything as I put my clothes back on.

"Row, where are you going?" he asks when I begin to unzip the tent.

I pause. "I can't stay the night here. The teachers will find me and we'll get in trouble. I'll see you in the morning."

But we both know it's a lie. From this moment on, I vow to do whatever it takes to erase myself from his life.

I sat up in bed, clutching at my chest as I struggled for air. My skin was damp with sweat and my hair stuck to my forehead. The dream—memory, I corrected myself—always did this to me. I wondered if there would ever be a time it didn't affect me.

I pushed the covers off and drew my knees to my chest.

Why couldn't I escape him?

Even when he was nowhere around, he still managed to weasel his way into my subconscious. Damn Wentworth.

I started to count—it was the only thing that seemed to calm me.

One, two, three, four, five, six, seven, eight, nine, ten.

The back of my neck was sticky with sweat, like the rest of my body, and I lifted my hair up to cool myself.

I looked over at the clock and groaned. It was only five in the morning, but I was the kind of person that once I was awakened I couldn't go back to sleep. I flicked the light on, blinking rapidly at the sudden brightness.

"Ugh," I groaned, rubbing my temples. I felt a headache coming on and that was the last thing I needed.

I had a prescription for my headaches, so I pulled the bottle out of my bedside drawer, popping one of the pills onto my tongue. With the stale water I'd brought to bed with me, I swallowed it down.

I placed my head in my hands, letting my long hair fall around me.

I was a mess. There was no other word to describe me.

I wanted to cry, but no tears came. It hurt too much to think about Trent. Everything had been perfect until he said those three words and ruined it all. *Why couldn't he keep his big mouth shut?*

I knew it was wrong to blame him. He didn't understand that those words didn't mean the same thing to me as they did to everyone else. Anyone that had ever told me they loved me was being deceitful. My mom. My grandparents. Everyone.

It was all a lie.

No one loved me.

I was nothing but a burden.

I WANTED to give Ivy and Tristan a decent breakfast, but there was barely any food in the refrigerator or small pantry. I got my paycheck from the library today and I'd use it to buy some groceries—hopefully, something I could use to make a decent meal out of.

"Sorry, guys." I frowned. "Looks like it's toast with butter for breakfast."

"I want Frosted Flakes!" Ivy cried.

"We don't have any." I sighed, brushing my hair out of my eyes.

"Fine," she grumbled, "toast is fine." She pouted for a moment, but it didn't last long. Unfortunately, all three of us were accustomed to not having proper meals and often going hungry. It broke my heart that I couldn't do more. But my paycheck wasn't large, since I spent the majority of my time at college trying to build a better life for us. No one knew, but my hope was to get a stable job, save enough money to buy a house and better car, then fight for custody of my siblings. I wouldn't leave them in this hellhole.

I handed each of the kids a piece of toast with butter. They ate it like it was the most delicious thing to ever pass through their lips.

I checked that their backpacks had everything in them.

When I was sure they weren't missing anything, I set the bags on the table. "Ivy, you needed to brush your hair," I said sternly.

She opened her mouth to argue but I pressed a finger against her lips. "No, Ivy."

Rolling her eyes at me, she stuffed the last of the toast in her mouth and sauntered out of the kitchen. I feared the teenage years with that one.

"Row, can you brush my teeth for me?" Tristan asked, wiping his hands on a paper napkin.

"Sure." I ruffled his hair.

Raising Ivy and Tristan had been a lot to take on, but they were worth it. I didn't understand how anyone could abandon their kids the way my mom had. But alcohol would always be the most important thing to her.

After I helped Tristan brush his teeth, it was time to get them in the car and drive them to school. Since I was either in class or working I was never able to pick them up, but I felt it was important that I at least drive them there.

"Ooh! Ooh! Turn it up, Row! I love this song!" Ivy chanted, bouncing in the back seat.

I sighed and turned the volume up. "Royals" by Lorde began to play and I was tempted to plug my ears. They played that song all the time and it was annoying. Why did radio stations insist on playing the same song over and over again? I mean, really?

Ivy sang along to the song. I had to agree with the lyrics, though. I didn't see how we'd ever be anything other than lower class, no matter how hard I might be trying to get to the top.

I pulled into the school's parking lot and circled around to the drop-off line.

"Have a good day!" I forced a cheerful tone as they got out of the car.

They said goodbye and then I was pulling away and driving across town to the university campus. It was nothing fancy, but it sufficed, and it was certainly expensive enough. I had the school loans to prove it. I was taking classes that might help me get into their nursing program. I was banking on getting accepted into it. If I didn't—well, I'd rather not think about it.

I parked in my usual spot in the back of the parking lot. I liked the walk. It allowed me to clear my head.

"Hey!"

I turned and found myself smiling as Jude jogged toward me. I didn't know how we'd ended up friends, but somehow, we'd clicked. He was tall with brown eyes and light stubble dotting his jaw. His straight brown hair fell messily over his forehead in a way that was effortlessly sexy. His long-sleeved green shirt hugged his muscular chest and jeans hung dangerously low on his hips. I'd be lying if I said I wasn't attracted to Jude, but what I felt for Trent was so much more—even if I insisted on denying it.

Jude wrapped his muscular arms around my torso and spun me around.

"Put me down!" I shrieked, beating his solid chest with my mitten covered hands.

"I missed you, Row." He grinned crookedly and planted a kiss on my cheek.

"You saw me yesterday," I replied, running my fingers through my hair after he'd set me down.

"So? I still missed you." He smirked, striding beside me.

"I didn't miss you." I looked up at him, fighting a smile.

"What?" he gasped, putting a hand to his chest. "How could you not miss me? Most women *wished* I missed them, and here you are wounding me for professing my feelings. Nice, Rowan. Real nice."

"Oh, please," I laughed, adjusting the straps of my backpack as we crossed from the parking lot onto the sidewalk. "We both know you were banging some girl's brains out last night."

"True." He winked. "Could've been you," he said with a chuckle.

I pretended to gag. "No, thanks."

"Are you a lesbian or something?" he joked. "I've never met a straight female that didn't want to hop on this and take a ride." He stopped walking and rolled his hips in a vulgar manner.

"Not a lesbian," I told him then shook my head, "just not into man whores."

"Baby, for you I'd change my ways." He threw an arm over my shoulder and hugged me against him. A girl passed us and glared at me. She had to be one of Jude's many conquests.

"And ruin our wonderful friendship? I think not." I removed his arm from my shoulders.

"That's true. I really value our friendship."

"Sure you do." I rolled my eyes, heading into the building.

"I do," he assured me, his voice suddenly serious.

We headed into the same classroom and he sat down in the seat beside me. It amazed me that Jude—womanizer, playboy, *Jude*—was studying to be a nurse. I'd think he'd be too selfish for that. But while I might joke about his slutty ways, Jude was a nice guy ... to me, at least. He was also caring and compassionate. Once, when we'd been working at a hospice, I'd seen him spend an hour just talking to one of the older ladies.

Jude propped his legs on the empty chair in front of him, crossing his legs at the ankle. Our classrooms were auditorium style, which I hated because that meant that the table attached to my chair was less than adequate workspace.

"Professor Hamilton is going to be pissed if he comes in here and sees your shoes on the seat," I warned.

"I don't give a fuck." He shrugged, eyeing one of the girls in the classroom. When she caught his gaze he licked his lips suggestively.

I kicked the legs of his chair and he glared at me. "What the fuck, Rowan?"

"Sorry, I couldn't control myself." I shrugged innocently. "I have muscle spasms."

"Yeah, right." He rolled his eyes and let his feet drop to the ground. "You disturbed my mojo."

"Your mojo?" I raised a brow.

"Yeah. Are you jealous or something?"

"Hardly." I propped my head on my hand, wishing the professor would hurry up and get here already. "I was trying not to throw up in my mouth."

He leaned back in the chair, his eyes sparkling with barely contained laughter. "You amuse me."

"Is that why you keep me around?" I replied. I was used to this banter with Jude. It's how our strange friendship worked.

"I keep you around because you're hot and it makes other guys think I'm not checking out their girlfriends," he said with a straight face and I knew he was being serious.

"Thanks, that makes me feel really good." I shook my head, trying not to laugh.

"Aw, Row" —he brushed my long hair over my shoulder— "you know I love you."

"I know." I smiled at him.

"Good." He leaned forward, drumming his fingers on the table. Jude was the kind of person that couldn't sit still to save himself. Sometimes that really irritated me since I was a quiet person by nature. I honestly didn't understand how we'd become friends. We'd met our freshman year at the university. He'd sat down beside me, flirting shamelessly, and I—of course—shut down his advances. From that moment on, he became my only other friend besides Tatum. "We should go out tonight," he suggested. I glared, so he added, "As friends, of course."

"I can't. I'm working, you know that." I sighed.

"You're always working," he grumbled, "when do you have time to just ... chill?"

"Never," I answered without hesitation.

"That fucking sucks." He rubbed his hands over his face and stifled a yawn.

"It's called life."

"You deserve a break, everyone does," he commented.

"I don't have time for breaks." I shrugged, pulling a pencil out of my backpack and a notebook. "It is what it is."

He opened his mouth to argue but the professor finally decided to make an appearance—ten minutes late, I might add.

I turned away from Jude and set about taking notes.

I WAS RUNNING LATE and I *hated* being late, but I had gotten stuck in traffic thanks to a train passing through town.

I ran into the library bathroom and locked myself in the wheelchair accessible stall. I changed out of the clothes I'd worn to class and into my work clothes, stuffing my jeans and sweater into my backpack so I could change into them again after my shift ended.

I opened the stall door, washed my hands, and jogged down the hall to the backroom where we stored our stuff.

I ran back up to the front—winded at this point—and stopped in front of Mary, the head librarian. She was an older lady, in her sixties, with short gray hair. She was one of the kindest people I knew, but I hated to disappoint her by being late, especially since she was the one who had hired me.

"I'm so sorry I'm late," I gasped.

She looked at me for a moment and her eyes flicked over to the clock on the desk. "You're two minutes late," she stated.

"I know, and I'm really—"

"Shush, child." She lowered her reading glasses. "I hardly constitute this as *late*, besides, you're usually early. Don't worry about it."

"But—"

She raised a brow and the look in her eyes silenced me. "You have nothing to be sorry for, Rowan. Now quit wasting my time with your apologies and put those books back on the shelves."

"I'm on it," I assured her, taking the cart and grabbing the first book.

"And Rowan?" she called before I was out of earshot.

"Yeah?" I turned to look at her.

"If you're late again, don't apologize. Just get to work."

"Sure thing."

I started the mindless job of replacing the books on the shelves. I loved being surrounded by books. They were the only thing in my life that always managed to make me happy. Reading allowed me to escape from my shitty life, even if it was only for a few hours. It was nice to ... disappear for a while.

Before I knew it, the cart was empty. I rolled it back and there was another waiting for me.

By the time I finished, the library was closed.

"Are you staying to study?" Mary asked, handing me the envelope with my check in it.

Technically, I wasn't allowed to stay after hours, but Mary trusted me and didn't mind.

"No." I shook my head, frowning. I *really* needed to study and get my homework done since I had trouble doing it at home, but I needed to stop by the grocery store and get some food. I knew my mom wouldn't have bothered to make Tristan and Ivy anything to eat—even if she tried there wasn't any food in the house. "I have to go to the store."

"Oh, okay then." Mary smiled and patted my arm as she flicked off the light on the desk.

"I'm going to change," I told her, already heading toward the backroom to grab my bag.

"I'll wait for you, sweetie." She shrugged into her winter coat.

"No, no, you go on ahead," I assured her with a wave of my hand.

"Don't be silly."

"Mary." I stopped with a hand on the door. "I leave here by myself a lot of nights. You don't need to worry about me."

"Don't be stubborn now, young lady," Mary warned.

"All right," I sighed. "Give me a minute."

I changed out of my clothes in record speed and met Mary at the front. She closed the large library doors behind us and locked them. The library was located in a historical part of town and first opened its doors in nineteen-thirteen. It was massive and one of the most beautiful buildings I'd ever seen.

Mary and I walked down the sidewalk and over to the parking lot. I waved goodbye and got behind the wheel of my ancient—but reliable—Honda Civic.

I was exhausted, but my day was far from over. I still needed to stop by the local Wal-Mart to get groceries before I went home. I'd have to deposit my check first thing in the morning so I didn't get a bill for overdrawing my account. That would majorly suck.

The parking lot was packed, even at six in the evening. I ended up having to park all the way in the back of the parking lot, which sucked since it was so cold out and my lightweight coat did little to protect me from the frigid wind and snow flurries. My long legs carried me quickly into the store. I grabbed a shopping cart and pulled the grocery list from my pocket.

My first stop was to get frozen lasagna. I would have rather gotten the ingredients to make it homemade, but it was far too expensive. I was used to living on a budget. I swung by and grabbed a package of deli turkey before heading down the bread aisle. I scanned the prices, looking for whatever was cheapest. Ivy and Tristan had learned early on that we couldn't afford to be picky. Whatever was the lowest price was what we ate.

I bent down and scanned the lowest shelf. "A-ha," I mumbled under my breath when I found what I wanted.

"I never knew bread was so interesting."

The hairs on my spine stood on end.

No. Freaking. Way.

I stood slowly, the plastic bag that held the bread was clasped tightly in my hand. I turned, shaking slightly, and my eyes connected with Trent's.

"Evening, Row." He smiled cockily, tilting his head. He was dressed casually in jeans and a black leather jacket with a baseball cap perched on his head.

"What are you doing here?"

Shit. I'd said the exact same thing when he'd shown up at the library. I really needed to stop talking around him.

"Getting bread, obviously." Looking at me, he reached out and grabbed a random bag of bread. Several other loaves tumbled to the floor, but neither of us moved to pick them up.

"Obviously," I whispered, at a loss for words. I looked behind me, hoping for a means of escape, but running away—again—would have been childish.

"Mind if I walk with you?" he asked, smiling crookedly.

My stomach did a somersault. Why did he have to affect me like this even after all these years?

"I don't think that would be a good idea."

"Why not?" He stepped closer to me, so close that I could clearly smell his cologne.

"Because …," I faltered.

Using my hesitation to his advantage, he moved around me and began pushing the shopping cart.

"Hey!" I called after him. He totally just stole my shopping cart, where my purse currently resided, like it was no big deal. *Ugh*. I wanted to punch the little cart caper.

"Come on, Row." His lips quirked. "What do you need next?" He nodded at my list.

"Pasta noodles," I found myself saying as I trailed behind him.

Trenton smiled and turned down the correct aisle.

I should've taken the cart from him and told him to get lost, but I couldn't make myself do it or form the words. Instead, I walked beside him, gripping the shopping list so tightly in my hand that it began to tear.

"How've you been, Row?" he asked, stopping in the middle of the pasta aisle—not caring that he was blocking people.

I swallowed thickly. "Is that what you tracked me down to ask me?" I countered.

"Tracked you down?" He chuckled, gazing down at me with those blue eyes that sent warmth flooding through my body. "That implies I wanted to find you."

I turned my face in the opposite direction so he couldn't see the heat infusing my cheeks.

"Hey." Trent stopped and grabbed my arm. "I was kidding, Row. I didn't mean to hurt your feelings."

"You didn't," I said too quickly.

"Liar." He eyed me, his jaw set.

"What are you even doing here?" I asked, trying to deflect the conversation from myself. "Aren't you off at UVA?"

"It's Thanksgiving break."

"Oh." How had I been completely oblivious to the fact that Thanksgiving was this week? I had no idea what I was going to do for the kids ... I needed to do *something*. Surely, I could find a cheap turkey? Or maybe Mary would help me out? She loved the kids, and while she didn't know the details of my home life, she knew it wasn't the greatest.

"Row? Rowan?"

"What?" I shook my head, clearing my thoughts.

"Where'd you go?" he asked.

"What do you mean?"

"You were completely lost in your thoughts. You couldn't even hear me."

"I have a lot to think about." I crossed my arms over my chest and stared down at my worn shoes.

Trent shook his head and pushed the shopping cart forward. "What kind of pasta do you need?" he asked, changing the subject, and I was incredibly thankful. Trent was good like that. He pushed me more than I liked, but he always knew when to back off. Maybe that's what scared me the most about Trenton. He knew me better than I knew myself.

"Whatever is cheapest," I muttered under my breath. I knew Trent had never had to live on a budget. His family was worth billions—they certainly didn't act like uppity rich people, though, so you had to give them credit there. In fact, they were the nicest people I'd ever met—even if I'd only met them briefly years ago. Years. Funny, it felt like a lifetime.

Trenton surprised me by reaching for the Wal-Mart brand spaghetti noodles and placing it in the cart.

We continued through the store, shopping for groceries together. I'd read something off the list and Trent would twist the cart in whatever direction we needed to go. I hated to admit it, but despite the fact that we barely spoke, I was really enjoying his company.

"So," I started, nervously fiddling with the buttons on my jacket, "what are you doing here? This isn't exactly the most glamorous place." I swirled my finger in the air for emphasis.

"I needed some ferret food." He shrugged, pushing the cart

forward and reaching up to push the brim of the baseball cap out of his eyes.

"Ferret food?" I questioned in disbelief.

"Yeah. I have a ferret and he has to eat."

"Do they even sell ferret food here? And there's a Pet-Smart right down the road, why wouldn't you go there?"

"So many questions, Row." He sighed, grabbing a container of orange juice and heading for the eggs. "Yes, they have ferret food here. I don't go to Pet-Smart because if I did that, then I'd want to bring home every furry creature I saw while I was there."

"You seriously have a ferret?" I continued to drill him.

"Yes, I seriously have a ferret. His name is Bartholomew and he's really cute. You should come over and play with him sometime. He needs friends." Trent grinned at me. "How are these?" He held up a carton of eggs.

"Those are great," I answered his question. "You know, I could see you with a snake or a lizard, but not a ferret."

Trent shuddered. "Don't tell anyone, because it'll ruin my street cred, but I hate reptiles. I'm not saying I'm going to go out and kill a snake because I hate them, I'm all for saving any little creature, I just don't want one living in my house."

I cracked a smile at that. "You're an interesting guy, Trenton."

He gazed down at me, studying my features. I found myself squirming at the intrusive stare. "Why did you stop talking to me?"

Shit.

I brushed past him and grabbed the handle of the shopping cart. I walked as fast as my legs could carry me, but Trent jogged after me.

"Whoa, whoa, whoa." He reached out, bringing the cart to a halt. "You're not getting away that easily. You don't want to answer the question? Fine, but I'm not going anywhere."

"Of course you're not," I grumbled under my breath. Trent would stick around and fester under my skin. He'd find a way into my heart, and when he did I'd have to tell him all my secrets. And when he found out what I had done he'd hate me, and I wouldn't blame him.

"I'm a Wentworth." He bumped me aside with his hip and took over with the shopping cart. "And we're incredibly stubborn, so get used to it."

"Believe me, I'm well acquainted with your stubbornness," I grumbled under my breath.

Trent glanced at me over his shoulder, grinning like the cat that ate the canary. Uh-oh. What had I said? "I like that you're admitting just how well you know me. This might not be as difficult as I thought."

"What might not be difficult?" I ground my teeth together. I swear, only Trent seemed to know what buttons to push to piss me off.

"Getting you to see that we're perfect for each other." He pushed the cart forward, and I had to force my gaze to the ground so that I didn't study the way his shoulders flexed beneath his leather jacket.

"We are *not* perfect for each other," I said vehemently. "So stop wasting your time."

"It's okay to fight what we have, Rowan. I like your spunkiness."

Ugh.

"Why now?" I asked. After what we did on the school camping trip, I'd avoided Trent. Yeah, he'd tried to pursue me but, eventually, he gave up and moved on. When we returned for our junior year of high school we'd both changed a lot and he'd left me alone. But for the last year or so, whenever Trent was home from college, he was constantly popping up when I least expected him. It was quite a talent he had.

"Now is our time. We weren't meant to be together back in high school, but now we're both older and ready." He stopped in the middle aisle and reached out to caress my cheek. I hated how good it felt to be touched by him. I didn't want to admit it, but I had missed him.

"Trent ..." I couldn't seem to make myself say the words to tell him he was wrong. Being with Trent had always been effortless. He had been my best friend, and I knew if I let him he'd easily step back into that role as well as lover but I wasn't sure I could let him. We'd both end up broken in the end. "I— Never mind."

He grinned crookedly. "I'm so happy you see things my way."

"Whatever." I rolled my eyes. Arguing with Trent was futile.

"What's left on the list?" He nodded at the piece of paper still clenched in my fist.

I unclasped my hand and looked down at the wrinkled paper. I could barely read my own handwriting I'd crinkled it so much.

"I need to get coats for Ivy and Tristan," I mumbled.

Trent raised a brow.

"My siblings," I muttered, casting my eyes to the ground.

"Yeah, I remember Ivy. But Tristan?" he questioned.

I kicked the toe of my worn shoe against the linoleum tile floors. "Yeah, he's my brother. He's only five. Apparently, my mom has never heard of condoms or birth control." My cheeks colored.

"Huh." He clucked his tongue. "So, let me guess, you're the one taking care of them?"

"Ding, ding, ding, we have a winner," I said in a flat voice. I'd confessed years ago to Trent that my mom was an alcoholic. I wasn't sure if he knew how bad she was, though—that she had basically been comatose since Tristan was born and that when she was awake she was violent.

"God, Row, you're not their mom. You have school, and a job. How do you do it?" He looked at me like he was really seeing me for the first time.

"You do what you have to do to survive. My mom doesn't take care of them, so I do."

His stare was penetrating, and I found myself squirming from the scrutiny.

He shook his head and the muscle in his jaw ticked, but he chose not to say anything.

He pushed the cart into the kid's clothing section and began scanning racks of coats. "How about this one?" He held up a blue coat with green dinosaurs on it.

I smiled at his effort. "Tristan likes dinosaurs, it's perfect."

Trent beamed at that. Trenton really did like helping people—particularly me, it seemed.

I grabbed a coat in the right size and dropped it into the cart.

I found a pretty purple coat for Ivy and deemed this shopping trip complete.

"All right, I'm done." I forced a small smile for Trent. "Should you go grab that ferret food you need?"

"Who said anything about ferret food?" He winked, heading toward the checkout.

I groaned, tilting my head back to look up at the ceiling. "You little liar. Do you even have a ferret?"

"Yeah, he just doesn't need any food right now." Trent shrugged, looking for a line that wasn't too long.

"Then why'd you tell me you were here for ferret food?" I continued to fire questions at him.

"It would be creepy if I said I came here because I saw your car. Ferret food seemed like a safe excuse."

"You're ridiculous." I shook my head, letting my long hair hide my face.

"Hey, I got to spend time with you, and you got to spend time with me. So, I'd say it was a win-win situation, wouldn't you?" He raised a brow as he reached into the cart to begin placing items on the conveyer belt.

"Who said I ever wanted to spend time with you?" I snapped.

His eyes flicked up to mine and hurt flashed briefly in the blue depths before being replaced by mischief. "You don't have to say it, Row. Your body does all the talking, and your body is attracted to my body."

"Keep dreaming," I mumbled, wrapping my arms protectively across my torso.

"Oh, I don't have to." His lips quirked up in a smile. "It won't be long till you see things my way. I've been told that I'm very persuasive."

"I'm guessing that you were the kid that was never told 'no' as a child," I quipped.

"Oh, I was told no plenty of times. Everyone knows my brother is the favorite. Personally, I don't get it. The guy dresses like he's going into the woods to cut down some trees, he says the *weirdest* things, and he's a pain in the ass." Shrugging, he added, "Don't worry, though, the lack of attention didn't ruin my childhood. I'm perfectly okay." He spread his arms wide. "There's no need to feel sorry for me, but if you'd like to kiss me and make it all better, I won't complain."

I rolled my eyes. "I'm not kissing you."

"You've kissed me before." Leaning in, so his lips brushed my ear, he whispered, "In fact, we've done *a lot* more than kiss."

My cheeks flamed and I put both of my hands against his muscular chest, giving him a shove.

He chuckled. "You can't deny the facts, Row."

I chose to ignore him, shoving the cart forward so I could start loading the plastic bags.

The cashier announced the total, and I reached for my wallet, but Trent was already pulling out a credit card.

"Nope, no way, put that thing away," I warned. I was *not* letting Trent buy my groceries. I didn't need his charity.

"Row, don't be difficult." He went to swipe his card.

"Don't even think about swiping that card, Trenton." My voice was icy cold. I was pissed.

"You mean like this?" He blinked his eyes innocently and swiped the card.

"Cancel that!" I pointed at the cashier. She looked at me like I had lost my mind. Maybe I had.

"Uh ..." She looked from me to Trent and back again.

"Don't listen to her." Trent waved a hand dismissively. "My girlfriend likes to assert her independence by buying the groceries. But I'm a man, and that's my job. She really needs to stop getting her panties in such a bunch."

My mouth fell open as the cashier handed him the receipt.

"I'm not your girlfriend." I don't know why those were the first words to leave my mouth.

"Oh, honey, you always say such hurtful things when you're on your period. I should've gotten you a brownie." He smirked, throwing a smile over his shoulder at the cashier. We sure were giving her an entertaining evening.

Trent pushed me aside and rolled the cart out into the night. He headed straight to where my car was parked and I wasn't surprised to see his shiny black car beside it.

"Open the trunk," he demanded, already grabbing up bags.

"I don't need your help."

He looked at me peculiarly. "I never said you did *need* my help, but I *want* to help you, and there's a big difference. Besides, Row, accepting help doesn't make you any less of an independent person. I know you're all for girl power and doing things by yourself, but it's okay to let someone else step in and take care of you."

I swallowed thickly, looking down at the ground so he couldn't see the tears in my eyes. I opened the trunk and stepped back, hoping he didn't see how upset I was.

No one had *ever* taken care of me. I was raising Ivy, Tristan, and myself. Nobody cared about me, and if I let Trent in I'd get spoiled to having him, then he'd leave and I'd be even more shattered than I was now.

He got all the groceries in the trunk and reached up to close it.

My breath fogged the chilly air as I forced myself to thank him. "Thank you," I finally squeaked after an awkward silence.

He laughed—and oh, my God, how I loved his laugh, it was husky and masculine, and perfect like him. "It really killed you to say that, didn't it?"

I shrugged. "No one ever helps me, so I'm not used to thanking people."

"That's really sad."

"It's the truth." I pushed my hair out of my eyes, heading for the driver's door. "I'll see you ... sometime."

"Row?"

"Yeah?" I turned back around and he was *right there*.

He reached out, caging me between his arms, his hands resting on the rusted hood of my car.

"Goodnight," he whispered huskily, and then he kissed me. It wasn't really a kiss, more a brush of his lips, but it was enough to ignite a fire in my body. I found myself leaning in, wanting more, but he was already gone.

I opened my eyes, which I hadn't realized I closed, and saw him getting into his car wearing a proud smirk.

He drove away and I still stood there in the cold. I was in a daze, shocked by his brazenness and how much I'd enjoyed the barely-there touch of our lips. My heart raced against my ribcage and I reached up to place shaking fingers against my lips. I was so screwed.

CHAPTER THREE

My car wouldn't start. It was completely dead. No lights. No clicking. Zilch.

I had stopped at the drugstore close to school before heading to class to pick up a few things and now I was stranded in the parking lot. If I had to, I could walk to campus from here, but it was a particularly windy day and my backpack probably weighed fifty pounds. I tried to comfort myself with the fact that today was a review day, but I still hated to miss a class. I prided myself on perfect attendance and grades.

I grabbed my phone, calling the insurance company so they could send for a tow truck. I was told to wait with my car and that a tow truck would arrive within thirty minutes to an hour. *Great*.

It was too cold for me to stay in my car, so I grabbed my backpack and headed inside Walgreens. I spoke to the cashier, explaining the situation, and asked if she minded if I worked on some homework while I waited. It wasn't an issue, so I picked a spot close to the door so I'd see the truck when it came, but far enough away that I wouldn't freeze every time it opened.

I had most of my homework done, only a review sheet left to fill out, so that took me no time at all. I pulled the book I was reading out of my bag and propped it on my knees. One of the perks of working at the library was the convenience of getting a new book to read. I couldn't afford a new book all the time—and I read fast—so it was nice to be able to check one out whenever I wanted.

Every time I read a page, I'd glance up in the hopes that the tow truck had arrived. But it wasn't here yet, and I'd been sitting here for close to an hour. It would be my luck that it would take closer to two hours to arrive.

Just when I was starting to get really pissed off, the truck pulled into the lot.

I shoved my stuff in my backpack and slung it over my shoulders. I stopped just as the automatic doors swooshed open. You had to be kidding me.

Wentworth Wheels, read the name on the side of the truck. It figured my insurance company would pick the *one* repair shop run by Trent's older brother.

I took a deep breath and forced myself to step outside and face this like a big girl.

"I believe I know you," Trace said as he climbed out of the truck. Trace was Trenton's older brother. They both looked alike with their dark hair and build, and both always seemed to forget to shave. The big difference between the two was Trent had blue eyes and Trace had green. "I haven't seen you in a long time. Rowan, right?"

I nodded, tucking a piece of hair behind my ear.

"Hey, Trent!" he called. "Come here! It's Rowan!"

My eyes threatened to bug out of my head as Trent rounded the front of the truck. Even when he wasn't trying to find me he was there. I couldn't escape him—and who was I kidding? I kind of liked seeing him.

He smiled an easy grin, casually leaning against the side of the truck. He didn't approach me like expected. Instead, he hung back, like he was waiting for me to make the first move. I had news for him, he'd have to keep waiting.

"Looks like you're in need of some help, Row." Trent nodded at my dead car.

"Yeah," I grumbled.

"Luckily," Trent spoke as he took a few steps forward, "my brother here knows exactly what he's doing, so you're in good hands." He clapped Trace on the shoulder.

Trace reached up to push his hair from his eyes and a wedding ring glinted on his left hand. I wondered when that had happened. "Don't worry. We'll get you fixed up in no time. The Wentworth brothers know *exactly* what they're doing." Something about the way he said it made me think he wasn't just talking about cars.

"You work on cars too?" I asked Trent.

He nodded, smiling crookedly. "Only when I'm home on breaks and during the summer."

"I didn't know that."

Trent stepped forward until we were so close that when the wind blew my hair brushed his chest. He grabbed a piece of my flying hair and rubbed it between his fingers, then reached up to tuck it behind my ear. "Remember, Rowan, there's a lot you don't know about me."

"I know plenty," I snapped, taking a step back to distance myself from him. The scent of his cologne was making me dizzy as memories of last night—his lips pressed so tenderly to mine—flickered through my thoughts. I wanted to deny enjoying the kiss, but I had. After I went home, it had been all I could think about.

"Ah" —he reached out, running the back of his fingers along my cheek— "but a person does a lot of changing in five years."

"You might have changed, Trent," I said as I pulled my hair back so it wasn't blowing in my face, "but so have I. I'm not the girl you remember from high school. She died a long time ago."

Trent frowned, a wrinkle marring his forehead. "I don't care who you were or who you've become. You're still *you*."

I shook my head. "I don't know who I am anymore, so how do you expect to ever know the real me?"

"I'll find her," he said triumphantly. "I always did like a challenge."

"Don't you see? I don't want to be a challenge for you—something to conquer and brag about." My eyes darted to the ground as I wrapped my arms around my body to protect from the searing wind.

"I never said I wanted to *conquer* you." He shook his head. "How do you always manage to misconstrue what I say?"

I shrugged, kicking a pebble with the toe of my worn shoe. "It's a talent."

He stepped forward again, grabbing my wrist so I couldn't get away. "I don't care what you say, I know you feel whatever this is that we have. Don't think for a minute that I haven't noticed the way your breath falters when I get too close or how your eyes flash with desire. I definitely can't forget the way you responded to me last night." His voice lowered to a husky whisper that had desire filling my belly, "You can't deny that you liked it when I kissed you."

He was right. I couldn't refute it. I *had* liked kissing him.

"That doesn't mean it's going to happen again," I countered.

"Why do you insist on denying what we have? Are you really that stubborn?" He narrowed his eyes. "I *know* you feel it," he whispered, stepping so close to me that my nose was pressed against his chest and his warmth enveloped me like a cozy blanket. His hand found mine, entwining our fingers together. "Don't fight it."

I jerked back, wrenching my hand from his. Disgust coated my tongue like a sticky syrup. "I can't do this, Trenton."

"What is it exactly that you think you can't do?" He pressed forward. He wasn't going to let me escape. I wished Trace would rescue me, but he was occupied in looking my car over.

I swallowed thickly, my pulse jumping. "I don't think you understand what I've been through." My voice was hushed with shame. "I'm … incapable of loving. Not just you, but anyone. The *only* people I love is my little brother and sister. It's like some fundamental piece of me is missing," I spoke fiercely, getting heated. "I'm. Not. Whole."

He took my face between his two large hands, staring down at me with a determined glint in his blue eyes. I swallowed thickly, my pulse fluttering in my throat. I thought for sure he was going to kiss me, but he didn't. "Then let me make you whole."

I was saved from answering by his brother calling us over.

Thank goodness I hadn't had to reply. I don't know what I would've said, probably something not very nice.

"Bad news, it's not the battery." Trace frowned, crossing his arms over his chest. "Your starter's gone out. It's going to be about two-hundred dollars to have it fixed."

Tears stung my eyes and I promptly closed my eyes so neither of the brothers could see how upset I was. I counted to ten, breathing deeply. When I had myself under control again I opened my eyes and said, "Tow it. It has to be fixed. I don't have any other choice."

"Row—"

"I'm fine," I snapped, cutting Trent off. "*It's* fine."

He appeared skeptical, but didn't say anything.

I went back inside the store while the brothers got my car hooked onto the back. I couldn't help and I was freezing anyway.

When they had it hooked up I was forced to get in the truck with them. I sat in the middle, caged in, and I began to feel extremely claustrophobic. "Can you drop me off at the university?" I asked.

"Sure." Trace shrugged. "Will you have a ride home?"

"Yeah." I knew I could get either Tatum or Jude to drive me to work and pick me up.

"I'll try to have this done tomorrow. I have everything I need to fix it, it's just a matter of how much time I have," he explained.

"If you could have it done today it would be so helpful. I always take my little brother and sister to school in the mornings, and we don't have a spare car," I rambled.

"It'll be done today," Trent assured me, leaning forward to eye his brother. "Today," he repeated.

Trace didn't say anything, he merely leaned his elbow against the window, and a small smile played on his lips. Clearly, his brother amused him.

Trace pulled into the parking lot and I directed him to where I needed to be dropped off. Trent hopped out of the truck and reached up to give me a hand to help me down. A part of me didn't want to accept his hand, but I didn't have much choice if I wanted to get out of the mammoth truck without breaking an ankle. I finally placed my hand in his, after an awkward hesitation. I forced myself to ignore the tiny zings coursing through my body at his touch.

I jumped down, stumbling to the side.

"Whoa." He grabbed my waist to steady me. "You okay?"

I nodded, embarrassment causing my cheeks to flush.

He reached inside the truck for my backpack and handed it to me. "I'll make sure he gets it done today. Even if I have to hold a gun to his head.".

"Thanks." I forced a smile, slinging my bag over my shoulder. "I really have to go. I'm already late."

"Of course." He climbed back in the truck. "See you later."

"See you later," I whispered, standing there and watching the truck disappear.

TATUM'S CAR was still being fixed, so luckily Jude was nice enough to be my chauffeur for the day. He pulled into the parking lot of Wentworth Wheels, and I took a deep breath as I prepared to see Trent again. This many times in only a few days was getting to be a bit much—especially since I hated how much I enjoyed seeing him.

"I'm gonna head out," Jude said, already putting the car in reverse, "if for some reason it's not ready, just call me and I'll come back."

"Thanks," I told him, slipping out of the car.

I headed into the shop through the open garage door. "Hello?" I called out, looking around. The place looked deserted. "Hello?" I ventured further into the shop.

"Hey!" Trent called from somewhere in front of me. "I'll be there in a second!"

I stopped where I was and waited for him. I looked around and found the garage to be oddly neat and tidy. Don't get me wrong, it was a repair shop so there were plenty of tools and the occasional grease spot on the ground, but it looked nicer than most. Trace had done a good job with the place; I remembered what a dump it had looked like before.

"Here's your keys." Trent grinned, appearing in front of me. He dangled them in front of my face, but when I went to grab them he lifted them too high for my reach. "Not so fast." He wiggled a finger in front of my face.

"What do you want?" I rolled my eyes, a disgusted breath whizzing past my lips.

"Well," he began, clutching my car keys in his fist, "since I was a good guy and stood over my brother all day to make sure he got this fixed for you, I think I deserve to be rewarded."

"Rewarded, huh?" I raised a brow in disbelief.

"Mhmm." He nodded, smiling crookedly. "Go to dinner with me."

"Yeah, um, no. I don't have time. I have to get home to take care of Tristan and Ivy, which means no time for dinner. Now, please, give me my keys." I held my hand out.

"Fine. Say no. Crush my dreams." He wiped away a pretend tear.

"I think you'll live." I rolled my eyes again, taking the keys from him. "How come *you* didn't fix it?" I questioned.

He smirked. "I would have, but my talents are more useful elsewhere."

"Talents?"

He shrugged. "Okay, that's a lie. I'm not very talented, at least when it comes to cars, Trace has got me beat there. All I can do is change oil and rotate tires. I assure you, though, I'm extremely talented in many other ways and if you'd like me to show you I'd be more than happy." He smirked, his tongue flicking out to moisten his lips.

"Uh ... no thanks." I shook my head. "I don't need a demonstration."

"Aw, too bad." He bit his bottom lip.

I shook my head. I really needed to stop being distracted by Trenton. "How much do I owe you guys?"

"I already paid him." Trent shoved his hands in his pockets.

"Why would you do that?" I asked through gritted teeth.

"Because I wanted to," he answered simply.

"Did you think for a second that maybe I didn't want your help?" My temperature was rising as anger filled me. "I don't need you to take care of me."

"Think of it as a friend doing a friend a favor." He shrugged casually. "Don't worry about it."

I don't think Trent understood how guilty I felt. I knew he had the money to blow, but that didn't matter to me. I didn't like being seen as a damsel in distress. This princess could take care of herself.

I didn't have time to stand there and argue with him, so I found myself saying, "Fine, but don't do it again."

He smiled triumphantly. "Your car's parked out front to your right," he said, backing away. I couldn't tell if he was angry that I'd turned him down or what. "And Rowan?"

"Yeah?" I turned back to face him.

"This isn't over. Not by a long shot."

CHAPTER FOUR

I tucked Tristan and Ivy into bed, kissing each of their foreheads, then I closed the door behind me and set about cleaning the kitchen. I was supposed to pick up Tatum in thirty minutes so we could hopefully get some homework done. I didn't know what went on at Tatum's house, but I got the impression that her parents didn't get along at all.

I hated leaving the kids once I got home, but they'd be asleep and never know I was even gone. If they woke up and needed me, I wouldn't be here, and that worried me. Only my mom was home, who was currently passed out in her bed, the floor littered with various bottles of alcohol. I had no idea where Jim was or if he was even coming home.

Once the kitchen was wiped down and the dishes were clean, I checked to see if the kids had fallen asleep. Both were snoozing peacefully and I knew I could make my escape.

As much as I hated to leave them, I needed to get out of the house more. My mom had been unbearable when I arrived home and didn't shut up until she passed out. I needed to get away from this toxic environment for a while. It was killing me, but I wasn't ready to escape yet.

I grabbed my backpack and purse from my room. I scribbled a note explaining where I was and shoved it under the kids' bedroom door in case they awoke.

When I pulled in front of Tatum's house she was already waiting outside. She hopped down the front steps and hurried to my car. "It's freezing," she shivered.

"Then why were you waiting outside?" I questioned as I pulled away.

"I couldn't get out of that house soon enough," she grumbled under her breath, looking out the window. "I hate it there. I just want to get away."

I didn't bother asking her about her home problems. It wasn't my business, and besides, I knew all about how easy it was to become trapped.

I drove to a local coffee shop that was open all night and that we'd often used for homework nights before. I ordered a latte and a muffin. I normally didn't indulge in such frivolous things, but since Trent had bought the groceries for me the other night I had the extra cash to treat myself.

I sat down at the table in the corner and Tatum left to order herself something. I pulled my books out of my backpack, sighing heavily at the amount of work I had to do. It never seemed to end. For once, I wanted to be like everyone else. I wanted to be able to sleep in and go out with friends. I wanted to let myself be with someone. But I couldn't do those things. I had to focus on getting through school and making high enough grades that I got accepted into the nursing program. I had to be able to take care of Ivy and Tristan. My mom and step-dad didn't do it now. It was all on my shoulders, and I was beginning to bow under the pressure. I was one person and I could only handle so much.

I removed the lid from my coffee so it could cool down. Tatum returned, pulling her blonde hair into a ponytail. She looked exhausted, with bruise-like shadows under her eyes. A part of me wanted to ask her if everything was okay, but I knew how much I hated being asked the same thing, so I kept my mouth shut.

I opened one of my books, flipping to the right page. I felt too tired to do homework, but I didn't have a choice. I only hoped we'd both be able to finish in two hours. I needed to get some sleep before class tomorrow. It was our last day before break and while we weren't starting anything new, I was sure they'd give us plenty to do for the few days we got off. I had learned early on that there was no such thing as a break.

I took a tentative sip of coffee, not wanting to scald my mouth. It was the perfect temperature though. Griffin, the owner of the coffee shop—that was really a coffee shop, restaurant, and a place for local musicians to perform—always got everything just right. I had never really talked to the guy—he was older and always pretended to be grouchy—but he seemed like a cool guy. He kept the place open 'round the clock. He and his wife mostly ran the place, with the help of a few employees. They did a really good business with all the local college kids.

An hour later I was out of coffee, had eaten my entire muffin, and thought if I read one more word I might fall over.

"I'm getting more coffee," I told Tatum as I stood.

She nodded in acknowledgement of my words but didn't look away from her laptop.

"Same thing?" Griffin asked as I approached the counter.

I nodded. "No muffin this time, it was delicious, though."

He punched something into the register and gave me the total. "Yeah, my wife makes them from scratch. Best muffins in the whole world."

I handed him the money and took my cup of coffee.

As I was turning I bumped into someone. "Shit," I cursed, doing a little dance to avoid spilling my hot coffee all over the person. Some sloshed on the floor, but I managed to miss the guy. "I'm so— You've got to be kidding me," I groaned. "Do you have a tracking device on me or something? This is so not cool."

Trent smirked, tilting his head as he studied me with those piercing blue eyes. "Maybe *you're* following me."

"I was here first," I responded, cringing at my words. I sounded like a whiny child. "Anyway," I said as I moved around him, backing toward the table, "sorry for almost spilling coffee on you."

"Apology accepted." He smiled, his eyes sparkling.

He turned to Griffin to place his order and once he wasn't looking I ran for the table, falling into my seat.

"What the hell?" Tatum exclaimed, surprised at my abrupt arrival. "No more coffee for you if it makes you that hyper."

"It's not the coffee," I whispered, letting my hair fall forward to shield me.

"Then what—" She looked over her shoulder to see what I was staring at. She smiled. "Ah, I see now." She laughed. "I don't know why you don't face facts, y'all so want to do each other, so get it over with already."

I spat out my coffee, surprised at her words. She ducked to avoid the spray, but some still landed on her shirt.

"I can't believe you said that." I grabbed a napkin, wiping up droplets of coffee.

"Hey, you two are the ones who have sex with your eyes."

"Who's having sex?"

I closed my eyes, my whole body flushing in embarrassment.

Trent grabbed a chair and pulled it up to the table. "Please, don't stop talking on my account. It sounded like you were getting to the good part."

Tatum sat forward, propping her head on her hand. "I was saying that clearly you're both attracted to each other, so you might as well do it and get it over with. It's going to happen eventually."

"Tatum!" I shrieked.

"It's true!" she exclaimed, throwing her hands dramatically in the air.

"Well ..." Trent tipped his chair back on two legs with a smirk gracing his full lips. "I'm happy to hear I have someone on my side. Not that I only want to *do* the lovely Rowan. I want much more than that."

I rolled my eyes. "Oh, please."

"What?" He raised a brow. "It's not possible that a guy might want more than sex? Come on, Row, you know I'm not some player looking to get in your pants for one night." He eyed me, daring me to refute him, but I couldn't. I did know Trent, and I knew he wanted much more from me than sex, and that's what scared me the most. Trenton wanted all of me, specifically my heart, and it wasn't something I could give away. I couldn't deny my attraction to him, though. I did yearn for him, but he wanted more than I was willing to give. "Go on a date with me," he pleaded. "You, me, and a delicious dinner. I'm not asking for anything else."

Tatum kicked my shin from beneath the table, willing me to say yes.

"No."

Trent stood, replacing the chair he'd sat in back to the table it belonged with, and grabbed his cup of coffee. Pointing a finger at me, he said, "I knew you'd say that. But it won't stop me from asking you again and again, until one day you do say yes. See you later, Rowan."

With that, he turned sharply on his heel, and headed out the door. The bell dinged above the door, signaling his departure.

"Why won't you go on a date with him?" Tatum asked, her mouth agape with shock. "He's hot and he's nice, that's a winning combination in my book."

"I don't date," I stated bluntly. "I don't have time for a relationship. It wouldn't be fair."

"Excuses, excuses." Tatum shook her head, a few strands of blonde hair escaping her ponytail to frame her face. "I know you're busy with school, and taking care of your brother and sister, but you have to find time to do something for yourself. What's so wrong with letting yourself have some fun?"

"It's complicated."

"I don't see anything complicated about it. You like him. He likes you. Go for it. Live a little." She smiled as she started packing her stuff up.

Live a little.

I pondered those words, wondering if I could do it—if I could branch out and let myself give in to my desires.

CHAPTER FIVE

Jude and I walked across the parking lot toward our cars. Today had been the last day of classes before our short break. Unfortunately, the professors hadn't been kind enough to cut us some slack so I had plenty of homework to occupy my time—which I had been sure would happen.

"Wanna grab something to eat before you go to work?" Jude asked me. "I'm starving and I'd really like to have a pretty girl to sit with me."

"Jude," I grumbled, "I really don't have the time."

"You have an hour before you need to be there." He bumped my shoulder with his as we stopped beside my car.

I stared up at him. "The fact that you know my work schedule is mildly disturbing. Don't you have better things to do to occupy your time than take me to dinner?"

"That would be a no." He grinned, adjusting the beanie he wore. "Come on, Row. I'll even buy your meal."

I *was* hungry, and while I'd been planning to use my spare hour of studying, I decided what the heck. I did deserve to have some fun now and then.

"Okay," I agreed.

Jude appeared taken aback.

"Excuse me, can you repeat that? I don't think I heard you right." He turned his ear toward me.

"I said okay."

"It's a miracle, folks." Jude began to clap like we had an audience.

I rolled my eyes. "You're ridiculous."

"And you're always turning me down. This is a moment that should be documented in history."

"Oh, whatever. You know I'm busy," I told him. I did feel bad, though, that I tended to ignore my friends, but I had so much going on and they didn't even know the half of it.

"Yeah, I know." He reached up and removed his beanie, twisting it in his hands. "But sometimes you need to be a normal twenty-one-year-old for a while. Otherwise, you might go crazy." He tweaked my nose.

I pushed his hand off of me, glaring at him. "We haven't even gotten dinner yet, and I'm already regretting my decision to say yes."

"Oh, Row, straight to the heart." He put a hand against his chest, dramatically acting like he'd been shot. People were beginning to stare.

"Quit it, Jude," I grumbled under my breath, not liking the unwanted attention.

"Aw, come on, Row, don't get so worked up." He slung an arm over my shoulders.

I shrugged his arm off. "Are we going to eat or not?

I *do* have to get to work," I warned him, grabbing a clip off my bag and using it to pull my hair out of my face.

"All right, bossy pants. Let's get some food in you. You get grumpy when you're hungry." He smirked.

"I'll follow you." I opened the driver's door of my car.

"I knew you liked looking at my butt, Row." He winked, sauntering away.

"Your truck! I'll follow your truck! Who said anything about looking at your butt?" I called after him.

He threw his head back and laughed, completely ignoring me.

Ugh. Jude could be so irritating sometimes.

I got in my car, tossing my purse and backpack onto the passenger's seat. I followed his truck out into the traffic and through the town. He parked on the street and I was lucky to grab a spot not too far away from his.

He jogged over to where I was, blowing air into his hands. "Fuck, it's cold," he groaned.

"It's not that bad." I shrugged. "There isn't even any snow."

He rolled his eyes, jumping in place. "It's cold," he stated. "You're crazy and feel nothing."

I chose to ignore his statement. "Lead the way. I don't know where we're going."

Jude shoved his hands in the pockets of his jeans and looked both ways before jogging across the street. I did the same, letting my long legs carry me to the sidewalk. He led me up a set of steps and in through the back of the restaurant. We passed a formal dining room and bathrooms, before it opened up into a large bar. I saw a door leading to a deck and outdoor patio, but of course it wasn't open in the winter months.

Jude picked a booth in the back corner. I took the seat across from him, looking around.

"You've never been here?" he asked.

"No." I shrugged, running my finger along the shiny lacquered tabletop. "I don't have extra money to go out to eat at nice places like this."

"Row..."

I looked up and flinched when I saw the pity in his gaze. I should've kept my mouth shut. I wasn't ashamed that I was poor. Lots of people were. But I hated when people looked at me like I was missing out on stuff because of my lack of money. I already knew I was, and I didn't need to see the reminder in their eyes.

"Just the two of you?" A waitress appeared beside our table, glaring at Jude. Geez, I couldn't go anywhere with guy. Had he slept with everyone?

"Yeah, just the two of us," Jude replied, leaning back in the booth with an easy grin.

She dropped the menus on the table and the plastic made a smacking sound as it hit the table. "What can I get you to drink then?"

"Water," I answered.

"Same," Jude replied, smiling at the waitress.

She rolled her eyes and turned sharply on her heel.

"She's so going to spit in my drink," I grumbled.

Jude chuckled, pulling off his beanie and running his fingers through his hair. "Nah, she won't bother you. It's me that'll be drinking her spit."

"Ew." I wrinkled my nose. "Anyway," I said as I picked up the menu, "what's good here?"

"Everything," he replied.

"That's real helpful, Jude."

"Hey, it's the truth." He chuckled, scratching his stubbled jaw.

Since I was starving and running out of time before I had to get to work, I ordered a turkey club sandwich. Jude ordered the same and cheese fries for an appetizer.

"Uh ... Rowan?" He leaned forward with both his hands on the table, looking at something over my shoulder.

"Yes?" I responded, inspecting my water for any foreign substances.

"Do you have a boyfriend?"

"God, no, Jude! You know that! And no, I'm not going to date you!"

"Hey." He raised his hands in defense. "I know you're not interested in me, that's why we're friends. But that dude over there is glaring at me like he wants to rip my balls from my body."

"Thanks for that disturbing visual, Jude," I groaned.

I looked over my shoulder to see who he was talking about, but couldn't see anything, because the top of the booth blocked my line of sight.

"Did he leave?" I asked.

"Nope." Jude picked up the wrapper from his straw and began playing with it. "He's still staring. I think he's planning to kill me and trying to figure out the best place to hide my body so no one finds me." He reached across the table and took my hand. "If I don't make it out of this alive, please tell my mom I love her."

"Are you sure you're not studying to be an actor?" I pulled my hand from his grasp.

"Oh, fuck," Jude paled as he spoke, sitting up straight, "he's coming over. I think he's pissed that I held your hand."

"Hello, Rowan." Both words were said through gritted teeth, telling me the person who spoke them was beyond mad.

A shiver danced down my spine as I recognized the voice.

"Hi, Trenton." I tried to keep my tone light and sound unaffected, even though my whole body was humming with pleasant zings at his close proximity.

"You know this guy?" Jude asked me, his mouth falling open in shock that I might possibly know someone other than him that possessed a penis.

I nodded. There was no way I could deny it, and I didn't want Trent to cause a scene. Well, an even bigger scene.

"Oh, she knows me better than I'm sure she knows you." Trent smiled—and there was nothing pleasant about it—as he slid into the booth beside me. "Who are you?"

"You don't have to say anything," I warned Jude, taking a sip of water.

Trent glared at me.

Jude swallowed thickly, looking like a deer caught in headlights. "I'm Jude."

"And are you on a date with my friend here?" Trent tilted his head toward me.

"No-o-o." Jude's voice shook. Scaredy-cat. "We're just grabbing a bite to eat." Jude was a tough guy, and I found the fact that he was scared of Trent to be hilarious. I'm sure with the way Jude got around he'd run into plenty of jealous boyfriends and had to fight his way out of a sticky situation, but something about Trent had him shaking in his boots.

"Yeah, and I bet you're trying to figure out how you're going to get her to go back to your place, aren't you? I bet she's just another conquest to someone like you. I know your type. You're always looking for an easy fuck. So, I suggest you look elsewhere."

My eyes widened and my jaw dropped at Trent's words. I punched his arm as hard as I could, forcing him to acknowledge my presence. I could tell Jude was pissed too and opened his mouth to say something to Trent, but I didn't need Jude to fight my battles.

"I can't believe you just said that to him," I spat at Trent, keeping my voice hushed so we didn't disturb the other people in the restaurant.

"Yeah, well." Trent reached up and ran his fingers nervously through his hair, obviously ashamed of his behavior. "I'm a bit pissed off that you keep wanting to brush me off, but you're out with this guy. You turned me down for dinner last night, but here you are with *him*." He pointed a forceful finger at Jude.

"This guy has a name, and it's Jude. J-U-D-E."

"Do I look like I care?" Trent glared, his nostrils flaring with anger.

"I'm *not* on a date, so stop being rude to him," I told Trent. I was tempted to kick him, but since he was beside me, that would've been quite difficult.

"Then what are you doing?" Trent looked from me to Jude.

"Why should I tell you? You're the one that came over here like a dog pissing on its territory," I seethed.

"Oh, this is good." Jude chuckled. I turned in his direction to see him shoving cheese fries in his mouth. "Please, continue."

I ignored Jude and went back to glaring at Trent. I was embarrassed by his behavior and I knew I'd have a lot of explaining to do, because Jude would want to know what was going on between Trent and me. I'd do my best to avoid that conversation for as long as possible. I didn't want to go into details with Jude about my past with Trenton.

"And you're the one that acts like you hate me, then I kiss you, and it's obvious you do want me," Trent countered, referring to the night after we shopped for groceries. "You can keep denying this as long as you want, but as long as your body continues reacting to me, I'll keep coming back."

"You kissed him?" Jude asked, dipping three fries in ranch. Of course, out of all of that the only part Jude noticed included kissing.

"*He* kissed *me*," I argued, glaring daggers at the two guys. "And it hardly was a kiss at all."

"Whatever you need to tell yourself to feel better." Trent smirked in my direction. "Can I have some of those?" he asked Jude, pointing to the fries.

"Sure, as long as you promise not to kill me and cut me up into tiny pieces." Jude shrugged, sliding the plate closer to where Trent and I sat. I guessed they were best friends forever now thanks to the magical bond of cheese fries. "Now, tell me about this kiss," Jude probed Trent for answers.

"There's nothing to tell," I spoke up before Trent could open his big fat mouth.

"It was a simple kiss goodnight." Trent shrugged, taking a fry as he talked over me.

"You naughty girl. I can't believe you didn't tell me." Jude winked.

"Why would I tell you?" I muttered under my breath. "You're a guy. Besides, it wasn't worth talking about."

"Burn," Jude coughed, eyeing Trent warily in case he decided to jump across the table and strangle him.

"Well, then." Trenton turned to face me, a challenge glimmering in his blue eyes. "I guess I'll have to give you something to talk about then."

"Huh?"

In a lightning-fast move, he grabbed my face between his large hands and pressed his lips against mine. The kiss was demanding and forceful, but somehow still passionate. It was the kind of combination that left your world spinning. I found my traitorous body responding to the feel of his tongue against my lips. I felt insecure and unsure what to do. I hadn't been with anyone since Trenton and that had been five years ago, so I was clearly out of practice. I found that my body seemed to know what to do, though. Despite my lack of knowledge. I grasped his sweatshirt between my fingers, curling the fabric into my fist. His tongue flicked against mine and a soft moan escaped me. My mind had gone completely blank and all I could do was feel. My lips followed his in a passionate dance.

Cold water flicked against my face and I pulled away from Trent. We both wiped our faces and looked in the direction the water had come from. Jude sat there grinning, wiping his hands on a napkin. "Y'all looked like you needed a cold shower. Seeing as how we're a little low on showers at the moment, I thought this would suffice—" he pointed to his glass of water.

My cheeks flamed. I couldn't believe I'd just let Trent kiss me like we were making a porno in the middle of a restaurant.

I pushed Trent's shoulders and he looked down at me. "What?"

"Get out." I pushed him harder.

"I'm not leaving." He refused to budge and he wasn't a little guy, so I was making no headway with my efforts to dump him on the floor.

"I need to go to the bathroom."

That got him to move. As soon as I was free, I ran to the bathrooms. I didn't want either of them to see me upset.

I turned the water on, lightly splashing my face. I counted to ten in my head—but it did nothing to calm me down. Trenton was the only person that had the ability to mess with my emotions. Normally, I was calm, cool, and collected. Trenton Wentworth turned me into some weepy, weak, little girl. I prided myself on being strong and not needing anyone. But being around Trent made me question what it would be like to have someone. Well, not *someone*. The only person I could ever see myself with was Trent. I knew it would be unfair to let myself be with him, even if it was only for a little while. Once upon a time he'd told me he loved me, and I knew I could never return that emotion. The only people I loved were Tristan and Ivy. I knew they'd never leave me but Trent? He would, eventually. Like all other guys, he'd get bored and move onto another plaything. I couldn't allow myself to get attached.

Oh, who was I kidding? I was already attached. I'd belonged to Trenton since I was sixteen years old.

The bathroom door creaked open and I looked up. In the mirror, my eyes connected with Trent's. My heart raced in my chest, thumping harshly against my ribcage. I didn't want to, but I did care about him. Maybe it was some silly teenage crush still lingering, or maybe it was just *Trent*, but I knew if he kept hanging around I wouldn't be able to ignore the temptation. He was dangerous for me, like a sweet intoxicating drug, and I was too dumb to tell him to leave—not that it would work anyway.

I was sick and tired of fighting my primal desire to own him. I was done denying myself what I wanted, and oh, how I wanted Trent. For so long, I'd put everyone else before me, and wasn't it time I did something that I wanted?

I licked my lips, my breath echoing against the tile walls. Neither of us said anything. We simply stared, chests heaving, waiting for the other to make the first move.

I swallowed thickly and forced myself to turn around and face him.

My eyes connected with his once more and butterflies took up residence in my stomach. I opened my mouth to speak, but nothing came out. I cleared my throat and tried again, knowing these very words could change my life.

"I want you."

His eyes flashed with desire and he stalked toward me. I found myself backed against the bathroom counter. He grasped my hips in his large hands and stared down at me. "You have no idea how long I've been waiting to hear you say that."

One hand stayed planted on my hip, while the other tangled in my hair, pulling my face toward his. His lips were against mine again for the second time in a matter of minutes. But this was nothing like the kiss we'd previously shared. While that one had been hot and demanding as he tried to prove a point, this one was a slow boil, simmering in my veins. I found my legs wrapping around his waist and suddenly my back was pressed against the tiled wall and my fingers were wrapped around the silky strands of his dark hair. His tongue twined with mine in a sensual duet. He groaned low in his throat and the sound sent a shiver down my spine. My legs wrapped tighter around his waist and his arousal pressed against me. *Holy shit.*

He nipped at my bottom lip, pulling it between his teeth and letting it go with a pop. I swore my temperature had risen ten degrees. Sweat broke out across my skin from the heat we were creating.

He dotted kisses down my neck and back up, latching his lips onto mine. I knew I wasn't just being kissed—I was being devoured—and I'd be lying if I said I wasn't enjoying it.

Being kissed like this was an all-consuming thing. I couldn't think about anything except the feel of his lips on mine and his body pressed against me.

He broke away, panting, and rested his head against the curve of my neck. He stayed where he was, holding me against the wall, with my legs still around his waist.

"Fuck," he breathed.

"Why'd you stop?" I panted, my fingers curling into his hair.

He pulled his head away from my neck to look at me. "I think it's pretty obvious that I want you." He pressed his hips into me and I gasped. "But not here and not like this. You deserve better than a public restroom and I—" He swallowed thickly, his eyes briefly closing. "I deserve to know that you do actually want this. I won't be able to handle it if you tell me you do and the next day you're back to ignoring me."

It hit me then that Trent was actually a pretty sensitive guy. What I had done to him—what I'd *been* doing—had hurt him. But I'd been hurt too and my heart was shattered beyond repair. I wanted him, though. That much was true. However, I didn't think I could give myself to him completely. I had to hope that what I had to offer would be enough for both of us—for now, at least, because I knew Trent would eventually find someone better suited for him than me. Besides, I'd never be able to let him in all the way. I couldn't tell him everything. It was wrong of me to want him for whatever time we could have. We'd both be better off if I spoke up and told him that I couldn't do this—that I had lied and I didn't want him. But I couldn't make myself form those words. Instead, "I do. I want this. I want you," came tumbling out of my mouth. A huge grin lifted his lips and he kissed me again.

Dread began to fill my stomach. I knew I'd just signed our death sentence, because there was no way my secrets would ever be able to stay buried, and when they surfaced we'd explode like a supernova. After that, it would be the end of Trent and me. No banter, no running from him, no kissing, no nothing, because I would never see him again. He'd remove himself from my life and it would all be over. Despite what I tried to tell myself, I did enjoy Trent's random popups. Seeing him made me feel alive when I was dead inside. Without those brief moments of aliveness, I'd become nothing. I was already nothing, but I'd cease to exist all together.

It was too late, though.

I couldn't take back my words.

I had sealed our fate and all I could do was enjoy this exhilarating ride until it came to an explosive end.

CHAPTER SIX

THE LIBRARY DOOR CLICKED CLOSED BEHIND ME. IT WAS late and I knew Tristan and Ivy were starving. I needed to get home and make them dinner. I hoped they both had their homework done so I wouldn't have to bother with that.

I started down the steps when a dark shadow to my right caught my eye.

I was starting to get scared when the person stepped fully into my line of sight. "Jesus, Trent!" I put a hand to my racing heart. "What are you doing creeping around here at night?"

He bit his lip, his hands shoved into the pockets of his coat. His breath formed foggy clouds in the cold air. "I'm sorry for showing up here like this ... although I'd think you'd be used to it by now." He chuckled, biting his plump bottom lip as he eyed me bashfully. "I needed to see you, though."

"You saw me at the restaurant," I remarked. I was still shocked that I told him that I wanted him. When we'd returned to the table he'd worn a proud smile and been the happiest I'd seen him in a long time. I still wasn't sure if it was the best idea to explore whatever this was between us. I felt we'd both end up hurt in the end.

"I needed to see you again," he repeated, taking a deep breath as his eyes briefly closed.

"Are you okay?" I questioned, my gaze carefully sliding over his body to make sure he wasn't harmed. "Has something happened?"

"Everything is fine," he assured me. "I needed ... I needed to see you before I went to bed. I have to make sure you're okay with this, whatever *this* is." He ran his fingers through his hair. "I won't be able to handle it if I wake up tomorrow and you're back to pretending I don't exist. I've waited five years for you to come back around. I can't—" He stopped, gritting his teeth like he was unsure if he wanted to continue with what he had to say. "I can't handle it if all you're doing is messing with me."

"Trenton, I ... I don't pretend to know everything and I certainly have no idea where we might be headed, but I'm yours."

His blue eyes flared brightly at my words.

I don't think he understood how much he *owned* me. Even at sixteen years old he'd ruined me for anyone else. He was all I knew and all I wanted. No one else could ever compare. I'd been through a lot over the years, and even then, I'd known I wasn't worthy of his love. I could never say the words back to him. I didn't know what it was to love someone that wasn't family. Regardless, that didn't stop my attraction. Although, many times I'd wished it had. Even after our night in the tent, when I'd started ignoring him, every time I saw him I'd been attacked by a major case of the butterflies. Over the years that feeling never went away. Trenton was the only man that was able to tempt me. He was like an intoxicating drug that I couldn't get enough of. I tried to stay away from him—because he might not know it, but we were bad for each other—but like any addict, I could only stay on the bandwagon so long. I was done being good. I wanted what I wanted, and that was Trent. He obviously wanted me too, so why deny myself any longer? It would end, I knew that, but at least I'd have experienced what it was truly like to be with Trent, and I'd be able to look back at those memories with fondness.

"Say it again," he breathed, reaching up to run his thumb over my bottom lip.

"I'm yours," I whispered. *For now, and forever.* "I'm done running. I'm done fighting what I feel," I spoke passionately. "I'm doing this for me."

"And what is this, Row?" Trent asked huskily, leaning so close to me that if I moved an inch my lips would be on his. "What are we?"

"I-I don't know," I answered honestly. "Why does it need a definition? Why can't we just be ... us?"

"Just us," he mused. "I like the sound of that."

I liked the sound of it too—almost too much, but I wasn't telling him that.

"As much as I'd like to stand here and chat, I've really got to go," I told him, already walking away.

He was quick to catch up to me, falling into step beside me. "We can walk and talk."

"What do you want to talk about?" I adjusted the strap of my purse on my shoulder.

"How about we figure out where we're going on our first

official date?" he suggested, jogging in front of me and turning around to face me as he walked backward.

"Surprise me." I rolled my eyes as he began to balance on the edge of the sidewalk.

"Hmm." He did a little hop, coming back to my side and throwing an arm over my shoulders. "I do love surprises. Whatever will I come up with?"

"Nothing too crazy, please?" I begged. "And don't drag me to another state. I do have to be home."

"I think I can come up with something in those parameters." He chuckled, reaching for my hand.

I skidded out of the way and pretended to be messing with my hair.

Trenton raised a brow in puzzlement. "You don't want me to hold your hand," he stated.

I swallowed thickly and nodded. There was no sense in denying it. I found there to be something oddly intimate about holding a person's hand, you were connected, twined together, and that scared me.

"Why?" he questioned.

"I don't know," I lied, starting forward. The parking lot was in sight and I could make my escape from this uncomfortable conversation. "I just don't."

"Oookay," Trent drew out the word, his legs carrying him quickly back to my side. "No hand-holding. I'm still allowed to kiss you, though, right?"

"Since when do you ask for permission?" I sighed, stopping beside my car.

"Good point," he whispered gruffly, stepping so close to me that our bodies lined up. He cupped the nape of my neck in one of his large hands and drew my face toward his. "This is me not asking for permission."

My eyes closed at the first touch of his soft lips. My body melted against him and I grasped his forearms for support. I had always prided myself on having little to no reaction to the things surrounding me, I was closed off and proud of it, but Trent managed to make me *feel*. He barreled right through the cinderblock walls I'd built around myself. He'd never get my heart, that was too well guarded, but I knew he'd try.

I forced myself to stop thinking so much and enjoy the feel of being in his arms. He backed me up against the car, towering above me. I wasn't short, but in Trenton's arms I felt small and dainty. His strong arms wrapped around me, protecting me from the cool wind.

I kissed him back with fervor. If I was doing this, whatever *this* was, I was certainly going to enjoy myself.

My skin began to feel heated and I forced myself to pull away. He rested his forehead against mine and we both breathed like we'd run a marathon. "I *really* have to go," I told him reluctantly. For a moment, while he'd been kissing me, I'd forgotten everything I was. I'd just been a girl—Rowan Sinclair. I didn't have all these strings tying me down. The moment his lips lifted from mine, though, reality came crashing back down. I wasn't a normal girl. I couldn't hang out with friends and spend time with my boyfriend—if you could even call Trent my boyfriend. I had children depending on me and a future to think about. I hated it. I wanted nothing more than to stay here in his arms in this warm bubble he'd created, but I couldn't.

"Not yet," he breathed. "Please, not yet."

I stared up at his handsome face. "I have to."

He nodded and took a step back. "What are your plans for tomorrow?"

"Uh ...," I paused, thinking. The kids were home from school and I had to work in the evening, so I had been planning to spend time with them. "I'm busy."

"What about the next day?"

"That's Thanksgiving," I sighed. This *thing* between us, it was going to be impossible. I could see that, and yet I wasn't leaving, or telling him that it wouldn't work out. Clearly, there was something wrong with me. I think maybe I was becoming a masochist.

"Friday, then?"

I bit my lip, thinking it over. I didn't have anything I had to do, but I'd have to find someone to watch the kids—I wasn't leaving them alone with my drunk mother.

"Friday should work." I nodded.

Trent brightened. "I guess I better come up with something to wow you then."

"I don't need to be wowed." I shook my head.

"Yes, you do." He slowly backed away from me, his eyes never wavering from mine. "Friday," he stated. "Don't even think of backing out on me. I'll hunt you down if you do." He winked, smiling in jest.

"I don't doubt your finder skills," I called after him as I opened my car door. I slid inside and gripped the wheel in my hands. I didn't pull away. I sat there thinking. There was a giddiness fluttering through my body. It was a feeling I hadn't felt since ... Well, since the night Trent and I were together in the tent.

Snow flurries began to fall on the windshield and I knew I

couldn't stay here any longer. I had to get back home ... back to reality.

"Row! Can I have that?" Tristan pointed enthusiastically at a bar of Hershey's chocolate as we stood in the checkout line at the grocery store. Since I'd forgotten about Thanksgiving, I hadn't picked up anything to make a meal while I was there with Trent. Shopping with Ivy and Tristan was exhausting. They wanted everything.

"Tristan, you know what the answer is going to be, so why do you keep asking?"

The little boy frowned, lowering his head.

I hated always being the bad guy and saying no, but I knew we couldn't afford special treats. Heck, I would've loved some Rice Krispies Treats, but that was a luxury, and we couldn't have those. Looking down at Tristan's sad face as he said nothing, threatened to crack my resolve, but I stood strong. I needed to save as much money as I could, because hopefully in a year, I could fight for custody of the kids. I needed to show the court that I was responsible.

We checked out and headed to the car. The chilly air seeped through my thin coat. If this weather kept up we were going to have an unusually harsh winter.

"Do we *have* to go home?" Ivy whined from the back of the car.

I frowned. Boy, did I know the feeling of not wanting to be at home. No matter how hard I tried to make it seem like a comforting place, the kids still didn't want to be there. When my mom and step-dad were home, you couldn't help but feel an icy chill like they wanted you out of the way.

"Uh …," I pondered. It was cold so I couldn't take them to the playground and there wasn't much else to do. "Do you want to go to the library and pick out some new books? It'll be warm and Mary should be there."

"Yes!" Ivy smiled widely in excitement. "Will she have cookies?"

Mary always made the best cookies and often brought them into work so we could all have some.

"Cookies!" Tristan exclaimed, hopping up and down in his car seat. "I want cookies!"

"Don't get too excited guys," I warned, "she might not have any."

"I hope she does." Ivy licked her lips, "I *love* cookies."

"Me too!" Tristan piped in.

I shook my head and pulled out into traffic, heading downtown to the library. I wasn't worried about the groceries since I didn't have anything that would melt, not that it would with how cold it was.

I parked and helped Tristan out of his seat. Ivy bounced excitedly on the balls of her feet. As hyper as she was today, I wasn't sure she needed any cookies.

"We have to hold hands when we cross the street," I warned them both. Tristan was already at the age where he didn't want to hold my hand, but I wasn't about to let them go running out into the road.

We crossed the street and bound up the steps.

Inside, Tristan looked around in awe. "Are we in a m-m-muzum?"

I laughed. "I think you mean a museum, and no, this is the library."

"Oh. I knew that." He smiled up at me. "I forgot."

"It's been a long time since you've been here." I bent down, helping him out of his bulky coat—the coat Trent had picked out. I draped the coat over my arm and stood up straight. "Come on, let's go find Mary and then we'll go to the kids' section."

"Cookies?" Tristan brightened, his little hand finding mine.

I shrugged. "Maybe."

Ivy was already at the information desk, hounding Mary. "Ivy," I scolded, "manners."

"Sorry, Ms. Mary." She stepped back from the counter. "But do you have any cookies? I'd really like one." I eyed her and she added, "Please."

Mary leaned on the counter, pretending to think. "I might have some cookies I can spare." She bent down behind the counter and rummaged around. "A-ha!" She placed a large metal tin on the counter. "Here's the cookies, they're peanut butter chip."

"I love peanut butter!" Tristan exclaimed.

"Shh," I hushed him. "We're in a library which means you have to be really quiet," I whispered.

"Oops." Tristan looked around. "Sowwy."

"It's, sorry," I corrected. "Use your R's."

"Sorry?" He tilted his head. "Did I say it right?"

"Yep, you've got it right."

"Does that mean I can have a cookie now?" he questioned.

"Yeah, you can have a cookie." I smiled at him.

"Yay!" he said in a hushed whisper, waving his arms in excitement.

"Thank you," I told Mary.

"You're welcome." She placed the lid back on the tin once each kid had two cookies in their hands. Whispering, she said, "Grab this on your way out. I made way too many and don't need them."

"I can't take your cookies." I shook my head.

"Thanksgiving is tomorrow, sweetie, my house is going to be full of sweets. I don't need them."

"Well, thank you."

"You know you're welcome to bring the kids and come to my house for Thanksgiving," she offered. Mary was one of the nicest people I'd ever met and she always wanted to help.

"Thanks for the offer, Mary, but I'm going to make dinner for them."

She smiled, glancing over at the kids who were sitting at one of the tables munching on their cookies. "What you do for them ... It's remarkable, Rowan."

"Hardly." I shrugged, brushing off her comment.

"No, really it is," she continued. "Most people your age ... they would've abandoned them, saying they have parents to look after them, but not you. You stayed."

"I have my reasons," I murmured, staring off into space.

"Regardless, I'm proud of you."

I looked up at her in surprise. Proud of me? No one had ever told me they were proud of me before. I'd always been told I was worthless, useless, and a pain in the ass. I wasn't called nice things, and unfortunately, I was used to it. Kindness wasn't something I experienced often, and when I did I clung to it with strong fingers. I let her words warm me all over. I didn't know it could feel so good to have someone tell you they were proud of you. It seemed like such a simple thing to say, but it could have such a profound effect.

"I-I ... Thank you," I finally said.

"For what?" She tilted her head.

"Nothing," I muttered. I couldn't explain to Mary how much her words had meant to me.

I sat down at the table with Ivy and Tristan as they finished their cookies. I cleaned up their crumbs and led them to the kids' section.

"There's so many books, Row." Tristan looked around in awe.

"There *are* so many books," I corrected.

"How do you expect me to choose just one?" He frowned. "I want all of them." He put his hands on his small hips.

"Well," I told him as I bent down, keeping an eye on Ivy, "you pick one now, we read it, and then we bring it back and you get to choose another."

His lower lip jutted out. "Can I get two? Please?"

"Yes, you can get two." It had been relatively easy to deny him a chocolate bar, but a book? No way was I telling the kid he couldn't have two books.

"Yay! I love you, Row." He wrapped his tiny arms around my neck.

I squeezed him tight, inhaling the scent of his baby shampoo. I wished he could stay this little forever—naïve of all the bad in the world.

"You're the bestest big sister."

"Let's get your books picked out. The library is closing early," I told him, pulling his shirt down to cover his stomach.

I let the kids each pick two books and play in the kids' area for a little while. I sat against a shelf with my legs brought up. I draped my arms over my knees. I watched them play and talk about their books, my heart swelling with pride. I didn't understand how someone like my mother could birth a child and not care about them. I knew there were plenty of other parents exactly like my mom, and my heart broke for those children. A child deserves to be loved, and without it, they'll shrivel into nothing—I think that's what happened to me. Without the love of my mom or any parental figure, I'd missed out on some fundamental development. I was closed off and emotionless. I knew it, and yet I could do nothing to stop it. Maybe one day I could learn how to feel, but I didn't see it happening any time soon.

I watched the clock, giving Tristan and Ivy a five-minute warning that we needed to leave. Neither was ready to go back home. Like me, they found solace in the peaceful library.

"All right, guys, we have to go."

Neither gave much protest, but they did frown, their heads slightly bowed.

I let them hand their books to Mary for her to scan them. She handed them back and thrust the tin of cookies at me, lest I forget it. "Have a good Thanksgiving, and the offer's still open if you want to come to my house."

"Thank you," I told her as I took Tristan's hand. "We'll be fine, though."

We headed straight home and I cringed when I saw my step-dad's truck sitting in the driveway. The last thing I needed was to deal with him.

The kids helped me carry the groceries inside. When I passed Jim, his hand shot out grazing the side of my butt. I cringed, bile rising in my throat. I wanted him gone from my life—him *and* my mom. I wanted to erase all the bad.

"You been to the grocery store?" he asked, spitting into a can and scratching his round beer belly.

I bit my tongue to keep from correcting his grammar. "Obviously," I said instead, my tone short and clipped.

He tilted his head, his hairy brows furrowing together. "Don't sass me," he warned. "You know how I feel about that," he said in his thick Southern drawl. I think Jim was from Alabama—I didn't really know and, frankly, didn't care.

I said nothing, heading into the kitchen and sitting the bags on the counter.

One, two, three, four, five, six, seven, eight, nine, ten.

I took deep breaths in and out, trying to calm myself. I felt like I was suffocating under the stress of being stuck in this house. I wanted out. I wanted to break down the walls and run away, never to return. It wasn't that easy, though, nothing ever was. I wouldn't stop trying to get away. My eyes landed on Tristan and Ivy. They deserved more than this shitty house and life. They deserved to have toys like other kids, and chocolate bars, but most importantly they deserved a future my mom could never give them. I didn't want them to have to work as hard as I did. I wanted them to have the chance to be kids and normal teenagers.

"Row?" I shook my head clear of my thoughts and looked down to see Tristan tugging on my sweater.

"What?" I asked.

"You did it again," he whispered, like he was letting me in on a secret.

"Did what?" I asked puzzled.

"You left me …" He shrugged his small shoulders. "Sometimes you leave, and I'm scared you're not coming back."

"But I didn't leave." I lowered, wrapping my arms around him, "I would never leave you, Tristan."

"He's talking about when you zone out," Ivy piped in, removing a box of stuffing from one of the plastic bags.

"You do it a lot." Tristan nodded. "I don't like it."

"I'm sorry. I didn't know I was doing it." I took his small face between my hands, looking into his blue eyes. "I'll try not to do it again," I assured him with a light kiss to the end of his nose.

"Stop babying the boy," Jim said loudly as he entered the kitchen. "If you want him to grow up to be a man you've got to treat him like one." He reached into the refrigerator for a beer. He took several long gulps and let out an obnoxious burp.

"I don't need your advice," I snapped. "I certainly don't want him turning out like you."

Jim's eyes flashed with anger. "I might not be the boy's father, but treatin' him like a fucking fairy princess isn't helpin' him."

I bit down on my tongue to keep from saying anything else. I knew if I ran my mouth it would only serve to get me in trouble later.

With his beer in hand, Jim headed back to the living room and to his beloved recliner. My mom was already passed out on the couch. One of these days she wasn't going to wake up—I was sure of it, and I didn't care. I don't know what that said about me.

With Ivy's help, I got all the groceries put away.

"Can I help you make dinner tomorrow?" she asked, bashfully looking at the ground.

"Of course," I said brightly, "I'd love your help."

"Can I help too?" Tristan piped in.

"Yep." I lightly poked his tummy, making him giggle. "I like it when you guys help me. You're the best helpers I know."

"We are?" Tristan asked with bright round eyes.

I nodded. "The best."

His small lips turned down in a frown. "Shouldn't we get a sticker? My teacher always gives me a sticker when I'm a good helper."

That got me to laugh. "Sorry, I'm fresh out of stickers, but not kisses." I grabbed him before he could run away and smacked my lips against his cheek.

"Ew, Row! You got lipstick on me!" He tried to wipe off the pink imprint left behind on his chubby cheek.

"It looks good on you," I joked.

"It's gross." He sent me the meanest glare he could muster, which was hardly a glare at all. I didn't think Tristan had a mean bone in his body.

"Fine then, I'll wipe it off." I stood and led him over to the sink. I wet a dishtowel and wiped the lipstick from his cheek. "All gone."

"I wish y'all would shut up!" Jim yelled. "I can't hear the damn TV!"

Tristan looked at me with wide eyes. "He said a bad word. He should get soap in his mouth," he whispered.

I couldn't help but crack a smile. "Since Jim is cranky, why don't we go do something in your room?" I suggested. "I can play a game with you guys." I looked up at Ivy so she'd know I wasn't only speaking to Tristan.

"Can we build a fort?" Tristan asked excitedly. "I love forts!"

"We can build a fort," I replied, smiling at his jubilance. Little kids, I had learned, didn't need much to make them happy. Some parents thought tossing a shiny new toy at a kid was what they wanted. That wasn't true. All a child wanted was someone to love them, to play with them, to make them feel special. I knew that from watching Ivy and Tristan. I'd also learned from my own experience. As a child, all I had wanted was for my mom to *notice* me. To be more than a nuisance. It never happened, though. I was always in the way. That's what made me determined to make Tristan and Ivy's childhood better than mine. I never wanted them to feel unloved or uncared for. I wanted them to know they were special, because it was true. Every child is special. A gift.

Tristan held out his small hand and led me to the bedroom he shared with Ivy.

I spent hours making forts and playing with dinosaurs beneath them. I understood the appeal to building a fort. You could pretend you lived in a different world, a world where nothing could touch you, and bad guys didn't exist. The blankets served as a cocoon, protecting you from everything evil. You couldn't stay hidden forever though and eventually the bad guys would find you. They always did.

"THIS DINNER LOOKS TASTY." Jim patted his round stomach as I leaned over to place the turkey on the table. As I pulled back his fingers grazed my breasts. I shuddered in response, revulsion clinging to me like the tendrils of vines.

I started counting in my head so that I didn't do or say something that would get me in trouble.

One, two, three, four, five, six, seven, eight, nine, ten.

After the numbers flitted through my mind I felt calmer and more centered.

Since a card table served as our dining table, I chose to stand by the counter with my plate of food after I'd helped Ivy and Tristan with theirs. Besides, I didn't want to be near Jim anyway ... or my mom. I was surprised she was actually eating something and not already passed out.

We all ate in silence. We didn't have anything to talk about, so there was no point in making idle chat. Even Ivy and Tristan said nothing.

My mom's fork clattered to the ground. "Fuck!" she exclaimed, her face going red with anger. She always got so angry over the dumbest things. "Rowan! Get that!"

I sighed, setting my plate down. I wanted to tell her to get it herself, but I'd rather avoid an argument.

I got down on my hands and knees, crawling beneath the table to retrieve the fork that was right beside her foot. I grabbed the fork and started to back out. My movements halted momentarily when Jim's hand landed firmly on my butt, squeezing. Oh, hell no. I was tempted to pierce his bare foot with the fork in my hand for that one.

"Ew! Jim has his hand on Row's butt!" Tristan exclaimed.

I hastily scooted all the way out and jumped up, tossing the dirty fork in the sink and grabbing a new one for my mom. She snatched it out of my hand so quickly that the prongs scratched my skin. "You little whore," she seethed, "always enticing the men, even my husband." Her hazel eyes—the exact same shade as mine—were full of hate. Of course she'd consider Jim touching my butt *my* fault, instead of seeing that the guy was a scumbag. Her thought process was so twisted. I preferred her when she was too drunk to cause trouble. She was ridiculous.

I knew better than to say anything. It would only serve to make her angry, and I didn't feel like hearing her spout hateful comments at me. If she got *really* mad her fists would start flying, and I didn't want the kids to see that. She'd never hit Ivy or Tristan, only me and even that was occasionally. If she laid a hand on one of those kids, though ... I don't know what I might do. Whatever it was, it would probably land my butt in jail.

"I don't know why the fuck you still live here," she continued, pulling out a cigarette and lighting it. She took a long drag and continued, "Ain't you eighteen now? I shouldn't have to pay for your sorry ass."

Anger simmered in my veins at that comment, and I couldn't keep my mouth shut. "For starters, I'm twenty-one, and *Mom*," I said in a condescending tone, "you haven't paid for my 'sorry ass' in a long time. You don't work, and he barely makes enough money to buy a loaf of bread. So, who's money keeps this roof over your head?" I glared at her, hatred for the woman that birthed me ate up my insides. "Me." I pointed at my chest. "I pay for this. All so you can blow your welfare check on booze and cigarettes. So, don't preach to me about values and certainly don't call me a whore." I let out a lengthy breath.

She shook with anger, her stringy blonde hair falling into her eyes. It looked like she hadn't washed it in a week, which was probably the case. I knew I shouldn't have spouted off the way I had. This wasn't going to be pretty.

She let out a roaring scream and knocked her plate to the ground. The glass shattered and food splattered against the walls. "Do *not* talk me that way!" she screamed. "Don't forget everything I've done for you!"

I swallowed thickly, anger rising inside me to match her. "What you've done for me?" I yelled back. I hated that the kids were seeing this, but I couldn't keep quiet any longer. I'd retreated into the shadows, never saying anything, for all my life and finally something inside me had snapped. "What you've done for me is ruin my life! You've taken *everything* from me!"

"You're nothing but an ungrateful *bitch*," she spat, shoving the table. It toppled over and food went everywhere. Ivy and Tristan began to cry. I couldn't do anything to comfort them right now. My mom stalked toward me, her hand raised to slap me. She didn't, though. "Thanks to me you have a *life*."

I shook my head. "You're wrong. What life I had thanks to you was destroyed a long time ago." My voice wasn't angry, mostly defeated.

"You really hate me, don't you, Rowan?" She stared up at me—I was at least a head taller than her.

"I suppose I loved you once, like all children love their parents, but I lost respect for you a long time ago. And after everything you've said and done to me ...," I paused, lifting my shoulders in a small shrug. "I guess I do hate you. How could I not?"

Her lips twitched into a smile. A freakin' smile. God, she was weird. "At least you own it."

"I am what I am. I feel what I feel. There's no sense in denying it," I stated.

"You really are my daughter." Her lips spread up into a wide smile, revealing her rotted teeth.

Hearing the word *daughter* come out of her mouth

repulsed me. I didn't belong to her, and I didn't like her staking claim to me. "I'm nothing to you."

Something about those words made her snap. Her hand shot out, smacking sharply against my cheek, pivoting my head to the side.

I raised a shaking hand to my stinging cheek. Tristan and Ivy's cries grew louder. "Try that again," I warned through clenched teeth, "and you won't like what happens. Me, them —" I nodded at the kids "—we'll be gone and you'll lose all this." I spread my arms to encompass the house. "Don't push me, Mom."

Her nostrils flared but resignation shone in her eyes. She knew that without me she'd have nothing. What she didn't know was that I was nowhere close to being ready to leave. The rent for this place was hardly anything—seeing at it was a dump and all. I couldn't afford a nice place yet and I knew legally I couldn't take the kids. I'd end up arrested for attempted kidnapping. But she was dumb and didn't know that. For now, threats were my only real weapon and I planned to use them to my full advantage.

Finally, she turned sharply on her heel and stormed out of the room. The front door slammed closed behind her.

"Fuck," Jim groaned, pulling at what little hair he had left. "Ronda!" He hopped up, running after my mom. I didn't know he could move so fast. I guessed he knew he needed to do damage control for groping my ass.

I sighed looking at the mess of food covering the floor, the walls, and the kids. This was not going to be fun to clean up.

I bent down on the floor to start the process of cleaning up but didn't get very far. Tristan launched himself into my arms and wrapped his around my neck. "You and mommy fighted. I don't like it when you fight. She said bad words. I don't like bad words." He looked at me with wide innocent blue eyes. "She hit you. She not nice. I don't like her. Why does she have to be my mommy? Why can't you be my mommy, Row?" My eyes closed at his words, my throat clenching. His small hand gently rubbed my sore cheek. "Hold still. I kiss it and make it better."

My stomach tightened painfully at Tristan's words. I held him in my arms as his soft lips touched my cheek—trying to take away my pain. If only sweet little kisses could make everything better. The world would certainly be a vastly different place.

CHAPTER SEVEN

HEY.

I stared at the text message flashing on the screen of my phone. It was from a number I didn't recognize and I wasn't sure whether I should respond or not.

It's Trent. The text came through a minute after the first.

How'd u get my #? I typed back. I knew I hadn't given it to him and I was curious to know who had.

Ran into my new best friend, Jude. Cool dude. Glad I didn't have to fight him for u. I would've though.

I rolled my eyes; slightly pissed that Jude had given Trent my number. Wasn't that breaching some kind of friend code or something? I mean, I'd been asked by more than one of Jude's conquests for his cellphone number and I never gave it away. I was nice like that. Apparently, Jude didn't return the same favor.

Don't be macho. I typed back. ***U went through all this trouble to get my # so what do u want?***

My phone began to buzz in my hand and I lifted it to my ear.

"I didn't feel like typing on that ridiculous keyboard any longer. It changes everything I type, so then I have to double check it before I click send so I don't say penis when I mean pens," he rambled without a breath in-between.

"Do you text about pens a lot?"

"I like pens," he stated, and I knew he was smiling that crooked grin that made my insides squirm. "Anyway, I didn't call to discuss the merits of a good ball-point. I wanted to discuss our date that's supposed to happen in three hours if you haven't backed out on me," his voice grew slightly sad.

"I haven't forgotten," I mumbled, staring at the clothes strewn about my room. I had never cared how I dressed before. Even when we'd dated in high school I hadn't cared what Trenton thought of my clothes. Suddenly, though, I wanted to be worthy of being seen with him. Pathetic, I know. Overnight I had turned into one of *those* girls. Irritated with myself I turned the phone on speaker and grabbed a pair of black leggings, shimmying into them.

"I'll pick you up at one—"

"No," I protested, clutching a loose teal sweater in my hands.

Trent huffed in exasperation. "I've been to your house before. I know the rules, stay in the car, and do not go inside. I'll be a good boy."

I swallowed thickly. "Okay," I agreed reluctantly.

"I'll see you then." With that, the line went dead.

I flopped on my bed. Why the hell had I ever agreed to this? Stupid Trent and his annoying knack for being persistent. Why couldn't he have left me alone? He knew even after all these years I still had feelings for him—it was pretty obvious in the way my body responded to him and the fact that I always ran away from him like a child with a schoolyard crush. I knew we would never make it as a couple, though. We were too different and there was so much he didn't know—that I *couldn't* tell him. Keeping my distance had been the only way, but he had to constantly pop up and chip away at the icy shield that blocked my emotions. I knew this was bad, but I had agreed, and I couldn't stop myself now. I wanted Trenton for as long as I could have him. Especially since no one else could ever replace him. Despite our differences, our connection was deep, it was the kind of connection most people never experienced. We understood each other better than anyone else did. Trenton had always been able to read my emotions when most couldn't.

I covered my face with my hands and let out a quiet scream so I didn't worry the kids. I had gotten myself into a sticky situation and there was no way out—not until the both of us shattered completely.

I forced myself off the bed and pulled on my sweater and boots. I picked up the mess of clothes strewn about my small room and returned them to where they belonged.

I dabbed on a bit of pink gloss and some mascara—it's all I usually wore.

I opened my bedroom door and jumped back when I saw Tristan standing there, peering up at me with curiosity shimmering in his blue eyes. "You were in there for a looooooooong time. Who were you talking to?"

"I was getting dressed," I told him, tugging on the bottom

of my sweater, feeling like I was about to get in trouble for something—funny, considering he was five.

He tilted his small head, taking in my words. Finally, he shrugged his shoulders. "Okay." At his age, he didn't need more of an explanation, and he'd probably already forgotten that he'd heard me talking to someone.

"What do you want for lunch?" I asked him, closing my bedroom door behind me.

"Sammy!" he exclaimed excitedly, running toward the kitchen as fast as his feet could carry him.

"What kind of sandwich?" I asked when I reached the refrigerator. "Do you want a sandwich, Ivy?"

"Mhmm," she responded from where she sat at the table drawing a picture. "Turkey, please."

I set about making the sandwiches, and made one for myself as well. I didn't want to assume Trent and I would be getting a late lunch, so it was better to eat. I sat down at the table with the kids. Tristan droned on and on about his toy cars and Ivy listened patiently to everything he had to say. I stared off into space, my eyes focusing on a stain on the wall I hadn't been able to remove after yesterday's disastrous Thanksgiving dinner. Jim had gone after my mom and hadn't returned last night or this morning. My mom had come back, and she was currently passed out in her bedroom, a trashcan full of vomit beside her. I didn't understand how someone wanted to live like that. I guessed that was the thing, though; you weren't really living.

The kids finished eating and I looked down to see that I'd only eaten half of my sandwich. I wasn't very hungry anymore. I cleaned up, wiped down the table, and looked at the clock. I still had a good two hours to kill before Trent arrived. I needed to get the kids to the babysitter, but I wouldn't have to do that for another hour and a half. Time had become my greatest enemy. If I allowed it, I'd end up talking myself out of this date ... or whatever it was.

I decided to kill the hour left by cleaning. Unlike most people I actually enjoyed doing household chores. It allowed me to keep busy.

Once the whole house was spotless I checked the clock again. I had enough time left to run the kids down the road to Colleen's—a nice older lady that occasionally kept the kids for me when I was in a pinch. She'd seen my mom in action and agreed with me that the kids shouldn't be left with her. Unfortunately, there was nothing I could do about the after-school time they were stuck with my mom. She was usually already passed out by that time and didn't bother them. I didn't know how long I'd be gone today with Trent and didn't think it would be all right to leave them home basically by themselves.

I packed a small bag with toys and snacks. Ivy had a book under her arm and waited by the door for me.

I buckled Tristan in his car seat and drove a block over to Colleen's. She opened the door when she heard me pull in the gravel driveway. Tristan hopped out and gave me a big hug before running into Colleen's house. Ivy hugged me as well, her eyes sad. I knew last night had really upset her and she still wasn't over it.

"Thank you for doing this," I told Colleen, handing her the bag. "I'm not sure what time I'll be back." I frowned. "I'll call you when I know something."

"No rush, sweetie." She took the bag from my hands and set it inside, using her foot to hold the glass storm door open. "I know you don't get out much. Have fun!"

It was pretty sad that everyone seemed to notice that I rarely got out. What was wrong with that? I *liked* being at home with my siblings. I wasn't missing out anything.

"Thanks." I forced a smile and backed off the porch steps.

I drove the short distance home and was getting out of my car when Trent's black car came speeding down the road. He didn't pull into the driveway; he parked on the street, like he had when we were teenagers. A part of me missed those days, when I'd been young and naïve. Trent had been the greatest thing to ever happen to me, but also the worst. Like an idiot here I was back for more.

He rolled down the passenger window and lifted his black Ray-Bans from his eyes. "Get in." The words were slightly demanding in tone, like he thought I'd run away and he needed to be bossy, but they were softened by the easy grin he wore.

I slung my purse over my shoulder and zipped up my jacket. Today wasn't as cold as it had been in the last few days and the sky was a bright clear blue.

I opened the car door and slid inside. My poor heart was beating so fast that I thought it might give out. I wasn't going to let Trent know I was nervous, though. I'd act like I was perfectly fine.

"Where are we headed?" I asked, buckling the seatbelt as he pulled away.

"Not far," was his vague reply.

"That's all I get?"

He smiled crookedly. "Yeah, that's all you get."

I stared out the window watching the trees and houses rush by. Familiar sights met me and I turned to him. "Seriously?" I questioned. "We're going to the library? They're closed."

Trent chuckled. "Oh, how you doubt me." He scratched his slightly stubbled jaw. "We're *not* going to the library, emphasis on the *not*. We're going to be in the vicinity," he said, turning down a street and into a parking garage.

"So," I drew the word out, "are you going to tell me what we're doing yet?"

He hopped out of the car without a reply. I followed him to where he stood, opening the trunk. He pulled out a small black bag and slung it crossways over his body.

"Is that a purse?" I questioned.

Trent let out a bellowing laugh that echoed around the parking garage. "A purse? Oh, that's a good one." He continued to laugh as he slammed the trunk closed.

"If it's not a purse, what is it?" I asked, walking beside him as we headed for the exit.

"Well, seeing as how this is our first real date ... as adults, that is, I wanted to do something different."

"And by different, you mean—?" I probed.

"I thought I'd introduce you to one of my hobbies." He stopped on the sidewalk, tilting his head up to let the sun's rays hit his skin.

"Are you purposely being vague to irritate me? I can always leave," I huffed, tossing my finger over my shoulder in the opposite direction.

"Oh, how I love your sassy mouth." He smirked, his eyes sparkling with mirth. "I love it even more when my mouth is on yours."

"So poetic," I droned. "It makes me want to rip off my panties."

"Hey, whatever it takes." He shrugged nonchalantly, unzipping the black bag at his waist. I peered closely to see what he was pulling out.

"A camera?" I questioned. "What are you doing with a camera?"

"Uh, isn't that obvious?" He aimed it at my face and there was a clicking sound.

"Did you seriously just take my picture?"

"I seriously did." He grinned boyishly.

"I'm so confused. What does a camera have to do with this date?" I asked, pushing my hair out of my eyes as a light wind ruffled it.

He held the camera up again, snapping another picture as he spoke. "I wanted to do something different for our date. Lunch or dinner, that's too basic. Go-karts is for teenagers—besides they're closed at this time of year," he rambled as he continued to snap pictures of me. I resisted the urge to shield my face, letting him snap away. "I was about to give up hope when I was playing with Bartholomew—that's my ferret, if you forgot—and I was struck by a genius thought. A photo shoot!" He grinned, clearly pleased with his so-called brilliant idea. I had to give him props, it was definitely a different date concept. "I would get to spend time with you, take your picture—you're beautiful, so you make an excellent model—and we could just ... hang out." His expression was suddenly vulnerable, and I hated that I was the reason for it. My constant rejections had genuinely hurt his feelings—so, why hadn't he given up on me?

"It's a great idea, Trenton." I smiled—it was a small smile, but at least it was a real one.

"Are you sure?" he asked, holding his camera at his side. "All of a sudden it seems kind of silly." He frowned.

He made like he was going to put his camera away and I stepped closer to him, reaching out and grabbing his arm to halt his movements. My hand tingled where it touched his skin. How could one person make my body feel so ... shivery? Nobody else, and I did mean *nobody*, gave me those same feelings. "Don't put it away," I pleaded softly. "It really is a good idea. Way better than go-karts."

Trent still seemed unsure of his idea. That was something I liked about Trenton. One minute he seemed like the most confident guy ever and the next he wasn't afraid to show his insecurities.

"May I?" I asked, sliding my hand down his arm to grasp the camera.

He swallowed thickly, watching with surprised blue eyes as he relinquished the camera to me.

I took it from him, looking over the camera. It was rather fancy, beyond my basic knowledge of cameras, but I finally located the correct button. I started taking pictures and felt myself begin to loosen up now that I wasn't the one under the scrutiny of the lens. "Smile, Trent," I coaxed, "you should be the happiest guy alive, since you're on a date with moi."

He laughed, and I snapped a picture. I stared at the large screen where the photo flashed for a moment. I liked seeing him like that, so carefree and happy, and knowing the reason he was like that was because of me. "Rowan Sinclair, did you crack a joke?" He grinned, playing with his sunglasses as I continued to take his picture.

"I believe I did, Mr. Wentworth." I smiled. This was actually pretty fun. Who would've thought?

He reached for the camera, but I wasn't ready to give it up. I started to run away, but I didn't make it far. Trent's muscular arm shot out, catching me around my middle. He spun me around. I couldn't help but giggle at the motion. I felt weightless and free. None of my indiscretions clung to me. I was nothing but a girl having fun with a guy. I hadn't realized until this moment how much I'd craved normalcy—and Trent was the only person that could give me that. He always managed to reveal the real me—the one that was normally a stranger to even myself. He was pretty amazing that way.

He kept spinning me around until I found my back pinned against the stone wall of one of the many shops lining the old town walking mall. He slung the camera strap over his shoulder, staring into my eyes. My arms weaved behind his neck like they had a mind of their own. One of his hands ventured to my waist, grasping me just above the curve of my butt. My body arched against his. His other hand found the nape of my neck and slowly drew my face to his. He gave me plenty of time to pull away—his way of letting me know I was in control of this. When I didn't pull away, his lips slowly pressed against mine. I hadn't realized it, but a part of me had been dying to kiss him—to *really* kiss him—without him surprising me or trying to prove something. This was all about us, and how we truly felt. His lips glided over mine like he'd done it a million times. I surrendered to the carnal feelings that always overwhelmed me when I was near Trenton. Our sexual chemistry was off the charts—I couldn't deny it. Fire ignited in the pit of my belly as his kisses descended down my neck. My eyes were closed and breathy sighs escaped me. I had no thoughts for the fact that *anyone* could be watching us. When Trent kissed me, I couldn't think about anything, I could only feel. I needed to let him kiss me more often. His lips claimed my mouth once more and my arms wrapped tighter around his neck.

"Row," he gasped, the sound of my name leaving his lips stirred my insides.

"Just kiss me." I took his face between my hands, pressing forward.

We were tangled together and I wasn't sure where I ended and he began. I let myself go and didn't worry about anything else. For now, it was only Trent and me.

His lips parted from mine and he backed two steps away from me. His chest rose and fell heavily with every breath. He pulled at the ends of his hair and looked down at the ground. I suddenly felt very unsure of myself.

"Did I do something wrong?" I voiced my concerns. My lips tingled and my body was still humming from the kiss, but could it have been possible that he thought it was awful?

He shook his head back and forth, forcing his eyes to meet mine. "No, not at all."

"Then why'd you stop?" I hated that my voice squeaked and I sounded like an insecure little girl. I needed him to answer my question.

"Because," he said, his hands on his narrow hips, "if I didn't stop, I never would, and I'm not prepared to go that far with you again just yet. We both need to be ready for *that*," he said significantly, "and when it happens, because it *will*," he voiced with the utmost confidence, "you're going to be in my house and in my bed. Not pressed against a wall out in the open."

My breath faltered as desire flooded my body. With a few words Trent had me imagining the two of us together once more. Something told me that the next time would be even better than the first. We were both older now and with our sexual chemistry ... it would be explosive. Hell, we were already explosive without sex involved.

"I—" I didn't know what to say.

He stepped forward again, cupping my cheek in one hand as one large thumb grazed my slightly swollen bottom lip. "Did my words scare you?"

"No," I answered honestly and without hesitation.

"Good." He grinned, lightly grazing his lips over mine. It was so quick that I wasn't even sure it could be called a kiss. Regardless, the simple touch sent a shiver skating down my spine. Five years of avoiding Trenton had only made me crave him more. Now that I'd given into my desires there was no turning back. "As much as I'd like to stand here and kiss you all day, we better get back to our date."

"Yeah, I guess so." I forced my body away from the wall, which was currently the only thing holding me upright. "So ..." I backed away. "Are we only taking pictures on this date?"

Trent grinned crookedly. "That's only part of it, dinner's involved, and kissing. Definitely more kissing."

I laughed, twirling around as he snapped pictures. "I thought kissing was dangerous for us?"

"Oh, it is. Luckily for you, I'm a man that can control himself. I won't ravish you until we're both ready to beg for it," he said huskily, hiding his face behind the camera lens.

I swallowed thickly at his words, pleasure rolling through my body. I hated to admit it, but I didn't think it would be long until I was begging him to devour me.

"Hey, let's go over there." Trent grabbed my arm and we jogged across the street. "Lean against here." He pointed to a brick wall with intricate graffiti covering its surface. "Look down a bit, yeah, like that. Cross your arms over your chest. Perfect." Suddenly, Trent had morphed from laid back to business mode. It was kind of cool seeing him in action like this. I hadn't known he was interested in photography. Back in high school his hobbies included video games and more video games.

"When did you get into photography?" I inquired, turning my head at a different angle as he snapped away.

"Uh ..." He seemed hesitant to answer. After taking a few more photos, he said, "After what happened with us ... I needed something to distract my mind. Pathetic, I know." He lowered the camera, giving me a glimpse of his vulnerable face. "You hurt me."

Those three words were like a slap. I was only beginning to realize how much I had hurt him. When I left, I'd assumed he'd be like every other guy on the planet and would move on in a millisecond. Not Trent. He was different.

"I'm sorry," I whispered after a lengthy silence. "I was scared," I admitted, nibbling on my bottom lip. "You don't ... You don't understand how I feel about love."

"It was a long time ago." He shrugged his shoulders. "I'm over it. You don't owe me an explanation."

I felt like I did, though, but I didn't know how I could ever make Trent understand that I felt like there was no such thing as real love. He had a wonderful mom and loving grandparents—his dad had already passed away when I met him. Someone that had grown up surrounded by such warmth, couldn't possibly understand why my heart was frozen—forever an icy tundra never to be conquered.

I simply nodded, taking the opening he gave me. Sometimes, it was better not to try to explain yourself. I'd only end up sounding like a crazy person.

"Anyway ..." He lifted the camera once more and I adjusted my pose, leaning slightly forward as my long hair whipped around me. "Photography became an escape for me. It allowed me to look at the world in a different light."

"Is that what you're studying at college?"

He nodded. "Photography and graphic design. I guess neither Wentworth brother is going to take over the family business." He lowered the camera so I couldn't miss his wink. "I can't imagine being chained to a desk all day. I think I'd shoot myself just to have something to do."

"What will happen to the business then?" I asked. Trenton's family had started an ammunition business a long time ago—the business had boomed and today the family was worth billions.

Trent shrugged. "I'm sure we'll keep it, but hire a CEO or something. My mom's running it now. When she's ready to retire, we'll figure something out." He sighed. "For now, it's not my problem."

I frowned, a little bit surprised by the sharpness of his words. They were so un-Trent-like. Normally, he was the guy coming up with a solution, not the one shrugging it off with mutters of it not being his problem. I guessed that worry was so far down the road that he didn't see the point in thinking about it, but ... God, I thought too much.

"Tilt your head up a bit," he directed, back to the task at hand. I did as he directed, my gaze sliding toward him. He looked down at the camera screen and a grin formed on his face. "Oh, that's a good one."

We moved on to another location—one where he had me sit on a crumbling half wall. I was afraid I might fall, but Trent assured me that if I started to tumble, he'd catch me.

I reclined back, letting my long hair blow around me in the light wind. I was getting cold, but I was having too much fun to tell him to stop. I'd thought this was silly at first, but it was actually pretty fun. For the first time in five years, I was enjoying myself.

I leaned back, closed my eyes, and let the sun's rays fan across my face. A small smile lifted my lips as I reveled in an emotion I so rarely felt.

Happiness.

TRENT CAME to a stop in front of my house. We'd been gone for hours and, sadly, I wasn't ready to say goodbye yet, but I had to. Cinderella's time at the ball was up. Reality had returned.

"Thank you for today." He turned to me, his eyes reading my face.

"I had a great time," I told him, my words sounding silly to my ears.

"Good." He smiled. His blue eyes darkened to navy as he watched me. "I don't want to leave you," he whispered so low I wasn't sure I heard him right. "I'm afraid ..." He swallowed, looking down. "I'm afraid when I get back, you'll ignore me again."

"Get back? Are you leaving?"

He nodded. "I have to go back to school. I have a few more weeks of classes before winter break starts."

Weeks. I would have to go a few weeks without seeing Trenton. Now that I'd agreed to this relationship, I hated to think I had to wait weeks before I saw him again. Trent was the only person that made me happy. Having him around brought me out of the dark space I'd been living in for so long. Without him here, I feared I'd retreat back into my dark hole—the hole that had become a suffocating pit. In fact, I could already feel my body drawing in and my mind shutting down. I didn't want to withdrawal into myself anymore. I wanted to be the girl Trenton believed I was.

"That's a while," I mumbled, picking at a loose thread on my sweater.

Trenton took my chin between his thumb and forefinger. "I know," his voice was deep with sadness, "but I'll be back. I'm not leaving you, Rowan."

I closed my eyes, absorbing his words. A week ago, I'd been avoiding him and now I was struggling to say goodbye. I didn't want to be this girl—the one dependent on someone else for happiness. That's why I knew in the end we'd never work. I was too messed up. I was broken ... Splintered and fractured beyond repair. I didn't understand why Trenton couldn't see that trying to mend me was pointless. Once so much damage has been done, there's nothing you can do to erase it.

"Rowan," he repeated my name, brushing his fingers over my cheek, "everything will be fine. I'll call you. and while I'm gone, I'll be planning something spectacular for our next date, because there will be a second, and a third, and a ... Well, you get the idea." He grinned and I couldn't help but smile in response. "Don't panic on me now."

"I'm not panicking."

"You're definitely over-thinking then." He tapped my forehead. "Thinking will only get you in trouble, so don't, just feel," his voice dropped to a deep tone and his face was so close to mine that I could have counted every eyelash if I wanted.

His breath fanned over my lips. I knew he was waiting for me to make the first move this time. I was trying to decide if I wanted to or not. I mean, that was dumb, of course I *wanted* to, but I wasn't sure if it was really the best idea. Kissing always seemed to prove to be dangerous territory for us. But I did it. I leaned forward that last little bit and rested my lips against his. Neither of us moved at first, then Trenton growled low in his throat, his fingers tangling in my hair. Both of his hands lowered to my waist and a small shriek escaped me as he pulled me onto his lap. He leaned the seat back and I landed roughly against his solid chest. Through the whole process our lips never broke contact. I grasped the fabric of his shirt tightly in my hands, needing to cling to something that would keep me grounded. His tongue pressed against my lips and my mouth opened in response. Damn, the man could kiss, and I really didn't want to think about the reason why he was so good. I wasn't naïve, but I didn't want to torture myself with images of Trenton with other girls either.

His hands ventured under the edge of my sweater, over my stomach, and up to my breasts. I gasped. Brave under the cover of the night sky I let him lift the sweater over my head, so I was left in nothing but my bra. Yep, we *so* shouldn't kiss. It always ended up going too far, but right then I didn't care.

My center pressed against him and heat flooded my body.

The light stubble adorning his chin and cheeks scratched at my skin, but I didn't mind.

"Trent." My gasp filled the confines of the car. I clawed at his black thermal shirt, desperate to remove it—to have nothing between us. A week ago, I'd been running from him—too scared to admit that I had feelings for him—but I was done being that girl. I was ready to take what I wanted for as long as he'd let me. I knew I wasn't worthy of him, and that I'd only end up hurt in the end, but some things are worth breaking for, and let's face it, I was already wrecked, so how much damage could one more fracture cause?

He tore the shirt off and tossed it somewhere behind him. My hands splayed across the warm skin of his muscular chest, his heart beating steadily beneath the palm of my hand. My hands ventured lower into the dips and curves of his abdominals—and holy hell did the man have abs to drool over. He certainly hadn't had those when we were sixteen.

His lips descended down my neck and over my shoulder—the little kisses making my body hum pleasantly. He pushed aside one bra strap and his lips continued lower, his hot breath causing my body to arch.

"Trenton, please," I moaned, my fingers in his hair, pulling him close.

"Fuck," he groaned, his hips pressing against me.

I felt him and I knew what I needed to relieve the pressure building in my body.

My fingers clumsily fumbled with his belt.

His hands ceased what they were doing to my body and grabbed ahold of mine. "Stop," he gasped breathlessly. "Stop," he repeated, and I wasn't sure if the word was meant for him or me. "We can't do this, not here like this. I already told you," he started, staring into my eyes so I saw that he wasn't mad, "we're not ready for that."

Boldly, I pressed my body down on him so that he knew I was very aware of the hard-on he was sporting. "You seem ready to me."

He released my hands and clutched my hips tightly in his hands. His eyes closed as he shook his head back and forth. "I can't. Not yet. I've waited years to get you back." He tucked a piece of hair behind my ear that had fallen forward to hide my face from his sight. "I won't ruin this by rushing things. I've proved how patient I can be, and I assure you, I won't make love to you—because, yes, it will be *making love*, not fucking or anything like that—until I know that you're not going to run from me the next day."

How could I possibly argue with that?

Looking into his eyes, I knew a part of him—a big part—believed I'd be gone when he got back for his winter break.

I'd have to prove him wrong.

CHAPTER EIGHT

I'D GONE A WHOLE WEEK WITHOUT SEEING TRENTON. I thought I might be relieved to have him gone—instead I felt slightly empty inside and I ... I missed him. Man, that was hard to admit, even to myself. I missed the way he always seemed to pop up when I least expected him and how his smile made butterflies flutter in my tummy.

I startled when someone's arm draped over my shoulders as I walked across campus. For a second there I dared to hope it was Trent, but when I looked over a laughing Jude met me. "Did I scare you?"

"You know you did." I shrugged off his shoulder. "That wasn't nice." I clutched my books tightly against my chest as I headed across campus toward my last class of the day.

"Are you sure I really scared you or were you hoping I was someone else?" He raised a brow as he fell into step beside me.

I frowned, looking down at my black ballet flats.

"I knew it!" He threw a fist in the air. "You really like him! And here I was beginning to think that no guy would ever strike your fancy. I'm relieved to know that your ovaries do indeed work."

I rolled my eyes, reaching up to adjust the hat on my head that was protecting me from the frigid air. "Trust me, my ovaries work just fine."

Jude jogged ahead of me and grabbed the door, holding it open for me. I stepped inside the warm building. "Thanks, that was rather gentlemanly of you," I noted, unwinding my scarf from around my neck.

"That's me. Jude the Gentleman." He grinned easily as we headed into class together. Since we were both studying the same thing, we shared most of our classes. Sitting down beside me, Jude asked, "Are you studying tonight?"

I gave him a *duh* look.

He chuckled, rubbing his jaw. "At the library?"

I nodded. "What's with all the questions?"

He shrugged. "I was wondering if I could join you. My roommate is always playing this heavy metal shit and I can't think straight. Plus, you're smart, so you can help me."

I rolled my eyes. "Jude, we both know you're way smarter than me, so flattery will get you nowhere. But if you'd like to join me, that's fine."

He smiled widely. "Thanks."

"What are you up to?" I narrowed my eyes on him.

"Nothing." He smiled innocently, crossing his arms behind his head.

"*Jude*," I warned.

He smirked. "I heard some pretty hot girls hangout at the library. I was thinking of branching out."

"Have you banged all the sluts you can handle? Moving onto the good girls now?" I mocked. "I've got news for you; smart girls won't fall for your charms. It looks like you might have to give it up, unless you want to fuck the same girl twice." I patted his shoulder in mock sympathy.

Jude laughed at my words. "Oh, Row, you don't know me at all. I can charm any girl I want out of her pants."

"Not me," I snorted, searching my bag for a pencil and my notes.

"Trust me, I could if I wanted to," he assured me. "I've never released my powers on you."

I eyed him doubtfully. "Is that supposed to hurt my feelings? Or should I be proud that you like me enough not to ruin our friendship with sex?"

"Proud." He nodded, fighting a smile. "Definitely proud."

I rolled my eyes, focusing on the professor as he strode into the room and began the lesson. Now wasn't the time to be thinking about Jude's sex life.

I PULLED MY HAIR BACK, securing it with a hair tie, and shoved the book away from me. I'd been reading the same sentence for the last thirty minutes, and that wasn't like me. I knew what my problem was. I kept waiting to feel the familiar tingles that announced Trent's presence. But they weren't coming. He was at school and I had at least two more weeks before I'd see him. Trent had succeeded in invading my every thought—just like he had when we were in high school. After our friendship ended I never stopped thinking about him or wishing for things that I knew would never come true. So, it was easy for me to fall for him—he already stole my heart a long time ago, and I never got it back. I think that was part of the reason I tended to feel so hollow inside.

"Are you okay?" Tatum's voice broke through my thoughts.

"Yeah." I forced a small smile. "I'm fine."

She rolled her eyes. "You are *so* not fine. I'm your friend, talk to me," she pleaded.

I wished I could, but I didn't know how to open up. Expressing my feelings didn't come naturally to me. My mom had made me feel like a worthless piece of shit—always wanting me to be invisible and never to speak. I didn't even know how to put into words what I was feeling.

"It's nothing." I shrugged, reluctantly sliding the book toward me so I could resume studying.

Tate shook her head, her pretty blonde hair swishing around her shoulders. "Sometimes, I just don't get you," she mumbled.

I flinched at her tone, knowing I should tell her that I missed Trent, but it wasn't that easy for me. I felt ridiculous for even missing the guy; to voice those words out loud made me feel weak, like I was admitting that I needed him … Which I didn't. I was perfectly fine on my own. I wouldn't allow myself to be dependent on someone else for my happiness, I'd only end up disappointed in the end.

I knew I should say something to Tatum, apologize for my inability to talk to her, but I couldn't.

I went back to my studies and only faltered when a little while later Tate muttered under her breath, "You have got to be fucking kidding me."

I'd never heard Tatum cuss before, so my eyes widened in

surprise. I put the book down to see what had made her suddenly so venomous and found her staring at Jude.

"You two know each other?" I questioned.

Tatum's eyes were murderous. "*You* know *him?*" she countered.

"He's my friend?" I don't know why my words came out sounding like a question.

"Well, if it isn't little Tate." Jude smirked, his eyes lingering on her chest, which was concealed by a thick black sweater, and finally venturing up to make eye contact.

"Jude," she spat out the word like it was something sour in her mouth. "I see you haven't changed since high school."

He chuckled, shrugging off his backpack, and dropping it onto the table. He pulled out a chair and plopped down across from Tatum.

"And I see you still have that same fiery attitude." He leaned forward.

"Don't think I won't kick you in the balls again," she warned.

"Once was enough." He grinned crookedly, eyeing her with mischief in his eyes. "I assure you I've healed, though, and I'm in perfect working order if you'd like to check it out."

She rolled her eyes. "You're a pig."

"And you" —he leaned forward, steepling his fingers— "are a tease."

I watched their back and forth banter like one would a tennis match. I was mesmerized and disgusted all at once.

"I don't think it counts as being a tease if you're only trying to avoid contracting some nasty disease," she sneered, gathering up her books. "You never could handle rejection."

"What can I say? I'm not used to it." He smirked cockily,

crossing his arms behind his head as he watched her stand and sling her backpack over her shoulder. "Don't worry, though, I quite enjoy a chase, and this one is only starting."

"Ugh." She rolled her eyes before leveling him with a glare. "I would've thought four whole years of rejection would have been enough for you. Don't waste your time with me because you're never getting these off." She dramatically lifted the bottom of her shirt and reached down to hook her thumb through the top of her panties.

She flipped her hair over her shoulder, stealthily flashing him her middle finger, then storming away dramatically.

Jude wore a funny smile—one I couldn't quite pinpoint—then he looked over at me. "She doesn't know it yet, but I'm going to marry that girl."

I snorted. "Your confidence amazes me."

"It's the truth." He shrugged, glancing over his shoulder as her form disappeared around the corner. "That girl ... There's something about her."

I couldn't help it; I busted out laughing at the absurdity of the situation. "Care to elaborate?"

"Not much to tell." He opened his book, eyes downcast.

"There's always something to tell," I pressed, my curiosity getting the best of me.

He looked up, flicking his straight dark hair out of his eyes. "Well, you see, when I was a freshman, I kind of ended up sleeping with her brother's girlfriend. He found out and spouted off to me, but it didn't go any farther than that. Until little Tate there found out. I didn't know who she was at that point. She sashayed up to me in the halls one day, laying it on thick I might add, and then kicked me in the balls. She started screaming about her brother and I figured out who she was pretty quick. I liked her spunk. From that day on, I couldn't get her out of my head."

I stared at him, mystified. "And yet you sleep around."

"Hey, while I'm waiting for her to wake up and see that we're gonna make babies one day, I don't see the point in not having some fun."

Boys.

I shook my head. "That makes no sense whatsoever."

"It doesn't have to." He shrugged, his brows furrowing as he read.

I let the subject drop, trying not to laugh at the ridiculousness. Tatum and Jude knew each other. What were the odds? And Tate had a brother? She'd never mentioned a brother to me. She didn't tell me a lot, just like I didn't tell her much. I guessed we both had our secrets.

Thirty minutes later, I looked at the time and cursed under my breath. I needed to change and clock in.

I explained to Jude where I was running off to and he lifted his head in acknowledgement.

I ran to the restroom, pulling my change of clothes out of my backpack. I shucked my jeans and pulled on the black pencil skirt. My sweater went next, replaced with a white button-down blouse that I tucked into the skirt.

I stuffed my school clothes into the bag and ran for the backroom to clock in. I knew Mary and none of the others would care if I was a little late, especially after the talk I'd had with Mary the previous time I was running behind. Besides, they already knew I was here studying.

Mary shook her head at me when I appeared at the desk. "Silly girl," she muttered, before dolling out tasks.

I relaxed into the tranquil monotony of replacing books on

shelves. Occasionally someone would ask me for help locating a particular book and I was happy to oblige. It made me sad that the library wasn't as busy as it once was. With computers and Kindles, most people didn't see the need to come to the library.

Hours passed and soon it was time to close. I changed back into my school clothes, replaced my contacts with my glasses, and sat down at an empty table to get more studying done. The professors were going easy on us, with winter break approaching so soon, but I didn't want to get behind. I needed to stay ahead of my studies.

Since the library typically closed early, I had a good hour of study time before I had to head home to feed the kids and get them ready for bed.

The times when I stayed late like this were the only break I seemed to get. Most would probably find the large library on the spooky side if they were here by themselves. I'd turned off most of the lights, expect for the ones in the section I occupied, and there was something eerie about the large black shadows casted by the bookshelves. I was never scared, though. This place ... It was the only place that truly felt like home to me. It was welcoming and it was easy to lose myself in the scent of book pages.

I finished studying, but lingered for a few more minutes, letting my fingers glide along the spines of the books as I passed them by.

The minute I walked out of these doors, it was back to reality, and I wanted to feel this comfort for a little while longer. Silly? Definitely. However, I didn't care.

My drive home was silent. I had no desire to listen to the radio. I knew when I walked in the door, I'd be assaulted by

Tristan and Ivy's endless chatter. I didn't mind it; I actually enjoyed talking to the kids. Right now, though, I needed silence—a clear head. My step-dad was back home, and my mom had been an even bigger bitch the last week than she normally was. I wondered if she'd seen me practically mauling Trent with my mouth and greedy hands in his car. If she had, she didn't say anything. Something was off about her. Well, she was always in a mood, but more so than usual. She was a confusing person. I'd never understood why she drowned her sorrows in alcohol. Now, too much damage had been done for me to ever care to find out. I didn't understand the lure of the bottle though. I wasn't the type to give up. I fought. Maybe that was something I inherited from my dad—a man I didn't even know the name of. My mom never talked about him. Supposedly, he'd bailed before I was even born. With the lies she told though, my guess was that wasn't even true. It sucked pretty bad when you couldn't believe anything that came out of your mother's mouth. She was the one person I should've been able to go to with anything, but I couldn't. The one time I did ... Well, that was a story for another time.

I sat in the car, parked in the driveway, my hands clenching the steering wheel.

When did my life get so fucked up?

Had it happened when I was born?

Or had there been a time when I was a normal kid who loved her mom?

I didn't know. I'd *never* know. For as long as I could remember I'd raised myself. Then Ivy, and finally, Tristan. I couldn't ever remember being a kid, playing with dolls, having sleepovers. All I had ever had was this hell.

I pushed my body out of the car, grabbing my stuff, and headed inside.

I moved mechanically.

The kids greeted me and I bent down to hug and kiss them both, holding them in my arms longer than normal as I soaked in their comfort.

"You're squeezing me too tight, Row." Tristan squirmed his small body out of my arms.

"Sorry," I told him.

"Row?" He tilted his head questioningly. "Are you going to cry?"

I hadn't even realized my eyes were filling with tears. The tears didn't spill over and I didn't even know why they were there in the first place—maybe for everything I had lost and was working so hard for my siblings not to have to experience. I had a suspicion that these tears were because of Trent too. He'd surged back into my life, making me *feel* again, and my emotions had burst forth like water from a dam.

"No, sweetie, I'm not going to cry." I forced a smile as he gripped my face between his two small hands, looking at me in fascination.

"I don't want you to be sad." His lips turned down in a frown.

"Sometimes you have to be sad," I told him, my voice shaky.

Tristan wrapped his arms around my neck and clung to me tightly. We had a special bond—one I didn't share with Ivy.

I picked him up to carry him to the kitchen when my mom opened her bleary eyes from where she lay on the couch. "Don't baby him."

"Whatever." I rolled my eyes as she passed out once more.

I was tired and didn't even feel like boiling pasta noodles, so I settled on peanut butter sandwiches that the three of us dipped in milk—don't knock it until you try it.

"This is yummy." Tristan grinned, smiling up at me. Ivy nodded in agreement to his words. Watching the two of them, my throat clenched. They deserved more than peanut butter sandwiches eaten at a card table. I didn't understand how a parent couldn't want better for their children. But my mom, she wanted us to suffer like she had, while she escaped into oblivion—the coward's way out.

Ivy helped me clean up from dinner, then I gave Tristan a bath and read them both a story. I fell asleep in Tristan's bed, my body wrapped around his, with Ivy beside me.

THE WIND BLEW my hair in my face, several long strands getting stuck on the gloss coating my lips. I pulled my hair way, my head lowered. When I looked up, my steps faltered. I couldn't believe what I was seeing.

This had to be a mirage or something.

Trenton stood straight ahead of me, his back leaning against a light pole with a coffee cup and something else in his hand. I was so confused. He was still supposed to be at school, what was he doing here?

He looked up then, a smile spreading over his handsome face as he spotted me. He was dressed nicely in a pair of jeans and a long black button-down coat. His dark hair was brushed out of his eyes. To me, he looked like he should be on the runway, not chilling on campus. He looked so sophisticated and out of my league.

He didn't jog up the steps. Instead, he waited for me to meet him.

I walked slowly to him, butterflies assaulting my stomach.

"Hi. What are you doing here?"

God, even when I wasn't trying to I still sounded like a bitch. There was something seriously wrong with me.

He chuckled, licking his bottom lip. "I brought you coffee." He held up the paper cup.

"I can see that, but why are you *here* on my campus," I hissed. "Aren't you supposed to be at school?"

He shrugged his muscular shoulders. "I finished my school work early and decided to head home. There was no point in hanging around there when I could be home." *With you,* the words hung there unuttered.

I reached for the coffee. "Well, thanks for this."

"It's caramel," he assured me before I took a sip. "Caramel's still your favorite, right?" he asked hesitantly.

"It is." I nodded. "I can't believe you remembered that," I whispered in awe, taking a sip of the hot liquid. It gave me a dose of much-needed caffeine and warmth.

"I remember everything about you," he whispered. "Oh, here's this."

My throat closed up as I looked at the shiny teal wrapper in his hands. I took the Rice Krispiess Treat from him.

"You really do remember everything," I gasped.

He chuckled. "Yep. Your middle name is Elise and you hate it because you think it sounds old-fashioned. I, on the other hand, love it. Your favorite color is green. Rice Krispiess Treats are your favorite sweet." He nodded at the wrapper in my hand. "You love to read anything and everything, and ... Shall I continue?" He raised a brow, waiting for my response.

I gazed at him in awe. I would've thought all these years later, we'd have to get to know each other again, but he hadn't forgotten anything about me. I certainly hadn't forgotten him, either.

"No," I squeaked as we walked side by side. I had to get to my last class of the day.

Trent fell into step beside me, both of us silent. I stopped outside the door to the building that led to my next class. "I have to go, I can't be late," I mumbled.

Trent nodded. "I know. I'll ... see you later." He smiled, leaning in to give me a soft kiss that left my whole body humming.

"Thanks for this." I held the coffee and Rice Krispiess Treat aloft.

He nodded, tipping his head at me as he backed away.

"Red!" I called at his retreating back.

He turned around, stopping in his tracks with one brow raised.

"Your favorite color is red," I breathed. "I remember things too, Trent."

CHAPTER NINE

Even hours later, I was still shocked by Trent's surprise visit and the sweet gesture of the coffee and Rice Krispies Treat. I'd greedily slurped down the coffee, finding it to be the most delicious thing I'd ever tasted. For some reason, though, I had found myself unable to devour the sugary treat currently residing in my backpack. Like a child, I wanted to hold on to it and treasure it for what it signified.

Five years.

One thousand eight hundred and twenty-six days.

It was a *long* time.

Yet, it was also like no time at all.

Neither one of us had ever been able to forget the other. I remembered things about Trenton that I *wished* I could forget. It would make ignoring him so much easier. But we had a past, a past that refused to let either of us go. We were tethered together and our bond was indestructible. My years of ignoring him had proven just how everlasting it was, because here he was—here, *we* were—back to pretty much where we'd always been.

A connection like ours—I refused to think of it as love, love was simply a fairytale—it wasn't easily broken. It stretched, it frayed, but it did not break.

I looked at the time on my phone, cursing under my breath. I had to get home, the kids were probably starving, and my "study time" had been pretty much non-existent.

I packed up my stuff and locked up the library on my way out.

I couldn't get home fast enough. I felt horrible that I'd completely forgotten the time. I might have to stop staying late at the library, but that meant I'd never get any school work done.

Technically, though, I shouldn't have had to worry about rushing home. They were my mom's responsibility, but the woman couldn't do anything.

When I walked in the front door and into the house I found the kids in their bedroom playing.

"Hey." I stopped in the doorway, a little breathless. "Are you guys hungry?"

They shook their heads.

"Ivy made me a sammy." Tristan smiled up at me, from where he played on the floor with little toy cars.

I frowned. "Oh. Okay."

I knew at Ivy's age she was perfectly capable of making a sandwich, but I didn't want her to have to do that. I wanted her to be a child, to know that I'd always be there to make everything better. I didn't want her to have to be ... me.

I smiled in Ivy's direction, and she frowned, feeling like she'd done something wrong.

"That was very nice of you, Ivy," I hastened to add. "If you two are okay without me for a bit, I'm going to shower."

Ivy nodded. "We'll be okay."

She didn't know it, but those three words hurt. It made me feel like they'd be just fine without me. Maybe I was being selfish by thinking they needed me.

I grabbed a pair of sweatpants and a loose shirt from my bedroom, locking myself in the bathroom. I leaned against the door, wondering why a stupid sandwich had made me upset. It wasn't the sandwich, but what it represented—that life went on without me around.

I sunk to the floor, resting my head on my knees.

One thought lingered in my mind.

Nobody needs me.

I WASN'T SURPRISED to see Trenton waiting beside my car when I left school. I had come to expect him to pop up wherever—and why would he stop now?

"Hi," I said hesitantly. After my breakdown last night, my emotions were raw and I wasn't ready to see him. I knew Trent would pick up on something being wrong and another day to quiet my mind would have been welcome.

"Coffee, Rice Krispiess Treat." He held each out for me to take.

Despite my efforts, I smiled, taking the items from him. "Is this going to become a daily occurrence?" I questioned.

He grinned, flipping his nearly black hair out of his eyes.

"Sure. It gives me an excuse to see you until I go back to school. Let's not talk about that, though." He seemed to sense my discomfort at the mention of him being away at school. "Are you okay?"

I nodded. "Fine." I brought the coffee cup to my lips and tried not to drop the Rice Krispiess Treat. I was determined to actually eat this one. Since it wasn't a very cold day I hopped up on the trunk of my car and tapped the empty space next to me. Trent quickly took the spot beside me, the car bouncing from the momentum. A small laugh escaped me. He kicked his legs out, and for once seemed unsure what to say.

"Today was your last day of classes?" he asked as I set the coffee cup between us and ripped the wrapper off the treat.

I nodded, taking a bite—and oh, my God it was the best thing I'd ever tasted. I hadn't had one of these in forever. I was beginning to regret not eating the one from yesterday.

"I never have asked you what you're studying," he probed me for answers.

"Nursing," I answered around a mouthful of food, using my hand to hide my mouth.

His eyes widened in surprise. "I didn't expect that."

"Why not?" I asked, finishing the last of the Rice Krispiess Treat and licking my fingers clean.

"I don't know." He shrugged, glancing at me out of the corner of his eye. "It just doesn't seem very ... you."

His statement didn't offend me. When I'd known him, I'd been convinced I was destined for bigger and better things. I'd been interested in acting. Oh, how dreams change when life gets in the way.

"And what seems like me?" I countered, picking up the coffee cup once more and holding it between my hands.

He peered at my thoughtfully. "Teacher ... Yeah, I could see you as a teacher. You're good with kids. I remember watching you with your sister once, Ivy, right?" When I nodded, he continued, "I thought I'd never seen anyone handle a little kid so well before. You'll make a great mom one day, Row." He looked at me wistfully.

I glanced away and out to the parking lot. I didn't want to talk about this.

I brought the lid of the coffee cup to my lips and let the warm liquid heat my suddenly bone-chilled body.

"Did I say something wrong?"

I turned to look at him and shook my head.

"You don't seem okay," he whispered. "Are you ...?" he left the question hanging.

"Having regrets? No." I rubbed at my tired eyes. "It was just a rough night." After my mini meltdown—minus actual tears —I'd showered and climbed into bed with Tristan. I'd needed to surround myself with the comfort of the kids. If I'd shut myself up in my room, I think I would've went crazy.

"Well," he started, and I swore a slight pink color stained his cheeks, "allow me to make tonight not so rough."

I raised a brow.

"Come over for dinner ... please," he tacked on, like he thought the *please* would make me give in.

"You know I can't." I frowned. "Ivy and—"

"It can be an early dinner then, and I'll make plenty, so you'll have leftovers to take home to them. Or you can bring them with you. I wouldn't mind. It would limit my time kissing you, but I'm willing to make the sacrifice."

"I'll need to go home and change, but I can be there in two hours." That would give me plenty of time to shower, change, and give myself a much-needed pep talk, because I was going to be at Trenton's place ... Just the two of us ... Oh, God.

Trent's grin was so wide that crinkles appeared at the corners of his eyes. He hopped off my car and started to back away. "I guess I better figure out what I'm making."

"I would've thought you'd already have a plan," I retorted.

He shrugged. "I figured you'd say no."

With that, he turned on his heel and jogged down the lot to where his black car was parked.

I continued to sit on the trunk of my car, drinking the delicious caramel coffee, and wondering what the heck I'd gotten myself into.

MY HAIR WAS clean and dry, hanging in a straight sheet down my back. I wore a pair of jeans, a loose black sweater that hung slightly off my shoulder, and an old pair of boots that had certainly seen better days but were so comfortable I refused to get rid of them.

The kids Christmas break didn't start for another week, so there was still a good hour before they'd be home, and they were used to being here alone anyway. Not that they were *technically* alone, since my mom was here, but still.

I brushed my teeth for the fourth time since I'd been home and forced my fingers through my hair. My heart was racing in my chest, at the possibility of what might be about to go down between Trent and myself. I sort of felt like a cocky dude, assuming sex was on the menu, but after the kiss in the car, I'd be lying if I said I didn't want more.

That didn't mean I wasn't scared, though.

I hadn't had sex, except that one time so long ago. I was sure Trent had had plenty of practice and knew exactly what he was doing. I, on the other hand, was pretty clueless. One time hardly made me a master. Sure, there were times over the years when guys had expressed interest in me, but I couldn't even make myself kiss them, let alone have sex. In the back of my mind, there was always ... Well, there was always Trent.

"Stop it, Rowan." I glared at my reflection in the mirror. "Stop this right now. It's only dinner. That's all."

Oh, God. Now I was talking to myself in the mirror. I was destined for the loony bin. *Shit.*

I forced myself out of the bathroom, shrugged on my coat, and grabbed my purse. I was almost out the door when I looked back and saw my mom passed out on the couch—sans trashcan.

I rolled my eyes, and strode back inside, grabbing the waste bin and sitting it beside her. I didn't want to come home and have to clean up her vomit.

I guessed the sound of the trashcan being sat down woke her, because her groggy hazel eyes opened to meet mine. "What the fuck are you doing leaning over me like that?"

I pointed to the trashcan. I didn't owe her an explanation. I didn't owe her *anything*.

"You're a worthless piece of shit! You know that!" she called after me.

I turned around, flipping her off. "Only because I'm your spawn," I spat. "So, you would know."

"You little bitch," she snarled, her greasy hair hanging limply in her eyes as she struggled to get off the couch and come at me.

I slammed the door closed and ran for my car, speeding

away before she could make it outside. A part of me hoped she'd come outside and be so drunk she'd forget how to get back inside, then maybe she'd freeze to death. Fuck. I was a horrible person. What kind of sane person *wishes* their mother would die? The sick kind, that's who. I was so going to hell.

Trent had texted me directions to his place, since he no longer lived at his family's mansion. As big as that place was I was surprised he hadn't stayed. Surely, he had plenty of privacy there.

I drove through town and turned into a nice neighborhood lined with brick three-story townhomes. My mouth gaped open. What kind of twenty-one-year-old guy needed a place like this?

I pulled along the road and checked my phone to make sure I'd remembered the right house number. When I was sure I had it correct, I drove forward and pulled into the driveway. I sat for a moment, a bit scared to get out and knock on the door.

"You have nothing to be scared of, Rowan," I mumbled to myself.

Great, not only did I talk to myself in the mirror, but now I did it in the car too.

I stepped out and locked my car—although, in this nice neighborhood, I doubted anyone would want to break into this jalopy.

I bound up the steps to the front door with a pep I didn't really feel. I reached out and hesitantly knocked on the door. No sounds greeted me, and when more than thirty seconds had passed without Trent appearing, I pushed the doorbell.

I heard Trent talking, but no one answered, so I was a bit confused about what was going on.

"Stay away from there, Dean!" he yelled as the door swung open.

"Hi," I said, but he wasn't looking at me, but over his shoulder.

That's when I saw the baby.

Holy shit.

Trent had a kid.

A fucking *baby*.

My throat closed up. He had a kid with some girl that was probably a whole lot prettier and nicer than I was. I wondered why he wasn't with her and why he was wasting time with me.

I didn't even realize I was doing it, but I turned around and ran toward my car.

Trent called after me, but I didn't stop.

I went to unlock my car, but I couldn't find my keys. Where the hell were my keys? I patted my pockets, looked in my purse, and they weren't there. So much for my quick escape.

The door to his townhouse was opening again and I turned to see him running down the steps with the drooling little monster in his arms. Normally, I went gaga over a baby, but seeing Trent's offspring from some whore was making me so angry I couldn't see straight.

"Stay away from me!" I seethed, ready to punch him in the nose if he took one step closer.

"Row, I don't know why you're freaking out. I'm sorry I didn't tell you about Dean. I forgot I was supposed to watch him."

The baby—which was really more a toddler—blew spit bubbles at me and waved. I hated to admit it, but he was pretty cute.

"You should've told me you had a kid!" I exclaimed, pointing at the child in his arms. "I deserved to know!"

Trent's brows furrowed in puzzlement. "You think Dean is my kid?"

I gave him a *duh* look, and crossed my arms over my chest. "I'm not dumb, Trenton."

"No, not dumb, but jumping to conclusions can get you in trouble. Dean isn't my kid."

"He's not?" I hated the fact that those words made me breathe easier.

"No," Trent chuckled. "He's my nephew."

"Nephew …?" *Oh. I'm a colossal idiot and just made a fool of myself.*

"Yeah, this is Dean." He pointed to the baby, outfitted in a red plaid jumper. "Trace's son."

I blushed profusely, embarrassed by my overreaction.

"Oh … I'm sorry … I thought …"

"I know what you thought." He laughed, clearly amused by my humiliation. "Anyway, when I invited you to dinner, I'd forgotten I told Trace I'd babysit so he and Olivia could have a night out. I hope you don't mind …," he trailed off, scratching the back of his head.

Dean started making a buzzing noise with his lips.

"No, I don't mind. Can I … Can I hold him?" I reached my arms out. My demeanor had completely changed once I knew the child wasn't his.

Trent quickly deposited the baby in my arms. "Maybe I can cook now. This little gremlin" —he smacked Dean's butt— "keeps trying to break Bartholomew out of his cage."

I laughed. "The ferret?"

"Yep." Trent nodded, heading back inside, assuming I'd follow—which of course I did.

The townhouse was really pretty, with shiny wood floors and light blue walls. It was airy and welcoming. There was a formal living room to my right, but it was empty. I followed Trent toward the back of the house, past a set of stairs, to where it opened up to a kitchen, dining room, and family room. The furniture was dark and manly, but everything was surprisingly neat and clean. There was nothing lingering out in the open that shouldn't be there. I didn't know why I expected a mess.

"So ... where's Bartholomew?" I asked. At this point, a part of me still believed he'd made up the pet ferret thing. He pointed to a cage in the corner, which was obscured by the large entertainment center. "I keep him in there when I'm down here, and he has a cage in my room."

"He gets lonely?" I laughed.

"*I* get lonely," he said with a straight face. "You wouldn't believe what a good snuggling partner a ferret is."

"You're a strange guy." I continued to laugh as Dean squirmed in my arms. I finally was forced to put him down before I dropped him. He immediately toddled over to Bartholomew's cage and tried to undo the latch. Trent hadn't been lying, the kid really wanted the ferret out.

"Now that you're here," Trent said as he looked through the refrigerator, "you can get Bartholomew out if you want and let Dean pet him."

"Uh ..." I didn't know why, but I felt a bit frightened of the furry brown and white creature peering lazily at me from a hammock in its cage.

"Oh, come on, Rowan," Trent goaded me, as he closed the

refrigerator door, setting items on the granite counter, "don't tell me you're afraid of him. He won't bite if you're nice."

I took a deep breath and stepped forward. I moved Dean behind me and opened the cage. The furry creature hopped out of the hammock and hurried to the open door. I grabbed him before he could jump out. He was surprisingly light and his fur was soft. I looked down at his face, and he was actually pretty cute.

"Come on, Dean," I called to the toddler as I took a seat on the couch. I held Bartholomew in one hand and reached down to help Dean up with the other.

"Mew Mew." Dean smiled up at me, displaying small white teeth as he pointed at the squirming creature in my hands.

"He can't say Bartholomew," Trent called, "just go with it."

I rolled my eyes and didn't reply. Did he really think I couldn't figure out what the kid meant by Mew Mew?

"Soft." Dean pet Bartholomew with a surprising gentleness. "Kiss." He lowered his head and kissed the furry critter on top of his small head. Bartholomew seemed used to the attention and didn't move. He'd stilled in my arms and I thought he might have fallen asleep. When I woke up this morning this was so not how I'd seen my day going. I mean, who expects to cuddle with a ferret? I still felt a bit bad about jumping to the conclusion Dean was Trent's son without asking questions. They looked so much alike. Dean had thick dark hair and his smile had Wentworth written all over it. I guessed Trace and Trent had some strong genes. There wasn't anything about Dean that didn't look like a Wentworth ... except maybe his slightly upturned nose. He was a cute kid with expressive green eyes. He did seem to drool a lot, however.

Dean crawled onto my lap and continued to pet

Bartholomew with his chubby little hand. "Mew Mew," he whispered again. Looking up at me, he asked, "Who you?"

Dean seemed to realize for the first time that I was a stranger. He was still burrowed against my chest though, and seemed to have no plans to leave. Unlike most kids, he obviously wasn't afraid to get cozy with a stranger.

"My name is Row," I answered him.

"Row?" he repeated, looking up at me with big green eyes.

"That's right." I smiled, lightly tickling his stomach and making him giggle.

I looked up and my gaze connected with Trent's. He was looking at me wistfully, and my heart raced in my chest knowing what he was seeing and probably imagining.

I quickly looked away. "Me, Dean." Dean pointed at his chest. "You, Row." He poked my breast. *Definitely a Wentworth.* "Dat Mew Mew, and he Rent!" He twisted to point enthusiastically at Trent.

Trent chuckled, shaking his head as he covered some kind of fish in a seasoning. "Good job, Dean. Thanks for making the introductions."

"Welcome," Dean beamed, turning back to me.

The little boy quieted, and went back to petting Bartholomew. I stretched my legs out on the ottoman, adjusting my hold on both the ferret and the toddler, since my arms felt like they were seconds away from falling asleep.

When I knew Trent was occupied with what he was doing, I watched him out of the corner of my eye. He was reading something off his phone. A recipe maybe? He kept flicking his head to keep his dark hair out of his eyes. His thumb scrolled the screen on his phone and his tongue stuck slightly out of his mouth as he concentrated. He muttered under his breath and began opening cabinets as he looked for something. He finally located it and added it to a bowl. As he worked he hummed under his breath. I didn't recognize the song—and wasn't even sure it really was a song, or just something he was making up as he went along.

He turned on two of the gas stove eyes and set something across it. It looked like he'd be grilling the fish; at least, I thought it was fish.

Feeling like a creeper for spying on him as he cooked, I glanced back down at the warm bundles in my arms. Both the ferret and the toddler were sound asleep. It didn't look like I'd be moving anytime soon. For once, I was okay with that. I didn't feel the need to run. I was actually enjoying myself, and I wasn't even really hanging out with Trent. But I was here, in his house, and I didn't have an urge to leave. I was ... comfortable.

"You okay?" Trent asked as something sizzled on the stove.

"Mhmm," I hummed. "I'm great."

Trent turned to look at me over his shoulder, and at his grin, I couldn't help but smile in response. "Good," he said, his eyes devouring me the way one would their favorite piece of chocolate.

Goosebumps broke out across my skin as he stared at me. That look ... It turned my insides to mush. It felt good to be desired.

With a wink, Trent turned back to what he was doing. I wondered if he was aware of the delicious feelings coursing through my body from a single glance. The boy was good, and he didn't even have to try. It was quite a talent he had.

I must have dozed off as well, because some time later I was awakened by Trent gently shaking my shoulder.

Bartholomew was gone, and I started to panic, but I immediately glimpsed him snoozing in his hammock. Dean was still curled in my arms, his body providing warmth to mine. His tiny lips were pursed in sleep.

"Dinner's ready," Trent told me.

I nodded, stifling a yawn.

Trenton picked Dean up off my lap and the little boy came awake with a start. "Rent?" he asked quizzically, looking at Trent with sleepy eyes.

"It's Uncle Trent," he assured the toddler, carrying him over to a highchair by the dining table.

"You have a highchair for him?" I tilted my head, taking in the sight of Trent tending to Dean.

"Well, *I* didn't buy it." He chuckled. "I watch Dean as much as I can when I'm home. Trace works a lot and Olivia's home with this goober all the time." He affectionately kissed Dean's cheek, making a loud smacking sound with his lips. "Sometimes they need a break, and I'm happy to help. I like kids. I even have a pack n' play for when we have sleepovers." he winked, ruffling the toddler's hair, and sauntering into the kitchen.

I sat down at the table in front of a steaming plate of deliciousness. My stomach rumbled as I inhaled the scents of rosemary and garlic. It was official, the man could do anything, he was perfect.

"Do you drink wine?" he asked, looking at me over his shoulder.

"I'm legal if that's what you're asking, but no, I've never drank any ..." After what I saw at home, how could I want to? I didn't want to become my mother.

"This is really good with our dinner." He held a bottle aloft. "Would you like to try some?"

I frowned, prepared to tell him no, but he was already pouring a glass. I didn't see how one glass could turn me into a raging alcoholic. Besides, if I hated it, I didn't have to drink it.

Trent set our glasses down and went back to the kitchen, returning with a plate of food for Dean. He took the seat beside the highchair and fed Dean a spoonful of mashed potatoes. "If I let him feed himself, he throws his food at me," Trent explained. "I'm really sorry about this." He tilted his head to Dean, who was making a humming sound as he ate a gob of mashed potatoes. "This wasn't at all what I had planned for tonight."

"And what did you have planned?" I ventured to take a bite of the grilled salmon—and holy shit, it was the best thing I had ever tasted.

"Dinner." He nodded to our plates. "Talking ... Kissing ..."

"Always with the kissing." I laughed—the sound surprising me. I was laughing, and if I recalled correctly, there had been other times when Trent had made me laugh. A real genuine laugh, not one I had to force. The man had superpowers.

"I like kissing you." He winked, feeding Dean a piece of roasted chicken that was specially prepared for him. I doubted a baby would want to eat fish anyway.

"Did you have anything else planned?" I questioned as I took a hesitant sip of wine. It was actually pretty good and went well with the fish.

"Nope." Mischief danced in his eyes when he looked at me.

"Really?" I raised a brow.

He nodded, finally taking a bite of his own food.

Embarrassment flooded my cheeks in an unflattering

shade of red, because I had been imagining more. Much more. What was wrong with me?

I should've known Trent wouldn't expect *that* yet, he wasn't that kind of guy. A part of me was disappointed though. I felt like maybe he was doing this on purpose—dragging it out until he knew I was so desperate with want that I'd jump his bones.

No, it wouldn't be like Trent to think that way.

More than likely, he wanted me to be sure that I did actually want this. Right now, though, I didn't want him to be a gentleman.

There wasn't anything I could do, though. Dean was here, and I couldn't exactly pull Trent away to have my wicked way with him.

I was okay with that.

Clearly, now wasn't the right time for our relationship to move in that direction. After five years, I felt like I was about to explode. It would be worth the wait. *Trent* was worth the wait ... I just hoped that finally admitting that I did have feelings for him wouldn't blow up in my face. Who was I kidding? It would. Once all my lies and deceptions were out in the open, he'd hate me. I had to tell him what I'd done. I should open my mouth up and let it all out. But I couldn't, and I was selfish anyway, wanting to spend more time with him before I didn't have him at all.

"How's your mom?" I asked him. I'd only met Lily a handful of times, but she was a lovely woman and had raised her sons well, especially after their dad died. She was the kind of woman I could admire. She was beautiful, but strong and independent. She didn't take shit from anyone. "Your grandparents?"

"Mom's good." He shrugged. "She's busy a lot now, running the business and all, but we have family dinner's once a week. I always come home for them." His eyes grew sad, and he added, "Gramps died a few years ago. Cancer. It's been hard losing him. He became like a dad to Trace and me after ours died. Gramps' death has been harder on Trace than me, but I miss him every day."

My heart broke seeing the pain in his eyes. Even two years later it was obvious he still missed his grandpa and that the wound would probably never quite heal all the way. I'd only met Warren once, but he was a nice man, and went out of his way to make me feel comfortable.

"I'm so sorry, Trenton," I whispered.

He shrugged, his lips turned down in a frown. "It was his time."

"That might be true, but it doesn't make his loss any easier."

Trent nodded, cooing to Dean. I knew he didn't really want to talk about his grandpa, and that was fine. I knew what it was like not to want to talk about things. I wouldn't push him.

We moved the conversation to more comfortable topics, like school and friends.

I laughed and smiled easily, something I seemed to only do around Trenton. He had some kind of magical spell over me that melted my icy exterior.

He refused to let me help clean up from dinner, instead putting me in charge of Dean once more. The little boy had renewed energy after dinner and I had to chase him down. He was a quick little thing.

"Do you need to go yet?" he asked, putting food into plastic containers.

I shook my head. "I still have time."

"Want to put a movie on?" he asked, stacking the containers one on top of the other.

"That's fine with me." I grabbed Dean up in my arms before he could crawl up the steps. "I probably won't be able to stay for the whole thing though."

"Any extra time I get with you, I'll take." He smiled. Pointing to the containers, he said, "These are for your brother and sister. I figured they wouldn't like fish, so I gave them the chicken I got for Dean."

Tears pricked my eyes. I hadn't believed him when he said he'd have food for Ivy and Tristan. But he did. He was remarkable.

I turned away from him so he wouldn't see the moisture building in my eyes and pretended to be playing with Dean.

"You can pick out the movie." I jumped when his hand pressed against my waist.

"O-Okay," I stuttered.

He took Dean from my arms and led me to the entertainment center. He brought up something on the TV and said, "Scroll through until you find one you want."

I gaped. I had never seen such a fancy TV. It was like a spaceship.

I was a quick learner so it didn't take me long to figure out how to work the fancy remote.

"*Thor*?" He chuckled, when I had made my selection.

"I always did have a thing for muscular superheroes." I winked. Oh, my God. Was I flirting? I was totally flirting.

Trent chuckled. "I remember all those superhero shirts you used to wear. Do you still have them?"

"I sleep in them."

He made a noise in the back of his throat, causing heat to rise to the surface of my cheeks. "I like those shirts. A lot."

"Me too," I squeaked.

Jesus Christ, the man was making me hot and bothered just by talking about my old ratty superhero t-shirts.

The movie started and Trent turned off the lights. "You want some popcorn?" he asked before he sat down.

"No thanks."

He picked up Dean and plopped down beside me, depositing the little boy in his lap. The couch dipped with his added weight and I slid toward him, stopping when my left side was firmly pressed against his right side. I *so* didn't want to watch a movie right now.

I forced myself to focus on the screen, and not on the way his warmth felt beside me, or how I really wanted to tilt my head up and kiss his jaw, then his lips, then …

You knew you had it bad when even the sight of Chris Hemsworth couldn't distract you.

I found my eyes growing heavy, and my head fell to Trent's shoulder.

I wasn't falling asleep. I wasn't. Okay, I totally was.

But he felt so good, and he kept humming, the sound calming me. Eventually, I couldn't resist it any longer, and fell asleep with my head rested on his shoulder, and a small smile on my lips.

I WAS BEING JOSTLED AWAKE, rather rudely I might add. I blinked my eyes open to find Trent's brother hovering above us.

"Trace, stop it, that's not nice," a female voice piped in.

"Dude, wake up." He smacked Trent's cheek.

Trent woke with a start. "What the—"

"Tsk, tsk," Trace waggled a finger in front of Trent's face, holding Dean. "Sleeping on the job, baby brother, that's not allowed."

"Sorry." Trent stood, reaching his arms above his head to stretch. His shirt rode up exposing his smooth and toned stomach. I itched to reach out and have that skin beneath my hands.

Trace cuddled Dean in his arms, the child completely undisturbed, his eyes still closed and his small thumb stuck in his mouth.

A woman, who didn't appear to be much older than me, peered around Trace. "Hi, I'm Olivia." She reached her hand out to shake mine. Her voice was light and pleasant, and there was something so sweet about her. She was the kind of person you couldn't help but instantly like. She was also beyond gorgeous with long, dark-brown, wavy hair, pouty lips, and an adorably upturned nose. It was obvious this was Trace's wife and Dean's mother.

"Rowan," I replied, taking her hand and shaking it.

"Oooh," she drew out the word, her eyes flicking to Trace. "I've heard about you."

"Why am I not surprised?" Trent grumbled under his breath.

I blushed at Olivia's words. They'd talked about me? That was embarrassing.

Olivia peered around Trace, who seemed to stand in front of her like a bodyguard, to see Trent. "We'll get out of your way."

"You didn't have sex in front of my kid, did you? That would be traumatizing for him," Trace asked Trent. I knew he was teasing, but I couldn't help the blush that only kept getting redder.

"Fuck, no."

"Oh, so you only cuss in front of him? Good to know. Uncle of the Year award right here." Trace pointed at his brother.

"Get out of my house," Trent grumbled, reaching down to grab the remote and turn the TV off.

"Who pays the bills? Oh, I do, that makes it *my* house," Trace retorted.

Olivia rolled her eyes and looked at me. "They argue all the time. I think they find it fun."

I didn't really know what to say to her. She was a stranger, and I wasn't the type to make friends easily.

"Come on, Trace." She put her hand on his muscular arm and lightly tugged. "Let's go home. I'm tired."

"You better not be too tired." He grinned, letting her lead him toward the front door. "I'm not done with you yet."

"Trace!" she scolded, looking back at Trent and I with an embarrassed smile. "See you guys another time." She waved, pushing Trace out the door.

As soon as the door was closed and the headlights of their car fanned across the front window, Trent whistled, giving me a funny smile. With his hands shoved into the pockets of his jeans, he said, "That was awkward."

I couldn't help but laugh. "You could say that again."

"That was awkward." He grinned impishly.

Noting the time, I frowned. "I have to go."

"I know." He headed for the kitchen, grabbing up the plastic containers. "I'll walk you out."

He didn't bother putting on a coat, and as soon as the cool air greeted us, goosebumps broke out on his skin. He jumped up and down trying to keep his body moving. I unlocked my car and he handed me the food. I leaned inside to set it on the passenger seat. When I straightened, I could've sworn his eyes had been glued to my ass.

I raised a brow at him and he smirked, not at all ashamed at having been caught.

"I'll see you soon," he said, leaning in to press his lips to mine. He ended the kiss quickly, before things could progress to a dangerous level, but I was no less affected.

I got in my car and watched him jog back into his house. With a shake of my head, I forced myself to back out of the driveway and return to reality.

CHAPTER TEN

I woke up early, determined to make the kids a hearty breakfast and spend some time with them. I scrambled eggs and made some of that microwave bacon. I popped three slices of toast into the toaster and gathered the plates. After I'd placed everything on the table I looked up to find Tristan standing there rubbing his eyes.

"Good morning," I told him cheerily.

"That smells good."

"I hope it tastes just as good." I bent, kissing the top of his head. I wrapped my arms around him and held him close. Tristan and Ivy were the only people I'd ever truly loved. Something told me that if I let myself, I could love Trent too. I didn't know if I'd ever be ready for that, though.

I released Tristan and he climbed onto the chair. Ivy came out of the bedroom next, sniffing the air. "Mmm," she hummed.

Based on their reactions, I was glad I had taken the time to make them a decent breakfast. Most mornings, I either didn't have the time, or we didn't have the ingredients.

I sat down with them, taking the time to talk to them. Tristan was excited about learning the alphabet, and Ivy kept mentioning a boy's name. I was going to have my hands full with that one.

I loved these moments I had with them where we were like a family. I really hoped I didn't have to wait much longer before I could take custody of them away from my mom.

As if conjured by my thoughts, she appeared in the doorway of the kitchen. Her hair stuck up wildly around her head and there were bags under her eyes. "Give me that!"

My mouth dropped open when she snatched Tristan's half-eaten plate from him. What kind of mother takes food from her child?

Tristan's bottom lip began to tremble with the threat of tears.

I stood slowly, glaring at my mom. "Give. That. Back."

"What?" she gasped, not because she hadn't heard me, but because she couldn't believe I had spoken.

"You heard me."

A piece of egg clung to her bottom lip. Everything about the woman was disgusting—even me, because I was a part of her. Her taint clung to me, and it was something I would never be able to shake.

She set the plate down on the counter, not in front of Tristan.

"This is my house," she seethed, the stench of her breath threatening to knock me down, "and the food in it belongs to me. I'll eat whatever the hell I want."

"*I* bought that food and *I* made it." I pointed to my chest. "You have no right—"

My head snapped to the side with the impact of her hand landing against my cheek. My teeth had bitten down on the sensitive inside of my mouth and I tasted blood.

Tristan began to cry, and when I looked at Ivy her mouth hung open in shock.

"You ungrateful brat!" she screamed at me, hatred filling her eyes.

I wasn't going to let her think that a slap would silence me anymore. I was done being passive. My mouth filled with blood and I wondered if it was possible to need stitches in your mouth. I really hoped not. "You've taken *everything* from me!" I couldn't seem to stop shouting. "I'm not your little bitch anymore! I'm not going to sit back and let you rule me! I'm done!"

She seemed shocked at my comeback. I always took her shit and never fought back, but she had done one too many things to me in the past, and I had finally snapped.

She didn't seem to have a comeback, so she grabbed the plate of food, glaring at me, and marched back into her bedroom. She slammed the door closed hard enough to rattle the whole house.

"Tristan," I whispered, bending down to take his small face in my hands. His cheeks were wet with tears and I hated that I'd been part of the cause for them. "It's okay, Tristan."

"You-you-you," he hiccupped, "bleedin'."

I reached up to my mouth and my fingers came away with a slight red mark. It wasn't bad, but to Tristan it seemed like the end of the world.

"I'm fine," I assured him.

He shook his head, his sandy hair falling into his eyes. "Not okay. You're bleedin'."

I took him into my arms, rocking him back and forth as he cried. No kid should have to witness what went down between my mom and me. Tristan was probably wondering when she was going to hit him and when I'd yell at him. I had to get them out of here. I just had to.

When Tristan's cries had stopped, I slid my plate toward him. "Here, eat mine."

He was hesitant at first but, eventually, hunger won out and he started eating what was left of my food.

Now that the adrenaline was wearing off, my cheek stung and the inside of my mouth was throbbing. I needed some Advil.

I went to the sink and filled a cup with water. I used it to swish out the lingering blood coating my mouth. The day had barely begun, and I already wished it were over.

Let's go to Griffin's. I'll pick you up in an hour.

The text was from Trent. A part of me felt like responding to him and telling him that I couldn't. My cheek and mouth were still sore, and I had a headache that didn't seem to want to leave—one that not even my prescription medicine could relieve. After I took the kids to school, I'd come back home and shut up in my bedroom with the curtains drawn. I wanted to block out the world. Leave it to Trent to make that impossible.

K. I typed back.

A moment later he sent a smiley face. I hadn't done anything after the showdown with my mom, so I knew I looked horrible. I took the quickest shower of my life, towel-dried my hair, and applied more makeup than I normally would to hide the red mark on my cheek.

He said he'd pick me up in thirty minutes, so I tugged on a pair of worn jeans and gray sweater. It had dropped into the teens, so I grabbed my warmest coat, black mittens, and my infinity scarf with the words BAM! and POW! on it with drawings of superheroes. I knew Trent would like it.

The door to my mom's room was closed. I didn't bother telling her where I was going or checking on her. I didn't care. I'd stopped caring a long time ago.

When I reached the front of the house and looked out the windows, Trent's black car was parked by the mailbox. I hurried outside to him, excitement filling my belly. A short amount of time surrounded by Trent was turning me into a completely different person.

I opened the car door and slid onto the warm leather seat. When I looked over at him and saw him watching me, my heart skipped a beat, just like they always talked about in romance books. The sound of my breathing filled the car and I couldn't be bothered to be embarrassed by it. Our eyes connected and neither of us moved. The silence swirled around us and I found myself desperate to shatter it.

"Why are we going to Griffin's?"

Jesus, Rowan, of all the things you could ask him, that's what comes out of your mouth? Brilliant.

He grinned, his eyes crinkling at the corners with amusement. "I'm not telling. You'll see soon enough."

He turned the radio up and "Goodbye" by Glenn Morrison sounded through the speakers.

We didn't really talk along the way. We didn't need to. That was something else I liked about being with Trent. There was no awkward silence, only comfort.

He parked across the street from Griffin's and hopped out to put change in the parking meter.

He opened my door for me and held out a hand for me to take. I stared at it with unease.

"It's just a hand, Row," he said, "you can let go as soon as you get out if you want. There's no obligation for you to hold my hand."

I placed my hand in his and he closed his fingers over mine. He helped me onto the curb, and went to release my hand, but I tightened my hold. He glanced down at me in surprise. I smiled up at him and he grinned in response, a dimple popping out in his cheek. I liked that dimple. A lot. I itched to stand on my tiptoes and press my lips to the indent, but I didn't. I wasn't brave enough yet. I'd take it one step at a time, starting with handholding.

Traffic zoomed by and we waited for the crosswalk to flash our turn. I itched to pull my hand away from his, but I forced myself to keep it where it was. There was nothing wrong with this.

When it was our turn we jogged across the street, our breath fogging the cold air. The sky was gray with the promise of snow.

Trent held the door to Griffin's open for me and I stepped inside. It was packed and I was taken aback by all the people.

"Come on." Trent took my hand again, reaching up to adjust his maroon colored beanie with the other. "Back here."

He pushed through the crowd and I didn't know how he got his body to fit through such small spaces.

In the back area of Griffin's there was a stage where musicians could perform. Someone was up there now.

A hand shot up, waving us toward a table.

I was trapped behind Trenton and couldn't see who it was.

It turned out to be Trace and Olivia. Trace was grinning from ear to ear, and Olivia bounced Dean on her lap.

"I'm so happy you guys could make it." She smiled, her cheeks flushed a rosy pink. There was a nervousness to her demeanor as she bit down on her bottom lip and glanced nervously at Trace.

"Are you okay?" I asked her, pulling off my black mittens and shrugging out of my coat.

She nodded. "I always get nervous before I sing." She began chewing on the side of her fingernail. Trace grabbed her hand, pulling it away from her mouth, and twining his fingers with hers. He looked at her with so much love that even I couldn't help but be affected ... Especially when I'd seen Trent look at me in a similar way.

"You're singing?" I asked her, a bit surprised.

"We're singing together," Trace clarified as Olivia tucked a piece of hair behind her ear, then proceeded to cover the top of Dean's head with kisses. She looked like she was going to be ill, poor girl.

"Do you sing?" I turned to Trent, who'd taken the seat beside me.

"No," he replied quickly. "I'll leave the singing to those two."

"Are you bad?" I asked.

His brows furrowed together. "I don't know. I've never actually tried to sing."

"Maybe you should try." I pointed to the stage.

"Um, yeah, no. If I *ever* sing, the first time will not be on a stage in front of a bunch of people." He shook his head rapidly. "No way."

I couldn't help but laugh at his reaction. "Would you guys mind watching Dean while we sing?" Olivia asked, holding tightly to the toddler.

"Isn't that why you asked me to come?" Trent retorted.

"Well, yeah." Olivia shrugged. "We have to use you while you're home. Dean doesn't like to be left with anyone else but you. Not even your mom or my mom."

"That's because Dean has good taste in people," Trent joked.

Griffin appeared by our table, asking if we wanted to order anything. Trent asked for a beer, and I asked for water. This was seriously the weirdest coffee house around. I mean, how many coffee shops have menus like a restaurant, a stage, and they serve beer? I think Griffin strove for uniqueness.

"They're calling our names. Oh, God," Olivia mumbled, looking like she might throw up.

"It'll be fine," Trace assured her. "*You'll* be fine," he reinforced, taking her face between his hands and giving her a kiss that shouldn't be legal in public. I found myself turning away, feeling like I was witnessing something that was best kept private.

Trace stood, as did Olivia, who reluctantly handed Dean to Trent as they headed for the stage.

"Row?" Dean asked, finally spotting me. His arms reached out for me as he tried to climb out of Trent's hold. I took the baby into my arms and he smiled goofily up at me.

I held Dean in my arms as I looked toward the stage. Trace picked up a guitar and sat down on a stool, scooting the microphone toward him. Olivia grabbed another stool and sat down. Her eyes were closed and she was taking deep breaths.

Trace said something into the microphone, no doubt charming the crowd, but I couldn't pay attention because Dean had grabbed a strand of my hair and was currently yanking on it as he tried to shove it in his mouth.

Trent noticed and began to laugh, but he was quick to help untangle me from the tight hold. I'm pretty sure Dean ripped out a few hairs.

"That's not nice," Trent scolded, tapping Dean on the nose.

My heart surged with an emotion I couldn't begin to describe. Seeing Trent with Dean was amazing and heart-breaking all at the same time.

Dean held his arms out for Trent and then proceeded to yank Trent's beanie off his head.

"He's about to hit the terrible twos," Trent explained. "Trace and Olivia are in for it with this monster." He tickled Dean's stomach.

I laughed, ruffling the baby's hair.

My ears finally seemed to register that Trace and Olivia were singing. Both of their voices were incredible, but together they sounded phenomenal. My mouth dropped open in surprise as they covered "Everything Has Changed" by Taylor Swift and Ed Sheeran.

"Wow," I gasped. "They're unbelievable."

"I know, right." Trent grinned, wrangling a squirming Dean.

I listened closely to the song and watched their interactions, how they sang to each other and not the crowd. It was a beautiful thing to watch. I was in awe, and I wasn't afraid to show it. When they finished and sat down across from us once more, I bit down on my tongue to keep from gushing. I didn't want to embarrass them or myself.

Trace took Dean and deposited the squirming child in his lap. I began to laugh when I realized the father and son were wearing matching blue plaid shirts. I wondered how they'd ever found a child's shirt to match.

"Mew Mew," Dean protested, reaching for Trent.

"That's Uncle Trent. Mew Mew isn't here," Trace told his son. "They don't let carpet sharks run around restaurants."

I spat out my water. Thank God none of it landed on Olivia. It just splattered on the table.

"Carpet shark?" I asked.

"That's what he calls Bartholomew," Trent explained. "He thinks he's so clever."

"I am clever, among other things, like the most amazing kisser in the universe, and the best sex you'll never have."

I blushed, but the stain in my cheeks in no way compared to the one infusing Olivia's.

"Ow," Trace groaned, and I figured Olivia had punched him in the leg.

"We're going to head out now," Olivia said, standing and pulling on her camel-colored leather coat. "Now that my husband has made me feel thoroughly uncomfortable, that's the cue that it's time to go home."

"Shit," Trace mumbled. "I'm in trouble."

"Oh, yes, you are." Olivia stared him down.

It was funny, though, because despite her obvious mortification, I didn't think she was actually really that mad at him, and more that she was putting on a show to scare him into never doing it again.

They grabbed up their stuff and disappeared into the

crowd, but not before saying goodbye. I really liked those two, and they were cute together. I also felt that given time I could end up being friends with Olivia.

"Do you want to stay? Or head out?" Trent asked.

I thought for a moment. "I'm ready to leave, but I don't want to go home yet."

He grinned at my words, clearly pleased with them. He finished his beer and slapped some bills on the table.

"Let's go."

It took me a moment to get my coat buttoned and pull my mittens on. Trent grabbed my hand again and we made our way outside.

I'd grown hot in Griffin's and the cool air felt like heaven against my heated skin.

"It's snowing!" I exclaimed, smiling at the large snowflakes falling from the sky.

I spread my arms out wide and stuck my tongue out in the hopes of catching one.

"Rowan, what are you doing?" Trent laughed as he watched me act like a little kid.

I continued to spin around, marveling at the sound escaping me. I was giggling. I don't know if I'd ever giggled in my entire life.

"I'm living," I finally answered as the snow swirled around us. I had never allowed myself to let go and be so free. I was finding that I really liked it. I felt like a weight was being lifted from my shoulders as I danced down the street, the snow falling into my hair, and sticking to my clothes. The cold didn't touch me. I was oddly warm, Trenton's gaze heating my body.

I wasn't paying attention to what I was doing and suddenly I started to fall right into the street, straight into oncoming traffic. Trent darted forward, wrapping a solid hand around my arm and yanking me against his chest before I could go splat. My body thudded against his with the impact and we stumbled back.

"Whoa," he said, one hand on my waist, trying to balance us and keep us from falling. I clasped the soft fabric of his coat in my hands. I looked into his eyes and I was overcome by the one emotion I fought so hard to keep dormant—desire.

"Row—"

I didn't think. I didn't hesitate. I took what I wanted. I was tall, but Trenton was taller, so I brought myself up to my tiptoes and crashed my lips against his. My heart raced in my chest at the intensity. The hand that was at my waist came up to cup the nape of my neck, his fingers gathering my long hair in its grasp. He lightly bit my bottom lip and growled against my lips, "I can't deny this much longer. I want your legs wrapped around my waist, and I want to bury myself deep inside you."

I gasped at his words. Boldly, I leaned up and whispered in his ear, "Then do it."

"Fuck," he groaned, his fingers digging into my hip. His eyes scanned my face, searching for something. A shiver passed over his body and he closed his eyes. Opening them, he bit his lip, and it had to be the sexiest thing I had ever seen. "Are you sure?"

"Do you even need to ask?" I gasped, looking up at him as snowflakes stuck to my lashes.

He didn't answer. Instead, he took my face between his two large hands and kissed me until I forgot about everything except him. My cheeks warmed from the heat of his hands and my lips moved against his like they had a mind of their own.

This was it.

This was our now.

———

I HAD THOUGHT MAYBE Trent was going to stand on the sidewalk and kiss me in the snow all day. Finally, though, he'd torn his lips away and pressed his forehead against mine. His chest rose and fell with unsteady breaths. Kissing the end of my nose, he'd asked, "Come home with me?"

I hadn't hesitated to take what I wanted and said yes.

He opened the garage door, parking outside since a sleek black motorcycle occupied the space. As soon as I was out of his car I found my back pressed up against it with his lips assaulting mine.

My legs wrapped around his waist and he gripped me just below my butt. His hips pressed against mine and my lips wrenched from his as I gasped.

He carried me into the garage, hitting a button to close the door. He fumbled for the keys to unlock the door that led into his house. I placed my hand over his to steady him.

He finally got the door open and we burst inside. He kicked the door closed with his booted foot.

My mouth never left his as he carried me up two flights of steps and into the master bedroom. All the while we were tearing each other's coats off.

He sat down on the end of the bed with me straddling his lap. His stubbled cheeks rubbed against the palms of my hands. I kissed him deeply—with every ounce of passion that possessed my body. I had to show him with my actions how I felt, because words could never compare.

My hair was slightly damp from the snow melting in it and he brushed the strands away from my face as he rained kisses down my arched neck. I was sure, even with the only the slight pressure of his lips, he had to feel how fast my heart was beating.

He tugged my sweater off and tossed it behind me. Scooting farther back on the bed he pulled me with him.

I placed my hands flat against his chest and gave him a slight push. He toppled onto his back and I lowered over him, kissing him deeply as my hair fell forward to create a shield.

His tongue played with mine and a soft moan escaped me.

I thought I'd wanted Trent at sixteen years old, but my feelings then in no way compared to how I felt now.

His hands were all over me, just as mine were with him. Both of us were feeling, tracing, and exploring the other's body. I didn't feel shy or hesitant like I thought I would.

My hands skimmed his chest, pushing up the shirt he wore until he sat up to tear it off. He flipped over so he was above me and kissed over my naked stomach.

His fingers found the button of my jeans and he stopped.

He looked up at me and his blue eyes met mine. He braced himself above me, his eyes flicking to my lips and back to my eyes as his fingers lifted my chin.

"Are you sure?" he asked, his eyes closing as if the question pained him. "Are you sure you want this?" He swallowed thickly. "Say the word, and we'll stop. But if this goes too much further, I don't know if I'll be able to. I need you to stop me right now if you're not okay with this."

"You've tempted me this far, why stop now?"

That was answer enough for him. His lips descended to touch mine as his fingers easily found the button of my jeans.

He pulled them down my thighs and I helped by kicking them off.

"You. Are. Beautiful," he enunciated each word while staring at a different part of my body. My lips, my breasts, and finally the skin peeking out above the top of my panties. When he looked at me like that, I believed him, in fact I would've believed anything he told me in that moment. "I want to love you in so many ways," he confessed, kissing his way down my stomach. I couldn't control the shiver that rocked my body. "But I'm scared I'll end up pushing you away." His blue eyes lifted to meet mine, stealing my air, my heart, my very soul. "I can't survive losing you," he admitted, and I could see how much it killed him to confess those words. "You're not the one that got away. You're *the one*."

It wasn't until the words had left his lips that I understood how much I had needed to hear them. A part of me that I fought hard to silence had wondered if that's all I was—*the one that got away*. He told me I wasn't, though. A weight was lifted off me, a weight I didn't even realize I was carrying, and I could breathe.

He looked at me, like he was waiting for me to say something, but I didn't know what.

I reached up and my fingers tangled into the hair at the nape of his neck. "Show me how much you love me." I swallowed thickly, shocked that the dreaded *L* word had passed my lips. But neither of us were declaring anything—we were simply showing—and there was a difference, right?

Trent's eyes closed and when they opened, what I saw there scared me. That kind of look consumes you, it changes you, it ruins you. Oh, yes, I was definitely ruined.

"Kiss me," I pleaded. A part of me hated that my voice

sounded so breathless with want, but the bigger part didn't care. I did want him, and I had nothing to be ashamed of.

He was more than happy to oblige.

He kissed me.

He touched me.

He loved me.

He didn't have to say the words, but I knew how he felt. I could see it clearly in his eyes. Unlike most girls, I didn't want to hear those three words—they'd only send me running again. In my opinion, there was something so much more magical, about seeing his love, rather than hearing it. Words are lies, but actions speak the truth.

He kissed me thoroughly, his lips exploring every crevice of my body, and eventually the last of our clothes fell on the floor.

Just when I thought I'd explode with want, he stopped.

"Trent?" I gasped his name, on the verge of begging. Jeez, since when did I beg?

"There's no turning back now," he growled low in his throat, his teeth lightly biting the skin of my neck.

"We reached the point of no return a long time ago," I breathed, closing my eyes as he leaned over me, grabbing a condom out of the drawer of his nightstand.

He fixed it on, and then pressed into me. A gasp escaped my parted lips and my hands sought something to hold, settling on the bed sheets.

"Fuck, you're tight." He gritted his teeth. With a joking smile, he took my cheek in his hand. "If I didn't know better, I'd think you were a virgin."

He braced his hands on either side of my head, easing into me a little bit further. I tried not grimace, but I couldn't help it.

"Rowan ...," he paused, unsure if he should continue with

his question. After a brief hesitation, he found the courage. "How long has it been for you?"

"Five years," I admitted.

"You mean ...?"

I nodded.

"You have no idea how happy that makes me." He lowered his head, kissing me so deeply that I couldn't think about anything else as he inched the rest of the way inside me.

His fingers entwined with mine and he pinned my arms above my head as he gently rocked in and out.

There was nothing rushed about his movements. Everything was slow, sweet, and sensual. It was perfect. Somehow, even more perfect than the tent.

He didn't make me feel like I was just another girl beneath him. He made me feel like I was *the* girl as he worshipped my body.

"You're mine, Rowan," he breathed against the skin of my neck, "one day you'll see that."

"I already know," I gasped, my hips lifting to meet his.

"Good." His lips crashed against mine, drawing a long moan from me.

His lips left mine as he trailed kisses down my body, his mouth closing over my breast. His hands still clasped in mine as he continued to slowly rock into my body, my legs falling open.

What I saw in his expression scared and exhilarated me all at the same time.

"I feel like I've been waiting forever for this," Trenton confessed, his lips brushing against mine. "Please, don't run from me this time."

In that moment, he was so vulnerable, and vulnerable

certainly wasn't one of the words that came to mind when you thought of Trent.

I didn't say anything, because I wasn't sure that I *could* make that promise.

I tilted my head up and kissed him, hoping that would suffice.

He kissed me back, his tongue brushing my open lips before caressing my tongue.

He released my hands and they skimmed down my body, making me shiver. His thumb found my clit and I clenched around him. "Trent," I gasped, clawing at his back like a wild animal.

His eyes were dark with pleasure as he watched me. "You're the most beautiful woman I've ever seen."

A blush dotted my chest, running up my neck, and over my cheeks.

"Your hair fanned out around you like this, the desire in your eyes, and those kissable lips …" His thumb brushed over my bottom lip and slightly into my open my mouth. "I never want to let you leave."

He shut up then, kissing me deeply, as his thumb found that special spot again. I gasped beneath him, my hips jerking. "Trent, I'm gonna—" My words ended on a gasp, and my arms wrapped around him, holding him tight like I was scared I might float away and he was the only thing keeping me anchored. My muscles were coiled tight, but I'd also never felt so relaxed.

Trent pumped into me a few more times and then his release stole over him.

He kissed me deeply, sucking on my bottom lip. He released it with a pop and rolled over.

I didn't think I could move, but I didn't want to either.

I closed my eyes, fighting a smile. That had been amazing. I hadn't expected him to be so sweet and tender. I should've known, though, it was Trent after all. It wasn't like him to be rough, although something told me he could be when he wanted to, and that excited me.

The bed creaked and I knew Trent had gotten up. It dipped again a minute later, and he pulled me against his body. With his other hand, he pulled the covers up over us.

He brushed my hair away from my neck, pressing kisses to the area where my neck met my shoulders.

"I don't deserve you," I whispered so low I was sure he couldn't have heard it.

"Why do you say that?"

All of my lies clung to me like a dirty, sinful, second skin that wouldn't wash away no matter how hard I tried.

Trent couldn't see it, but once he did he'd never look at me the same.

I had lived this lie for so long that it felt like the truth.

It wasn't.

And once it was out in the open, none of our lives would ever be the same.

"No reason," I finally said, letting his warmth wash over me. "You're just too good for me."

"That's where you're wrong," he said, his lips gliding over my shoulder. "You're unable to see the goodness that resides right here." He placed his hand over my heart and it sped up at his touch. "You're one of the kindest, most giving people I know. I wish you could see that. Until you do, I'll have to remind you every single day." His words were punctuated by light kisses to my arm.

"I should go," I mumbled, trying to pull out of his arms.

"You're not going anywhere." He tightened his hold. "You're staying right here until the last possible second."

I closed my eyes, clasping my hands under my head. "You're bossy, you know that, right?"

"Not bossy." He snuggled close, burying his head into the curve of my neck, his breath tickling my skin pleasantly. "I just know what I want."

I rolled over, so we were face to face. I lightly traced my finger over his cheek and around his lips. There were so many things I wanted to say to him, but when I opened my mouth no sound came out.

He tucked my head under his chin and I decided that it wasn't time to say any of those things. Unfortunately, there probably never would be a good time.

CHAPTER ELEVEN

I closed the door to the library and eyed the stack of books I still had to put away. I'd been unusually slow working, my mind distracted with a million and one thoughts. I hadn't seen Trenton in three days. We'd talked on the phone and text, but the kids' Christmas break had started and it made it nearly impossible to get away. I didn't want to leave them home with my mom if I didn't have to, and I couldn't bug Colleen every day.

I hated to admit it, but I missed him. Damn Wentworth. He was impossible not to succumb to. He was just so ... Trent.

I changed into my favorite loose gray sweater and jeans before I grabbed the cart of books and began putting them away. Since we were on break, I obviously wouldn't be staying to work on homework, but I had hoped to get some personal reading time in. It didn't look like that would happen now.

I hummed a song I'd heard on the radio this morning, inserting a word here and there.

Somebody laughing had me jumping out of my skin. Everyone was supposed to be gone and I hadn't heard anyone approach.

I turned sharply, a book clutched to my chest in case I needed to use one of the sharp edges as a weapon.

"Trent," I gasped, unable to hide my smile. I rarely smiled, but Trent seemed to always be able to make me happy. "How'd you get in here?"

"Some idiot left the door unlocked." He eyed me.

"Shit," I cursed. "I normally lock it. I forgot." I shrugged, still holding tightly onto the book for some reason.

"I was planning to text you to let me in, but since the door was conveniently left unlocked," he said, stalking toward me and lowering his head, "there was no need." His lips brushed against my jaw. "It feels like forever since I've seen you." He placed a hand against my neck and grinned crookedly when he felt my pulse jump.

"So ... you thought you'd just stop by?" My fingers grasped his leather jacket, drawing him closer.

"Mhmm." He nodded, his eyes hooded.

"To talk ...?"

"I just wanted to see you," he said huskily, his breath tickling my neck. "But now that I'm here, I want to do a whole lot more."

My heart skipped a beat. "You mean—"

He didn't wait for me to finish. He claimed my lips with his, asserting his dominance and control. He lifted me up, my legs wrapping around his waist, and he braced one of his hands against the bookshelf my back was pressed against. It certainly wasn't the most comfortable position, but it was hot as hell and, frankly, I didn't care. It felt so good to be in his arms again.

"I want to take you right here," he growled, nibbling on my earlobe.

"Do it," I pleaded, desire filling my body at his words.

He didn't have to be told twice.

He had us undressed in under a minute and put a condom on. My body was already buzzing with want and need. He lifted me up again and I sank down on him, both of us moaning in response.

I took his face between my hands and lowered my mouth to his. I never would've thought I'd be into something like this, but the spontaneity had me feeling like this was pretty damn hot. For once, I wasn't thinking. I was letting myself go and doing what I *wanted*, not what I felt like I *should* do.

Being in Trent's arms felt so good—better than I wanted it to.

I had been trying so hard to guard my heart all these years, but there was nothing I could do to prevent Trenton from staking claim. I belonged to him.

He pressed my back against the shelves and the books began to rattle. I might have laughed if I hadn't been enjoying myself so much.

This was definitely rougher, than the other day, but with Trent there was always an underlying sweetness.

He sped up his thrusts and— "Oh, my God!" My head fell back as a soft cry escaped me. "Trent!"

Trent watched me with lust-filled eyes, smiling at what he was doing to me.

"I like it when you scream my name," he whispered, lightly

biting my neck before placing a kiss there. "You have no idea what seeing you like this does to me." His eyes were dilated, only a thin ring of blue showing.

"I think I have some idea." My voice was breathless as I wiggled my hips, my fingers finding the soft strands of his hair.

"Oh, fuck, you feel so good," Trent gasped, his hands on my hips as he guided me up and down. My eyes closed as I let myself succumb to the pleasure coursing through my veins.

Trenton holding me like this, it was like he filled every part of me, and our eyes rarely strayed from each other's—creating an intimate bubble.

He grasped my thighs in his hands, and said, "Hold on."

I held on tightly to his muscular shoulders as he started carrying me, and I soon found myself lying on a table. The wood was cool and my sweat-dampened skin wanted to stick to it.

Trent pushed into me and I gasped, my nails digging into his arms.

"Did I hurt you?" He stilled.

I shook my head. "No, it feels really good. Do it again."

He did, and my back arched off the table as he reached down and took my breasts in his hands. "You have no idea how happy it makes me that this" —he stared at my body— "hasn't been seen by anyone but me."

I didn't answer, because I didn't have anything to say except, *you own me*, and there was no way I was saying that out loud.

"I never want anyone else to see you like this, spread out beneath them," he continued. "I want you to belong to me and only me," he growled, lowering his lips to mine as he staked his claim. He didn't need to, though; I had been his from the moment I met him. There were too many other circumstances standing in our way, keeping us from a happy life together. I had made so many mistakes and my regrets continued to pile up, slowly suffocating me from the inside out.

"What's wrong?" he asked, gazing down at me with a puzzled expression. "You look upset."

I shook my head, reaching up so my fingers wrapped around the back of his neck.

"Rowan ..." he pressed.

"Make me forget," I whispered in his ear.

"Forget what?" he questioned, looking at me worriedly.

"Everything."

―――――

TRENT HAD DEFINITELY BEEN able to make me forget. After the table, we'd sunk to the floor and started the whole process over again.

Now, we lay spread out on the floor, still naked, and my body was wrapped around his. I never wanted to move, because once I did I'd have to return to my messed-up life.

His lips pressed against my forehead. "I have something I want to ask you ... and, please, don't get mad, hear me out."

"Okay ..." I ventured hesitantly. "Usually when someone says, "don't get mad" it's because you're going to get mad."

He swallowed thickly, looking up at the ceiling of the library. "Come to New York with me."

I was not expecting *that* to come out of his mouth.

"Trent, you know—"

"I know, you have to look after your siblings. But can't you find someone else for a week? We could go over Christmas, and return in time to go to my family's annual New Year's Eve party, then I would reluctantly take you home."

I bit my lip, chewing on it nervously. Since I'd been able to drive, I'd been taking the kids to our grandma's and spending a few days to a week there for the holidays. That's what I had been planning to do this year, but ... I could always drop them off and go with Trent. I knew they'd be in good hands with her. I wouldn't have to worry, and I could enjoy myself. I deserved to do something for myself, right?

"I ... I need to think about it," I whispered, tracing my finger along his chest and down his abs.

"Well," he sighed, "thinking about it is certainly better than a flat-out no."

I really did want to do it—even though the thought of being alone with Trent for a full week scared me. I knew that winter break would end soon and he'd be gone for a while. His university was only two hours away, but when you have classes and homework, it could be hard to find time to visit. I certainly didn't want to be one of those clingy girls begging him to come home every weekend. I would miss him, though, and I wanted to spend as much time with him as I could.

"Why New York?" I asked, truly curious.

"We have a place in the city, and it's spectacular this time of the year. Plus, I'd like to spend more time with you, and New York City seemed like a good place. We're far enough away that you can relax and enjoy yourself without worrying about your brother and sister, but close enough to get back quickly if we need to."

"You've really thought this through." I glanced up at him as he twirled a lock of my hair around his finger.

He nodded with a grin. "I understand if you can't ... or even if you don't want to."

"I didn't say I didn't want to." I sat up a bit to look at him, my hair falling forward to conceal my breasts. "I need to think about it, though ... okay?"

"Take your time, but if we're going to do this, we leave in four days." He held up four fingers like I couldn't count.

My heart was already beating wildly at the thought of spending a whole week alone with Trenton. I wasn't sure it was the best thing for us—at this point, I didn't want to let myself get any more attached—but if I didn't go, I'd always wonder what might have happened.

"I need to see if my grandparents are okay with keeping Tristan and Ivy that long. The three of us normally spend Christmas with them and come home a few days before New Year's, so they'd need to keep them longer than normal."

"Don't be worried about disappointing me." He reached up, cupping my cheek.

"I want to go," I assured him, putting my hand over top of his.

"If you can't go, maybe ... Maybe you'd come over to my family's place and bring your siblings?" he suggested, biting on his lip, and giving me a look that didn't have me thinking about what he just said.

I lowered my head and pressed my lips to his. His fingers tangled in my hair as he kissed me back.

"What was that for?" he asked, panting slightly.

"You looked so kissable that I couldn't resist," I admitted, looking down shyly. I wasn't one to spout my feelings or to admit to such things.

"I like this side of you," Trent remarked, watching me steadily.

"What side?" I questioned with a raised brow.

"The free one." His thumb rubbed over my bottom lip. "You're always so closed off, but lately you've been opening up more. Laughing, smiling, being ... free," he repeated.

"I've been through a lot," I whispered, shame causing me to look down at the carpeted floor.

"I know you have." He grabbed my chin, forcing me to look at him. "And I hope one day, you'll trust me enough to tell me everything. Until then, I won't push you, but I will be here for you. I will *always* be here."

I closed my eyes, wishing his words were true. I knew he meant them, in this moment, at least, but if he knew the truth of what I had done he'd leave and never come back.

I FINISHED CLEANING up from breakfast and ran around trying to get ready. Before she left last night, Mary had offered me more hours today. More hours meant more money, and I needed all the money I could get.

I pulled on a red button-down jacket to brighten up my black skirt and white top. I opened the door to the kids' room and kissed them on top of their heads. "I have to go in to work, but I'll be home early today. Be good."

Tristan clung to my neck. "Don't go, Row."

"I have to," I told him, unwinding his arms from their stranglehold. At Tristan's age, he couldn't understand that I was doing this for him, for *them*, in the hopes of giving them a better life. I was doing the best I could, but most times it seemed like I wasn't trying at all.

I kissed his small hand and ruffled his hair. "I'll be home before you know it."

His sad face made it hard to push myself out the door but I had to.

Outside, the cold air whipped around me, blowing my hair in my face. I pushed the strands away and got in my car, rubbing my hands together for warmth as I waited for heat to pour into the frigid vehicle.

I backed out of the driveway, wondering where my stepdad was. He was gone more and more lately, and I was sure yet another divorce was in my mom's future.

I parked and hurried into the library, ready to be out of the cold.

I was headed to clock-in when Mary called out for me. "Yes?" I turned, searching for the older woman.

When I spotted her, she crooked her finger, motioning me to her.

"Yeah?" I asked, when I stopped in front of her.

The way she was looking at me had me breaking out in a nervous sweat. "Honey, I have some bad news." She patted my arm. It was obvious she didn't want to continue to speak further, but had to. "We have to let you go."

"What?" I gasped, stumbling back. I *needed* this job. Without it, I was screwed. "Why?" I couldn't understand. Was this some cruel joke? I was a hard worker and I never caused trouble.

"Honey," her voice was hushed, "there was ... something on the security tapes."

I closed my eyes. This couldn't be happening.

"We can't have someone working here that would do something like that." She looked at me sadly, not with disgust, which surprised me.

I nodded. "I understand." I cringed at the fact that Mary, someone I respected, had seen me like that. I wasn't sure I'd ever be able to look at her ever again.

I walked away from her and out the door, straight to my car. My posture was stiff and I was completely stunned that that had just happened. I couldn't seem to process the fact that I had just gotten fired. I knew what Trent and I had done in the library was wrong, and I had to pay the consequences.

I leaned my head against the headrest.

Unlike most people, I was more upset over losing my job than I was about them having watched Trent and I have sex. Without a job, I was screwed. Simple as that.

I picked up my phone, my fingers clumsy with my anger.

"Hello?" Trent answered and he sounded half-asleep.

"I got fired," I seethed. "I need that job, Trent! I don't know what I'm going to do!"

"Whoa, slow down," he sounded slightly more alert, "why'd you get fired?"

I frowned, staring up at the ceiling of my car. "They saw us, Trent, on the security tapes."

"A library has cameras?" he asked in disbelief.

"Yeah," I said slowly, angry with myself. "I have to have a job, Trent." My head fell against the steering wheel, honking the horn.

"Did you just honk your car horn?" He chuckled.

"It was an accident," I mumbled.

"So ... they seriously have it on tape?" He cleared his throat. "Us having sex?"

"No, they fired me because I let a bunny loose around the library!" I was getting pissed now. "Of course they have it on tape!"

"Think they'd let me buy it?" His voice was serious.

"Trent!" I exclaimed.

"What? I didn't say I was going to watch it," he said, and there was rustling in the background. "But I'd hate for something like that to get out. I can tell you're upset. Let me fix this."

"I don't care about the sex tape! All I care about is the fact that I'm jobless!"

Trent chuckled. "You are such an unusual woman. As for your 'jobless' problem, I think I have a solution for that."

"You do?" For the first time since Mary had said they'd have to let me go, I could breathe again.

"Yeah," he mumbled and there was more shuffling. "Meet me at Trace's."

"Uh ... I don't know where he lives."

He laughed at that. "I meant at his shop."

"Oh, okay. I'm pretty close," I muttered, already backing out of the parking lot.

"Just wait in your car until I get there," he told me.

"I can do that," I breathed, relief flooding my body.

Wentworth Wheels was only about five minutes from the library. I parked on the street, instead of the lot. I didn't want Trace coming out and asking me why I was there before Trent arrived.

I stayed alert, watching for Trent's black car. When it pulled into the lot across the street, I got out of my car, braving the cold.

He was already out of his car and grinning as I jogged across the street. Thank God I'd worn flats today.

"I can't believe the librarians watched us have sex." He laughed with a smirk.

"Stop talking about it." I gagged and pointed a warning finger at him. "And don't you dare say anything to your brother about this."

"Trust me, I won't." He raised his hands in surrender. "I'd never hear the end of it from him. Come on." Trent waved for me to follow him into the garage.

In my skirt and button-down jacket, I felt extremely overdressed. Plus, my legs were cold.

"Trace?" Trent called out. "Where are you?"

Something metal clanged to the ground, and then we heard, "Over here," coming from our right.

"What are you guys doing here?" Trace asked, sliding out from under a car and scaring me half to death.

"I have a solution to your problem," Trent smirked, shoving his hands in his pockets as he rocked back on his heels.

"What problem?" Trace slid out even further so he could sit up.

"The one where the phone's always ringing and you have to stop working to answer it." Trent's grin widened further if that was even possible.

"And how have you solved it?" Trace pushed his dark hair out of his eyes before draping his arms over his knees.

He pointed to me. "Rowan."

"Me?" I gasped.

"She needs a job. You need someone to answer phones and check inventory. It's a win-win." Trent shrugged. "Feel free to thank me and shower me with your affections." He bowed dramatically.

"Why do you like this guy?" Trace looked up at me. "He's really dumb."

"Remember," Trent said as he leaned against the side of the car Trace was working on, "we both came from the same sperm and egg."

"And that was unfortunate." Trace jumped up and ruffled Trent's hair. "I got all the good looks. Sucks for you."

Trent shook his head. "Whatever you need to tell yourself to feel better."

Ignoring his younger brother, Trace eyed me. "Can you handle answering the phone and setting up appointments, plus keep track of parts I need to order?" There was a challenge in his eyes, like he didn't think I could really do it.

"That's easy," I said sassily. I was the kind of person who always rose to the challenge, and this was no exception.

Trace smiled crookedly. "Welcome to Wentworth Wheels." He held out his hand for me to take. "Just don't have sex in the office and we're good."

My eyes threatened to bug out of my head. How did he know? He was making a joke about Trent and me in the library, right?

"I'm kidding, Rowan. Relax. Have all the sex you want, as long as I don't have to walk in on it. That's happened one too many times with Avery and Luca, and let me tell you, that's something no one wants to see."

With that, Trace sat back down and slid under the car. "Can you start tomorrow?" He slid back out so just his head poked through from beneath the car.

"Absolutely."

Then he was gone again.

Trent and I walked back outside. "What was with the sex comment?" I asked him. "Did you tell him what happened at the library?" I'd thought he'd said as we came in that he didn't want Trace knowing, but he seemed to be aware of something to make that sort of remark.

I was about ten seconds away from being *pissed* if he'd told his brother what happened. I'd never be able to look Trace in the eye ever again.

"What? No, of course not." He stopped walking. "Why would you think that?" he asked, his thick brows furrowing together.

"Um, because of the no sex in the office comment." I tossed my thumb over my shoulder, pointing at the garage.

"Oh, that's because of Luca and Avery." He shrugged as he started walking toward his car.

"They're real people?"

"Yeah," he laughed, stopping by his car and crossing his arms over his chest. "Luca is Trace's best friend, which I seriously don't understand since the guy barely speaks, and Avery is his fiancée ... wife." He shook his head, scolding himself for the mistake. "They're gone on their honeymoon now."

"And they both work here and have sex in the office?"

I was so confused.

Trent laughed, clearly amused by me. "Luca does. He helps Trace. Avery's just hornier than a guy and can't leave him alone."

"That's not very nice of you to say." I frowned.

Trent shook his head, giving me a small smile. "Once you meet Avery, you'll see what I mean."

I wasn't so sure I wanted to meet this Avery. She sounded like she'd get on my nerves.

"I'll see you later." I wasn't sure if I should kiss him, or hug him, or I don't know what, so I turned and walked away. That seemed to be the safer option.

"Wait!" he called, the gravel crunching beneath his boots. "Why don't we go to lunch?"

"I should really go home," I mumbled.

"But if you were working you wouldn't be home."

He was right. "Fine," I relinquished without any fight. "I'll follow you."

Ten minutes later, I found myself sitting at the same booth in the same restaurant I thought Trent might kill Jude in. I couldn't help but feel a bit nostalgic when I thought of it and what had then happened in the bathroom.

I also couldn't believe I'd just gotten fired. I couldn't care less about the "sex tape" as Trent kept calling it. Did it really count as a sex tape if it was caught on a security camera? Probably.

"I'll have the club sandwich," I told the waiter, handing over the menu.

Trent placed his order and eyed me over his glass of water. "Didn't you get that last time?"

"I did, and it was delicious. That's why I got it again."

"Why not try something new?" he suggested, his smile widening so that I caught sight of the small dimple in his cheek—it didn't always show, but when it did, it was adorable.

I squeezed the lemon, dropping it into my water before taking a sip. "If I like something, I don't see the need to try something else."

Trent cleared his throat and wiggled in his seat, like he was unsure if he wanted to ask something. "Is that why you ... uh ... haven't been with anyone else ... since me?" His voice was hushed so it didn't carry through the restaurant.

I traced my finger over some words carved into the table. "I guess you could say that." I shrugged.

"If you had feelings for me all these years," he ventured, "why did you stay away?" His eyes were truly inquisitive and I knew he genuinely didn't understand why I had avoided him.

"I had my reasons," I answered vaguely.

"Your mom?" he pressed me for more information.

"She was part of it." I sighed, swirling my finger around the condensation shimmering on top of the table from my water glass.

"You can talk to me about her, Rowan."

I looked up at him and his eyes pleaded with me to open up to him. I couldn't do it, though. I wasn't the kind of girl to confess her feelings and seek comfort in the arms of another person. I preferred to fight my demons on my own. I didn't need Trent to slay my dragons and be my knight in shining armor. I could save myself; I didn't know if I wanted to.

"Rowan?" he repeated my name when I didn't say anything.

With a sigh, I said, "I know I *can*, but I don't *want* to. It's not something I like to talk about." I stared down at my water glass and away from his eyes that always saw too much.

"Fine, I won't push you." Tapping his fingers along the back of the booth, he asked, "Have you thought anymore about going to New York with me?" he questioned.

"You asked me last night! This morning I lost my job! So, no, I haven't thought about it," I snapped.

"Sorry," he chuckled. "I really want you to go."

"I want to go too," I admitted, crossing my arms over my chest, "but I have to work things out with the kids."

He nodded. "I understand."

"No, you don't," I muttered. "You don't get it at all."

"Why are you in such a mood today?" He eyed me. "Is this a PMS thing or something?"

"No, it's called a 'you're being annoying' mood," I countered, looking around the restaurant. I began to feel bad; I shouldn't have been taking my anger out on him. "I'm sorry," I apologized. "I didn't get much sleep, and getting fired was the icing on the cake for this craptastic day."

Trent grinned.

"Why are you smiling?" I asked.

"Because, I don't think I've ever heard you say that you're sorry."

"Well, there's a first time for everything." I sat up straighter.

"There most certainly is."

CHAPTER TWELVE

"I don't want to go to Grandma's without you!" Tristan protested, stomping his foot.

"You love Grandma's." I kneeled on the ground so that we were eye level. "You're going to have so much fun and bake cookies for Santa!"

"I want *you* to help me," he pouted.

"I'm sorry, Tristan," I ran my fingers through his sandy hair as I spoke, "but I need to do this."

Watching the tears brim his eyes was tearing me apart. Maybe I could tell Trent I had changed my mind. I knew he'd understand.

"Okay," Tristan finally agreed as he hugged me. Just as I was beginning to talk myself out of it, he'd finally agreed. He was such an easygoing child, and so easy to love.

I kissed his cheek and he squirmed. "Ew, Row! Don't kiss me!"

"Get in the car," I told him. "Grandma is waiting for us."

I checked the trunk again to make sure I had all their stuff and the gifts from Santa that I had carefully hidden.

My grandparents lived over an hour away in a much nicer neighborhood than the one we lived in. We didn't visit them much. My mom didn't like for them to help us. I'd been bringing Tristan and Ivy to their house for Christmas since I could drive, and our mom always stayed behind. I knew Ivy still remembered previous Christmases we'd had with our mom, and it never ended well. Tristan was lucky enough to have never experienced it.

I pulled into the driveway of the nice two-story home. I wasn't surprised when the door opened and my grandma appeared, her arms spread wide to welcome Tristan and Ivy into her embrace. I grabbed their suitcases, watching her chat happily with them as they beamed up at her.

I didn't have a very good relationship with my grandparents. It was nothing like what I had with my mom, but I didn't really know them. I'd never allowed myself to. My mom had made me wary of other people, and because of it I'd shut off my emotions. If you didn't feel, the things people did to you could never hurt you.

As my mom got worse, I had reached out to my grandparents for Ivy and Tristan's sake. I did enjoy being here, though; it was peaceful, and I didn't have to worry about my gross stepdad or my drunk mother.

I wheeled the suitcases up the pathway, the bag with the presents slung over my shoulder. Tristan and Ivy had gone inside, but my grandma waited, holding the door open for me.

"I'm sad you won't be staying." She smiled kindly, her eyes

crinkling at the corners. "I was looking forward to spending time with all of you."

"I'm sorry I can't stay." I placed the suitcases and bag by the steps, shoving my hands in the back pockets of my jeans. The house was clean, warm, and welcoming. The scent of cinnamon hung in the air. "Are you baking something?"

She nodded. "Cookies. Would you like some?"

I started to say no but, instead, I found myself nodding.

"Come on then." She closed the door and waved for me to follow her down the hallway to the kitchen.

I ran my finger along the marble countertops, smiling at the kids as they devoured the cookies.

Being in this house, and seeing how *nice* my grandparents were, made me question how my mom had become such a monster.

"Here." She held out a baggy filled with snickerdoodle cookies. I gladly accepted them as she patted my cheek. "You've grown into such a beautiful young woman. I wish we saw you more often. All of you." She smiled at Tristan and Ivy. "Please, don't let your mom keep you away from us."

I frowned. It wasn't my mom that kept me away, it was my fear of abandonment. Keeping at a safe distance meant you couldn't be disappointed by someone's actions. I'd given Trenton a chance, though, so why not them?

"We'll try to visit more often." I smiled. "I have to go." I looked over at Ivy and Tristan. "Give me a hug."

They dove at me, getting cookie crumbs all over my shirt and on the floor.

"I'm so sorry." I lowered, stretching my arm out to pick up the crumbs.

"Don't worry about it." My grandma reached down, grabbing my arm and helping me up. Stray pieces of gray hair fell into her face. "Can I ... Can I hug you goodbye?"

"Yeah, of course," I mumbled as I hugged the woman. Was I such a horrible person that my grandma felt like she had to ask for my permission to hug me?

"I love you, Rowan." She smiled as she led me back to the front door.

Love. There was that word again, the word that made me cringe and feel like my insides were curling in on themselves. Love was nothing but a lie in my mind.

"Mhmm," I mumbled. Pointing at the bag I'd dropped on the floor earlier, I said, "Their presents are in there. Be sure to hide it."

"I will," she assured me, standing in the doorway as I headed to my car. "Have fun!"

I waved my hand and got in my car. I sat there for a moment, staring at the house and the happy picture it made. When had I gotten so messed up? When had my childhood innocence transitioned me into this hardened shell of a person? Would I ever be able to break free of myself?

BACK HOME, I still had an hour before Trent was picking me up for our evening flight. I hadn't packed yet. I had stared at my closet, willing the clothes to magically appear in the open suitcase, but so far that wasn't working. Everything I owned didn't seem like it was enough, but it would have to do. I didn't have the money to go out and buy a whole new wardrobe.

I packed what I had that I felt would be acceptable for a city like Manhattan and zipped the luggage.

"Where are you going?"

I jumped at the sound of my step-dad's voice. I hadn't heard him come home. I guess since he'd been gone for a few days I expected him not to come back.

"I'm leaving for a week," I answered.

"That's not what I asked you." He stepped further into my room and it felt like the aqua walls were closing in around me.

"I don't see how where I'm going is any of your business." I stood up straighter. I would not be intimidated and I would not act afraid. I was a strong woman and I wouldn't let this insignificant piece of shit frighten me. Jim preyed on the weak, and I certainly wasn't that.

He reached out, wrapping a strand of my hair around his finger and tugging—hard. My teeth ground together as I fought to control the wince that so desperately wanted to twist my face.

"Don't. Touch. Me."

The words were hissed between my teeth and they barely sounded human. I was sick of being afraid in my own house.

Jim clucked his tongue. "You can't talk to me like that."

He pushed me onto my bed, and all the air left my lungs as his body fell on mine, pining me to the mattress.

Panic shook my body. I couldn't breathe. I couldn't move. I couldn't think.

One, two, three, four, five, six, seven, eight, nine, ten.

The counting calmed me and helped to clear my head.

Jim pinned my wrists down and despite the fact that he was a scrawny man he was still strong.

One, two, three, four, five, six, seven, eight, nine, ten.

I counted again and then again.

His lips were sucking on my neck as he ground his hips

into me. I knew screaming was futile. My mom was passed out drunk in bed, and the neighbors would never hear. I was on my own.

"Stop." I tried to wriggle my arms free. "Stop it!"

"Shh, I know you want it." He continued to suckle my neck. I was going to throw up.

"You asshole. Last time I checked, 'stop' didn't translate to somebody wanting something!" I squirmed some more, but his hold didn't lessen. "Let me go!"

I'd given him the perfect opportunity for this. Tristan and Ivy were gone, and he knew my mom would never wake up. If only I had already been gone.

A part of me had been anticipating something like this happening for a while. Disturbing, I know, but the guy was a creep.

My phone vibrated in my pocket and I prayed it was a text from Trent, saying he was here.

Counting on Trent to be outside waiting, I kneed Jim in gut. He grunted, releasing my wrists. His face was red with anger. He pulled his fist back to punch me, but I head-butted him in the face first. Blood spurted everywhere, and he fell to the ground, clutching his broken nose. "Bitch!" he spat.

My heart racing, I grabbed my suitcase and ran out of the house.

Trent wasn't parked outside, like I had expected.

I felt myself beginning to panic. I turned around, looking behind me to see if Jim was coming after me. He wasn't. I knew he wouldn't, but I was still scared. I was out in the open, where any of the neighbors would see him attack me, and Jim wasn't stupid.

My head throbbed painfully where I'd bashed my head

against his nose, and I knew I'd end up with a killer headache. As I pressed my hand against my head, I happened to look down and see blood—*his* blood—on my shirt.

My panic escalated, making my heart race painfully in my chest.

I needed it off.

One, two, three, four, five, six, seven, eight, nine, ten.

I dropped to my knees, my hands shaking as I wrenched off my shirt and tossed it somewhere in the snow-covered yard. I didn't care if one of the neighbors looked out and saw me in the yard in only my bra. I had to be rid of that shirt. I opened my suitcase and pulled out a sweatshirt, yanking it on.

I had just zipped my suitcase closed when I looked up to see Trent's black car coming down the street. Thank God.

I wheeled my suitcase down to the end of the driveway. Trent was quick to hop out and take it from me, putting it in the trunk.

"Are you okay?" he asked, as he got in the car and looked over at me.

My knee was bouncing restlessly and I couldn't stop my hands from wringing together. I knew I couldn't play this off like it was nothing. This wasn't my normal behavior and Trent wasn't stupid.

"Just drive. I want to get away from here."

"Row—"

"*Please*, Trenton," I begged, my lower lip trembling with the threat of tears—tears I was determined to never let spill over.

He nodded and didn't say anything as he put the car in drive.

I let out a sigh of relief, relaxing against the seat as we left my house and the horrendous people inhabiting it, behind.

A few minutes had passed before Trent spoke. "Now that we're a safe distance from your house, can you tell me what happened?"

I scrubbed the palms of my hands on the fabric of my ripped jeans. I knew I had to tell him something, but I didn't know what. If I opened up and told him what Jim had done, I knew Trent would turn around and go back to my house, most likely killing the man. Trent ending up in jail because of me, wasn't something I was willing to let happen.

"It was nothing." I waved my hand dismissively. "I got in a fight with my step-dad."

He glanced at me out of the corner of his eye before turning onto the interstate. The muscle in his jaw ticked and I knew he was contemplating what to say next.

"Did he ... hurt you?"

"It was nothing I can't handle," I mumbled, propping my head on my hand and looking out the window.

"Rowan, you can tell me."

"It was nothing," I repeated yet again. Maybe if I said the words enough I'd start to believe them.

He sighed, scratching his jaw. "I know you're not telling me something. I'm not dumb, Row, but I'm not going to push you for information, either. I want you to open up to me because you trust me, not because I'm pressing you." He sighed, turning down the music in the car.

I closed my eyes, leaning my head against the cold glass.

I couldn't love.

I couldn't trust.

And without those two very important factors, how could I ever live?

"Rowan?"

I opened my eyes and lifted my head to look at him. "Yeah?"

"I want us to have fun on this trip, okay?" He waited for me to nod before continuing. "I understand that there's things you don't want to tell me, and I'll respect that ... for now." He eyed me. "Whatever happened with your step-dad, let's just put that behind us."

I wanted to kiss him. That was how thankful I was to know he was dropping this. I knew Trent had to be itching to ask me more, but for the sake of not pushing me too far, he was going to let it go.

"Thank you." I smiled at him gratefully, reaching for his hand.

His eyes flickered down to where I had entwined our fingers together. I knew he was a bit shocked by the gesture since I wasn't the biggest fan of handholding.

He gave my hand a slight squeeze, his eyes watching the road ahead of us.

"Have you ever been on a plane before?" he asked.

I couldn't contain my laughter at his very poor change of subject. "Never," I answered, choosing not to call him out.

"So, I'm taking it you haven't been into the city either?"

"No." I shook my head, looking out the side window at the farmland rushing past us.

"This is going to be fun." He laughed, sounding like an excited little boy.

"Something tells me I should be afraid of your excitement." I couldn't help but smile. Now that so many miles were between my home and us, I was feeling looser ... free. It helped that Trent wasn't pressing me for information. I was happy that, for now at least, he was respecting my privacy.

"I promise you have nothing to be afraid of."

"Mhmm," I mumbled doubtfully.

"We'll do some sightseeing, but in all honesty, I'm really not that interested in showing you the city." He grinned.

"Oh, really? And what is it you're so excited to show me, then?"

"The bed."

"The bed?" I laughed.

He nodded excitedly. "It's a big bed. With fluffy pillows."

"And are we just going to lay on this bed?"

"Hmm," he hummed while he pretended to think, "I might kiss you ... if you're nice to me."

"Is that it?" I smiled, liking this game.

"If you appreciate my kisses, and you're *really* nice to me, I might take your clothes off." He tapped his fingers on the steering wheel.

"What about your clothes?" I countered.

"Oh, they'll come off in time, if you're *really, really* nice to me. I have to make you work for it." He chuckled. "This—" he took his free hand off the steering wheel for a moment to wave at his body "—is a work of art, and only special people are allowed to feast their eyes upon its magnificence."

"So, what happens once we're both naked?" I bit down on my lip to stifle my laughter.

He bit his lip. "I *might* touch you, but only if—"

"I'm really, really, *really*, nice?" I interrupted.

"You're catching on."

He released my hand, his skimming up my thigh and

resting dangerously close to where I needed him most. "I'd really like to touch you here," he whispered huskily, his fingers skimming over the seam of my jeans and making me squirm. My legs snapped together and he chuckled. "Open your legs."

Slowly, I did as he asked.

His fingers brushed against *there* again and my eyes closed as my breath faltered. After another stroke, his fingers were gone. I opened my eyes and looked over at him. He wore a smug smile. "Don't worry, there's more where that came from, but you're going to have to wait."

THE WENTWORTHS HAD A PRIVATE PLANE.

I mean, *of course* they had a private plane.

But I hadn't been expecting it.

I had been nervous for the flight, having never been on a plane before. Trent was an excellent distraction, though. Well, his lips were.

We departed the plane and a sleek black car was waiting for us. I felt like I had stepped into a dream or something. Surely, this wasn't real life.

One man placed our luggage in the trunk of the car, while the driver got out to open the door. Trent slid inside and I followed him.

I looked around the dark inside of the car like it was the coolest thing I had ever seen. Trent watched me, a smile playing on his lips that he tried to hide behind his hand.

"To the penthouse, Mr. Wentworth?" the driver asked, driving toward the exit.

"Yes." Trent smiled at my wide-eyed expression.

Penthouse.

This was too much.

I didn't belong in this kind of world—fancy houses and cars. I was certainly wowed by the luxury surrounding me, but it also served as a reminder as to how different we were.

My mouth dropped open as we drove into the city.

The skyscrapers, the lights, the people ... all of it didn't seem real.

"Wow," I gasped, turning in my seat to see better.

"Are you happy you came?" Trent asked, brushing my hair off my shoulder.

I nodded. "Thank you. This is amazing."

"Don't thank me yet." He grinned, twisting the leather bracelet around on his wrist. "The fun hasn't even started."

The driver made a sharp turn and suddenly we were descending into darkness. I hadn't even noticed the parking garage I'd been so absorbed by everything else.

The driver parked beside an elevator and hopped out to get the door for us. He offered me his hand and helped me out.

"I'll have someone bring up your bags, Mr. Wentworth," the man said, smoothing his fingers down his emerald green tie. He appeared to be in his fifties with graying hair and kind brown eyes.

"Thank you, John," Trent said, shaking the man's hand. I wasn't sure, but I was positive I saw Trent slip some money into his hand. "Come on, Row." His hand touched my waist, guiding me to the elevator. "Let's get settled before I show you the city."

He pushed the button for the elevator and I looked over my shoulder to see John pulling away.

The elevator doors opened and my jaw fell.

I never knew an elevator could be so fancy. The floors were covered in marble and the walls and ceiling were covered in a dark wood paneling.

"Based on how fancy this is," I remarked, looking around the elevator in awe as we stepped inside, "I'm a bit scared to see what the penthouse looks like."

Trent chuckled, inserting a key into a slot and turning it, then pushing a button.

The elevator began to ascend and with each floor we got higher, my heart raced faster.

It finally stopped on the very top floor and I held my breath as the doors opened.

I let out a gasp as Trent grabbed my hand, leading me inside.

The foyer had marble floors, similar to what was in the elevator, and a round table sat in the middle with a large flower arrangement.

He pulled me through an archway and I gasped at the view. Windows spanned the whole back wall, and it felt like the skyscrapers were inside the room. "This is stunning." I walked up to the windows, placing my palm against the glass. There was a small terrace with a fancy table and chair set.

"So, you like it?" Trent asked, stepping up beside me. His eyes were on the view as well, his hands shoved into the pockets of his jeans.

"How could I not like it?"

He chuckled. "You're not like other girls." He shrugged his wide shoulders. "I thought you might hate it."

"This view is incredible." My eyes took in all the cars and people bustling below, trying to get somewhere.

"It's my favorite part about this place."

I looked over to find that he had his arms braced above his head, leaning against the glass.

A month ago, I never would have thought I'd be standing here with Trenton, but now there was no place I'd rather be.

For the first time since we'd entered, I took in the décor. I had been so distracted by the spectacular view of the city, that I'd been unable to appreciate the beauty inside.

It wasn't white and sterile like I had expected. There was a comfy looking sectional couch with heavy wooden tables and a leather ottoman. There were built-in wood shelves with tons of books covering the available surface. Of course, there was also a large TV. The floors were a dark hardwood, carrying into the kitchen that was surprisingly large with black cabinets and shiny white countertops. Everything was beautiful, but didn't give off the vibe of "look but don't touch".

Trent's fingers brushed against my cheek, bringing me back to reality. "I'm so happy you're here," he breathed.

"Me too," I whispered, my eyes closing as his thumb grazed my bottom lip. It was hard for me to admit how good it felt to be here with him. Being with Trenton was effortless—as easy as breathing—and if I let myself, I'd never want to let him go.

His lips brushed lightly against mine—the touch so soft I wasn't sure it could even be considered a kiss. "I really want to show you my bedroom now." His voice was husky with want and I found a quiet whimper escaping my throat as he pushed the collar of my sweatshirt over so he could kiss the bare skin of my shoulder.

"I'd like to see it." I sounded breathless, like I'd just run a mile, but it was simply the power Trent's lips had over me.

"Let me show you then."

He picked me up, carrying me like a groom would carry his bride.

He pushed open the third door in the hallway and kicked it closed behind him. He laid me down on the soft surface of a massive bed. "I'll show you around the room later," he growled against the skin of my neck, "for now, I'd like to acquaint you with my bed."

His fingers found my hips and he slowly inched my sweatshirt up, exposing my stomach, and then my breasts hidden behind a plain black bra. I sat up and lifted my arms in the air so he could pull the garment off of me.

"I could never get tired of looking at you, Rowan," he confessed, his blue eyes filled with an emotion I refused to define.

I swallowed thickly.

"I—"

I silenced his next words by grabbing him by the neck and kissing him. I knew what he was going to say and I couldn't hear it. I wasn't ready. I'd never be ready.

He kissed me back, his large hands grasping me around my sides. One hand slid up the skin of my back and landed on the strap of my bra. With a flick of his fingers he had it unhooked and sliding down my arms. His eyes feasted on my naked breasts and I refused to be embarrassed.

I slid away from him, propping back on my elbows and giving him a look. "Your turn."

He chuckled, the sound low and raspy, making my body fill with pleasure at the promise of what was to come. He hooked his thumbs in the back on his long-sleeve shirt and yanked it over his head, musing his hair. My tongue flicked out to moisten my lips as I greedily eyed the sight of his defined chest and the dark smattering of hair that disappeared below the belt holding his jeans up.

"Happy?" he asked.

"Not quite." I smiled seductively. I wasn't as shy now in the sex department, and I wasn't going to let him completely be in control this time.

"I can make you *very* happy." His eyes narrowed, the blue turning to black with desire.

"Then do it."

He grinned at the challenge in my tone.

I squealed as he grabbed my hips, pulling me down the bed toward him. In a matter of seconds, he had my jeans and panties off. His eyes lingered on my lower body and I counted to ten in my head, hoping that the gesture would keep me from blushing.

"I'm going to touch you, Rowan, and kiss you, and you're going to like it," he growled low in his throat.

I let out a small mewling sound as his fingers traced my folds. "Trent," I whimpered.

"Shhh," he hushed. "The best is yet to come."

I gasped as his fingers plunged inside me. "Oh. My. God."

My eyes closed and my fists grasped the soft white bedspread. His free hand landed on my stomach, holding me down so my hips couldn't buck. "Hold still," he commanded, and something about his bossy tone only served to turn me on more.

His fingers pumped into me as he kept his thumb pressed against my clit.

Just when I was about to come, he moved his thumb, and — "Holy shit."

His tongue was on me and I had never felt anything like it.

I whimpered as the pressure built in my body. His tongue flicked against me and I thought I might burst into tears it felt so good.

His fingers continued to toy with me as he sucked and it wasn't long before I found myself gasping as pleasure roared through my veins.

He stood above me, grinning at what he had done to me.

Then he held out his thumb. "Suck."

"Wh-What?" I gasped, my chest rising and falling sharply.

"Suck," he repeated, his thumb brushing against my bottom lip.

I finally understood what he wanted, and opened my mouth. He stuck his thumb in my mouth and my lips closed around it, my tongue swirling around. I tasted myself on him, and surprisingly, it didn't gross me out.

He pulled his thumb from my mouth, his eyes dark with desire. "Fuck," he whispered.

I sat up slowly, reaching for his jeans. "My turn."

I undid his belt and had his jeans off before he realized what I intended to do.

"Whoa, you don't need to do that." He pushed gently at my shoulders, trying to stop me.

"I know." I smiled at him. "But I want to."

He swallowed thickly, his eyes closing briefly. "I'm serious. I don't expect you to return the favor."

"I know," I repeated as I stood and then knelt. I looked up at him, suddenly feeling shy. "You have to tell me if I do it wrong. I've never ... I've never done this."

"Trust me, Row, I don't think you could ever do anything wrong."

I hated it when he said things like that. Trenton put me up

on a pedestal like I was this great person who never did anything wrong. He had no idea just how mistaken he was.

I eyed his thick length, carefully hidden behind his black boxer briefs and swallowed thickly. I could do this. I *wanted* to do this.

I pulled the fabric down and gasped as he sprang free. I had never been this close before, and he was just as beautiful here as he was everywhere else.

I took him in my hand, stroking slowly.

"Fuck, Row," he groaned, throwing his head back, "you don't have to do anything but that and I'll be a happy man."

"I doubt that." I smiled, then took him into my mouth.

I felt uncomfortable at first with my lack of knowledge in situations like this. I swirled my tongue around the tip and then took him deeper into my mouth. He let out a growl, his fingers winding into my hair as he held it away from my face. I felt his eyes on me and it spurned me on.

"You have no idea how fucking hot you look right now," he murmured.

My eyes flicked up to look at him watching me.

"It feels so good," he whispered, his eyes briefly closing as he swallowed thickly.

It pleased me that I seemed to be doing it right.

I stroked him and he threw his head back. "If you keep doing that with your hand and your mouth, I'm not going to last long, and I really want to come inside you."

I pulled away and climbed onto the bed. I lay down, my hair spreading around me.

"Then do it," I repeated my words from earlier.

His eyes roamed over my body like he was memorizing what I looked like.

"With pleasure." He grinned crookedly with a fire lighting his eyes.

He grabbed a condom, rolled it on, then grabbed my hips again. He pulled me until my bottom was hanging off the bed and he was holding onto me.

"You're not coming up here?" I asked.

He shook his head.

"No, I think I'll stay right here." He winked.

He thrust inside me and I gasped as he filled me.

He slid out and back in quickly.

Now I understood why he was standing.

He rolled his hips against mine and I bit down on my lip to stifle the cry that threatened to escape me.

"Harder," I pleaded.

"You want it rough?" One brow rose in disbelief.

I nodded, trying not to whimper.

"Well, then ..."

I couldn't quiet my cries after that.

His thrusts were quick and powerful, shaking the bed. The veins in his arms stood out and his fingers dug into my skin.

"Trent!" I screamed his name as I came. I'm pretty sure I screamed some other things too, and maybe even in another language, because nothing I said made sense to my own ears.

Trent growled and I felt him twitch inside me with his release.

He collapsed on top of me, careful to hold his weight off of me. He pressed sweet kisses to my face, neck, and across the tops of my breasts. "That was fucking incredible," he murmured, wrapping his arms around me and burying his face into the curve of my neck.

I nodded in agreement. I had no words.

"I promise I didn't bring you here for sex," he continued, "but I'd be lying if I didn't say it was worth it." He chuckled, kissing the corner of my mouth. "Rowan?" He paused. "Are you okay?"

I nodded.

"Can you speak?"

I nodded.

"Rowan?"

"Give me a minute," I finally managed to force words from my lips.

He laughed. "Was it that good?"

Good was the understatement of the century. That had been mind-blowing.

"Can we do it again?" I asked, turning my head to look at him. I was breathing heavily and my body was covered in sweat, but I didn't care.

He laughed. "We most certainly can. Just give me another five minutes."

"You don't need longer?" I questioned.

He laughed. "With you? No. Trust me, it won't be long until I'm ready again." He wiggled his hips and I gasped, realizing he was still inside me. "Especially if I don't move."

I wrapped my hands around his neck, lacing my fingers together. "Don't move, then."

"Trust me, if you told me I never had to, I wouldn't," he said seriously, brushing my hair away from my eyes. "I want nothing more than to stay here with you forever."

"And by here, you mean inside me?" I joked.

He laughed heartily. "I wouldn't complain about that."

I glanced down at our joined bodies. "I think you're ready," I whispered.

"How about that?" He chuckled. "I told you it wouldn't take long. Now, lie back and let me love you."

And he did.

Again.

And again.

And again.

CHAPTER THIRTEEN

My whole body was sore, but in the best way possible.

I stretched my toes, pointing them down, then raised my arms above my head. Sunlight streamed into the bedroom from the floor to ceiling windows. Last night I'd been occupied by more important things and hadn't noticed any details about the room.

It was painted a medium gray color and all the furniture was black. The bedding was white and fluffy. It was so soft that I wasn't sure how I'd feel about returning to my own sheets.

"That makes your breasts look more amazing than usual."

I startled, lowering my arms, as I looked over to see Trent standing in the doorway. A pair of navy sweatpants hung loosely off his lean hips and his hair stuck up wildly around his head from sex and sleep. He held two cups of coffee in his hands.

He padded across the room and climbed into the high bed. "Here." He handed me the coffee.

I took a sip, unable to contain my moan. "This is delicious."

He winked. "It's caramel."

He leaned back against the mountain of pillows, looking out the windows. His gaze was thoughtful and I knew he was contemplating something.

"Whatever it is, just spit it out," I told him.

He laughed, ducking his head. "Am I that predictable?" He smiled and his dimple showed.

"I know you." I shrugged. "You don't have to be predictable for me to pick up on your body language. Now, out with it." I blew on the hot coffee, eyeing him over the rim.

"Can I take your picture?" he asked.

I laughed. "Trenton, I'm pretty sure you've already taken my picture plenty of times."

"No, not like this." He shook his head, his dark hair falling into his eyes.

"Not like what …?"

"You, naked, in my bed." He bit his lip. "And then I want to take your picture while I make love to you."

I shivered at his tone.

"You can say no, if you don't want me to," he assured me, "but I'd really like to."

"I …" I drew my knees up to my chest, contemplating. Finally, I met his unwavering gaze. "Okay."

"Okay?" he repeated, smiling slowly like he was afraid at any second I'd scream that I was only kidding.

I nodded. "It's okay with me."

He set his coffee cup on the table and then reached for

mine. "You want to start now?" I asked, reluctantly handing over the cup.

He nodded with a small grin. "I thought I better get started before you change your mind."

"I won't."

"I don't care," he laughed, picking up his camera. I realized that our suitcases were now in the bedroom. Someone must have dropped them off last night and he'd brought them in this morning.

He aimed the camera and started taking pictures.

"Lay down," he said huskily.

I did as he asked.

Before taking another picture, he reached down and spread my hair around, then lifted one of my arms above my head. "Don't move," he warned me like one would a child.

My heart was beating so fast in my chest that I was sure he could see its thumps.

"These are beautiful," he whispered, looking down at the screen of his camera.

He posed me in a different position and snapped my picture again. He continued that way for a good thirty minutes.

"Now," he said before he lowered, taking my bottom lip between his teeth and then releasing it, "I'm going to make love to you."

He held tight to the camera and kicked off his sweatpants. He was hard and completely ready for me. He slid a condom on and climbed on the bed. His fingers found me and when he felt that I was wet, he grinned. "I'm glad that turned you on as much as it did me."

"How could it not?" I breathed.

"Good point." He kissed me as he took ahold of his length

and slowly slid it inside me just a bit. I squirmed, letting out a small shriek from the soreness left over from yesterday. "Are you okay?" His brow creased with worry. "Do I need to stop? You know I will," he assured me.

"Just go slow," I warned him. "I-I'm sore down there."

"Trust me," he said, kissing me deeply and making my head spin, "this is going to be slow, and you're going to love every second of it."

My heart sped up even further at his promising tone.

He inched inside me ever so slowly, and when he was all the way in he stopped, taking a picture. I'd completely forgotten about the camera, but seeing it in his hand as he was braced above me made me excited.

"You can move," I whispered.

"Not yet." He took another picture.

He slowly inched back out, taking my picture again as my mouth fell open in an O.

He rocked his hips in and out at a leisurely pace that somehow managed to drive me crazier than what we'd done last night. I also found that there was something extremely erotic about having him above me, taking my picture as he made love to me. I couldn't hide my emotions. They were plain for him and the camera to see. I was baring my soul to him, and I hoped he knew that, and understood the gift I was giving him. I was letting him *see* me.

Sweat dampened my body as I edged closer and closer to that cliff I was desperate to fall off of.

"Come for me," he breathed, his voice barely above a whisper. "Let me see you."

He drove into me with shallow thrusts and I clawed at the

blankets as I felt my orgasm begin to take over. All the while, he took my picture.

"God, you're so fucking beautiful and you don't even know it," he growled.

I wished I believed him. I had never been a person concerned about my outward appearance, but I knew on the inside that I was ugly. Scarred. Disfigured. I was diseased. Poison, known as lies, ran through my veins, suffocating me.

"Rowan?" he questioned, noticing the look of disgust on my face. "What's wrong?" His movements stilled as he gazed down at me questioningly. "What did I do? What'd I say?"

"It's nothing," my voice cracked.

"Row ..." He cupped my cheek in his hand. "Did I hurt you? Is it the pictures? You have to tell me what's wrong so I can fix it." His eyes pleaded with me to speak, to tell him what was going on in my head, but it was so hard.

"You didn't hurt me," I assured him. "But I'm not beautiful, Trent."

"Yes, you are," he said sternly.

I shook my head. "I'm not talking about what I look like," I spoke fiercely. "I'm talking about what's in *here*." I placed a hand over my heart. "If you knew who I was, what I had *done*," I croaked, "you'd know I wasn't beautiful."

"Don't say such horrible things about yourself," he whispered, tracing his fingers over his lips. "I don't know who has planted these lies in your head, but they're wrong."

"No one had to tell me anything," I whispered with a frown. "I can see my own darkness."

"Row ..."

I knew he didn't know what to say to me, and that was perfectly okay. I didn't need to hear him try to convince me that I was *good*. He didn't know what I had done, so in his eyes I was good. Eventually, I'd have to tell him—he deserved to know—and then he'd see how bad I was. I couldn't hide the evil residing in my heart forever.

I pushed his shoulders, rolling him onto his back so that I was on top.

"Take your pictures." I took his chin in my hands, pressing my lips to his, sealing us together.

Because soon, those pictures will be all you'll have left of me.

———

"And this is Times Square," Trenton said, as if I hadn't already figured that out. I twirled around, my jaw hanging open in awe.

The lights, the sounds, the people ... None of it was like home. It was easy for me to believe that Trent and I were in a whole new world. One where only the two of us existed.

Somebody bumped into me, propelling me into Trent. He wrapped his arms around me to keep me from falling on the sidewalk.

"Well, that was rude." I glared at the retreating back of the man that had pushed me.

"That's New York City." Trent laughed. "Get used to it."

He didn't release me, if anything he tightened his hold. The air was cold and there was a slight wind. I was thankful for my heavy black coat, yellow scarf, and hat. Trent was dressed similarly, only his scarf and hat were red.

"Let's get a picture," he pleaded with me.

At this point, I was used to Trenton and his pictures, so I obliged.

He positioned me in front of the jumbotron and stood beside me. He held his arm out with the camera. "Smile," he warned me.

I wrapped my arms around his neck and gave the camera the biggest, cheesiest smile I could muster. Then I kissed his cheek. In the last photo he took, he kissed me squarely on the mouth, his tongue finding its way past my lips. I took his face in my hands, the scruff on his cheeks rubbing against the soft cotton of my mittens. He nipped my bottom lip and I couldn't help but giggle.

He kissed the end of my nose, his breathing unsteady. "I know I wanted to show you the city, but I'm beginning to think leaving the penthouse was a really bad idea."

"How about this, take me to see the Christmas tree in Rockefeller Center, then we can go back there and take a really long shower ... together."

"That's a really good idea." He grinned. "I wish I would've thought of it."

"Come on." I took his hand. "The sooner we get a taxi, the sooner we see the tree, and the sooner we see the tree ...," I trailed off, letting him finish my thought.

"The sooner I can have you wet and pinned against the shower wall." He winked. "I do love showers."

"And cameras," I muttered.

He laughed. "Pictures are worth a thousand words, but those ... Something tells me they're worth a million."

A taxi finally stopped and I slid inside. Trent told the man where we wanted to go and I stifled my cough. The taxi reeked of cigarette smoke.

I crinkled my nose in displeasure at the nasty smell. I'd

never understood the appeal to smoking. I mean, who wants to suck on a death stick? Obviously, our cab driver.

He dropped us off and Trent handed him cash. "Thanks," Trent called and the cabby simply grunted in response.

"Such a lovely fellow," I joked. "I think he wants to be your new best friend."

Trent's arm wound around my waist. "Hardly."

The crowd around the tree was thick, but not as bad as Times Square had been. I didn't think we'd be able to get very close to the tree, but I was okay with that. It was lit up with multi colored lights and the ornaments were huge. I wondered just how tall the thing was. I had to crane my neck back to see the top of it.

"Excuse me," Trent said, stopping a man passing by. "Would you mind getting a picture of me and my girlfriend?"

My heart stilled.

Girlfriend.

Trent had called me his girlfriend.

We had never defined what we were, but obviously Trent had his own idea, and I liked the sound of him calling me his girlfriend a bit too much. I should've told him I wasn't okay with him calling me that, but it would've been a lie. I did want to be his girlfriend. In fact, I wanted to be even more than that. But I knew it would never last, so I didn't see the point in defining what we were to each other.

The guy seemed pissed that Trent had stopped him, but agreed. Trent handed him the camera and brought me close against his side.

The guy held the camera up and I smiled.

"Thanks." Trent nodded, taking the camera from him.

Without a word, the man left.

"Can I see it?" I asked, pointing at the camera.

Trent nodded, handing it over.

On the screen was the picture with the tree sparkling behind us. I smiled at the camera, but Trent was smiling down at me like ... like I was his whole world. It was a beautiful picture, one that I wished I could imprint in my mind so I could look back on it years from now and remember how he'd felt.

I handed the camera back, swallowing down the sudden lump that had taken up residence in my throat.

"Are you ready to go?" Trent asked. "Or do you want to stay a little while longer?"

We'd already been gone from the penthouse for a while, I was chilled, and while the tree was pretty I didn't see the sense in staring at it any longer.

"I'm ready to head back," I answered, wiggling my chilled fingers. The black mittens did little to warm them, so I shoved them in the depths of my coat pockets.

Trent hailed a cab and we headed back to the penthouse. He dropped us off at the front of the building and we entered that way. I hadn't seen the lobby area yet, and I was stunned. Everything was so shiny and expensive looking. I didn't want to know how much their penthouse must cost.

"You've got a little drool there," Trent joked, wiping my lip for effect.

"This place is so amazing," I gasped, turning around and around to take in everything.

"I like it here." Trent shrugged. "The city vibe has always suited me, but I'd have a hard time leaving home. It's nice to have this place to get away to, though."

"How many other places do you have like this?" I questioned as we waited for an elevator.

"A few," he answered vaguely.

"Something tells me it's more than a few." I laughed, stepping into the elevator.

He pulled out the key again, inserting it in the slot and twisting. "So maybe it is more than a few." He shrugged casually. "I can't tell you what they are, because I have to have something to keep you interested."

"You know I don't care about your money, Trent," I said seriously, "or how many cars and houses you own. None of that matters to me."

"I know." He cupped my cheek, lowering his mouth to mine. "It's one of the reasons why I—"

The elevator doors opened into the penthouse and I grabbed his hand, pulling him after me. "About that shower?" I smiled seductively, and what he had been about to say was forgotten.

THERE WAS a library in the penthouse. Every wall was covered with shelves filled with books of every genre. On one wall, there was a window with a built-in bench seat covered in a fluffy white cushion and pillows. I had grabbed a blanket from the family room and I draped it over my legs as I looked out the window, brushing the wet strands of my hair.

Trent was making us dinner. I'd offered to help, but he'd declined, telling me to relax.

Since I hadn't gotten much of a tour yesterday, I had taken

it upon myself to look around the penthouse. When I'd come across this room, I'd been delighted. I'd always found comfort in a library. It made me sad to know I wasn't going to be working at the library anymore. I probably wouldn't be welcome there to study, either. It looked like I'd be stuck studying at the university's library. I'd have to come up with something creative to tell Tatum as to why I was fired. She was my friend, but I wouldn't be able to bring myself to tell her the truth.

Luckily, I'd gotten a few days of work in at Trace's car shop before Trent and I left. It certainly wasn't the library, but it was nice. He was easy to work for and he paid well, so I had nothing to complain about. The guys that worked for him in the shop could get a little rowdy, but he was quick to shut them down and order them back to work. For being so young, Trace was handling being a business owner very well.

I tapped my fingers on top of my knees and laid the hairbrush aside, letting the long damp strands hang down my back.

I was overcome by a sudden sadness, knowing that in a matter of days we'd have to return home and this bubble surrounding me would burst. Being here alone with Trent made it all too easy for me to hope for a future with him— a future that I knew could never be. I vowed that when we got back home I'd end things. I'd walk away before it got messy. When he dropped me off, I'd lie and tell him that this week with him had shown me that my interest wasn't there. I'd lie, because it was easier. They always say the truth can set you free. In my case, the truth was my prison.

One day, when I was older and wiser, I would find him and explain to him why we would've never worked out.

It wasn't that day yet, though, and for now, I'd enjoy myself.

A patter on the open library door had me looking up. Trent stood in the doorway, his dark hair had dried from our shower and he was shirtless, just those same low hanging sweatpants on his hips.

"Why am I not surprised to find you here?" He grinned crookedly, crossing his arms over his chest as he leaned against the door.

"I like this room." I forced a smile, wrapping my arms around my knees. "It's ... peaceful. I find it so easy to seek comfort in books," I murmured, looking around at the packed shelves. "The books ... they can't hurt me, not the way people can."

Trent frowned at my words. "Rowan," he whispered my name as he took a step into the room, "I know there's a lot you're not telling me." He crouched in front of me, looking into my eyes. "I understand what it's like not to want to talk about certain things, so I've respected your space, but I want you to know that I'm here anytime you need to talk to someone."

"I know."

There was so much that I did want to tell Trent, but I knew once I opened up I'd have to tell him everything, and I couldn't tell him all my dirty secrets yet.

"Dinner's ready," he said, and I was thankful for the change of subject. I knew Trent was curious about the demons that haunted me, but he respected me enough not to force my secrets out of me. That right there showed me how much he cared for me—more than I wanted to believe he did.

"I'm not very hungry," I muttered, laying my head on my

knees.

"You need to eat." He looked at me with worried eyes. "Are you getting sick?"

No, not unless you could grow sick from lies. "I feel fine," I assured him. "Just tired."

He frowned. "That's my fault. I'm sorry." He stood, holding out a hand for me. "Eat some dinner and go to bed. Please?"

I nodded, placing my hand in his outstretched palm. There was no reason to argue with him. He grabbed the blanket, draping it over his arm.

Out in the open living and kitchen area I saw that he had dimmed the lights and set the table. He'd even lit candles. It was beautiful.

He didn't take me to the table, though; he guided me to the couch and told me to sit. He draped the blanket over my lower half and pushed a button on a remote, which ignited a roaring fire. I hadn't noticed the fireplace yesterday. It made the room seem cozy.

He pushed another button, which closed the large blackout curtains.

He blew out the candles and brought our plates of food and glasses of wine to the couch.

He raised his glass for a toast, so I mimicked.

"To us." He smiled.

"To us," I echoed.

To our demise, I thought.

"TRENT, WHERE ARE YOU TAKING ME?" I groaned as he held onto my hand, running down the street. He grabbed a door, pulling me into a fancy upscale store.

"Shopping." He grinned like a small boy, a little bit of his excitement rubbing off on me.

My mouth fell open as I got a look at the clothes.

"No." I wrenched my hand from Trenton's. "This place is too expensive, I don't even want to *look* at anything for fun."

"Rowan," Trent said my name in a calming tone, "I want to buy you a dress."

"A dress? Why do you want to buy me a dress?" I asked, my eyes shifting around me, taking in all the people dressed in fancy clothes. I didn't belong there in my leggings and gray sweater. I looked like a hobo, and Trent wanted to buy me a dress? Was he crazy?

"Remember the New Year's Eve party I mentioned?" When I nodded, he continued, "Well, it's formal, so you need a dress."

"I have a dress," I mumbled, even though I *so* didn't have a formal gown. I hadn't even gone to prom.

"Rowan," he warned, "I'm buying you a dress, a new dress, and you're not going to say anything about it."

"You're so bossy," I grumbled.

"It's the only way I can get anything done with you." He chuckled. "Now, please don't make this difficult."

I frowned. I didn't want Trent spending his money on me, but I knew that determined glint in his eye all too well, and there was no way I was getting out of this.

"Fine," I reluctantly agreed.

He grinned, pleased to have gotten his way. He didn't take my hand, probably scared I'd slap it away, and nodded for me to follow him.

It was obvious Trent had been here many times before. He

led me to the ladies' section, or did they call it something else in fancy stores like this?

A woman greeted him and they shook hands. "Row, this is Sherri. Sherri, this is my girlfriend, Rowan, and she needs a dress for a party."

Sherri shook my hand, her eyes starting at my feet and roaming up my body as she sized me up. "Hmm," she grunted. I took it she didn't think I was good enough for Trenton. That made two of us.

"What kind of party?" she asked Trent. Her voice was oddly nasal sounding, like she had a cold.

"A New Year's Eve party. My family has one every year and it's very formal."

Sherri tapped her chin in thought.

She was a petite woman with fiery red hair that was in no way natural and aqua glasses. Her lips were plump and shimmered with a cherry-red gloss. Her clothes were nice and probably cost more than what I paid for rent in six months, and she *worked* there.

"I think I have some things that might work."

It didn't escape my notice that she addressed Trent, not me, like I was nothing.

She turned briskly on her heel, flicking her hand over her shoulder for us to follow.

"I don't think she likes me," I muttered under my breath to Trent.

"I'm not sure she likes anyone," he replied with a shrug.

"She likes *you!*" I exclaimed in a hushed whisper.

"I can't help it that I'm so charming." He winked, his eyes scanning the racks of clothing warily. "I know this was my idea, but I hope this doesn't take long. Shopping is not my thing."

"It's not my thing, either," I assured him.

"Wait here." Sherri pointed to a fancy couch that was covered in amethyst velvet.

Trent and I took a seat while she went to pull some dresses.

I looked up, noticing an intricate crystal chandelier hanging above us. I wasn't sure what store he'd dragged me into, and looking around at all the fancy finishings and clothing, I was pretty sure I didn't want to know. My stomach was already churning at the thought of what this dress would cost, and I'd *have* to let him buy it. I certainly wasn't spending the money in my savings account on a dress—that money was going to be used to get me and the kids away from my mom and step-dad.

Sherri returned with a rack of dresses. They were all in different styles and lengths, but most were shiny.

She crooked a finger at me and I stood to inspect the dresses she had pulled.

"Do you see any you like?" she asked, her voice full of false sweetness. Someone had woken up on the wrong side of the bed.

I reached for a long black evening dress that was strapless. It had jeweled detailing on the top and the bottom was plain. "I like this one," I said.

"All right then, try it on." She led me down a hall and opened a door into a dressing room.

She closed the door so she was left in the small room with me. "Uh ..." I eyed her warily. "I don't need any help. I'm fine on my own."

"Okay." She nodded, leaving me to myself.

I stripped out of my clothes and shimmied into the

black dress. Once it was on I decided I didn't like it as much as I had on the hanger, but I knew Trent would want to see. So, I forced myself to leave behind the comfort of the dressing room and venture out to the waiting area.

Trent sat up straighter when he saw me.

"I don't like it," I declared quickly, "but I knew you'd want to see." I turned, brushing my hair over my shoulder so he could see the dress at all angles.

"It's pretty, but not you," he commented.

"Try this one." Sherri pulled a dress off the rack and handed it to me. She didn't even look at it, maybe she knew what she'd pulled that well, or maybe she didn't care to help me. Regardless, I really didn't like the woman.

I held the new dress in one hand, and lifted the hem of the one I was wearing in the other.

I didn't like this dress either. It was skin tight and silver. It wasn't me at all. When I showed Trent, he was quick to shake his head in disapproval.

I skimmed through the dresses Sherri had chosen, lingering on a short champagne-colored dress. It was covered in sequins, which wouldn't normally be something I'd like, but it worked. I also liked that the neck came up higher and it had three-quarter sleeves, so despite the short length I wouldn't feel like I was naked.

I took the dress back with me and as soon as I looked at my reflection I knew I had found the one. It was tight, but not glued to me like the other dress had been, and I felt comfortable in it, not like a little girl playing dress up.

When Trent saw, he sat back, a grin lighting his face. "That's the one."

"I love it," I said, unable to keep the slightly giddy tone from my voice.

Trent stood, his hands falling to my waist. "It's perfect."

I smiled, pleased that he liked it as much as I did.

"We'll take it," he told Sherri, not even bothering to look in her direction. "While you're at it, get her some shoes to match."

Sherri asked me what size I wore and I told her. "I'll change and then we can get out of here," I said to Trent. "I'm ready for lunch."

I don't know if it was the fact that we couldn't keep our hands off each other, or what, but I was hungry all the time.

I closed the dressing room door behind me and reached around to undo the zipper. It started to fall off my shoulders and I gasped when I looked into the mirror and found Trenton standing behind me.

"Trent, what are you doing?"

He didn't use words to answer me. He picked me up and my legs automatically wound around his lean waist. He backed me against the wall, using it to support me as his lips ravished mine. "You look fucking gorgeous in this dress and I wanted to be the one to get you out of it," he growled against my lips. He sucked on my neck and a gasp escaped me.

"Trent," I breathed, pushing against his shoulders, "we can't do this here."

"Yes, we can." He kissed his way over my collarbone and to the other side of my neck. "But you'll have to be really quiet."

"What if someone finds us?" I protested.

"So what?" he countered, covering my lips with his and effectively cutting off any further protests.

He undid his belt buckle and pushed his jeans down,

careful to hold me up.

"This is going to be hard and fast," he warned. "Are you okay with this?" He cupped my cheek tenderly in his hand.

I knew if I told him to stop, that this wasn't okay, he would, but I didn't say that. I nodded, giving him permission, unable to ignore the rush of adrenaline coursing through my veins. I knew we could get caught at any moment, but that only added to the excitement.

"Hold on tight." He chuckled, pushing the dress up and ripping off my panties. Like, he literally *ripped* them off. I didn't know guys did that in real life. It was kind of hot.

Once he had fixed a condom on, he was inside me in one smooth hard stroke and I gasped. I reached up, covering my mouth with my hand to stifle any sounds I made.

He hadn't been kidding when he warned that this was going to be hard and fast. I kept one hand over my mouth, and clung to him with the other.

Knowing that we could be caught at any moment had my excitement building.

I held my breath as my orgasm grew closer, it was so hard not to make any sounds, but there was something intoxicating about it too.

Trent's gaze found mine and I knew he was close too. Looking into his eyes, I let myself fall off the edge, knowing he'd be there to catch me.

He came too, his fingers digging into my hips to keep me from falling. Slowly, he brought his head up, kissing me deeply, and braced one hand beside my head. "You're the only one I want," he whispered, nibbling on my chin.

My eyes closed as I swallowed thickly.

And the only one you can never have.

CHAPTER FOURTEEN

Kisses were tenderly pressed against the skin of my neck, down over my breasts, and then a hand eased my shirt up and even more kisses were pressed against my stomach.

"Trenton," I groaned, trying to roll away, clinging to the soft pillows. I had been sleeping so well and I didn't want to wake up, even with such sweet kisses. "I'm tired."

He pinched my waist and pulled my body back over to the edge of the bed. "We need to go," he whispered in my ear. "We're going to miss our flight."

Flight.

Shit.

I'd completely forgotten we were heading home today. My heart stopped in my chest for a second before resuming its beat at a frantic pace. If we were going home, that meant tonight was the New Year's Eve party, and tomorrow I'd have to tell him that this was over between us. I couldn't keep doing do this to him—to myself. The longer we were together, the more it created a false hope for a future we could never have.

I suddenly never wanted to leave New York, because as long as we stayed, I could pretend the outside world no longer existed.

"I don't want to go home," I mumbled, burying my face in the pillow.

I didn't see how I could force myself out of this bed to get ready and have to act normal. I had less than twenty-four hours with him, and I knew I needed to make every moment count, but I wasn't sure I could do it. It would be easier to resort to how I had always been in the past when things bothered me.

Withdrawn. Emotionless. Broken.

I took a deep breath and rolled onto my back, cracking my eyes open.

Trent was smiling above me. "We have an hour to get packed and to the airport."

An hour was plenty of time for me. I wasn't one of those girls who had to do her hair and pile on gobs of makeup. I didn't care what I looked like.

Trenton headed out of the room and I was left alone. I forced myself to stand, reluctant to leave behind the comfy bed, and I hated to shed the borrowed t-shirt of Trent's that I was wearing.

I yawned, stretching my arms above my head.

This had been the greatest week of my life, but also the worst. This had given me a taste at what life with Trent would be like, and I liked it a bit too much. Being with him was so easy. He was well-aware of my flaws and he could see past them. He brought out the best in me, something no one else had ever been able to do. Without him in my life, I'd become a drone, simply going through the motions on a daily basis—just like I had done before he came back into my life for a second time.

I padded into the bathroom, brushing my teeth and hair, and packing things into my toiletry bag. I pulled my hair into a bun on top of my head and secured it with a hair tie. I took a quick shower, washing my body with the sugar-scented body wash.

I dropped the shirt of Trent's that I'd been wearing on top of his bag.

I dressed casually for the plane ride in leggings and sweater. I slipped my feet into a pair of flats and checked the bedroom to make sure I'd packed everything before zipping the suitcase closed.

Since Trenton hadn't returned I took the time to pack his bag too and wheeled them both out to the foyer.

Trent was in the kitchen making us breakfast.

I smiled, taking a seat at one of the barstools. "You know," I said as I smiled, taking a sip of freshly-squeezed orange juice from the glass he'd had waiting, "a girl could get used to this."

He smiled, handing me a plate with scrambled eggs and toast. "Well, if I had my way, you would."

Guilt threatened to suffocate me. Here I was, smiling and joking with him about a future I was well-aware I was about to extinguish.

After that thought hit me, I found it nearly impossible to eat my breakfast.

"Hey," Trent started, bumping my shoulder with his, "are you okay?"

I felt like he was always asking me if I was okay, and I almost never was.

"Just tired," I replied, using my fork to push the scrambled eggs around the plate.

"I guess that's my fault." He winked, taking a bite of toast.

Besides the near constant sex, Trent had shown me different places around the city nearly every day. He was familiar with the city, so he didn't waste much time on the touristy things, instead showing me the heart. He'd also taken me to one or two different restaurants every day. I was sure I had probably gained ten pounds in the last week, but I didn't care. I had enjoyed myself too much to regret even a single moment.

Trent finished eating, and when he saw that I wasn't going to force any more down my throat he cleaned my plate as well.

"I want to warn you," he said, his words instantly making the hairs on the back of my neck stand up, "that this party can be a bit ... stuffy ... if you know what I mean. Just stick with me, okay?"

I nodded, too relieved to know his warning had been about the party and not anything else.

"Trace and Olivia will be there with Dean, so of course you know them." He shrugged, bracing his hands on the counters. I couldn't keep my eyes from the way the muscles in his arms flexed with the motion. "But if it gets to be too much, you can tell me, Row."

Row. I loved it when he called me by my nickname, treasuring the way it sounded leaving his lips.

"I know," I answered, sliding from the barstool. I don't know what made me do it, but I found myself wrapping my arms around his middle and hugging him. He seemed shocked at first but his arms eventually wound around me as well. I felt his lips press tenderly against the top of my head.

He grasped my arms so I couldn't pull away, and looked down at me, studying my face like he was searching for something. Finally, he said, "I feel like there's something you're not telling me."

There was *everything* that I wasn't telling him.

"You must be imagining things." I laughed, schooling my features into a mask that even he couldn't see through.

I hated lying to him, I really did, but I didn't have a choice. One day, I hoped he'd see that.

Trent nodded, and it was obvious he didn't believe me, but he wanted to.

He looked at the shiny silver watch adorning his wrist and muttered, "We have to leave or we'll miss our flight."

"Can you actually miss a flight when you own the plane?" I joked, hoping to distract him.

"Good point," he chuckled, heading for the foyer, and running his hands nervously through his dark hair. "We'll simply be *delayed* then."

He wheeled our suitcases into the elevator and I looked around the penthouse one last time.

I wouldn't be returning, I knew that, and I wanted to take this moment to remember everything.

"Row, come on," Trent called, his arm keeping the elevator door from sliding closed.

I took a deep breath and stepped in beside him.

The doors closed and I was overcome by sadness as the penthouse disappeared from my sight. I had created some really great memories in that place—memories that would last a lifetime.

When the doors opened, the lower garage appeared, and the same car and driver that had dropped us off waited.

The driver opened the car door for us and then deposited our suitcases in the trunk. I leaned my head against the leather seat, wishing I didn't *feel* everything. I wasn't talking about physical touch. No, I was referring to the emotions I felt at the moment. I had so many emotions rolling through my body that I felt dizzy. It seemed impossible to feel so happy, sad, angry, and a billion other things all at one time.

"Are you getting sick?" Trenton asked and I turned to look at him. I knew I needed to get my act together or he wouldn't leave this alone.

"Like I said, I'm just tired." I rested my head against the cold glass window as the driver pulled out of the garage and into the busy traffic.

Trent and I didn't speak on the way to the airport. I pretended to be sleeping and he read something on his phone.

The flight back was almost as quiet. I knew I should make use of every moment I had left with him, but it would only remind me further that our end was near.

Once midnight struck, and the New Year began, I'd have to say goodbye.

Damn.

I really was like Cinderella.

Only, instead of two wicked stepsisters, I had the kindest, sweetest, kids waiting for me back home. They'd hold me together through my grief, they wouldn't understand what had upset me, but they'd be there to offer their quiet comfort.

When we got off the plane one of the crewmembers loaded our bags into Trent's car. I couldn't quite get used to the fact that Trent had other people to do such simple tasks. I felt like I should help the man with my suitcase, but I knew that would only offend him, and I didn't want that.

"Something's wrong with you," Trent stated once we were driving home. His jaw was stiff and his knuckles had turned white where he gripped the steering wheel.

I opened my mouth to assure him that I was fine, but he spoke over me.

"Don't you fucking *dare* say you're okay." He reached up, adjusting his sunglasses. "I know you, and you can't lie to me. You're hiding something from me. I wish you could see that you can trust me. I'd never betray you, Row, *never*." He beat his fist against the steering wheel. "I can feel you pulling away from me again, and I fought so hard to get you back. Don't fucking do this to me again," he pleaded.

I didn't know what to say as he ranted. I didn't think there was anything I *could* say. If I opened my mouth, only lies would spill out, and there was already an ocean of them between us.

"I know you don't want me to say it, Rowan, but I love you. Do you hear me?" He glanced at me. "I love you! I love you! I. Love. *You*. Whatever is going on with you, you can tell me and we'll work through it together. *Nothing* could ever change my feelings for you."

I swallowed thickly, choking on the sudden lump that had lodged itself in my throat. "I know you think that now, but there are some truths about me that you don't want know." Tears filled my eyes, but they didn't spill over. Trent's mouth fell open in shock as he noted the shimmering in my eyes. He knew me well enough to know that I never cried, and rarely came even close to it.

"I want to know everything about you, damn it!" He

slammed his hand against the steering wheel. "The good, the bad, *everything*. None of it will change how I feel about you."

"That's where you're wrong," I whispered, looking down at my shaking hands.

He thrust his fingers through his hair, making it stick up in uncontrollable directions.

"Just tell me. Whatever it is, just tell me," he pleaded with me, but it was to no avail.

"I *can't!*" I screamed. "Do you understand what I'm saying? I *can't*! I didn't say I *won't*, I said I *can't*," my voice lowered to a softer tone, but my breathing was accelerated, my loud breaths currently the only sound in the car.

"What ...," he paused. "What does that mean?"

"It means that I was a naïve child and I put my trust in the wrong fucking person," I growled, and he stiffened at my use of foul language. I wasn't one to cuss, at least out loud, and I never spoke this passionately. "I signed my fucking life away, Trenton!" My lower lip trembled with the threat of tears, tears I had refused to cry for five years. "I gave up *everything* for no reason! I'm legally bound to my silence! I gave up my entire *life* for *nothing!*" My breath was coming out in short shallow gasps. "Pull over." I gripped the door handle tightly in my fist. "Pull over!"

He did, watching me with shock on his face as I broke down.

As soon as the car was stopped I was out, pacing the side of the busy road.

I couldn't believe I'd told him all of that.

I should've never opened my mouth.

Oh. My. God.

I sunk to my knees, gravel digging into the thin cotton of

my leggings, and let my head fall forward into my hands. None of my tears fell, even though I willed them too.

I clutched my stomach, letting my head fall forward as a scream tore through my throat.

I couldn't do this.

This lie was suffocating me.

It was going to kill me.

And I was going to let it, because I had no choice.

Everybody thinks they have a choice in life.

Not me.

All my choices were taken from me at sixteen years old.

I wished I had been strong enough to stop it, to stand up for myself, but I hadn't. The one person I should've been able to trust, took my powers and my choices away from me. I wished I had done things differently, but I hadn't, and now I'd have to spend my whole life suffering for one wrong decision.

"Rowan?"

"Leave me alone!" I screamed at him. "Just leave me alone!"

A part of me wanted to stand up and run into his arms, to let him comfort me, but he was the last person I deserved comfort from.

I leaned my head back, looking up at the blue sky, wishing I could disappear into the clouds so I didn't have to deal with this pain.

"Rowan," he said my name softly, placing his hand on my shoulder, "please get back in the car."

"I can't," my voice cracked. *I don't deserve to. I don't deserve you.*

"Yes, you can." He was so calm with me. There was no anger in his tone, only concern.

If he knew what I had done he wouldn't be talking so sweetly to me. He'd leave me here to let my sins eat me alive.

"Please, come back to the car," he pleaded, like he was talking to someone who was about to jump off a building to their death.

I inhaled the cold air, letting it sear my lungs.

One, two, three, four, five, six, seven, eight, nine, ten.

"Okay."

I REFUSED to look at Trenton or even speak to him as we drove to his family's home. When he asked if I wanted to go home and skip the party, I shook my head no. It was selfish of me, but I wanted this last night with him. I would need it to carry me through the rest of my lonely existence.

My fingers twisted together as he turned down the unmarked road that led to his family's mansion.

"Rowan?" he said my name hesitantly, like he was afraid I'd start yelling again.

I had news for him: I was too tired to scream and yell. My breakdown had drained me of energy.

I nodded, letting him know he could continue with what he had to say.

"Whatever happened to you, we can fix it," he whispered, glancing at me out of the corner of his eye.

"There is no fixing this." I stared straight ahead, biting down on my tongue. "This isn't something that can just be undone, Trenton."

"I don't know that, though!" He raised his voice. "You

refuse to tell me what it is, so I have no way of knowing what I can do!"

The trees disappeared and I saw the mansion up ahead, its large lawn covered in snow, but the driveway clear.

"Let it go, Trenton," I warned. "I mean it."

He let out a sigh, pinching the bridge of his nose as he pushed a button and pulled his car into the garage.

"How do you ever expect us to have a lasting relationship if you're keeping secrets?"

I don't.

I didn't say anything. I simply opened the car door and got out. I wrapped my arms protectively around my chest.

Trent got out too, slamming the car door closed. He crossed his arms and rested them on the hood of the car. He watched me carefully, not saying a word. With a sigh, he shook his head, looking away from me.

He grabbed our suitcases and wheeled them to the door. "Come on." He flicked his hand for me to follow.

I could feel him pulling away, and it hurt. I knew it was for the best. I was already planning to end things. But the last thing I wanted was for Trenton to hate me. I guessed I was delusional, because of course he'd hate me.

"Hey, Mom!" He called out and I stilled.

I hadn't seen Lily Wentworth since I was a teenager.

"Trenton." She smiled at her son. She was beautiful with long dark hair and pixie features. "Hello, Rowan," she greeted me brightly, and surprised me by opening her arms for a hug. "Did you enjoy New York?" she asked me.

I nodded. "It was lovely."

Why the heck do I sound so formal? It must have been the

mansion giving me the impression that I needed to be more proper.

"I'm glad you enjoyed yourself." She smiled, stepping away. "Well, I have a lot to do before the party, so I'll leave you two alone."

Her heels clicked on the shiny floors as she disappeared down one of the many halls in the mansion. Seriously, how did nobody get lost here? Or maybe they did and they were never heard from again.

Trent picked up our suitcases up and started up the steps. I knew the luggage had to be heavy, but he acted as if they weighed nothing.

"Do you want to get ready in a guestroom, or my room?" he asked, walking ahead of me.

"Your room is fine." I shrugged, looking around. "I mean, after this past week, I don't think either of us have anything to be shy about."

He chuckled and the sound of it relieved me. "I guess you're right about that."

He bumped his shoulder against a door, and muttered, "This is my room."

The only time I had been here before, I hadn't seen his bedroom.

The walls were red, a stark contrast to the yellow walls in his bedroom at the townhouse, but I knew this was his favorite color. The bedspread was a charcoal gray and all the furniture was black. Posters for different bands plastered the walls. It definitely suited the teenage Trenton that I remembered.

"So ..." He sat down on the end of his bed, making it bounce. "This is home."

"I like it."

He shrugged, looking around the large room. "It's okay. I prefer my place; this room seems like it's stuck in a time capsule, but it's nice to still have a place at home." He chuckled. "It makes me feel like that no matter what happens, I'll always have this place."

"I'm sure you will," I glanced around, noting a bookcase in the corner, there was a picture sitting there and something about it drew me closer.

I reached out, wrapping my hand around the frame.

I gasped as I recognized the people in the photo. It was Trent and me on our school trip, the one where we lost our virginity. We were both sitting on a log. I was smiling and he was laughing at something I had said. It was raw and beautiful and completely unexpected. I studied my face, the happiness shining there. That day was the last day I had felt true happiness.

"I can't believe you have this," I gasped. "Who took it?"

"One of the teachers." He stepped up behind me, his body almost touching mine. "Mr. Jones, I think. He gave it to me, he thought I'd like to have it."

"And you've kept it for this long …" I breathed. "Trent …" I placed a shaking hand to my mouth.

He took the picture frame from my hand and replaced it on the shelf. "Of course I kept it. Just because you stopped speaking to me doesn't mean I stopped having feelings for you. Emotions aren't something you can turn on and off, Row. Although, I wished many times that I could."

I closed my eyes, unable to look at him and see the hurt in his eyes. I *hated* that I had hurt him, but it was what I had had to do. At first, it was because he told me he loved me and that scared the shit out of me then. It still did. But then other things had happened and I'd pushed myself even farther away from him.

"Trent, I know you probably don't believe me, but I am sorry for how I treated you."

"It's okay." He picked up a strand of my hair, rubbing it between his fingers. "We were young and foolish, and I scared you with my words. I meant them then, though, and I mean them now."

I took a shaky breath. "I don't deserve your love."

I didn't want to believe in love. Hell, I'd spent most of my life not believing in it. I had seen so much bad that it made it hard to see the good. But I did love Tristan and Ivy. I also knew that there was only one word to describe the look in Trent's eyes, and that was *love*.

Love, the very thing I had been running from five years ago when I left that stupid tent.

Now that I was ready to accept love, to let myself be free, I knew I had to end things.

Trent would think I was running again.

Maybe I was.

But I had to.

"I don't know why you think no one could love you," he whispered, taking my cheek in the palm of his hand and caressing my lips with the pad of his thumb.

I placed my hand over his. "My own mother doesn't love me. If she can't, why would anyone else?"

His eyes filled with sadness. "No one should ever feel unloved."

I shrugged. "I did … I *do*."

His eyes closed and pain flickered across his face. "That breaks my heart." His blue eyes shimmered with tears. His arms caged me against the bookcase as he stared unwaveringly down at me. "I want you to know that you're not unloved. I know your brother and sister must love you very much. You've been the only mother they've known and your heart is so good and pure how could they not?" He leaned his forehead against mine, his breath tickling my face as he spoke. "And I love you, Row. More than my next breath."

I cracked a smile. "That's really cheesy."

He grinned. "That's me, a giant cheese ball." He chuckled. Pressing his lips tenderly to my forehead, my eyes closed, and he said, "I meant it, though."

I grasped the soft fabric of his blue sweatshirt in my hands. "Don't we have a party to get ready for?"

"Why, yes, yes we do."

HOURS LATER, I stood at the top of the grand staircase, grasping Trent's elbow.

I had washed my hair, and styled it in an up-do. I had put on more makeup than usual, but nothing overly dramatic.

"Ready?" Trent asked, tilting his head to look down at me.

I nodded, wishing my heart would slow its frantic pace. I was beyond nervous. I was downright terrified. This was *way* out of my comfort zone, and knowing that tomorrow I'd have to sever all ties with Trenton left a sour taste in my mouth.

"Breathe," Trent warned as we descended the steps and made our way to the ballroom. Yes, a legit ballroom. What kind of house has a ballroom? Apparently, this one.

The doors were open and I gasped as I glimpsed my first

sight of the expansive space. Everything seemed to shimmer and sparkle with the light from the chandeliers. There was a live band playing orchestra music in the corner, and many couples danced, while more sat at one of the numerous round tables occupying the space. Waiters came around with food and laughter filled the air.

My mouth fell open in shock.

This was straight out of a movie.

"Would you like to dance?" Trent asked.

I nodded.

He led me onto the dance floor, and gave me a little spin, before holding me in his arms. He easily led me, like a proper dancer, so I didn't look like an incompetent fool.

"I didn't know you could dance like this," I commented.

He laughed, bashfully glancing at the ground for a moment and then met my gaze. "My parents made us learn when we were boys. It doesn't keep Trace from dancing like a fool, though." He winked, nodding in his brother's direction.

I looked where he indicated and couldn't contain my laughter as I spotted Trace shaking his hips in a wild circle and his arms flailing above his head. Dean giggled as he mimed his father, and Olivia simply shook her head, obviously used to this behavior. Lily watched in horror, embarrassed by her oldest son's actions. She finally waved her hand in dismissal and went to speak to someone.

My heart stuttered in my chest as a realization rocked me.

I loved this family.

Most importantly, I loved Trent.

Somehow, Trenton had shown me how to love. Love wasn't meant to come with strings; it was free and uncomplicated—as easy as breathing. That's what we had, and I'd tried so hard to fight my true feelings, but they were there. He taught me how to love, and now I didn't know how I would survive breaking our hearts for a second time.

"What's wrong?" he asked, falling out of rhythm to grasp my chin and force me to look at him. He was so in tune with me and my body that he always knew when something was wrong. I wished I were capable of hiding my emotions from him like I could everyone else.

"Nothing's wrong," I lied. Knowing that wouldn't suffice with him, I hastened to add, "It's just ... your family ... They're amazing, Trent."

He smiled. "Yeah, they are. I'm lucky."

He had no idea how lucky he was. Most people didn't have families like his. I hoped, when I broke his heart again, that they'd be there for him to help him heal. As much as it killed me to think of Trent with another girl, I hoped he moved on, fell in love, and built his own amazing family one day.

We danced to one more song, then he led me to the table Trace and Olivia currently occupied. Dean was trying to climb up Trace's shoulders and yank on his hair.

"Dean," Trace scolded, "pulling hair isn't nice." He grasped the boy's small fist and removed it from his hair.

Dean then proceeded to smack Trace's cheek. Those two definitely had their hands full with that kid.

Lily came breezing up to the table and sat down just as a waiter came by with a tray of food, depositing plates in front of all of us.

Everyone talked and chatted easily with one another.

Except me.

I was retreating into myself once more, and I felt like an

outsider looking in. I didn't belong here. I liked all of them, I really did, but they were so different from me.

"You okay?" Trent leaned over to ask.

"Yeah," I replied with a small shrug, trying to figure out how to eat the lobster I had been presented with.

"Since we're all here." Trace took a sip from his wine glass, waving his hand at his family gathered at the table. "There's something I'd like to tell all of you."

We all perked up with interest at whatever the oldest Wentworth brother had to tell us.

"I'm so happy to tell you guys that Olivia has once again let me plant my sperm inside her and have the joy of watching a baby grow."

"*Trace!*" Olivia exclaimed, her cheeks a bright red.

"Congratulations," Trent raised his glass, as his mom and grandma squealed in delight. "Another baby will be exciting ... especially if it's anything like that little devil." He pointed to a grinning Dean who was clapping his hands together and blowing spit bubbles.

"I'm so embarrassed," Olivia muttered, hiding her face behind a napkin.

Lily wiped away a tear from her cheek. "I can't wait for another grandbaby," she sniffled.

"Oh shit," Trent muttered under his breath. Turning to me, he grinned crookedly, "Next she's going to expect me to get you pregnant."

I spat out the sip of wine I had just taken and maroon colored droplets of liquid stained the pristine white tablecloth.

"I was just kidding, Row." He chuckled, beating my back as I struggled to breathe.

I managed to recover in time to see Trace's grandma

hugging him and then Olivia. I couldn't remember her name though.

"That's Grammy," Trent said, pointing to the older woman. It was like he could read my mind or something. "Her name's Ellie, but she'll prefer for you to call her Grammy."

About that time, I heard someone behind us call, "Hey, bitch!"

Olivia's eyes widened and her cheeks turned even redder than they had been. Poor girl.

"And that," Trent said without turning around, "is Avery."

The woman appeared at our table, draped over a tall brawny guy. She had pretty red hair, styled in waves, and her red dress was beautiful but skin tight. I was surprised her boobs didn't fall out. The man beside her—Luca, I assumed—was tall with wide shoulders and shaggy dirty blonde hair that fell over his forehead. A black fedora was perched on top of his head.

"How was the honeymoon?" Olivia asked as the couple pulled up two chairs to the already crowded table. "I didn't realize you were getting back today."

"It was beautiful!" Avery exclaimed loud enough that people at other tables heard her. "I didn't want to come home! It was so nice to be at the beach, and now we're back home to this crappy snow." She frowned. Noticing me, she leaned over the table and raised a brow. "Who the hell are you?"

Olivia let out a sigh. "Avery," she muttered, "manners."

"It's fine." I smiled at Olivia. "I'm Rowan. Who the hell are you?" I mimicked her words and tone.

She smiled. "I'm Avery, this one's wife, so don't get any ideas." She grasped Luca's shoulder in one hand, and let the other venture territorially over his crotch area. *Ew.*

Luca, who sat beside me, gave me an apologetic smile but didn't speak.

"I wasn't planning on it," I assured her.

"Good. We can be friends then." She flipped her hair so that it cascaded over her chest and went back to talking to Olivia.

"Sorry about her," Trent murmured. "That's just how she is. Don't take it personally."

"I didn't."

"This is Luca." Trent pointed to the man beside me, who I'd already figured out the identity of. "He doesn't talk much, so don't expect him to introduce himself. I think I've only heard the guy speak a total of twenty words since he and Trace became friends."

"Uh …" That was strange and I had no comment. I scooted my chair a little closer to Trent's and he chuckled.

They all continued to chat effortlessly, and while Trent tried to engage me in conversation I just wasn't feeling it.

I felt so disconnected and out of place.

"Where's the bathroom?" I asked Trent, interrupting whatever he had been saying.

He gave me directions and I muttered, "Thanks," as I pushed my chair away from the table.

I walked briskly out of the ballroom and down the hall.

Luckily, the bathroom he'd given me directions to was empty.

I closed the door behind me and started counting.

One, two, three, four, five, six, seven, eight, nine, ten.

The counting didn't calm me the way it normally did.

So, I counted again and again and again, until I thought I might go crazy.

I paced the length of the bathroom, muttering under my breath.

Finally, I stopped, grasping the pedestal sink in my hands.

I glared at my reflection.

I didn't recognize the girl I saw there.

The dress.

The hair.

The shoes.

None of it was me.

I was an imposter.

I didn't belong there.

This life wasn't mine.

I didn't deserve to be surrounded by these people—to laugh and smile with Trent.

I was tainted.

I continued to glare at the girl in the mirror.

I hated her.

I hated *me*.

Before I could stop myself, my fist cocked back and flew into the mirror.

It shattered everywhere, slicing my knuckles painfully and making me scream.

I crumbled to the ground, some of the shattered mirror shards digging into the bare skin of my legs.

My knuckles were on fire and blood dripped from my fingers onto the floor.

Oh, God.

What have I done?

"Rowan!" Trent pounded on the door.

Of course he'd come to check on me. Someone had probably heard the mirror break and my scream.

"Rowan! Open the goddamn door!"

I couldn't move if I wanted to.

I sat there, cradling my injured hand in the other.

"I'm going to break down this fucking door if you don't open it!"

I shook my head, despite the fact that no one could see me, my throat constricting painfully.

He pounded on the door and then silence fell.

I stared down at the blood dripping from my knuckles and down my fingers. The pain filled me with an odd sense of satisfaction. The physical pain drowned out what I felt inside. I liked it.

The door burst open, splintering from the hinges. Trent stood there, cradling his shoulder, his chest rising heavily with each breath. His mouth fell open as he caught sight of the shards of mirror littering the black and white tiled floor and my bleeding hand.

"Row," he gasped, dropping to the ground and reaching for my hand.

I whimpered as he inspected my bloodied knuckles. "We need to get you to a hospital."

I shook my head rapidly. "No. No hospital. Please." My words came out short and clipped as I winced from the stinging pain in my hand.

"You might need stitches. You should go to the hospital," he pleaded.

"I'm not going." I pulled my hand away from his hold and cradled it once more.

He sighed, reaching up to run his fingers through his hair and then wincing from the pain in his shoulder.

"Fine," he relinquished, "but at least let me clean you up."

After thinking it over for a moment, I nodded in agreement. "Okay."

He grasped my arms and hauled me up. He eyed the mess on the floor and then my hand. "What were you thinking?"

That I hated myself.

"I don't know," I said instead.

He wrapped one arm around my shoulders and helped me stumble out of the bathroom. My legs were shaky from the leftover adrenaline.

We made our way slowly up the steps and some guests lingering in the hall and foyer eyed us with curiosity.

Once in his bedroom he pointed at the bed. "Sit." The tone of his voice told me not to argue with him.

He shrugged off his tuxedo jacket and tossed it on a chair in the corner, then proceeded to undo the first three buttons on his crisp white shirt. He eyed my hand, which had stopped bleeding, and a frown marred his face. He muttered something under his breath and strode into his bathroom.

I heard him rummaging through a drawer and when he found what he was looking for he came back into the room, kneeling in front of me. He opened the first aid kit, pulling out a set of tweezers, and laying a towel to the side.

"I need to get the shards out of your skin before I clean it," he murmured, holding my hand up and twisting it in the light so he could search for the small pieces.

I winced as he began to pick them out. My skin was raw and tender and the metal points of the tweezers hurt as they pinched at the debris.

"I don't understand," he whispered.

"You don't understand what?" I asked, my voice hoarse as if I had been crying.

"Why you would do this," he answered.

I looked down, letting the stray hairs that had fallen loose from my up-do hide my face. "I guess you don't know me as well as you think you do."

A muscle in his jaw ticked. "Why do I feel like I'm losing you?" His eyes flicked up to meet mine and those pretty baby blues rooted me to the spot.

"Can you lose something if you never really have it?"

His teeth smashed together. "Don't say that."

"It's true," I whispered as he laid the tweezers aside. He picked up the rubbing alcohol and dabbed it on a cotton ball before cleaning my knuckles. I winced from the burning sensation.

"Why are you so fucking scared of *us*?" He pointed at his chest and then me. "We're good together, we're happy. Why would you run from that?"

I'd been scared the night I left the tent, but that wasn't my reason for running now.

"I'm not running, Trent." I shook my head as he cleaned the blood from my hand.

"That's exactly what you're doing," he spat, reaching for the gauze to tape around my wound.

With my hand that wasn't injured, I reached for his face, rubbing my fingers against the slight stubble on his cheek. "I'm not running," I repeated. "I'm protecting you."

"Protecting me?" He laughed, but there was no humor in it. "From what?"

"From me."

"I'm pretty sure I can handle you, Row." He tenderly lifted my hand as he secured the gauze in place.

"It's not about *handling* me," I retorted. "I think you know after what I said today that there's a lot I can't tell you. I can't allow you to ..." My gut clenched painfully. "I can't allow you to love me with these secrets standing between us." My voice cracked painfully. I hated doing this to him again. I felt like my insides were curling in on themselves.

"Why can't you tell me?" He looked at my quizzically, wishing I would spill my secrets to him. "Does it really matter if you do?"

I closed my eyes. I *wanted* to tell him. There had been several times where I had come close to spilling the beans, but I always stopped myself, because I was protecting him from the repercussions of my sins.

It had been selfish of me to give in to my desires. No matter how much I had wanted this time with him, it wasn't fair to either of us. I was ruined for anyone else and he'd never understand why I had to do this.

"Yeah, it does," I finally answered. "I wished it didn't, but it does matter. One day," I rubbed his cheek softly as I spoke, "I'll be able to tell you, but until then, I can't say anything. I wish I could."

"Fuck," he groaned, his eyes closing as he swallowed painfully, "did you sign some contract or something?"

I nodded.

His eyes widened in surprise at having guessed right. "What the hell did you get yourself into?"

"I didn't kill anybody," I joked pitifully, "and I'm not in the witness protection program."

"I don't understand," his eyes pleaded with me to speak the truth.

"Good," I responded.

I lowered my head to his level, where he was bent, and

tenderly kissed him. Sadness clung to both of us, as we both knew this was goodbye. He knew me so well that I didn't even need to tell him.

Trent kissed me back fiercely as he climbed onto the bed. "I'm not okay with this," he whispered, his lips caressing the skin of my cheek as he spoke, "but because I love you, I'm going to set you free."

A sob threatened to escape me at his words. He kissed me as his hands found the zipper on the back of my dress. Cool air hit my back as it became exposed and he drew away from me as he pulled the sleeves off my arms and then the dress down my hips. Once it was off I was left in nothing but a pair of lacy black panties and a bra. His eyes feasted hungrily on my body.

"If this is our last night together," he murmured, gently tugging on my bottom lip with his teeth, "then I'm going to make every second count."

My heart clenched painfully. A part of me was happy that he had accepted that this was it, that there could be nothing more between us, but another part of me was immensely sad. Trenton Wentworth had ruined me for all other men. He owned me, heart, body, and soul. I loved him, I did. I knew that now. But I couldn't tell him, or he'd never stop fighting for me, and I needed him to let me go.

He took his time kissing me all over and undressing the rest of my body. My fingers shook as I unbuttoned his shirt and pushed it off his lean shoulders. His arms wrapped around me, protecting me with their warmth and security.

"I love you," he whispered in between kisses. "I love you. I love you. I love you." I wondered if he thought by saying those words he could change my mind.

I wished it was that easy.

He rolled on a condom and slowly eased inside me. Our fingers entwined together, and he rested his forehead against mine, staring into my eyes and straight down to my soul as he made love to me.

His lips placed tender kisses along my face, down my neck, and over my shoulders and breasts.

Everything was so sweet and tender.

It was the perfect goodbye.

If only goodbyes lasted forever ...

CHAPTER FIFTEEN

When I woke up, Trent's arms were wrapped around me and our legs were twisted together. It was like in his sleep he'd thought I might escape and he needed to bind me there.

His face was pressed into the crook of my neck and his forehead was wrinkled as if he was dreaming of something unpleasant.

I watched him sleep, studying his features—the elegant arch of his nose, his pouty lips, the nearly invisible scar on his cheek, even the light freckles on his nose that you couldn't see unless you were up close to him like this. They were all such simple things, but they were a part of him. What I loved the most about Trenton, though, wasn't what he looked like, it was his heart—he was the kindest, most giving person I knew. He cared so deeply, it was a rarity to see that in a man—I would know with all the men my mother had brought around as I grew up. Despite the distance in our social classes, Trenton understood me. At a time when I'd been the scared new girl, he'd taken me under his wing and made me feel comfortable. He'd been my best friend. I had trusted him more than I ever had anybody. He'd tried to claim my love before I was ready to give it, and it sent me running. Because of it, I had made some horrible decisions I could never take back. Regret is funny and it does terrible things to you. It robs you of happiness.

As if he felt me watching him, his eyes cracked open and he smiled sleepily. His smile quickly turned to a frown though as memories of last night flooded him.

"I'm ready to go home," I whispered sadly. I had to force myself to say the words. I didn't really want to go back to that place, back to my shitty mom and my sleazy step-dad. I wanted to stay right here with Trent. However, I knew if I let myself linger much longer, the pain I'd feel later would be even worse. The sooner I got away, the sooner I could grieve this loss and move on. Well, there never really would be any moving on for me. Every day I'd be reminded of what I had done, and what I had lost because of it.

Trent swallowed thickly and nodded. He clearly didn't want to let me go, but he knew he had no choice.

He extracted his body from mine and stood, pulling on his boxer briefs and then rummaging around his suitcase for a pair of jeans. "I'll take you home." His voice was thick, whether from still being sleepy or emotions he was fighting, I didn't know. I held the sheet to my chest and sat up, looking around his room for my own suitcase.

He glanced over his shoulder and saw what I was searching for. He grabbed my suitcase, which had been hidden from my sight by the mountain of blankets on the bed, and deposited it in front of me.

I dressed as quickly as possible and pulled my hair back in a messy ponytail. My eyes were bothering me from having fallen asleep in my contacts, so I went to the bathroom and removed them, perching my glasses on the end of my nose.

My hand hurt like a bitch this morning, but its constant throb helped diffuse the other pain inside me.

I eyed my tired reflection for a moment. My eyes were sunken in with dark circles beneath them and my mouth was turned down in a frown that I couldn't force into a smile no matter how hard I tried. Yesterday had been a trying day for me. I still couldn't believe I'd had that meltdown in the car, and then again in the bathroom. It wasn't like me, but everything was catching up with me and I didn't know how to process my feelings.

I finished in the bathroom and found Trent waiting by his bedroom door with both of our suitcases. "Let's go," he muttered without looking at me.

It killed me that he couldn't bring himself to look at me. This had to be done. We had to end. He couldn't find out what I had done and I wanted to tell him so bad. Some secrets have to be kept quiet and I was bound to mine.

He carried the suitcases down the steps and out to the garage. All the while not saying a word to me. I wanted him to look at me, to say something ... *anything*. Silence, ultimately, was better.

He drove me home, his jaw tight with anger, but sadness too.

I knew he'd hate me for this—for breaking his heart a second time.

But better he hate me for that than the truth.

He parked in the driveway, not the street, and hopped out to get my suitcase.

I knew better than to argue as he wheeled my suitcase up to the front door. I walked slightly in front of him and jumped in surprise when the door opened. I expected it to be my mom or step-dad, since they should've been the only ones home, but instead it was Tristan.

"Row!" he cried my name with joy as he came barreling into my arms.

My heart stuttered in my chest.

They aren't supposed to be home yet! I'm supposed to pick them up tomorrow! Tristan shouldn't be here!

"Hi." Tristan released his stranglehold on me and turned to greet Trenton.

Trent's mouth fell open in shock as his eyes landed on the little boy. His eyes narrowed in puzzlement, then flickered to me, and back to Tristan again. Recognition lit his eyes and my throat closed up.

He knew.

There was no denying the resemblance.

"Hello," Trenton finally responded, his voice slightly squeaky as he stared down at Tristan.

I knew what he saw. I saw it every single day. Tristan had the same light-colored hair I'd had as a child, but everything else about him had Trenton Wentworth written all over it—especially his vivid blue eyes.

"You need to go inside now." I gave Tristan a slight shove. He didn't need to be here to witness this.

"Why?" He peered up at me with inquisitiveness.

"Just do it," I said, my voice harsher than how I normally spoke to him.

He frowned, but finally went back inside, waving at Trent before closing the door.

"That's my son," Trenton stated, his eyes full of anger. His face was growing red and his nostrils flared.

I nodded. I couldn't refute it.

"That's my son," he repeated, rubbing his jaw. His face was clouded with disbelief. "My son," his voice grew soft with shock. "Why the fuck did you never tell me?" he suddenly roared, pointing an accusing finger in my face. His eyes were full of hatred for me. Despite knowing if he ever found out that he'd hate me it still hurt to see that look in his eyes.

My voice seemed to have stopped working. I opened my mouth to speak but no sound came out. My worst nightmare was playing out before me and I was powerless to stop it. This was exactly what I had been trying to avoid for the last five years. I knew letting Trent back into my life, no matter how brief, would have lasting consequences.

"I have a son," his voice was full of wonder as he glanced at the closed door. "What's his name?" His eyes stayed glued to the door, like he was willing the small boy to come back outside so he could see him again.

"T-Tristan," I stuttered, finally finding my voice.

"You gave him a T name," he whispered under his breath so low that I wasn't sure I heard him right.

He stared at the closed door, his jaw clenched, and his hands fisting at his sides. He seemed to be battling some internal war.

"I don't understand why you didn't tell me!" He twisted back to face me, and I flinched at his harsh tone. I didn't like him yelling at me, but I understood. This was a shock for him. He had every right to be angry and hate me.

"I couldn't tell you," I cried softly, itching to reach out and touch him, but knowing that was the last thing he wanted right now.

I had known there was the possibility he might find out about Tristan, it was a small town after all, but I'd hoped to avoid this. I had been forced to keep this a secret, and it had slowly been killing me inside to stay silent, but I'd had no choice. I wasn't allowed to say anything to Tristan until he was eighteen, which meant Trent couldn't know until then, either. I had always planned to tell him, knowing that he'd hate me when he found out, but having him see Tristan and find out the truth like this was horrible. I knew he wouldn't understand why I did it.

"Like hell!" he spat, shoving his fingers forcefully through his hair. "I can't fucking believe you, Rowan! *This*—" he pointed at the closed door "—is what you've been hiding from me! This is the reason you wanted to end this! Didn't you think I had a right to know?"

"Of course!" I reached for his arm, but he flinched, backing away from me. "I couldn't tell you, Trent," I pleaded with him to understand. "I wanted to, so bad, but I couldn't."

"I can't even look at you," he muttered, his voice growing quiet once more. "I have to go."

"Trenton! Please, let me explain!" I screamed as he darted around me, running for his car. "Trent!" I begged. I needed him to stay and hear me out. I had to make him understand. I knew he wouldn't want anything to do with me after this, but I deserved to explain myself.

"I don't want to hear it!" he yelled, turning to point an

accusing finger at me. "I'm so fucking angry right now! Guess what?" He spread his arms wide. "You're getting your wish! From this moment on, I'm out of your life!"

He climbed in his car, slammed the door closed, and sped away.

I sunk to the ground, snow seeping into my jeans and chilling me. A sob escaped me, and then tears. I reached up, feeling the wetness with timid fingers. I hadn't cried in five years, not since I found out I was pregnant and my world came crashing down around me.

I thought I had been broken before ... and I was ... but Trenton had managed to carefully piece together the shards of me. Now, I was breaking all over again, and this time I knew the pieces would be too small to ever be reassembled.

My hand shakes as my gaze drops to the slender white stick in my hand. I slide to the floor, my back against the bathroom door.

Pregnant.

Holy shit.

How am I going to raise a kid?

I already take care of Ivy, I don't see how I can raise my little sister and a child of my own.

Tears coat my cheeks with sticky dampness.

I will the test to change to negative, but of course that doesn't happen.

I'm going to have a baby.

Trent's baby.

After how horrible I've been to him I don't see how I can tell him. I've said so many mean things to him the last few weeks. Things I'll never be able to take back. I'm sure he already hates me, and why would he want a baby? We're sixteen, nowhere near ready to be parents. We're both kids ourselves.

I sit up and toss the stick in the trashcan. I wash my hands and splash my face with water.

I have to tell my mom.

She hates me.

But she's my mom.

She'll be there for me ... right?

She'll make this better.

Surely, she'll know what to do.

She has to.

I crack open the bathroom door and venture into the living room. Ivy is asleep, but my mom shouldn't be drunk yet. She doesn't start drinking until late ... although, in past weeks she's been starting earlier.

I'm not surprised to find her sitting on the couch drinking a beer as she speaks to her latest fuck buddy. I don't even remember his name. John? James? Jim? I think it's Jim.

"*Mom,*" *my voice cracks.*

She looks up at me, anger causing her to snarl. "*What do you want, brat?*"

I don't like it when she calls me that. It makes me feel like nothing I do is ever good enough, and I try so hard to get her to love me. I know she's going to be angry when I tell her I'm pregnant. But she had me when she was young, so I think she'll understand. Maybe it'll make us grow closer.

"*I need to talk to you,*" *I whisper.* "*Alone,*" *I add as my eyes flick toward the man in the recliner.*

"*Whatever you need to say to me you can say in front of Jim.*"

She sits back, taking a large gulp of beer. "Spit it out. I don't have all day."

My eyes squeeze shut. Now I'm wishing I had waited to tell her, to let it sink in more, so I could process it.

I didn't though, and if I don't tell her something, she'll get angry and hit me.

It was foolish of me to think she'd take me into her arms and make it better. She didn't care about Ivy or me. We were nothing to her, nothing but a burden.

I decide to tell her the truth. After all, that's why I came out here in the first place.

"I'm pregnant," I say, choosing not to sugarcoat the words.

Her mouth falls open. "I always knew you'd turn out to be nothing but a slut." She glares as she looks me up and down.

Her words hurt, but I've learned to keep my face void of emotion.

"I'll take you the clinic and we'll have that thing taken care of." She points at my stomach.

"What?" I stumble back, protectively clutching my stomach and the baby residing there.

"For an abortion," she says unnecessarily.

"No," I gasp. "I don't want that. I want to keep it." I'm shocked that she would even suggest such a thing.

"Honey," she leans back on the couch, "I'm just trying to save you from my mistake."

I flinch. She's talking about me. She's basically saying she wished someone had been there to tell her to get an abortion.

"I won't do that," I say fiercely. I'll run away before I let her kill my child.

"You could put it up for adoption," she suggests with a slight chuckle. It amuses her that I've made such a colossal mistake.

"No. I won't do that."

"What the fuck are you going to do with a child, Rowan?" She tilts her head. "Huh?"

I don't know. But I do know that I'd rather struggle and have my baby than kill it or hand it over to strangers. Maybe it's selfish of me, adoption would give the baby a better chance at a happy life, but I want to keep it.

I suddenly feel like I should've sucked it up and went to Trent. But my mom's next words silence those thoughts.

"The way I see it, you have two options. Abortion or adoption. Ain't no way you can raise a child, you're too dumb for that." I want to disagree with her and tell her that I basically take care of Ivy, but I know she'll only have a well-thought-out argument for that. "No way is that baby's daddy going to help you. Teenage boys run from commitment, Rowan. And a baby? That's a life sentence no boy wants."

Is she right? She sounds like she's speaking from experience, and I'd basically deduced the same. Trent wouldn't want to be a dad, and I had school to think about, and with a baby I'd need to get a job to buy it things, and what about college? I wanted to get out of here. A baby would keep me trapped in a life like this, a life just like my mom's.

"How about this?" She smiles, and I let out a sigh of relief that she's going to help me. "I'll adopt that baby. That way, you can go on and live your dreams, without a baby tying you down. I'm doing you a favor here, baby girl, take it or leave it."

I think it over for a few seconds.

"Deal."

I WIPED my face free of tears as the memory evaporated. I'd been so silly and naïve thinking my mom could fix the mess I had made. I wanted to believe that she was helping me.

She wasn't, though.

She was simply manipulating me.

I'd signed my life away when I put my signature on the adoption papers. She'd added stipulation after stipulation to the contract.

Basically, she wanted me to raise the baby, but he could never know I was his mother and I wasn't allowed to speak a word to the father.

I wondered now, if she knew Trent was Tristan's dad, if she would have been different because of the money they had. Knowing her, she might've tried to sell them the baby.

I never should have signed those papers.

I knew as soon as I did that I had made the biggest mistake of my life.

The contract stated that I couldn't reveal to Tristan that I was his mother until he was eighteen, unless extenuating circumstances permitted it.

So, he'd become my brother, and eventually, I started to believe it was true.

As long as Tristan didn't know I was his mother, then Trent couldn't know of his existence.

If I told Tristan that I was his mother before he turned eighteen, I wouldn't be allowed to see him.

If I had gone to Trent in the very beginning, none of this would have ever happened. Hindsight was a pain in the ass. I had believed that Trent would be like every other teenage guy and not want anything to do with me or the baby. I knew that wasn't true now. Trent wasn't like other guys, seeing him with his nephew proved that. He would've owned his mistake—*our* mistake ... and God, it killed me to even think of Tristan as a mistake. I loved that little boy with everything I had.

Now, I valued Tristan too much to tell him the truth. I couldn't imagine not seeing my son every day, so I kept quiet, refusing to breach the contract, letting my guilt and misery eat me alive.

I had so many regrets, but my biggest was not telling Trent I was pregnant before I signed that contract. I'd believe he'd already hated me after the way I pushed him away, and it was believable to think that a sixteen-year-old guy wouldn't want a baby.

"Rowan?"

I turned to look behind me and saw Ivy and Tristan standing in the doorway.

Ivy frowned. "It's cold, and you're getting wet. Come inside."

She sounded so mature and wise beyond her years. It broke my heart and tore me up inside. I had tried so hard to give her a childhood, but growing up with a mom like ours made that impossible.

I forced myself to my feet, drying my eyes with the sleeve of my sweater.

My suitcase still sat outside where Trent had left it. I grabbed it, bumping it along behind me.

"I made some hot chocolate." Ivy smiled, but her eyes were filled with worry. "Would you like some?"

I nodded, letting my eight-year-old sister take care of me.

The door to my mom's room was closed and the sounds of her having sex with either Jim or some guy she'd picked up at a bar filled the air.

I hated that Tristan and Ivy had been home listening to that. I left my suitcase by my closet door and climbed under the covers. Tristan scurried in beside me, his arms winding around my neck.

Ivy came into my room a few minutes later with hot chocolate.

"What's wrong with you?" she asked softly. "Are you sick?"

I knew it must have been a shock for them to look outside and see me having a break down like that. They'd never seen me cry and I was sure it had frightened them.

"I'm okay," I whispered, kissing the top of Tristan's head and sliding our bodies over to the other side of the bed so Ivy could join us. "Why are you guys home?" I finally asked.

"Mom wanted us home." Ivy shrugged. "I don't know why."

That woman. I hated her. I really did. She'd only wanted them brought home to punish me for leaving.

"How long have you been here?"

"Since last night." Ivy climbed into my bed beside Tristan.

"I'm sorry I wasn't here," I whispered.

"It's okay." Ivy reached for my hand. "I love you, Rowan. I wish you were my mom."

"I wish you were my mommy too," Tristan piped in.

And then I began to cry again.

CHAPTER SIXTEEN

I WAS SUPPOSED TO WORK TODAY.

Seeing as how Trace was my boss now, I wasn't sure if I was welcome back at Wentworth Wheels.

I was sure Trent had told his family by now. They were close, so why wouldn't he? They all probably hated me, and I couldn't blame them.

I wrestled with what to do, not knowing what would be the right thing.

In the end, I made myself get ready and take the kids to school. I'd never forgive myself if I didn't show up and Trace expected me to be there, and I already had enough stuff to be angry at myself for without adding something else.

I dropped the kids off and drove to work. All the while chewing nervously on my bottom lip. It was raw and sore feeling by the time I arrived.

When I put my car in park, my heart was racing in my

chest. I expected Trace to hear the sound of my car and come running out, yelling that I was never welcome here again.

That didn't happen, though, so I was forced to get out of the car.

I didn't see Trace when I stepped into the building. I called out for him, but heard no reply.

I turned to leave, thinking he was ignoring me, but the door to the office opened then and he waved. "Don't leave," he said, noting that I had turned on my heels to flee.

I braced myself for whatever he had to say. I prepared for him to yell and tell me how horrible I was, but that didn't happen.

"Are you okay?" he asked.

I was confused. *Why is he asking if I'm okay?* "I don't know what you mean."

"Well," he began as he crossed his arms and legs, leaning against the open doorway, "I'm assuming after what my brother figured out the other day, that he said some not very nice things, and so, I'm going to ask you again. Are you okay?"

I nodded.

"Don't lie."

"I'm miserable," I muttered.

"That's what I thought." He nodded. Pushing his hair out of his eyes, he added, "So is he."

I flinched. I didn't want to hear about Trent, about what my secret had done to him.

"I don't understand why you did it." Trace pushed away from the doorway and strode toward me. "But I'm sure you had a pretty damn good reason."

I didn't have a good reason, not at all.

"I couldn't tell him," I whispered. "Tristan doesn't even

know that I'm his mom. He's not allowed to know." I bit my lip as tears stung my eyes. I was *not* going to cry in front of Trace. "I'll just ... leave now," I muttered, turning to leave.

"Whoa, whoa, whoa," Trace said, reaching for my arm. "I never said anything about you leaving."

"What else do you have to say?" I snapped.

"Nothing, but I am paying you to work for me."

"You mean ... I still have a job?" I asked in surprise, hope flooding my body. I had been sure Trace was seconds away from telling me to get off his property and never come back.

"Of course you do." His brows furrowed together. "Am I pissed because you didn't tell my brother that he's a dad? Yeah, I am. But I offered you a job, you're good at it, and I see no real reason to fire you." He shrugged, bending down to pick up something from the floor. "You're family now, Rowan. You're not going anywhere."

"Thank you," I gasped, flinging my arms around him and surprising us both with the gesture. He patted my back awkwardly.

When I released him, he smiled and said, "Get to work."

I grinned, pleased that I still had my job, but my heart panged in my chest with the knowledge that Trenton was hurting.

I headed toward the back of the building where the office was located and Trace called for me. "Yeah?" I stopped, turning to face him.

"Trent's really pissed right now ... but in a few weeks, when he cools off, I think you should visit him and explain things to him. Make him understand."

"I will." And I would, even though it would kill me to face Trent and explain everything to him, it had to be done. Right now, all he knew was that he had a son that I had never told him about, and that was it. He needed to know why I couldn't tell him, and understand how much I had suffered because of my decision. I would regret what I had done every day for the rest of my life, and I knew when I died, I'd burn in hell for it too.

I WATCHED TRISTAN CLOSELY.

I saw him with different eyes now that Trent knew the truth.

I could allow myself to truly see the things about my son that were so clearly inherited from his father.

Like his eyes, they were exact same shade of blue that Trent's were.

And sometimes, when Tristan was concentrating on something his nose would crinkle, and I'd often seen Trent do the same thing.

It was amazing that Tristan had never even met Trent and acted so much like him. Most things really were inherited.

I had always tried to force myself not to notice things about Tristan that were like his dad and me. It killed me inside to see things about him that were so clearly us when Tristan didn't know the truth. It had been easier to make myself believe that he was my brother. It lessened the pain.

"Rawr!" Tristan hollered, playing with his toy dinosaurs, having one attack the other.

He played for a few more minutes before laying the toys aside.

"Row?" He looked up at me with wide questioning blue eyes.

"Mhmm." I nodded for him to continue.

"Who was that guy?"

"What guy?" I asked, picking at lint on the carpeted floor.

"The guy that said hi to me?" he questioned.

I frowned, not wanting to answer. "No one. It was no one."

"But I saw him!" Tristan cried.

"I know you did," I said soothingly to calm him, "but he's no one important."

"Oh." Tristan frowned.

"Why were you asking about him?" I pressed, wondering why the boy's mind had ventured to think of Trenton.

"I thought he might like to play dinosaurs with me." Tristan frowned. "Or cars." He pointed to his basket of Matchbox cars. "I think I like cars more than dinosaurs now."

I laughed. "Why is that?"

"The dinosaurs always eat each other," he complained.

"Then why do you make them eat each other?" I countered with a small smile as I crossed my legs.

"They're dinosaurs," he looked at me like I was dumb as he spoke, "it's what they do."

Real laughter burst out of me at Tristan's words. Leave it to the little boy to be the one to make me feel better.

"Why are you laughing?" he asked, dumping the basket of cars everywhere.

"Because you're funny." I reached over and pinched his cheek.

"Don't do that." He rubbed his cheek. "I'm not a baby anymore."

No, he definitely wasn't, and Trent hadn't been able to see

our son grow up like I had. He didn't know what Tristan looked like when he was born. He'd missed out on everything—Tristan crawling, walking, talking. All of it.

It was my fault.

I couldn't take back those years he'd lost with his son. But I could try to give him a glimpse.

I knew I still needed to give him more time before I saw him, though.

But I had to get him to understand.

I was prepared to accept the fact that he hated me, but I didn't want him to hate Tristan. I wanted him to see what an amazing kid our son was. How even at this age, he was wise like his father, and curious like I had been as a child. He was a little piece of the two of us that would always bind us together.

"Wanna play?" Tristan asked, holding out a car for me.

"Sure." I took it from him.

He sat on the floor, driving his car around. "Vroom! Vroom! Vroom!"

I stared listlessly at the floor as I half-heartedly pushed the toy car around.

"Row ... Row!"

I looked up to find Tristan halted in his playing. "Like this, Row." He raced his car around in a circle as far as his little arms could reach. "Vroom!"

I laughed, making the noise with him as I drove the car around the room.

"What are you doing?" Ivy appeared in the doorway.

"Playing cars," Tristan answered. He laid his car to the side and grabbed one from the pile. "Here, you play too."

Ivy took the car and sat on the floor to join us in play.

It tore me apart that Tristan didn't know I was his mom.

In his eyes, and Ivy's, I was, though, in all the ways that counted.

"What are you still doing here?" Trace asked, stepping in the office as he brought a bottle of water to his lips. "I thought you already left."

I shook my head. "I'm trying to organize your schedule for called-in appointments and make sure I've left time for emergency requests." I pointed to the appointment book I was scribbling in.

"I don't know what I did before you came along," he admitted, jumping up on the other desk in the corner, his legs swinging. He leaned over, opening the top drawer, and grabbed a bag of ketchup-flavored chips. "Want some?" he asked, holding the bag out for me. I shook my head as my nose wrinkled in disgust. *Ketchup flavored chips? Um, gross.* "Suit yourself." He shrugged, munching on one of the crunchy potato chips. "They're delicious."

We fell into an awkward silence, and I found myself opening my mouth and asking something I shouldn't. "How's Trent?" My eyes raised to briefly meet Trace's before they fell to the paper in front of me once more.

"Honestly?" he asked. "I don't know. He hasn't talked to any of us since he went back to school. He's ignoring our calls too. My mom was thinking about driving up to his school to check on him, but I talked her out of it. He just needs time." He crunched on another chip. "He'll come around."

"No, he won't," my voice was full of sadness. "Trust me." I swiveled in the chair to force myself to look at Trace. "I accepted a long time ago that when Trenton found out the truth he'd hate me. I've had five years to prepare myself. You don't need to try to make me feel better by spouting lies."

"I wasn't lying to you." Trace set the chip bag aside, rubbing his salty fingers on his already dirty jeans. "He will come around, and he will forgive you, because he loves you. Right now, he's hurt, and he can't think straight."

"He can't possibly love me after what I did," I whispered, pain clenching my insides. "What I did was *horrible* and I know he must hate me."

Trace shook his head. "I'm sure he *wishes* he hated you, but he doesn't."

"How can you be so sure?" I questioned.

"Because, love does crazy things to you. I love Olivia more than I ever thought it was possible to love another person, and if she did something like this to me, I'd definitely be angry at first. *Really* angry. But I'd get over it, and I'd let her explain, and we'd move on from it. Love makes forgiveness easy."

"Forgiveness is never easy," I whispered, "especially when it isn't deserved."

Trace hopped down from the desk and patted my shoulder as he passed. "I'm sorry you think that way, but my little brother is going to prove you wrong. Definitely not today or tomorrow. One day, though."

"What if one day doesn't come soon enough?" I asked him.

"Then that's Trent's loss." He shrugged, edging out the door. "Go home. It's late."

I nodded, closing the book and standing. I pushed the desk chair in and grabbed my purse. Trace flicked the office light off and closed the door. He locked it, and then we headed outside where he shut the garage doors and locked that as well.

As he started toward his car, he suddenly stopped and looked back at me. "Give him another week."

"Then what?" I asked.

"Then you explain yourself and hope for the best."

In my life, I'd learned that the best never came, and I expected this to be no different.

CHAPTER SEVENTEEN

I SAT WITH MY HANDS CLENCHING THE STEERING wheel.

I'd spent the last thirty minutes sitting in my car unable to back out of the driveway. It had been almost a month since Trent had left and I knew it was time for me to face my fears—to face him—and get everything off my chest.

I knew any chance of a relationship between us had been blown.

I also knew that I owed him an explanation.

I had asked Trace for Trent's dorm information and where best to wait for him last week. Trace hadn't pushed me to go after his brother, but he wanted me to. He was optimistic that Trent would get over this, and sweep me into his arms, but that was merely a dream.

"You can do this, Rowan," I started giving myself a ridiculous, but much-needed pep talk, "there is nothing to be afraid of. It's just Trent. He hates you, but you have to explain yourself. He deserves an explanation."

I let my head fall against the steering wheel.

"I'm an idiot," I stated.

Staring down at the dark dashboard, since I hadn't started the car, I counted. The counting calmed me and gave me something to focus on besides the thoughts in my head.

"You can do this," I said, not caring if I looked like an idiot sitting in my car talking to myself.

I started the car, turning up the radio and blasting it as I made the two-hour drive to Trent's campus.

My fingers tapped restlessly against the steering wheel. I was scared to face him now that the truth was out there between us, but I had to. I was definitely scared that he'd refuse to talk to me, or even look at me. I had to try—even if it crushed me.

I pulled up to the campus and parked my car.

One, two, three, four, five, six, seven, eight, nine, ten.

I took a deep breath and forced myself to open the car door and step out into the frigid winter air. I reached back inside for my mittens, hat, and the book I'd brought with me to give him. I slipped my hands into the warm mittens as I strode across campus, muttering Trace's directions under my breath. I'm sure to passersby I looked like a crazy person. Maybe I was.

I found a bench outside the dorm that Trace said was Trent's. Trace had written down his schedule and given it to me, so I knew that Trent should be coming out of the dorm any minute.

One, two, three, four, five, six, seven, eight, nine, ten.

I prepared myself to see him. I wasn't sure I was ready. But this had to be done.

I sat down on the bench, my eyes refusing to wander from the dorm door. I couldn't miss him.

"Hey."

I jumped, startled by the voice. I looked up to see a guy standing in front of me. He had shaggy blonde hair and he was tall with wide shoulders. He looked like a football player or something. He was good looking, sure, but there was only one guy for me.

"Hi," I replied, knowing I had to answer him.

"I'm Ben," he introduced himself.

"Mhmm," I muttered, peering around him at the dorm.

"Are you not going to give me your name?" he questioned.

"No."

He chuckled. "So, you want me to work for it?"

"No, I want you to move," I snapped, looking up at him.

"Are you looking for someone?" He turned to look behind him.

"Yes," I said, my tone cutting.

"Mind if I keep you company?" he asked, smiling cockily. He clearly thought that if I spent a few minutes with him I'd completely forget the person I was currently searching for.

I glared at him as he sat down beside me, not waiting for me to respond to his question.

God, the guy couldn't take a hint.

Luckily, at that moment, I saw Trent start out the dorm doors ... but he wasn't alone. There was a girl with him. She was beautiful, with raven-colored hair, olive skin, and dark eyes. She was the complete opposite of me.

He was smiling down at her as she spoke, obviously engrossed in whatever she was telling him.

Tears stung my eyes.

He had moved on.

I knew I should've expected it, but when I knew that there would never be anyone for me but Trent, it hurt to see that he'd been able to move on in a month.

"I have to go," I muttered to Ben.

I started to jog away, but I didn't make it far.

"Hey! Pretty girl!" Ben called.

I halted my steps. "*What?*" I screamed, loud enough that I drew attention to myself. "Can't you leave me the fuck alone?! I'm not interested!"

"You left this," he replied with a chuckle, not the least bit annoyed by my outburst. He jogged up to me with the book tucked under his arm.

I took it from him and muttered, "Thanks."

Bowing my head, I turned to leave and ran smack into someone's chest.

"Ow," I reached up to rub my forehead where it had clunked against the person's chin.

"Rowan, what the hell are you doing here?" Trent growled, grabbing my elbow as I stumbled.

Ice slithered down my spine.

"Nothing." I wrenched my arm from his grasp. "I was just leaving. Get back to your new girlfriend," I spat, my tone full of venom I couldn't contain.

"Rowan!" he called as I ran away.

Steps thudded behind me, and then I was forcibly turned around.

"Don't run away from me." He glared down at me. "You must have come here for a reason, so spit it out."

"Let me go!" I wrenched my arm out of his grasp. My chest heaved with angry breaths and tears stung my eyes. I was embarrassed and angry with myself for even coming here. What had I been thinking? I wasn't ready to have this confrontation, and clearly, he wasn't ready to see me. either.

He raised his hands in surrender. "You're the one that showed up at *my* campus," he seethed, his eyes so full of hate that it made me feel like I was going to be sick. "I think I have a right to know why you're here. Let's get this over with." He crossed his arms over his chest, his foot tapping impatiently against the ground.

"Not here," I whispered as the need to fight left me, my eyes bashfully darted to the sidewalk concrete beneath my feet. I knew we'd drawn quite a crowd, and there was no way I was having this conversation here.

"Fine," he growled.

He grabbed my arm once more and dragged me behind him to his dorm. He pulled out a keycard and swiped it. Forcing open the door, he all but shoved me inside. The muscle in his jaw ticked, reminding me once again that he wasn't happy to see me. I'd expected that, but it still stung worse than a slap from my mother.

"Follow me." He stormed up a set of steps, his heavy boots slapping against the tiled floor.

I'd come this far, so there was no turning back. I reluctantly followed behind him as I counted in my head.

One, two, three, four, five, six, seven, eight, nine, ten.

He stopped in front of a door and waited for me.

He opened the door and waved me inside first. I think he thought I still might try to leave.

"Sit." He pointed at the bed covered in a navy bedspread. I assumed it was his side of the dorm, as the other was covered in dirty clothes and other junk. Trent wasn't that messy.

I perched on the end of the bed, taking a deep breath.

He pulled out the chair from his desk and sat in it backward. "Talk."

Apparently, he was so angry that he could only speak to me in short curt sentences.

"I don't know where to begin," I whispered, forcing myself to look at him.

"I don't know." He scrubbed a hand over his face. "How about at the beginning." I noticed that his eyes were tired, like he hadn't been getting much sleep. His cheeks were scruffier and his hair had gotten longer, curling at the ends.

"Well, I-I got pregnant."

"Yeah, I figured out that part." He rolled his eyes, tapping his fingers nervously along the top of the chair.

"Who-Who was she?" I forced the words out of my mouth. I needed to know who the girl was that he had been with before I continued. "Is she your girlfriend?"

"Huh?" His brows furrowed together. "Who? Oh—" His face lit with recognition. "That was Kelsey," his tone was soft, not harsh like it had been. "She lives down the hall. We're friends. That's all."

My eyes closed as relief flooded my body. It had been tearing my insides apart to think he'd moved on so quickly.

"I shouldn't have asked," I whispered, my eyes reluctantly meeting his, "but I needed to know."

"Rowan," he said my name slowly, "I might be angry at you right now, but I'm *not* that kind of guy."

I nodded. "So ... I guess I better ... uh ... explain."

"That is why you came here, isn't it?" he questioned, sarcasm lacing his tone. I wanted the sweet Trent back from the moment before.

"Well." I rubbed my sweaty palms over the fabric of my jeans. "I-I found out I was pregnant ..." I swallowed thickly. "I'd already pushed you away before that. It scared the crap out of me when you told me that you loved me," I admitted. "I knew you meant what you said, but I didn't believe in love. My mom, who should love me, only hurt me. I thought if you loved me you'd only hurt me in the end too. I was scared and I wanted to avoid that." I took a deep breath, gazing at the ceiling for a moment as I gathered my thoughts. There was a water stain there and I stared at it as I counted. "When I found out I was pregnant, I've never been so frightened in my entire life. I was just a kid myself, Trent, and so were you!" I exclaimed furiously. "I was already raising my little sister. I didn't see how I could take care of a baby too." Wetness coated my cheeks. I had never told anyone this, and it was liberating to finally tell the truth. "I had been so mean to you, after what we did and I thought you had to hate me by that point. Besides, you were a sixteen-year-old guy, why the hell would you want a baby?" I laughed, but there was no humor in the sound. "I felt so alone. So *alone*," my voice cracked. "My relationship with my mom was already pretty much non-existent, but some part of me believed she could make it all better. Boy, was I wrong."

Trent's eyes never wavered from my face as I purged myself of my sins.

"She wanted me to get an abortion," I admitted, looking at the tiled floor. "I couldn't do that, Trent. I couldn't kill our baby." Tears stung my eyes but I dammed them back. Tears were a sign of weakness, and the last thing I needed was to be vulnerable in front of him. "So, she suggested that she adopt the baby. I thought that was the best option."

I took a moment to catch my breath, counting to ten in my head before I continued.

"I was so, so wrong." I shook my head, wringing my fingers together. "Tristan doesn't know I'm his mom."

Mom.

I was his mom.

I hadn't ever allowed myself to refer to myself as his mom before, but I was.

"The contract I signed for the adoption," I paused, momentarily overcome by sadness, "he can't know anything until he's eighteen. Once I signed that, I knew there was no way I could tell you."

"Why not?" he growled. "I would've fought for him! I would've gotten our son back!" he yelled, his chest heaving. "I wouldn't have let him suffer with that wretched woman! I may not know your mother, but I know enough to understand that she is the *last* person that should have custody of our child!"

"I know that, now," I whispered. "I regret it so much." I couldn't contain my sob. "*Every day* for the last five years, I've had to live with what I've done. It's *killed* me to live with this. You don't know what it's been like!" My whole body shook with the force of my emotions.

"Of course I don't," he tore angrily at his hair as he yelled, "because I didn't fucking know!"

"I can't take back what I did, Trent," I whispered, unable to look at him. "What's done is done, and I have to suffer for my decision for the rest of my life."

"How did you hide it?" he asked.

"Huh?" I was confused of his meaning.

"We went to school together. I saw you five days a week and I never knew you were pregnant. I didn't even suspect it. How did you hide it?" he repeated his question, looking straight at me, daring me to look away.

"I-I always wore baggy shirts, and I didn't get that big. So, it was easy to hide," I stammered, my hands wringing together with nervousness.

"When you were out with mono for like two months, that's when you had him, isn't it?"

I nodded, chewing on my bottom lip.

"Did anyone else, except your mom, know you were pregnant?" he continued to fire questions at me. I had expected this, but they were still hard to answer.

"Just my mom and Jim, my step-dad." I shrugged. "And Ivy, my sister, was too little to remember."

"Were you ever going to tell me?" he asked, rubbing his face, and his voice suddenly sounded exhausted.

"Of course," I gasped, offended that he thought I'd take this secret to the grave. "I had to wait until Tristan turned eighteen, but I was going to tell you. Please, never doubt that, Trenton."

"I just ... I don't know what to think of you." He scrubbed a hand tiredly over his face. "I can't believe you didn't trust me enough to tell me when you found out. I told you that I loved you! I would've loved our son too! Fuck," he groaned, burying his face in his hands, "I already love him and I don't even know him. I've only seen him once." His voice grew soft, his eyes far away. "I-I want to see him again." His gaze met mine with a steely determination.

"No." I shook my head. "No, I'm sorry, but I can't let you see him."

His face reddened. "He's my *son*, I deserve to see him!" He exploded with anger and I was surprised he didn't jump up from the chair and storm across the small space toward me.

"He can't know. Oh, God, he can't know," I repeated, my fight or flight senses kicking in, meaning I was about ten seconds away from running out the door.

"Jesus Christ, Rowan!" he exclaimed, making me jump. "I'm not asking you to tell him that I'm his dad! I just want to see him! I want to talk to him, please," his tone softened as he begged. "When I saw him, everything was such a shock that I don't even really remember what he looks like."

"I don't know," I whispered, my hands shaking. "My mom—"

"You can let me know when your mom's gone and I can come over then," he interrupted me. "I know you're …," he trailed off. "Anyway, she doesn't have to be around."

"She never leaves," I mumbled, picking at my fingernail so I didn't have to look at him. I'd looked at him all I could stand. It hurt too much seeing him. I'd suffered enough pain, I didn't need to add to it.

"Then meet me somewhere with him. Please," he begged, his eyes pleading with me to give in.

"I don't know if I can." I bit my lip. "Tristan might say something, and if it gets back to my mom …" Bad things would happen. Things Trent couldn't, and wouldn't, protect me from.

"Fine," he ground out through his teeth. "Don't let me see him."

He stood, pushing the chair back against his desk with a calmness I knew he didn't really possess. "I think you should leave now," he whispered with his back to me.

I nodded, even though he couldn't see me.

I stood, laying the book on the bed. "That's ... that's for you," I said slowly, as he peeked around at me.

He swallowed thickly, turning around fully, and his eyes landed on the photo album.

"I was making it for you," I squeaked. "It's ... it's pictures of Tristan from when he was born, till now. I was going to fill it until he was eighteen and knew the truth, and then give it to you. But seeing as you know the truth now ..." I lifted my shoulders in a small shrug. "I don't see the point in keeping it."

He didn't say anything, but I couldn't mistake the telltale glimmer of tears in his eyes. I hated that I had hurt him. I had been a naïve child and put my trust in a woman that had never given me a reason to trust her before. I had been foolish. I couldn't take back that fateful decision, and I was stuck living with the consequences. I always knew that if Trent ever saw Tristan he'd see the resemblance, so there was never any chance of us having a relationship. I had let myself get tangled up in him again, though, because I couldn't help myself when it came to Trent.

I took a deep breath and forced myself to put one foot in front of the other so I could leave. I stopped with my hand on the doorknob, unable to make myself twist it.

One, two, three, four, five, six, seven, eight, nine, ten.

I refused to turn and look at Trent, but I had to get this off my chest. He deserved to know my true feelings, even though it was too late for us.

I bit down on my lip until I tasted blood.

Our breaths were the only sound in the otherwise quiet room. Time appeared to stand still as I prepared to say three very important words.

I swallowed thickly and didn't bother to look at him. I couldn't bear to stare at his angry face as I finally spoke these words out loud.

My eyes closed, and I murmured, "I love you, Trent."

He gasped.

And with that, I swung open the door, tears falling from my eyes as I ran away from everything.

CHAPTER EIGHTEEN

"Rowan, are you okay?" Tatum asked, her blonde hair falling forward as she leaned across the table to peer at my face.

I didn't answer her.

Was I okay?

Yes.

No.

I suppose.

I don't know.

Did it matter if I was okay or not?

"I think she's comatose," Jude piped in, snapping his fingers in front of my face.

I didn't blink.

"Should I get someone?" Tatum whispered to Jude, but I heard her.

I must have looked bad if those two were speaking civilly

to one another. They bickered like an old married couple. Well, Tatum did. Jude usually just smirked at her as she went on a tirade about what a man whore he was.

"I dunno." Jude shrugged, tilting his head and squinting.

"You're the one that's studying to be nurse." She smacked his shoulder. "You should know if we need to call someone."

Jude grinned. "It pleases me that you know what I'm studying."

"Oh, down, boy," she muttered, crossing her arms over her chest, "stop fluffing your damn peacock feathers. I only know what you're studying because it's the same as Rowan."

Jude rolled his eyes. "Liar. You know you go home and stalk me on Facebook. I bet you lick your computer screen when you see pictures of me shirtless." He licked his lips suggestively. "Ow!" He exclaimed, rubbing the back of his head where Tatum had swatted him.

"Focus," Tatum hissed. "I'm really worried about her."

I frowned. I hated that I was worrying them, but I had nothing to say.

"Look—" Tatum pointed to me "—did you see that? She moved her face."

Jude rolled his eyes. "She's not fucking dead, Tate, of course she can move her face."

"Don't you ever call me Tate," she seethed, loud enough that several people in the library shushed her.

Jude raised his hands in mock surrender. "Sorry," he muttered. "I didn't know I couldn't."

"Only my *friends*," she emphasized, "can call me Tate."

"Oh, so we're not friends?" He grinned, propping his head in his hand and pushing the beanie he wore up his forehead a bit.

"We're not *anything*," she countered, glaring at him.

"We'll see about that." He chuckled under his breath.

Watching those two argue was like watching a really competitive tennis match play out. "Will you guys shut up?" I snapped.

"Finally!" Jude tossed his hands dramatically in the air. "She speaks!"

I rolled my eyes. "I'm not mute," I muttered.

"What's going on with you?" Tatum asked, her lips turning down in a frown. "You haven't been yourself for like two months now. I mean, it's not like you're normally a peppy person, but you're not normally this ... depressing, either."

"I've had a lot going on," I muttered, looking down at the book I should have been reading.

"Rowan," Tatum continued, "we're your friends." I wanted to laugh at how she reluctantly said, *we're*. She didn't like that Jude was my friend too and was hanging around all the time. "You can talk to us."

"There's nothing to talk about." I sighed. "Honestly."

"Did something happen with Trent?" she questioned, refusing to let up.

I flinched. Even hearing his name was painful. I hadn't heard from him since the day I left his apartment a month ago. I told him I loved him, and he did nothing. Not that I was expecting him to run after me, kiss me passionately, and take me back. I knew that was silly, but selfishly I had expected something. A call, a text, *something*. But I got a whole lot of nothing.

He didn't care about me.

Once he found out about Tristan, that shattered anything

we had or could've been. I'd known it would, but that didn't stop it from hurting.

"It did!" Tatum clapped her hands together.

"Why are you clapping?" Jude nudged her. "Obviously something bad happened, or she wouldn't be moping like this."

"Oh." Tatum's shoulders slumped. "Riiiiight."

I rolled my eyes and stood, packing up my books. "This has been … fun, but I'm going home."

"No, don't leave," Tate begged.

"It's late. I need to get home anyway," I muttered, heaving my heavy backpack onto one shoulder and then the other.

"I'll see you tomorrow then," Tatum said sadly.

I didn't reply. I needed to get out of there. I didn't want to hear or talk about Trent. I wanted to file all my memories of him in a box and only peek at it when I needed to be reminded of my love for him. I wasn't ready for that yet. For now, it was easier to pretend he didn't exist.

I got in my car, letting out a shaky breath.

I missed him.

It killed me to admit that to myself, but I did.

I missed his smile. His laugh. His warmth. Everything.

I needed to move on, though. I couldn't live in the past forever, and that's all he was to me.

I knew I would never love anyone else, and I couldn't see myself with another man, but I needed to move on in some way. It would help if I could focus on school and the kids, but it was impossible. No matter how hard I tried, I couldn't block Trenton from my thoughts. Thoughts of him always popped up when I least expected it.

I drove home, keeping the radio silent. I couldn't remember the last time I listened to music, because even a song could trigger a painful memory that I was trying so desperately to avoid.

When I stopped in the driveway, the house was dark, the only light was the one shining in the kids' bedroom window.

I grabbed my backpack, locking my car.

I stepped inside the house and found Ivy and Tristan waiting for me. They stood in the darkened living room by the door, waiting for me.

"Uh ... what's going on?" I asked, easing the door closed. I was irked by their strange behavior.

"Mom's cold," Ivy whispered.

"What do you mean?" I asked, fumbling through the dark for a light.

"She's cold," Ivy repeated. "I think she's sick. She won't wake up."

Oh, shit.

I finally got the light on and rushed over to the couch my mom always occupied. Ivy was right, she was cold. Too cold. Her skin had turned an icky blue-gray color and her eyes were closed, giving the impression that she was sleeping. I knew better, though. It didn't take any medical training to figure out that she was dead. I still felt for a pulse, but no fluttering met my fingers.

"Ivy, bring me my phone." I kept my tone as calm as I could. "It's in my purse."

"Is sumfing wrong wif Mommy?" Tristan asked, his words unrecognizable from his tears.

"She's not feeling well," I explained, not sure how to tell him that she was dead.

Ivy handed me my phone. I dialed 911 and pressed the phone to my ear. "Ivy," I took the girl into my arms, hugging her as I spoke, "I want you to take Tristan to your room and play for a little while, okay?"

She nodded. "She's dead, isn't she?" Ivy whispered in my ear.

I nodded. There was no point in lying to her.

She reached her hand out for Tristan's and spoke to him sweetly as she coaxed him out of the room.

"911, what is your emergency?"

"Uh ..." What the heck was I supposed to say?

"Ma'am, what's your emergency?" the operator asked again.

"I, uh, my mom, she's dead. An overdose, I think," I muttered, feeling so exhausted.

And shouldn't I have been sad? Or remorseful? *Something*? The woman who was my mom was *dead* and I didn't even feel like crying. I'd stopped caring about her a long time ago and after everything she'd done to me I felt nothing but relief at her passing.

"What's your address?"

I rattled it off.

"I'm sending an ambulance and a police officer to your house. They should be there in ten minutes," the woman said.

"Okay," I said slowly, my voice sounding as dead as the woman lying on the couch. I was in shock.

I hung up the phone, dropping it to the ground and crawling across the floor to the other side of the room where I sat with my legs drawn up to my chest and my arms wrapped around them.

One, two, three, four, five, six, seven, eight, nine, ten.

I couldn't take my eyes off her body slumped on the couch. Empty bottles lay beside her.

She could no longer be a pain in my ass, or smack me around, or hold those wretched legal papers over my head. I was free to tell Tristan that he was my son, but at his age, was that the right thing to do? Was he ready for the truth? I didn't think I could live with this secret anymore, and now that she was gone, I didn't have to.

"Row?"

I looked up to see Tristan standing beside the couch with Ivy behind him, looking from my mom to me.

"We heard the sirens," Ivy whispered, like she was afraid I'd be mad they left the room.

I shook my head, slowly coming to my feet.

Sirens?

I forced myself to focus, and I could indeed hear sirens in the distance.

"I need you guys to stay in the bedroom," I slowly came to my feet. "Wait there for me, okay?"

Tristan ran forward, wrapping his arms around my leg. "I don't want to leave you, Row."

I squatted down so I was at his eye-level. "I know you don't, but I need you to be a big boy and do this for me." I ran my fingers through his sandy hair. "Can you be a big boy?"

After a minute, he reluctantly nodded.

"Good." I kissed his cheek, steering him back to Ivy.

They went back to their bedroom and I heard the door shut.

At that moment, there was a knock on the door, announcing the presence of the paramedics and police.

I opened the door, letting them inside.

It didn't take the paramedics long to pronounce her dead.

The police came inside, looking around, and asking me

questions. I knew it was all standard procedure, but it still bugged me. I wasn't a criminal, and I most certainly wasn't a murder, so I didn't see why they thought they needed to interview me.

When they finally finished their questioning, it was beyond late. I wanted nothing more than to get in the bed and be done with this day. I was still numb to the fact that I'd come home to find my mom dead. It didn't seem real, and I felt like a despicable person for being happy that she was gone. She had done horrible things to me, and I didn't have an ounce of love or even gratitude for the woman. She'd destroyed every good thing I had in life.

"We're going to have an autopsy done," the police officer said, heading for the door. "We shouldn't rule out foul play yet."

In other words, I was a suspect and I shouldn't leave the state. Good to know.

I nodded. "Okay," I forced the word out of my mouth as the two officers descended the front steps. I closed the door, locking it.

I turned around, my back against the door, and bile rose in my throat. I couldn't take my eyes off the couch where she had died. I ran for the bathroom, collapsing in front of the toilet as I emptied my stomach contents into it. I heaved, unable to breathe, and tears stung my eyes.

I flushed the toilet and leaned against the sink, needing the support as I brushed my teeth, and then splashed my face with cold water.

I needed to get out of this place and find somewhere for us to live. We couldn't stay here. *I* couldn't stay here. It already held so many unpleasant memories, and knowing she had *died* here freaked me out even more. But it was close to midnight now, so there was no way I could find us a place to rent this late, and a hotel was too expensive. I didn't have class tomorrow, but I did have to work. Maybe Trace would let me off early to go house hunting. I didn't think he'd mind, especially once I informed him of the situation.

I grabbed a hand towel, using it to dry my face. I looked in the mirror and found my eyes bloodshot, my hair hanging limply, and my face gaunt. I didn't look good at all. The police officers probably thought I was a drug addict and killed my mother for some dumb ass reason.

It wasn't drugs that had made me this way.

It was my broken heart, because I'd been foolish enough to fall in love.

I'd never make that mistake again.

I laid the towel aside and walked across the hall to the kids' room.

I opened the door and they both barreled into my chest.

I wrapped my arms around them, holding on tightly, and wondering how someone couldn't love their child.

I hadn't believed it was possible to fall *in* love, but I had always loved my sister and son. It was a different kind of love than what I felt for Trenton, but nonetheless, it was love.

"What's going on?" Tristan asked. "Tell me, Row!" he cried, tears streaming down his cheeks and dripping off his chin.

I took his small face between my hands. "Tristan," I whispered his name, "Mom's dead."

His little face crumpled and he squeezed his arms tightly around my neck. "Does this mean you're our mommy now?" he asked, his tears soaking my shirt.

I kept quiet, because I didn't know what to say.

"Can we sleep in your bed tonight, Row?" Ivy asked. "I don't want to sleep by myself," she whispered.

"Of course," I replied, my eyes connecting with hers as I hugged Tristan.

They were both already in their pajamas so I fixed them in bed and set about fixing them something to eat. I wasn't hungry after everything that had happened tonight, and they probably weren't, either, but I wanted them to at least try to eat.

I found some microwave chicken nuggets and the fries you bake in the oven. It would do in a pinch.

As the food cooked, I carried bottles of water back to my room.

I smiled when I saw Ivy speaking to Tristan, her arm draped protectively over his shoulder.

I wanted so desperately to tell Tristan that I was his mom, but I wasn't sure that was the best thing. Would it be better to let him be older before I told him? Or was now okay? There wasn't a proper procedure for this, and I felt so clueless. I wanted someone to tell me what to do. I was sick and tired of always being the person that had to figure things out.

Their food finished cooking and I fixed them plates. It smelled good, and I found my stomach rumbling, so what was left I put on a third plate for myself.

"We're having a picnic in Row's bed!" Tristan clapped his hands.

I laughed, shaking my head.

The horror of our mom having been dead in the living room had already left Tristan. The woman had been awful, and children processed things differently than adults.

I didn't have a TV in my room, so the three of us sat lined

up in my bed eating our food and filled the silence with our chatter.

Since the ambulance and police officers left, a weight had been lifted off my shoulders. I didn't have to lie or worry about pissing off my mom anymore. I was beginning to feel the first inkling of freedom and I wanted to grasp onto it and never let it go. I wouldn't be imprisoned any longer.

"What's going to happen to us, Row?" Ivy whispered once the lights were off and we'd laid down to go to sleep. "Are they going to take us away from you?"

I reached over Tristan's body, since he was snuggled between us, and grasped Ivy's hand. "I will *never* let anyone take you guys from me," I spoke fiercely. "I promise."

"I love you," she sniffled, and I knew she was crying.

"I love you too."

CHAPTER NINETEEN

After I took the kids to school, I packed up everything that belonged to us—which wasn't much. I had no plans of sleeping there tonight. I knew it would be pretty much impossible to find a place to rent on such short notice, but if it came to it, I knew Colleen would be happy to let us stay with her. My grandparents lived too far away for them to be an option, because of Tristan and Ivy being in school.

I packed what I could into my car, having to leave some things behind because there wasn't room. Once I found a place to stay it would only take one more trip back here to have everything.

Even though I'd showered, I felt dirty from having been in that house. Its nastiness clung to me and I wanted it off—but that wouldn't happen until I was gone and never had to come back.

I was thankful that I only had to work today and didn't have classes. I didn't need the added stress on top of what I already had to deal with.

My mom was dead—this lone thought played on repeat in my mind.

I think a part of me was still shocked.

I'd believed someone as vile and despicable as her would never die. I felt like she'd stick around, always reminding me of my sins, and what I lost.

But she was gone, and I was free of my binds. I could be Tristan's mother. I didn't have to lie, or disappear from his life when it became unacceptable for me to be there if he believed I was merely his sister.

Now that Trenton knew the truth, and Tristan would know soon, I felt ... at peace.

The moment I signed those damn papers, I lost my freedom. Now, thanks to a stroke of luck, I had it back. I had been stuck in a prison for so long, that I didn't know what to do with myself. I didn't have to work so hard now, and hide money, because I didn't have to fight for custody.

Everything was falling into place for me.

Well, almost everything.

I had lost Trenton, and I was never getting him back, so there would always be damage to my heart.

That was okay, though, because I no longer had to live a lie. The truth was out there and I didn't have to hide behind the story I'd been coerced into telling.

It didn't take me long to get to work. Trace was already there, his boots sticking out from beneath the car he was working on.

I inhaled the scent of motor oil—something that had become familiar to me in the short time I had been working here.

"Can I ask you something?" My voice was hesitant as I stopped beside the car.

"Sure." He slid out, scaring me half to death with how quickly he did it. "What's up?" He grinned, running his fingers through his unruly hair. Trace was always so ... unusually peppy. Did the guy ever get mad?

"My mom died last night," the words slipped from my mouth. That was *not* what I'd been planning to say.

"Oh, I'm sorry." He jumped up, his arms winding around me before I knew what he was doing. I couldn't make myself hug him back, I was so in shock by the gesture.

"Don't be sorry," I muttered. "Seriously." I stared at the ground, frowning.

"Oh ...," he paused. "Was she ... not a good mom?"

I laughed at his awkward question. "You could say that."

"Do you need the day off?" he asked. "You could've called me. You didn't need to come in."

"I know." I shrugged, still looking at the ground. "I wanted to come in, though. Work will help take my mind off things." I forced a smile. "I was wondering if I could leave early? I need to find a place for us to live. I can't stay in that house."

Trace's eyes filled with sympathy and compassion. "Of course," he told me without any hesitation. "Wait ...," he paused and for a moment I thought he had changed his mind and my stomach dipped with worry. "I might have a solution to your problem."

"Really?" I was a bit afraid as to what his solution was.

There was no way I was staying with his mom and grandma at the mansion or at Trent's townhouse. Even if he was away at school that would be beyond awkward.

"Follow me." He stepped around me, striding out of the garage. He didn't look back to see if I was coming, he knew I would.

He led me around the side of the building and up a set of steps to the floor above the shop. I didn't know what was up here and never bothered to ask. He dug a key out of his pocket and opened the door.

He reached inside, flicking a light on, then reached out and grabbed my arm to yank me inside. I stumbled, and he tightened his hold so that I didn't fall.

It was a small apartment. The kitchen was surprisingly nice and clean. I saw a bedroom and a bathroom to my right and the living room was straight ahead.

"You guys can stay here," he beamed, his hands resting on his hips. "I know there's only one bedroom, but for a temporary thing, it'll work. I can get some bunk beds for your sister and Tristan, and they can go here." He pointed to the space where a dining table had probably once sat. "This is where I used to live." He smiled, looking around the place with a fond look in his eyes. "I like it. Once Olivia got pregnant, it wasn't suitable for a newborn."

"How much?" I asked.

"Huh?" His brows furrowed together. "What do you mean?"

"How much do you want to rent it out for?" I clarified.

He looked at me like I had lost my mind. "I don't want anything."

"Trace," I groaned, knowing I was going to have to fight

him on this. "I have to pay you something. I won't feel right if I don't."

"Rowan," he said my name slowly, staring me down with unwavering green eyes, "this place is sitting here empty and I'm not making any money off of it. You're not paying me."

"I have to pay you," I whispered, crossing my arms over my chest. "I won't feel right if I don't. You already let me keep my job, and after everything that's happened with your brother, I won't feel right if I don't."

He shook his head back and forth forcibly, like a child would. "Nope." He popped the 'p' as he rocked back on his heels.

"Well," I said as I turned to leave, "I'll find somewhere else."

"Wait!" He reached out, grabbing my arm. "Tristan is my nephew, please let me help." His eyes pleaded with me to give in. "I want to know that you're all safe. Not just him, but you and your sister too."

When he put it that way I didn't see how I could say no. I'd been forced to keep Tristan from him and his family long enough. I didn't need to do it anymore.

"Fine," I relinquished. "But if you change your mind and want me to pay, just say so."

"I won't change my mind." He winked, tossing his arm over my shoulders like we were old friends as we walked out the door. "Luca will be here any minute. I'll leave him here, and we'll get your things packed and moved in."

"I already packed everything," I admitted, shrugging off his arm as I descended the steps. "Most of it's already in my car, I couldn't fit everything, but there's not a lot left."

It was really quite sad how little the three of us had.

"Cool." He rubbed his hands together. "We'll get your car unloaded and you can go get the rest of your stuff."

"Thank you," I told him, finally allowing myself to sigh in relief. I had a place to stay with the kids. We didn't have to spend one more night in that house that haunted me. We could start over new.

"You don't ever need to thank me." He smiled, walking toward my parked car.

"Yes, I do, believe me," I muttered under my breath. Trace didn't understand how much his simple acts of kindness had meant to me. "It's unlocked," I told him, since he stood by my car waiting. I hadn't bothered to lock the piece of junk when I arrived at work.

He opened the back door, grabbing one of the clear plastic bins I'd used to pack our stuff. I hadn't had boxes and I'd gotten crafty.

"These are heavy," he said, unnecessarily, seeing as how I'd loaded them in the car and knew what they weighed, "so let me carry them. It's a long way to the apartment."

He was right, but I hated being useless. As soon as his back was turned, I grabbed one.

I knew I wouldn't make it up the steps without dropping it and spilling the contents, so I left it at the bottom of the steps. At least he wouldn't have to walk as far with it. That counted for something.

I unloaded the rest and found Trace waiting for me, staring at the bins as he shook his head. "Didn't I tell you not to help?" He eyed me, a smile playing on his lips—lips so similar to the ones I missed.

I forced a smile, tucking my hair behind my ears. "I'm not the type to sit back and not do anything. I have to help."

"I've figured that out." He laughed, wetting his lips. "I'll get these brought inside, why don't you head home and get the rest?"

"I can do it later." I shoved my hands in my back pockets. "I need to work."

He shook his head, his dark hair falling into his eyes. "Take today off. Get your stuff, come back, unpack, and get yourself settled. Make a home for my nephew."

How could I argue with that? The man knew how to guilt trip me.

I nodded. "I won't be long."

"Take your time." He shrugged, tapping his fingers on the stair railing. "We'll be fine here."

I didn't reply. I was overwhelmed by Trace's generosity, especially considering I'd kept Tristan a secret. Trace was an understanding guy, though. He didn't hold grudges.

I wished Trenton were the same way.

I didn't expect, or deserve, forgiveness for what I had done. Still, I would've loved to hear from him, something ... *anything*. Hell, I would have been happy with an angry phone call at this point. I wanted him to acknowledge my existence. Selfish, I know, considering what I had done. But love made you that way. Even if the other person hated you, you still wanted them.

I PACKED up the last of our things. Jim wasn't home, and I had no idea where he was, nor did I care. He was a piece of shit, and I was glad I could be rid of him and my mom. This was my chance at a clean slate. A new Rowan Sinclair was emerging.

I didn't have to lie and deceive anymore—and that was a really good feeling.

I loaded the last of our things up and didn't bother looking back at the house as I left. I was closing this chapter on my life, and starting a whole new one. I only hoped it got better.

"THIS IS OUR NEW HOME?" Tristan asked as I opened the door to the apartment. He clutched his stuffed dinosaur tightly in his hand, his eyes taking in the new space.

Ivy looked around, much the same way, a Barbie doll dangling from her fingers.

After everything that had happened last night, I'd decided to indulge and taken them to Target to get a new toy and then out to dinner at a nice restaurant.

"Yep, this is our new home."

I gasped when I spotted the bunk bed. Trace hadn't been kidding.

Tears pricked my eyes at his kindness. While I'd been gone, he'd bought a bed and put it together for the kids. Wow. To say I was touched didn't even cover the way I felt.

"Are those for us?" Tristan's eyes lit up when he spotted the bunk bed. He danced excitedly on the balls of his feet as he pointed at it.

I smiled. "It sure is."

Tristan giggled, running for the bed. "I get the top!" he shrieked.

I knew Ivy would want the bottom bunk anyway, since she was afraid of heights.

I set the groceries I'd picked up on the counter and then began un-bagging them. I hadn't gotten much, so it didn't take me long to put everything away.

Once the food was in its proper place I scoured the bins for the kids' bedding. I finally found it—in the last bin I checked—and forced them to vacate the bed.

Tristan pouted, upset at being evicted from his new favorite place.

"Don't you want your sheets on the bed?" I asked when he kept staring at me with mopey eyes as I made Ivy's bed.

He nodded. "I guess so." His fingers tightened around his stuffed green and orange dinosaur.

My breath caught for a moment as I looked at him. I so desperately wanted to tell him the truth—so why not tonight? What difference would waiting make? It wasn't like the woman he believed was his mom had ever acted as such. I was scared to tell him though. He was a child, and they could be so incredibly fragile. I didn't want to cause him pain. I had only ever wanted to protect him, which had led to the adoption in the first place. That had been a major screw-up, so I didn't want the same thing to happen again. I felt that waiting until he was older would only bring more heartbreak. There had been enough lies, and I'd carried them for so long. I was ending this tonight.

The new Rowan Sinclair wasn't going to keep quiet.

I finished making their beds and turned on the TV that had been left in the apartment from when Trace lived here. There was also a couch, and a bed was in the bedroom. Everything else had been cleared away.

As soon as I sat down, Ivy cuddled against one side, and Tristan burrowed against my other. I guessed playing on his new bunk bed wasn't a priority anymore.

I ran my fingers through his light hair and kissed the top of his head. I loved him so much—and that love had led me to make the worst decision of my life. I'd thought I was doing the right thing.

"Tristan." I swallowed thickly as his blue eyes—Trent's eyes—raised to meet mine. "There's something I need to tell you," I whispered, my voice cracking as I spoke. God, this was hard.

Ivy sat up too, watching me curiously. She knew from my tone that I had something important to say.

I didn't know quite how to approach this. Shit. I should've Googled this or read a book about it. I was sorely unprepared to have this profound conversation with my son.

Finally, I reached out, lovingly stroking his cheek. "A long time ago, I had a baby." I took a deep breath, closing my eyes. "A baby boy."

"You had a baby?" Ivy gasped.

"Baby? Where?" Tristan looked over his shoulder like one was magically going to appear.

"Here." I tapped his chest.

"The baby's inside me?" His light brows wrinkled together, looking like a fuzzy caterpillar.

"No, silly." I couldn't help but laugh. "You're the baby."

"I'm the baby? I'm not a baby, Row." He shook his head in disgust that I would suggest such a thing.

"Not now, but once you were a baby. My baby. I carried you in my tummy." I touched my stomach.

Tristan reached out, his little fingers touching my now flat stomach through the soft cotton of my shirt. "I was in there?" He tilted his head.

"Mhmm." I nodded. "I was a kid myself," I continued, brushing his hair out of his eyes, "and didn't think I could take care of you. So, my mommy became your mommy. She adopted you."

"Huh?" he questioned.

I shook my head. At his age, there was no need to go into detail. He wouldn't understand.

"What I'm trying to say, Tristan, is that *I'm* your mommy." I couldn't hold back my sob. When had I turned into such a blubbering mess? I didn't like this new development.

Tristan grinned, showcasing his slightly crooked little white teeth. "I always knew you were my real mommy." He surprised me by flying at me with open arms. I wrapped mine around him, holding on tight. I never wanted to let him go. I wanted to cling to him forever.

"Does this mean you're my mommy too?" Ivy's soft voice spoke up.

I looked over at her, not releasing my son, and found her crying little sniffling tears.

I frowned, wanting to cry harder for my sister. "No, sweetie."

Her face crumpled. "I want you to be my mommy too!"

I let go of Tristan with one hand, and wrapped it around her, pulling her in for a group hug. "I am, Ivy. In all the ways that count, I am your mom. It isn't blood that makes someone a mother, it's how they care about you." I dotted kisses all over the top of her head.

The three of us continued to cry, clinging to each other. I was glad Tristan knew the truth, that they both did. Now, it would be easy to move on ... I hoped.

Chapter Twenty

"Why do we have to go?" Tristan stomped his feet as I tried to fix him in his dress clothes.

I was losing my patience with him.

I had been trying to get him ready for my mom's funeral for the last twenty minutes and he was being impossible.

"Because, she's my mom and your grandma. It would be wrong not to go," I explained, trying to get his pants on but he was wiggling too much.

"She was mean! I don't want to go!"

"Tristan," I warned.

Somebody knocked on the door and Tristan scampered away, courtesy of my distraction.

I groaned, rising to my feet, and striding across the small apartment to see who was there.

I wasn't surprised to find Trace standing there in a pair of black slacks and a white button-down shirt.

"Hey." I ran my fingers through my hair to get the long strands out of my line of vision. "We're not quite ready yet," I pointed over my shoulder at the shrieking Tristan, who was running around in nothing but a pair of robot underwear.

"Uncle Trace!" he shrieked, running toward the door.

"Hey, buddy." Trace bent down, scooping Tristan into his arms. "Dude." He tickled my son's stomach. "Why are you naked?"

"I'm not naked, silly." Tristan giggled. "I've got my big boy underwear on."

"That you do." Trace laughed, walking into the apartment. "I wish Dean wore those."

"But Dean's a baby!" Tristan screamed exuberantly.

"I still wish he didn't poop himself," Trace groaned, spinning Tristan through the air before dropping him on the couch, much to the boy's delight.

"Mommy! Uncle Trace said poop!"

I dropped my head in my hands. I didn't think Trace showing up was going to help things.

"Yeah, yeah," Trace groaned, reaching for the clothes on the floor that I'd been trying to wrestle Tristan into wearing. "It's time to get you dressed."

"I don't wanna!" Tristan tried to climb over the back of the couch, but Trace grabbed him.

"You don't want to dress all fancy like me?" Trace asked him.

Tristan's lips pursed in thought as he studied his uncle. "Well, okay."

"That's what I thought." Trace chuckled, helping Tristan into his clothes.

I was already dressed and ready to go. So was Ivy.

She'd been struggling with the fact that I was really Tristan's mother, but not hers. Seeing as how I continued to treat them exactly the same as I did before the truth came out, she was coming around.

Trace finally got Tristan dressed and then we had to go.

After the coroner had performed an autopsy, they'd discovered my mom died from a lethal mix of alcohol and drugs. I had obviously been ruled out a suspect then—if I really had been one.

Trace's family was paying for her funeral since I couldn't afford it, and that pained me. I didn't want them feeling obligated to help me, especially with something like this, but I'd had no choice but to let them.

Outside, Olivia waited in their Land Rover, waving enthusiastically when she saw us leaving the apartment. I saw Dean in the back, banging his hand against the window and leaving smudged prints.

"Thanks for doing this," I whispered to Trace, "and thanks for coming here so we don't have to go alone."

"We're here for you." Trace pulled me into a hug when we reached the end of the steps. "We're your family. Don't ever doubt that."

"I don't know what I'd do without you," I confessed.

Ever since things blew up with Trent and then again with my mom, Trace had become my savior. He looked out for the kids and me. It meant a lot to me—more than I could express, especially since I wasn't the type to appreciate help. Trace had a way about him that made it so you couldn't help but like him. I could see why Olivia fell for him.

"We'll see you there." Trace smiled, getting in the Land Rover.

I buckled Tristan into his booster seat and Ivy climbed into the spot beside him, buckling her seatbelt.

I closed the back passenger door and stood outside for a moment. I inhaled the fresh spring hair, thankful that this late March weather was surprisingly warm. I needed that warmth on a day like today to blanket me in comfort.

One, two, three, four, five, six, seven, eight, nine, ten.

I could do this.

There was nothing to be afraid of.

We were burying her today.

That was it.

Nothing bad was going to happen.

She was gone.

It was over.

It was over; I repeated the thought. I wanted to cry out with joy. Today truly did mark the first day of the rest of my life.

I got in the car, smiling at Tristan and Ivy as I looked back at them in the rearview mirror.

"Everything is going to be okay," I whispered. "I promise."

Ivy smiled. "I know."

I spoke to the kids about random things as I drove to the cemetery. I wanted to distract them from what we were about to face. They'd never had to deal with death before, and while neither of them missed the woman we'd all once called mom, I knew it would be a difficult experience full of curious questions. I hoped I was prepared.

I parked behind Trace's Land Rover and walked with the kids across the cemetery lawn to where I knew the casket would be waiting.

Trace and Olivia were already there. I was shocked to see Ellie, Trent and Trace's grandma, as well as their mom, Lily.

Lily held a squirming Dean, while Trace and Olivia stood a few feet away. I couldn't help but smile as I watched Trace stare at his wife lovingly, his fingers stroking her small baby bump.

I was touched by the gesture of them all being there. Trace was right. They were my family, and I needed to stop acting like an outsider. Tristan would forever be a part of their lives, which meant I would be too.

My mouth fell open as disgust clogged my throat. Jim was there, dressed in stained black pants and a white t-shirt. There was nothing remotely nice about what he wore—not that it mattered, but I couldn't believe he was daring to show his face here after what he'd tried to do to me. Besides, I didn't think he'd ever loved my mom. They'd both used each other for different reasons, reasons I didn't want to even contemplate.

As I met the group, I refused to look at or acknowledge Jim. He was scum and didn't deserve my time. Just looking at him was giving me the creeps. After today I'd never have to see the man again.

I took my seat, which was unfortunately beside Jim, and settled the kids.

The others sat down in the chairs behind us.

I heard voices, and for a brief moment hope sparked and I believed that Trent had heard about my mom and shown up. It wasn't him, though. It was Jude and Tatum, making their way through the dewy grass. Tatum's shoe got stuck and Jude grabbed ahold of her arm to keep her from falling. She leveled him with a glare, shouting something about not needing his help. Those two were ridiculous.

"I'm glad you guys are here," I stood to greet them, hugging each of them. I was overcome with a feeling of ... completeness. Trace and Olivia were there, as were Ellie and Lily, and now with Jude and Tatum joining us, I realized that I wasn't as alone as I'd always believed. I'd been so blinded by my mom's hatred for me, that I didn't think anyone else could ever care for me. I was wrong though.

After about ten minutes, my grandparents arrived, and it was time to get the short ceremony underway.

It didn't take long. There wasn't much to be said, and I couldn't bring myself to tell lies for the sake of not speaking ill of the dead. The woman lying in that casket might have birthed me, but she was nothing to me. You have to earn love, and she'd never bothered to try. I'd been nothing but a hindrance to her, and then Tristan had become a way for her to trap and guilt me. She couldn't do that anymore. It was harsh to say, but she'd gotten what was coming for her.

We stood to place flowers on her casket one at a time.

"Mommy." Tristan tugged on the skirt of my dress. It warmed my heart that he'd had no hesitation in calling me Mom instead of Row once I told him the truth. The little boy hadn't even batted an eye.

"What is it, baby?" I asked, looking down at him.

"That man keeps staring at me." He pointed toward a tree behind us, enough distance away that it was difficult to see, but there was no mistaking that form. My mouth parted with a gasp.

Trenton.

He knew and he was there.

I dared to hope that a part of him still cared for me. In reality, though, he was probably only there because of Tristan.

"It's okay." I smiled at Tristan. "That's your daddy."

Tristan's blue eyes widened with surprise. "That's my daddy?" he echoed my words back to me.

"Yes," my voice was soft as I played with the silky strands of his nearly blond hair.

"Wow," Tristan gasped.

It was time for me to place my flower on the casket, so our conversation was cut short.

When I stepped back in front of my chair I gasped as Jim's hand found my butt. That dirty fucker—

Trace cleared his throat, placing his hand on Jim's shoulder. "Take your hand off of her *now*." His tone spoke of dire consequences if Jim didn't comply.

Jim's hand dropped from my butt and he stared ahead as if nothing had ever happened.

When I looked back to where Trent had been standing, I saw his form retreating, his head bowed.

I guessed he couldn't stand to look at me any longer.

I had to be okay, though. I'd known this would happen and now that the truth was out there, there was nothing I could do. He knew of Tristan and he knew I loved him. I couldn't keep fighting for something that was never going to happen. It was pointless.

"Mommy?" Tristan asked. "Where'd the man go? I thought you said he was my daddy? Doesn't he want to say hi to me?"

Tristan's words broke my already shattered heart into pieces that more closely resembled dust than shards.

I bent so I was at his level—I always hated towering above him when I spoke.

"I know he wants to say hi to you but he can't right now. Okay?"

Tristan nodded. "Is he going to live with us?"

"No, sweetie." I kissed his forehead. "He's not. One day, when you're older, you'll understand this better."

Tristan tilted his head, shrugging his small shoulders and that was that. Kids could let things roll off them better than adults could. They didn't understand the harsh sting of rejection.

"Come on, Tristan." Trace reached for the boy. "Want a piggyback ride?"

"Yay!" Tristan shrieked in delight as Trace hoisted him onto his back. It should have been Trent doing that, not Trace, but I was still thankful for the gesture.

Ivy's hand clasped in mine and I glanced down at her. She looked so much older than an eight-year-old, more like a teenager. Her light hair was long, curling down her back, and her hazel eyes were wide and expressive. She looked like a miniature version of me. I knew we both had different dads—like mine, hers hadn't stuck around—so we both inherited our looks from our mom. I had seen pictures of my mom when she was younger, and she had been beautiful, but her attitude and lifestyle had turned her into an ugly person.

Trace ran toward the cars, with Tristan's arms wrapped around his neck in a stranglehold. Tristan's giggle carried back to us with the breeze. It made me smile watching Tristan interact with his uncle.

Ivy peered up at me as we walked along. Olivia was beside us with Dean propped on her hip.

Ivy didn't say anything, but I could tell she was thinking really hard about something. She was a lot like me in that way. We were both deep thinkers who rarely spoke our thoughts out loud.

She stopped walking and I halted with her. She bit her lip,

looking around, and I knew she was nervous to ask whatever was on her mind.

"What is it, Ivy?" I prodded. "You can ask me anything, you know that."

She nodded, but still didn't say anything. After a moment of thought, she looked up at me. "Are you really going to be able to keep me?" she squeaked. "Tristan's your kid, but I'm not." She frowned. "I don't want them to take me away from you." Tears pricked her hazel eyes. "I don't want to be a foster kid."

"Oh, Ivy." I crushed her to my chest. "I will never let anyone take you from me," I vowed.

I knew the night my mom died that this was a thought weighing heavily on Ivy's mind.

"You have nothing to worry about," I assured her, smoothing my fingers through her soft hair.

She nodded, but the look in her eyes told me she didn't quite believe me.

That was okay, though, because soon enough I'd be able to prove her wrong. I wasn't going to let anyone take the kids from me—not that I thought they'd try. I was an adult, I had a roof over their heads, and I made enough money to support them. The court had no reason to find someone more suitable.

Trace unwound Tristan's arms from around his neck and lowered the little boy to the ground.

Tristan ran to me, jumping up and down excitedly, asking if he could ride in Trace's car. He was completely unaffected by the fact that we'd just been by the side of a dead person.

"Uh …" I looked up at Trace.

"It's fine." He grinned crookedly. "Why don't we all head to my mom's place for an early dinner? Your grandparents, Jude, and Tatum can come too." He leaned against the side of his large black SUV with his arms crossed over his chest.

I thought it over for a moment. I hated to be a burden, but I really didn't want to be alone right now. Besides, he'd extended an invitation.

"Sure," I replied.

"Yay!" Tristan shrieked, running into his uncle's arms.

It amazed me how quickly Tristan had embraced Trace—but at his age, the kid never met a stranger.

I removed Tristan's booster seat from the car and put it in Trace's. I buckled him in while Trace tended to Dean. Ivy had already gotten in my car. I let Jude and Tatum know what we were doing and that they were welcome to join us. They both seemed unsure if they should or not. They knew the truth about Tristan now. Neither had said much to me about it, but I knew it shocked them.

My grandparents had been stunned when I told them the truth about Tristan. I noticed they'd already left. I knew they were hurt that I hadn't confided in them about my son and how horrible my mom was. They'd been relatively clueless to her actions. They'd known she drank, but not that she hit me.

As I sat behind the driver's seat and prepared to leave, my eyes landed on the parking lot across form the funeral home. A very familiar black car was parked there and a shiver ran up my spine. Even though he was so far away, and I couldn't see him through the tinted windows, I felt his eyes on me. It was like his gaze alone was a caress.

"Row, they're leaving," Ivy warned, snapping me back to reality.

I put the car in drive, following Trace's large black SUV so that I didn't get lost on the way to the mansion. My body hummed with a nervous energy, wondering if Trent would show up. A part of me hoped he did, and another part hoped he didn't. I wasn't ready to face him yet, after I told him I loved him and he did nothing. In fact, I didn't think I'd ever be ready to face him. I felt like everything had been said between us and there was nothing left.

"You look sad," Ivy remarked from the backseat. "Is it because of Mom?"

"No," I answered, probably too quickly considering it was my mom who was dead and I should feel a tiny bit remorseful.

"Then what is it?" she asked.

Ivy was far too observant for her own good.

"It's nothing," I replied. I didn't need to go into details with her of the fucked-up-ness of my life.

Ivy's plump pink lips turned down in a frown and her fingers clasped together as I watched her briefly from the rearview mirror. Her gaze left me and she propped her head on one hand as she looked out the window. I knew she was mad that I wasn't telling her what was wrong with me. But she was eight years old. It wasn't that I didn't want to tell her, but more my need to keep her a child. I'd had to grow up fast, and I didn't want the same fate for her. Unfortunately, I was afraid it had already happened.

Unless you've experienced it, you didn't understand what growing up in a household like ours did to a person. You constantly had to live in fear of doing or saying the wrong thing. My mother—as far as I knew—had never laid a hand on Ivy or Tristan, but she had hit me in front of them on more than one occasion. If I had left, what would have stopped her from taking her anger out on one of them?

When we turned down the narrow drive that led to the mansion Ivy sat up straighter. "Where are we?"

"This is where Trace and his brother grew up," I answered.

"Why don't you ever say his brother's name?" she commented, peering around the seat at me. "Is it because he's Tristan's dad?"

Since Trace was constantly hanging around, and wanted to be a part of Tristan's life, I'd been forced to tell both of the kids about Trenton. It had been hard, especially because Tristan didn't understand.

"You miss him, don't you?" she continued when I didn't answer.

I swallowed the sudden lump in my throat. "Yeah," I squeaked.

She nodded, tapping her fingers against the glass window. "Why don't you tell him that?"

"It's complicated," I ground out—not angry with her, but at myself, because I still cared.

"When you love someone, it shouldn't be that complicated." Her hazel eyes met mine in the rearview mirror.

Leave it to an eight-year-old to be wiser than most adults.

"Whoa!" She bounced excitedly in her seat as the mansion came into view. "This is a house?" she exclaimed, her eyes round with awe.

"Yeah," I replied, parking the car.

"It looks like something from a movie!"

I couldn't help laughing, but she was right. The large house didn't seem like it could possibly be real, and once you got inside, that seemed even truer. It was so easy to get lost in there.

As we followed the Wentworths inside, Tristan and Ivy both looked around with their mouths hanging open.

"Wow," Tristan gasped. "Can we live here?"

I laughed, ruffling his hair as we entered the foyer, heading for the dining room. "We have a home."

"I like this one more," he pouted.

"You can visit anytime you want," Trace piped in. "We have a pool ... Two, actually."

"Two pools?" Ivy exclaimed, then slapped her hand over her mouth. "Sorry," she muttered, looking nervously at the shiny floors. Ivy had been very shy around Trace and his family—she was a cautious person—so her outburst clearly embarrassed her.

"Yep!" Trace clapped his hands together, before pushing open the door to the dining room. "They're great!"

Ivy's smile was small as she tried to hide behind me. I think Trace's exuberance always frightened her. She wasn't used to someone like him.

We sat down at the table, and I wasn't surprised when Tristan stole the seat beside Trace. Tristan thought he was the most amazing person ever. If only he knew his dad. I doubted Trent was going to reach out to me, and with my mom out of the picture, I knew I should contact him and let him see Tristan. I was scared he had changed his mind and wanted nothing to do with our son. So, I hadn't done anything.

Someone I didn't recognize brought out a meal that had already been prepared in anticipation of our arrival. My eyes widened at the delicious looking grilled chicken sandwich. My stomach rumbled. I hadn't even realized I was hungry until food was set in front of me.

"This looks yummy." Ivy smiled shyly at the people seated around us.

"I hope you think it tastes as good as it looks." Lily smiled back.

It amazed me how Lily, Trent's mom, had embraced Ivy, Tristan, and me. I thought she'd hate me for what I did, but she never looked at me like it mattered. She was always nice and went out of her way to look after us. Despite the fact that Ivy was of no relation to her, she seemed to genuinely want to get to know her and make her feel comfortable. The Wentworths were truly the greatest people I had ever met. They didn't let their status affect them, and it was a beautiful thing to see.

I took a bite of the sandwich and my eyes closed. That had to be the greatest thing I had ever tasted. I wish I could cook that well.

"It's as good as it looks," Ivy said after she'd taken a bite, causing all of us to chuckle.

Her cheeks flamed pink and I bent my mouth to her ear to whisper, "It's okay, Ivy. You didn't say anything wrong. It was cute."

She nodded, but didn't speak again through the rest of the meal.

I kept waiting for Trenton to appear, but he never did. I wasn't sure whether I should be relieved or disappointed.

I guessed it didn't matter.

CHAPTER TWENTY-ONE

Hours later, I had Tristan and Ivy put to bed and was crawling into bed myself.

I was exhausted.

Attending the funeral and seeing Trent had really taken a toll on me. I'd tried not to show it, but now that I was alone, I let my face crumple. I didn't cry, but I did allow myself to hurt and that counted for something.

For so long I had kept my feelings on a tight leash, not allowing myself to feel any emotion. I had been dead inside. Like he had when we were teenagers, Trent had woken me up and broken down all my carefully constructed walls. He hadn't meant to, but he taught me it was okay to feel. We're human. It's okay to be happy, sad, or angry. It's a part of life. I had allowed my mom to make me into a drone—always going through the motions where nothing could hurt me. I had been wrong to let her do that, but it had been my coping mechanism. It would be easy, almost too easy, to allow myself to fall back into that destructive pattern of not feeling. I was fighting it though. I was trying really hard to let myself feel—to *hurt*.

I was realizing that emotions aren't a bad thing.

Passion isn't wrong.

What *is* wrong is when you let those feelings build up and you lash out. I always thought that if I let myself feel too much I'd end up like mother. I never wanted to hurt anyone the way she hurt me—her words more cutting than her fists.

I wanted to be a better person and this was me trying.

A VICIOUS POUNDING woke me up.

I came awake quickly, sleep slipping away like a loose blanket around my shoulders.

A quick glance at the clock told me it was after one in the morning. I had no clue what kind of crazy person could be at our door at this time of night. I grabbed my phone so I could dial 911 if I needed to.

Ivy and Tristan had been awakened by the noise and both looked at me blearily as they rubbed their eyes.

"What's that noise?" Tristan asked.

"Why's somebody at the door?" Ivy questioned, stifling a yawn.

"I don't know." I frowned. "Just stay there," I warned, holding my hand out in a gesture for her not to leave the bed, "and keep quiet."

I typed 911 into my phone and held my finger over the dial button. There was no peephole, so I would be forced to open the door to see who was there. I suddenly wished I had some pepper spray or a gun. I was utterly defenseless and at the mercy of the person on the other side of the door.

"Rowan! Open the door!"

I knew that voice.

I threw the door open. "Trace," I gasped as relief flooded my lungs at hearing his voice and then seeing him. "What are you doing here?"

"We have to go," he spoke quickly, his eyes darting around. "Get the kids, we have to go *now*." His body hummed with a nervous energy.

"What's going on?" I drilled him as he pushed past me into the apartment.

He ignored me. "Come on, kids." He reached for Tristan on the top bunk. "We have to go. Grab some toys. Rowan," he called to me, "you might want to get dressed."

"Where are you taking us?" I asked, panic lacing my tone. He was so frantic—not like Trace at all—and I couldn't begin to fathom why. He acted like the place was about to blow up or something.

He finally stopped, and that's when I saw the tears in his eyes.

"What's going on?" I repeated in a soft tone, backing away, my hands braced protectively in front of me. Something told me I wasn't going to like what he had to say.

"It's Trent," he sighed, his voice cracking.

"Is he okay?" I asked, my breath catching as my heart clenched painfully behind my ribcage. Oh, God, something bad had happened. I knew it. I could feel Trent slipping through my fingers like a fistful of sand.

"Get dressed and then we'll talk." He turned away from me, grabbing up some of the kids' toys.

I rushed into the bedroom, dressing as quickly as I could. I'm pretty sure my socks didn't even match. When I left the room, the apartment was empty. I rushed outside, my fingers fumbling as I locked the door.

Trace was waiting in the Land Rover, he tapped the horn, urging me to hurry.

I ran down the steps and into the empty passenger seat. Olivia wasn't with him.

"*Please*, tell me what's happened," I implored as I fumbled with the seatbelt. "It's bad, isn't it?"

He nodded, the muscle in his jaw visibly tightening. "He confronted your step-dad and he shot Trent."

"Oh, God." I hadn't expected Trace to be so blunt with what he said, but I should've known, that was Trace—no sugar-coating.

I doubled over, my stomach clenching painfully.

"I think I'm going to be sick," I mumbled, sweat breaking out across my forehead as bile rose in my throat. I had expected something like Trent had been in a car wreck, not that he'd been *shot*.

"It's not good," Trace continued, his body taut with tension, "my mom just got the call, so of course she called me, and I came to get you. He's been in surgery for several hours." He rubbed his stubbled jaw angrily.

"And they just now called you?" I gasped.

Trent, *my* Trent, he'd been alone this long, fighting for his life? That wasn't right!

Trace nodded. "He didn't have his phone on him, only his wallet, so it took them a while to track us down. Our numbers aren't exactly listed publicly."

"Is he going to make it through the surgery?" I forced the

words out of my mouth, terrified of the answer he might give me.

"Honestly?" Trace asked, his eyes venturing to mine before returning to the road ahead. "They said it was a fifty/fifty chance. The bullet barely missed a vital artery in his heart, and he's lost a lot of blood." Trace's breath turned shaky. "We'll know more once we get there."

In the back of the car, the kids were sniffling as they cried, but I couldn't make myself shower them in words of comfort.

I was numb once more, drowning in an ocean of pain and solitude. I was going to lose him—I already had, but this was worse, because this was forever.

Everything was a blur as we arrived at the emergency entrance of the hospital. I forced myself to stay calm and follow Trace.

Inside, he asked the information desk about his brother and they directed us to the correct floor—the intensive care unit. This was so fucking bad.

My hands shook with panic. I couldn't imagine a world in which Trenton Wentworth didn't exist. Thoughts of him consumed me—his smile, his laugh, the first time he over spoke with me, every memory flitted through my mind in rapid succession.

We rushed through the wide white halls, our shoes squeaking on the tile floors.

Ivy and Tristan each held onto my hands, as I all but dragged them along.

We burst through the set of double doors and into the main hallway of intensive care.

"Trace," his mom breathed in relief when she saw us. Her eyes were red and puffy from crying. She looked horrible, and that scared me. Had she gotten bad news? Was he gone? Were we too late?

I released the kids' hands and dashed into the bathroom I spotted to my right.

The door slammed closed behind me as I fell to my knees and emptied the contents of my stomach. Tears stung my eyes, one trailing down my cheek and under my chin.

I felt like my whole world was crumbling around me.

I'd always prided myself with being *okay*. I had always been able to cope with bad things, but this was something I wasn't prepared to handle.

I flushed the toilet and cleaned myself up, wiping my face free of tears. I kept making a strange stuttering gasping sound as I tried to hold back more tears. I couldn't fucking breathe. I clutched the fabric of my shirt in my hand as I forced myself to calm down.

One, two, three, four, five, six, seven, eight, nine, ten.

Calm down, Rowan, I warned myself. *You need to be strong.*

But the last thing I could be in this moment was strong. I'd thought I'd escaped the hold of my mother and Jim, but it had all been a façade. I could never escape them. Jim had managed to take away something that mattered dearly to me. Trent might not have liked me at all anymore, but I took comfort in knowing he was out there somewhere thriving. If he didn't make it through this ... I was pretty damn sure he'd take a piece of my soul with him.

I loved him. God, I loved him so much that it felt like my heart was being ripped out of my chest and stomped on.

I reached for more paper towels, drying my still damp face. I couldn't stop the tears. I knew I needed to get myself under control before I left the sanctuary of the restroom.

One, two, three, four, five, six, seven, eight, nine, ten.

I wasn't okay.

This wasn't okay.

Nothing about the fact that Trent was here, fighting for his life, was *okay*.

One, two, three, four, five, six, seven, eight, nine, ten.

I took deep breaths, inhaling in through my mouth and out through my nose. I needed to get my shit together and be strong. Breaking down like this wasn't going to help Trent.

I turned the water on, splashing the cool liquid onto my face.

My eyes were swollen and red from crying. I didn't care, though. I no longer saw tears as a sign of weakness but of strength.

I took a few more calming breaths to make sure I was ready to face this.

I opened the bathroom door and looked down the hall. Trace was waiting for me and he waved me forward. With my head bowed, like a child in trouble, I hesitantly stopped in front of him.

"The kids are with my mom." He pointed over his shoulder to the waiting room before continuing, "He's out of surgery now." Trace hesitated, his eyes filled with pain. I had only ever seen the guy happy and smiling, so seeing him like this was shocking. "He's not in the clear yet. There's still plenty that could go wrong."

"He's not going to make it, is he?" I forced myself to ask, my lower lip trembling.

"I don't think so," Trace's voice cracked and tears began to spill from his eyes. He looked up at the ceiling, clearly hating that I was seeing him break down like this.

I found myself stepping forward that last little bit and wrapping my arms around his torso. My ear was pressed against his chest where I could hear his heart racing with panic and anger at the thought of losing his brother. My tears soaked the fabric of his shirt as he lifted his arms to wrap them around me.

"This hurts so bad," I confessed, my voice thick from my tears. I sniffled, trying to hold them back, but it was pointless.

"I know it does," his voice shook. "I almost lost Olivia once, so I know exactly how you feel right now, and it's the worst feeling in the whole world."

I hadn't known that, but now wasn't the time to ask questions about Olivia and his past. Right now, our focus needed to be on Trent.

"I fucking hate this hospital," Trace groaned, his voice muffled by my hair.

"Why?" I asked.

"This is where they brought Olivia, then Gramps passed. Although, the stubborn old man made them release him so he could die at home." I felt Trace crack a small smile but it quickly crumbled. "And now Trent's here, fighting for his life. If it wasn't for the fact that Dean was born here," he said, pulling away and I let my arms drop to my sides, "this place would only hold bad memories for me."

"Your family has really bad luck," I remarked, trying to bring some light to the situation, but it was pointless. I knew we both felt like falling apart.

"Yeah, something like that," he muttered, glaring at the tiled floor.

We stood there a few moments longer before joining his mom and the kids in the waiting room. I felt like I didn't deserve to be there. After what I had done they should've hated me, not embraced me like family.

Tristan sat on Lily's lap and she talked to him, forcing a smile here and there for his benefit.

I settled into the uncomfortable plastic chair, figuring we'd be waiting awhile before we knew anything.

Trace took the seat beside me, resting his elbows on his knees with his head in his hands.

Ivy was seated in the other chair next to me and laid her head on my shoulder.

"It'll be okay, Row." She looked up at me with innocent hazel eyes. "Love conquers anything, right? Even death?"

God, I wished that was true.

I nodded for her benefit as I leaned my head back against the wall and closed my eyes. If I slept, maybe I could convince myself that this was all merely a nightmare.

HOURS LATER, with no sleep, a doctor finally appeared in the doorway.

"He's awake now if you'd like to see him."

The hesitation his voice destroyed what hope was left inside me. His tone said, *you might want to say your goodbyes now.*

"Mom and I will go first," Trace whispered, grasping the chair arms and using it to heave himself to his feet. He stretched his arms above his head, cracking his back. He reached for his mom, wrapping his arm around her shoulders as they followed the doctor.

Tristan crawled into my lap, burrowing his head under my

neck. "What's going on, Mommy?" He asked, lovingly stroking my hair. Even at five years old he could sense the tension in my body and was trying to relieve it.

"Trent—your dad—has been hurt," I whispered. It pained me to say those words.

"Is he going to be okay? Can I say hi?" Tristan looked up at me with wide eyes.

"I don't know," I answered, kissing the top of his head, his hair soft against my lips.

I wrapped my arms tightly around him, closing my eyes as I rested my head on top of his. All my regrets were piling on top of me in this moment and I felt like I was suffocating. Because of what I had done, Trent had missed out on being a part of Tristan's life, and now Tristan might never get to know his dad.

I had been horrible and selfish to make the decision I did without telling Trent. I had been so young and stupid. Now, I was suffering the consequences.

I should have been the one in there fighting for my life, not Trent.

I didn't want to lose him.

Even if he didn't belong to me, and I'd have to watch him love someone else eventually, I'd rather deal with that pain than this.

I hummed under my breath, rocking Tristan in my arms.

Tristan took a piece of my hair and twisted it around his finger. "It will be okay, Mommy," he whispered in his sweet voice.

"I hope so." I felt tears sting my eyes once more. I didn't know how someone could keep crying like this. Eventually you had to run out of tears, right?

Trace and his mom returned ten minutes later, their faces pale.

"He wants to talk to you," Trace said, his eyes refusing to meet mine.

My stomach rolled with nausea once more.

"I'll be right back," I told Tristan, lifting him off my lap. He went scampering up to Trace, asking him a bunch of questions. "Tristan," I warned, "leave Uncle Trace alone right now. He's upset. Maybe you could give him a hug and make him feel better?" I suggested, knowing Tristan would like it if I gave him a task to perform.

Tristan nodded, wrapping his arms around Trace's legs. Trace reached down and picked him up, and his cries pained me.

I wasn't sure I could do this.

If Trace was breaking down like this, things didn't bode well for me.

The doctor was waiting to lead me back. His face was grim, so I let my eyes follow the lines of the tile as he took me to Trent.

He opened a door and nodded his head for me to go inside.

One, two, three, four, five, six, seven, eight, nine, ten.

I breathed in through my nose and out through my mouth. I knew that once I got a look at Trent—at what was my fault—what was left of me would finally shatter completely.

I was that broken vase that kept being fixed in vain, only to topple off the table and break again. Eventually, the pieces grew too small to fit back together.

I took one step further into the room, then another, until I stood beside Trent's bed.

His eyes were closed and his skin was a sickish gray color.

Where the front of his hospital gown dipped down I saw a white bandage over his heart.

I bit down on my fist to stifle my sobs.

This was my fault.

All because of my stupid step-dad, I was going to lose the love of my life.

My body was so full of hate at that man, and myself, that I thought it might obliterate me.

Trent's eyes slowly blinked open and I wrapped my arms around myself so that I didn't try to touch him. He wasn't mine and I knew the last thing he wanted was for me to be here.

"Don't." He swallowed, wincing at the dryness in his throat. "Cry."

"I can't help it." I wiped the tears away, looking out the windows where the sun was beginning to come up. It pained me to see him lying there so... battered. Trent had always been full of life, and seeing that stripped away from him was heartbreaking. I had done nothing but ruin his life from the moment I entered it. He would've been better off if he'd never met me.

"L-Look at me," he stuttered.

Unable to deny him his request, I did.

We stared at each other, neither of us saying a word.

"Come. Here," he forced the words out, trying to scoot over to give me room in the bed.

"No." I grabbed his hand. "Don't hurt yourself."

His eyes closed with tiredness and his Adam's apple bobbed as he swallowed painfully. It tore me apart to see him hurt so badly. I felt so helpless. I had no idea what to do or say to make any of this better.

"I'm an idiot," he forced the words out.

"Because you got shot? Yeah, you're an idiot." I made myself laugh to lighten the situation.

"No." He shook his head, wincing in pain. "For letting you go."

My breath caught and I didn't know what to say.

"I should've gone after you that day." His forehead wrinkled with effort as he spoke.

"Trent," I pleaded, "don't talk. Please, don't strain yourself."

"I need to say this," he continued, his light blue eyes connecting with mine. They seemed so alert and alive—not like he was fighting for his life. He stared up at me and I couldn't help but feel like he was making some deathbed confession. "I love you, Rowan." He wet his lips. "I've tried so hard to hate you, but I can't. I fucking can't. Every time I close my eyes I see *you*." His hand gave mine a light squeeze, and it didn't escape me how weak his grasp was. "I see our son. I see the life we could have together. You're it for me, Row. I know we have a shit ton of problems to work out, but that's okay. We're a family."

"Trenton ..." I shook my head, tears pooling in my eyes. "You don't mean that. It's only the drugs talking." I knew he had to be on some major painkillers and they'd clearly made him loopy.

"It's not—" He winced in pain. "It's not the drugs. I was coming to see you tonight, but um ..." He looked down at his chest and the bandage winking at us. "I kinda got shot."

Only Trenton could crack jokes after a gunshot wound.

"Are you sure?" I whispered, daring to hope that he loved me enough that we could move past this, and letting myself believe he was going to be fine.

He nodded. "I've loved you since I was sixteen and nothing

can ever make me stop. Once you stole my heart, it belonged to you and only you."

"You're such a cheese ball." I cracked a smile—a genuine one as I remembered saying something similar to him months ago.

"That's me, I like cheese," he joked, smiling half-heartedly. "Now, since I got shot protecting your honor and all, I think you owe me."

"I'm not having sex with you in a hospital," I gasped, appalled that he'd suggest such a thing after everything he'd been through. "Especially after you just had surgery! You're not in the clear yet, Trent," my voice cracked painfully.

He rolled his eyes at me. "Who said anything about sex, Row? I'm tired, but I don't want you to go. Lay with me, please," he begged, and when he looked at me like that I was unable to resist the temptation.

I climbed into bed beside him, resting my head on his shoulder. I kept waiting for one of the nurses to bust in here and make me leave, but no one came.

He reached over, wincing with the effort, and placed his hand on my stomach. I was about to ask him what he was doing when those pretty baby blues lifted to meet my gaze. "I should have been there for you. I should've been able to see my child grow inside you and take care of both of you." A sadness lingered in his eyes at what he had missed out on.

"I know," I squeaked.

"I understand why you did it and I'm ready to forgive you. I'm ready to move past this."

I nodded. I wanted nothing more than that, but I was afraid tomorrow might never come for us. He was lying there *dying*. I knew he was a fighter, though, so I had to believe he'd pull through this for me—for our family.

"Why the hell did you go after my step-dad, Trent?" I questioned, staring up at the crinkled white ceiling. Everything in here was white and sterile.

Trent coughed, his breath wheezing with effort. "I-I saw him touch you," he admitted, slowly turning his head to look at me. I felt his eyes on me, but I couldn't seem to stop looking at the ceiling. "He's a fucking p-piece of shit and I wasn't going to l-let him get away with that." His words ended with another strangled cough.

I made myself look at him then, my brow furrowing with worry. "Are you okay?"

He nodded, his hand over his mouth as he stifled the cough.

"Do you know what happened to my step-dad?" I asked softly, reaching over to stroke his cheek. His eyes closed in response and he made a pleased humming noise in the back of his throat. "Did the police get him? He's not on the loose, is he?"

"After he shot me he took off running and that's the last thing I remember," Trent said sleepily. "Don't worry, though. Trace will take care of everything."

"Yeah," I yawned, feeling sleepy too as the days' events caught up with me, "he's good like that."

"Should I be worried you're falling for my brother?" Trent's lips brushed against my forehead. "You know he's married."

I laughed. "No, there's only one Wentworth brother for me and he's right here."

"Good," Trent murmured. "I love you."

"I love you, Trent," I whispered, kissing his jaw. "Thank

you for teaching me that love isn't a myth. It's real and we have it."

———

I WAS AWAKENED by a shrill noise. It pierced my eardrums, making me flinch. What the heck was that?

I sat up, blinking sleep from my eyes as the bland hospital room came into view.

The doors to the room burst open and someone pulled me from the bed.

"He's flat lining!" was all I heard as doctors and nurses bustled about in a flurry of activity.

I stared in horror at the lifeless body lying in the bed.

My hand came up to cover my mouth as sobs raked my body.

"Trent!" I screamed as a nurse tried to pull me out of the room. "Trent!" I screamed his name over and over again—at least it felt like it. "Come back to me! Trenton! Please! You can't leave me! *Trent!*"

But the line stayed flat.

The nurse shoved me out the door and slammed it in my face.

I pounded on the small glass window in the door, which was covered in black paper so that no one could see in. I continued to shout his name until I lost my voice and felt like I couldn't breathe.

Eventually, I left, unable to stay there and continue to hear the high-pitched shriek of his heart not beating.

I didn't quite make it back to the waiting room. I guess my feet decided to stop working. I sunk to the ground, my back against the wall. My wails filled the halls. I didn't care who heard me or who saw me. I couldn't stop them. I needed to let it all out. I couldn't keep this pain bottled inside me as I was tormented with one thought ...

Everyone leaves me.

I pulled at my hair, kicking my feet against the floor.

My cries began to draw attention.

I saw Trace come out of the waiting room to investigate the noise, and when his eyes landed on me his mouth fell open in horror.

I shook my head, my throat clogged with tears, to tell him that Trent hadn't made it.

Tears streamed from his eyes as he shoved his fingers through his hair, making it stick up wildly around his head.

He looked back at the waiting room and then at me.

I watched as he walked a little ways down that hall from me. He reared his hand back and it shot forward, punching the wall repeatedly. His anger and sadness was palpable. A male nurse came running toward him and restrained Trace so he couldn't do any more damage to his hand. They led him away —no doubt to clean it up, and maybe even stitch the wound closed.

It made me think of the injury to my hand on New Year's Eve—when Trent had so tenderly taken care of me. It had been our last night together. It was sweet and perfect and over far too soon. Here we were four months later. He'd found out the truth and now he was dead.

Fuck.

Dead.

He was gone.

Like, *really* gone.

As in never coming back *gone*.

My heart hurt and my soul felt incomplete.

How on Earth could I be expected to live the rest of my life without him?

I'd have to.

I was going to have to take every day one step at a time. I'd live and love that much harder, because Trenton couldn't.

He'd always live on in our son.

And in my heart.

EPILOGUE

Three Months Later

THE WARM SUMMER BREEZE TICKLED MY FACE AND I couldn't help smiling as I closed my eyes, lying back in the tall grass. It scratched my skin, making me itch, but the sun felt so good on my body that I refused to move. I felt so peaceful—something that had been rare in the past few months.

I reached out, smiling as I pulled a dandelion from the dirt.

"Row!" Ivy yelled and I sat up to see her running toward me. She crashed into my arms and then fell to the ground giggling.

"What are you doing, silly girl?" I asked her. "Where's Tristan?"

"He's fine." She shrugged, looking around. "I like it here. It's pretty."

"Mhmm," I hummed. "It's like a little oasis."

As if she didn't hear me, she smiled widely, pointing to the flowers surrounding us. "Can you make me one of those braided crown thingies with flowers?"

"I'll try." I grinned, picking the flowers surrounding us. "It's been a long time since I've made one of these."

Ivy sat down beside me, crossing her legs as she watched my movements. I finished the crown and laid it delicately on top her head. "Now, you're a real princess, Ivy." I ran my fingers through her long wavy hair.

She beamed at my words. Since my mom died, Ivy had really come out of her shell. She was always so happy and smiling. She thrived on words of praise and I tried to give them to her as often as I could.

"Now, you need one, Row." She stood, skipping around to gather more flowers. "Then you can be a queen!"

I laughed, adjusting the skirt of my dress.

Once she'd gathered enough flowers she sat down once more. "Can I help make this one?" she asked.

"Of course." I carefully showed her how to braid the stems together. In no time, she had it mastered and I let her finish it.

When it was done, she placed it on my head in the same manner I had done hers. "All hail, Queen Rowan!" she squealed, jumping up and running in circles around me.

I laughed, turning my head to watch her run.

I marveled at how much a few months of not being in a toxic environment had changed her. She wasn't as timid and shy anymore. She was blossoming, and so was I.

For the first time in all my life I finally felt like ... *me*.

I was no longer a ghost, drifting through the shadows.

Trent had given me that gift, and I was thankful for it every day.

I'd done a lot of growing since New Year's when Trent found out about Tristan. With the loss of my mom, it had been easy for me to become the person I was always meant to be. She couldn't harass me anymore, and Jim was serving life in prison for what he'd done to Trent.

Life wasn't perfect for me, not by a long shot, but it was getting there.

Ivy skipped through the field, picking wildflowers and arranging them into two bouquets. When she deemed them perfect, she returned to my side, handing me one. "For you, my Queen." She giggled, her cheeks rosy with happiness.

"Thank you, Princess." I took the flowers from her, inhaling their scent—then trying not to sneeze.

She twirled some more, her dress fanning out around her legs.

"Oh, look!" She pointed toward the back of the Wentworth mansion. "Here comes the King and Prince now!"

I smiled, enjoying her little game. All I had wanted for so long was for her and Tristan to have the opportunity to be children. I'd finally gotten my wish.

"Mommy!" Tristan cried, running straight for me, much like Ivy had when she'd found me hiding out back here.

I liked the shade and privacy that the tall grasses provided. When I was here, in this spot, I felt like I was in a new place all together. There was something magical about this place. Once the weather had warmed I'd claimed this area as mine since I had been spending so much time with the Wentworths. Lily and I had grown close, and she was beginning to feel like the mother I never had.

Tristan collapsed onto the ground beside me, his chest heaving with every labored breath from his long run.

"What's that you've got there?" I pointed to the leather-bound book in his small hand.

"Daddy told me to give it to you." He smiled proudly, holding out the book for me.

My eyes raised, connecting with Trent's as he approached. God, he was beautiful. He wore a pair of long tan colored pants, and a white t-shirt. He grinned as he caught me staring at him. I stared at him a lot. I had almost lost him that day in the hospital. I always had to remind myself that he was there and he was alive.

Trent reached us and sat down beside me. He draped an arm over my shoulder, kissing my cheek.

I took the book from Tristan's outstretched hand.

Ivy reached for him, and the two took off running through the field, their laughter dancing through the air.

"Open it," Trent murmured, his lips grazing my ear.

I shivered at his touch, my body humming.

I opened the book to the marked page, a breath escaping my lips.

The emerald green ribbon that had been used as a bookmark had a ring tied around it, and written on the page in Trenton's scrawling handwriting was:

Will you marry me?

"TRENT," I gasped, my hand flying up to cover my lips. I was shocked, to say the least, but I should have seen this coming.

After Trenton was released from the hospital, we had

talked through things and pieced ourselves back together. It hadn't taken long for us to become a family. Trent and I already loved each other—and after countless hours of talking, of me telling him everything I'd been through since I was a child, we'd been able to move past what I had done by keeping Tristan a secret. Things had settled into normalcy for us the past few months and it felt like we'd always been a family, not like this was anything new. Trent showered Tristan and Ivy with love and a father's affection, even though Ivy wasn't his. He was the greatest man there ever was, I was sure of that.

After he'd been shot, things had been touch and go for a few weeks, but he'd healed. He'd had to drop out of college since he wasn't fit to go back. He said that he didn't need his degree; he had enough schooling to open his own photography studio and go from there.

"Rowan," his voice was hesitant. "Say something, please."

"Yes," I gasped, my cheeks flushed with happiness. "Yes, yes, yes!"

I let the book fall off my lap, and wrapped my arms around his neck, kissing him passionately. His tongue found the seam of my lips, slipping inside. I moaned in pleasure as my fingers grasped the soft strands of his hair.

"Ew!" Tristan exclaimed. "That's disgusting! Bleh, kissing is gross!"

With a laugh, Trent pulled away, swiping his thumb over his lips.

He reached down, untying the diamond engagement ring from the ribbon. I held my hand out for him and he slipped the ring on.

His eyes filled with satisfaction as he stared at the ring glimmering on my finger.

His fingers tangled into my hair, cupping the back of my neck as he pulled my lips to his, kissing me sweetly.

Breathing rapidly, he rested his forehead against mine as he stared straight into my eyes so that I was powerless to look away.

"You're mine now, Rowan Sinclair," his voice was husky and his eyes sparkled with mischief.

I brought my hand up against his where he cupped my cheek. "Always."

ACKNOWLEDGMENTS

Wow, I have so many people to thank with this book. I really hope I don't forget anyone. That would be embarrassing.

First, I have to thank my entire family for being there and supporting my dream. I'm glad you guys don't think I'm a crazy person for writing stories.

A BIG thanks to my BAFFs Harper James and Regina Bartley. Your support means the world to me. I don't know what I did before I had you. You keep me sane and I'm so happy that I can go to you when I'm struggling with my plot. Our random chats also help to keep me from working myself to death. Thanks for dealing with my crazy.

Thank you Emily W. for always being there for me. Also, thanks for suggesting that Trace eat ketchup flavored chips instead of plain ones. Genius. Trace does love ketchup.

Thank you to my beta readers, Kendall, Stefanie, Haley, and Stephanie. I appreciate your feedback... even if I'm a nervous wreck when I send you chapters. I truly believe that Tempting Rowan is a better book thanks to your suggestions.

Thank you to all the bloggers that took time to participate in the blog tour for Tempting Rowan. It means so much to me that you'd take time away from your friends and family to read and support my book. What you guys do for authors is remarkable and I want to hug each and every one of you.

A big thank you to Regina Wamba for the photography and stunning cover design. I think it perfectly captures the 'feel' of Trent and Row.

Thank you Eli and Hannah for bringing my characters to life. You guys did a wonderful job and I couldn't be happier.

Eli, I'm so honored that I had the opportunity to meet you. You're going to go so far with your photography and modeling. (And I really think you could make it in acting too, haha) One day, I know I'm going to see you or your photography on a billboard somewhere and I am going to scream, "I know him! I KNOW HIM!" But despite your awesome photography and modeling skills, you're just a really great person. Your attitude and vision is going to take you far.

Last, but certainly not least, the biggest thank you goes to my fans. Without you, I couldn't do what I love. I'm thankful for you every day. I love getting to speak with you guys via Facebook or through email, and I'm so happy I've had the honor of meeting some of you recently. I hope I get to meet many more of you in the coming years.

www.ingramcontent.com/pod-product-compliance
Lightning Source LLC
LaVergne TN
LVHW031609060526
838201LV00065B/4782